Stranger in Paradise

*Also by Eileen Goudge
in Large Print:*

One Last Dance
Blessing in Disguise
Such Devoted Sisters
Garden of Lies

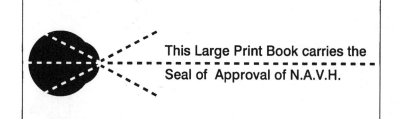

This Large Print Book carries the
Seal of Approval of N.A.V.H.

Stranger in Paradise

A CARSON SPRINGS NOVEL • BOOK 1

Eileen Goudge

Thorndike Press • Waterville, Maine

Published in 2001 by arrangement with Viking Penguin, a division of Penguin Putnam Inc.

Thorndike Press Large Print Basic Series.

The tree indicium is a trademark of Thorndike Press.

The text of this Large Print edition is unabridged.
Other aspects of the book may vary from the original edition.

Set in 16 pt. Plantin by Minnie B. Raven.

Printed in the United States on permanent paper.

Library of Congress Cataloging-in-Publication Data

Goudge, Eileen.
    Stranger in paradise / Eileen Goudge.
        p.   cm. — (A Carson Springs novel ; bk. 1)
    ISBN 0-7862-3446-6 (lg. print : hc : alk. paper)
    ISBN 0-7862-3447-4 (lg. print : sc : alk. paper)
    1. Mothers and daughters — Fiction.   2. Middle aged
    women — Fiction.   3. Pregnant women — Fiction.
    4. Young men — Fiction.   5. Widows — Fiction.
    6. Large type books.   I. Title.
    PS3557.O838 S76 2001b
    813′.54—dc21   2001041500

To Jon,
the other man I wake up to
in the morning

Whereupon she grew round-wombed, and had indeed, sir, a son for her cradle ere she had a husband for her bed. Do you smell a fault?

— From *King Lear*
by William Shakespeare

Acknowledgments

No novel is completed without a journey. And no such journey can be made without the help of others. To all those who assisted me along the way, I'd like to say how much I appreciate your help and guidance. I even have a jar of honey to show for it, which sits on a shelf above my desk.

I am forever indebted to the following people:

My old friend Tom Mogensen, once and always mural monitor. Tom, you rule.

Ed and Boots Thrower of Nantucket, for kindly opening their home and apiary to a perfect stranger.

Earl Bates, for sharing his extraordinary archives on Ojai without waiting to be asked.

My editor, Molly Stern, for her enthusiasm in launching into unknown territory with only a hand-drawn map.

Louise Burke, who is everything a publisher should be, and then some.

My dear friend and agent (in that order), Susan Ginsburg, who is the guiding light in every port.

My husband, Sandy, who's always there. It's half the work with him, and wouldn't be half the fun without him.

Eric Koperwas, for his limitless patience and unfailing good humor in the face of a particularly thorny problem.

And last, but not least, my doctors, George Lombardi and James Clarke, as well as the dedicated nurses on Ten South, Greenberg Pavilion, New York Presbyterian Hospital. Without their expert care and compassion I wouldn't have made the most crucial journey of all: from my bed to my desk.

Prologue

She chose a seat in the back of the bus so as not to draw attention to herself, a girl just shy of sixteen who could have fit the description on any one of a hundred missing person posters: 5 FEET 7 INCHES, BROWN HAIR, BROWN EYES. LAST SEEN WEARING JEANS AND NAVY SWEATSHIRT. A girl with nails bitten to the quick and a silver stud in her nose, an army-green backpack wedged between her grubby sneakers. It contained a change of clothes, forty dollars in crumpled fives and ones, a pack of Winston Lights, and keys to an apartment on Flatbush Avenue, where at that moment a man lay dead in a pool of blood.

She sat bolt upright until the bright lights of the city had dissolved into the flickery, undersea darkness of the interstate. She was long past exhaustion, but sleep was out of the question. Tiny muscles jumped under her skin. Her eyes were like dry, hot stones pounded into her skull. She would start to drift off only to be jolted awake as if violently shaken, her head teeming with nightmare images: the dark hole in Lyle's chest, the red circle widening across his ribbed white undershirt. It hadn't fully registered at the time, but now, in the sluggish current of heat that rose from the vents at her feet, she couldn't seem to stop shivering. She held herself braced against the gentle rocking of the bus, muscles tensed to the point of cramping. As if her life depended on staying alert. Which, in a way, it did.

The girl was asleep nonetheless by the time the bus reached Harrisburg. She slept straight through to Columbus, curled on her side with her nylon windbreaker pillowed under her head, unaware of the zipper that by morning would leave a row of red welts like stitches down one cheek. In the darkness, with the highway's fractured lights flitting across her slackened face, she looked far younger than her age: a peacefully slumbering child with someone to meet her at the other end.

At the rest stop in St. Louis, with the sun a lurid smear along the low horizon, she got out to stretch her legs. Snow dotted the pavement in scablike patches. She lit a cigarette and leaned against the cold cinderblock. Her eyes were empty, staring out at nothing. Smoke rose in a thin gray scrawl from the Winston Light cupped in her loosely dangling hand. When it had burned down to her fingertips she blinked and straightened. The butt made a sizzling sound as she flicked it onto the damp pavement. Shivering with cold and holding her thin jacket wrapped about her like an old peasant woman's shawl, she shouldered her way inside.

After a trip to the ladies' room she joined the line in front of the vending machine, which grudgingly coughed up a packet of beer nuts and a Mountain Dew. She wasn't all that hungry, though she hadn't eaten since breakfast. It was just to prevent her stomach from growling, keep others from casting curious sidelong glances. Long experience had taught her what most kids her age never had to know: how to be invisible. The rules were simple:

Don't raise your voice when speaking around adults.

Don't drink too much water (or your frequent trips to the bathroom will arouse suspicious looks).

Don't linger over expensive merchandise in stores.

Don't ask too many questions.

Don't give any more information than necessary.

In Topeka a middle-aged lady with hair the color of a rusty pipe sat down next to her. After a few minutes, she turned to inquire, "Going far?"

The girl tensed. Did she look like someone on the run? She muttered something unintelligible and curled on her side with her face to the window, burying her head in the crook of her arm. When she finally dared lift her head the rust-haired lady had moved to an empty seat two rows up, where she was loudly extolling the virtues of Metamucil to a stout black woman with a powder-blue raincoat folded neatly across her lap.

The girl turned her face to the window. The road was an endless river banked by fields of corn. A road that seemed to be carrying her backward. She remembered when she was little. She would play this game where she'd scan the mothers on the sidewalk after school, and choose the one who looked the nicest. She'd imagine the woman taking her by the hand, even scolding her in a motherly way about some stupid little thing like leaving her shoelaces untied or forgetting her lunch box. Over the years she'd gradually outgrown the game. It made her too sad. But now she wondered what it would be like to have someone waiting at the other end. A woman with a warm smile and stories to tell of what had happened while she was away.

But there was no one to meet her in Oklahoma City or Amarillo or Albuquerque. She'd been on the road nearly three days by the time she worked up the nerve to buy a newspaper. Though the murder of a small-time drug dealer in Brooklyn wasn't likely to make national news, she was vastly relieved even so when she found no mention of Lyle. Relief tempered by a perverse disappointment. Her name in print would have made people pay attention at least. Kids she'd gone to school with, to whom she'd never been anything other than The New Girl. Caseworkers who'd shunted her bulging file, with its ladder of crossed-out addresses, from one gray metal cabinet to the next. Even if it meant going to jail — wasn't that better than being invisible?

By the time she reached Bakersfield the endless stretches of desert and scorched brown hills had given way to green orchards and citrus groves. Even the fast-food restaurants looked more inviting somehow. Her mouth watered at the thought of a Big Mac. But when she checked in her backpack only a few crumpled bills remained. She'd have to hold off for now. Who knew how long the money would have to last?

At a service station just east of Santa Barbara she splurged on another newspaper. She was settling back in her seat when a glossy real estate flyer slipped to the floor. The old man beside her stooped to retrieve it.

"Prettiest place in the world," he said peering at it.

She glanced over his shoulder at a photo of a tree-shaded ranch house. Behind it was a fenced pasture in which horses grazed. Snowcapped mountains rose in the distance. "It looks too perfect to be real," she said.

He looked up as if he'd just noticed her sitting there. "Carson Springs? It's just beyond those hills." He raised a crooked finger to the window, an ancient man, his bald head flaking in spots, his body drooping like an old coat from its hanger. In the weathered ruin of his face, his blue eyes burned brightly. "I take it you've never seen the movie."

"What movie?"

"*Stranger in Paradise.* It was shot there."
He smiled. "Course that was way before
your time."

"I think I saw it on TV."

He brightened, and she saw that he'd
once been handsome. "Well, I directed it."
He extended a hand that felt like an old
baseball glove that'd been left out in the
rain. "Hank Montgomery's the name."

"That's where I'm going. To Carson
Springs." The words were out before she
realized it.

The old man fixed his keen gaze on her.
"That so?"

"My aunt lives there." *This is crazy,* she
thought. As far as she knew she didn't have
an aunt, and until just this minute she'd
never even heard of Carson Springs.

"Ever been out this way before?"

"No." That wasn't a lie, at least.

"Well then, you've a real treat in store."

The girl didn't know what had come
over her, but the idea had taken hold
somehow. Besides, it wasn't like she had
anywhere else to go.

When they reached Santa Barbara, she
used the last of her money to buy a ticket
on the local bus to Carson Springs; two
hours later she was once more en route,
traveling north along a steep, winding

highway. She'd just begun to doze off when they crested the ridge and a wondrous sight panned into view. A valley ringed with mountains on all sides, like a huge green bowl into which hills and pastures tumbled. Orange groves crisscrossed the floor in neatly stitched rows, and to the east a Crayola lake reflected the cloudless sky. The town itself, a cluster of red-roofed buildings in candy-heart shades, might have been a page from a storybook.

Minutes later they were cruising down the main street. Huge old trees shaded sidewalks lined with Spanish-style shops trimmed in colorful tiles. Miniature trees in clay pots dotted the curb. A red-roofed arcade stretched along one side of the street, ending in a stone arch festooned in flowers, through which she caught a glimpse of sunlit courtyard.

Several blocks down, the bus wheezed to a stop. The sun greeted her like a welcoming arm as she stepped onto the sidewalk. She saw that she was standing in front of the library, a squat adobe building framed by trees resembling tall green candles. People in short-sleeved shirts and sandals strolled past, looking tanned and well fed. With her pale skin and rumpled clothes would she stick out like a sore thumb?

She made her way back to the arcade, where she paused in front of an ice cream parlor. A little boy sat licking a cone on a wooden bench out front while his mother peered into the window of the book shop next door. Did he have any idea how lucky he was? The closest she'd had to a mother was plump, henna-haired Edna. Her earliest memory was of curling up next to Edna on the sofa, watching her leaf through a fat book filled with bird pictures. Edna knew them all by heart, and in time they became almost as familiar to the girl.

She continued along, hunger mounting with each step. Tantalizing aromas drifted toward her: freshly ground coffee, baking bread, a sweet scent she would later learn was lemons. Not like the ones in supermarkets back home, which had almost no smell, these hung like Christmas ornaments from the potted trees along the curb.

She paused in front of a shop with an enormous wheel of cheese in the window. Just inside was a deli case on which platters of thick, crusty sandwiches were displayed. Her last meal had been a bag of potato chips washed down with Coke, and it took every ounce of willpower to keep from darting inside and grabbing one of those sandwiches. With an effort she moved on, past a Mexican restaurant with a garland of dried chiles on the door. It wasn't until she reached a saddle shop with a wooden merry-go-round horse out front that she paused until her head stopped swimming.

At the first corner she crossed the street to the park. She still had no idea of where she was headed, but had the strangest feeling of being drawn to something. In the park, wandering amid the cool embrace of ancient trees, she stopped to slip off her sneakers. The grass was soft against her soles. There were no manicured flower beds or bronze statues gazing imperiously off into the distance. Here flowers poked from clumps of ferns and tangled vines, and stone fountains murmured sweetly.

Everywhere she looked there were birds. Tanagers, jays, bluebirds, juncos. She spied a small brown bird with dull red markings on its breast. A purple finch. It was fluttering about in a birdbath, sending up drops of water that caught the sunlight like sparks. She was so entranced she didn't notice the children playing nearby until one of them bumped into her. She caught him before he could fall, a bundle of sturdy limbs that wriggled briefly in her arms before pulling away.

A small, towheaded boy peered up at her. "Hi, I'm Danny. What's your name?"

The girl hesitated. She didn't appear to be on the FBI's ten most-wanted list. Still, it paid to be cautious. Her gaze fell once more on the jaunty little bird. She watched it take flight, scattering bright droplets as it disappeared into the branches of the tree overhead. "Finch," she said without thinking. She rolled it about in her mind like a new taste on her tongue. Yes, it would do.

The boy didn't seem to find it the least bit unusual. He held out a grubby fist, opening it to reveal an even grubbier penny. "You can have it if you want."

She pocketed the penny with a smile. "Thanks." Maybe it would bring her luck.

The boy darted off to rejoin his playmates.

She followed the winding path until she reached the other end of the park. Across the street, atop a shady rise, sat an old adobe mission. Pale pink with chunks of plaster missing here and there, it was topped by an arched belfry trimmed like a cake. The girl stared, transfixed, as the bells began to peal and a pair of stout wooden doors swung open. A white-gowned bride and her tuxedoed groom appeared on the sun-dappled steps, followed by a stream of wedding guests spilling out to join them.

Friends and family that she imagined for an instant were her own. She smiled even as tears filled her eyes — a brown-haired girl of medium height in frayed jeans and a faded maroon T-shirt, a girl with nowhere to go and no one to welcome her who had the oddest feeling she'd somehow arrived at her destination.

Chapter 1

How did I end up here? Samantha Kiley wondered. A forty-eight-year-old woman in a peach chiffon dress watching her youngest daughter get married. Wasn't it only a few years ago she'd walked down the same aisle, arm tucked through her father's? Since she'd stood with her babies at the baptismal font? Time doesn't just fly, she thought, it leaves you stranded in places you never expected to find yourself. Nearly two years since Martin's death, yet she still had trouble thinking of herself as a widow, a status conjuring images of the old *abuelitas* garbed in black who led the candlelight procession up Calle de Navidad each Christmas Eve.

It saddened her, Martin's not being here, but she'd made up her mind she wasn't going to let it spoil the day. She focused instead on the poised young woman at the altar, a vision in ivory taffeta and clouds of white tulle, her honey-colored hair smoothed back in a Grace Kelly-like chignon. *My daughter . . .*

Light streamed from the high clerestory windows flanking the nave, illuminating the altar's carved gilt reredos. Father Reardon, striking in his black cassock and snowy surplice, had turned the page on the Song of Songs and was heading into the choppy waters of vows. Sam reached for her handkerchief. She'd managed to keep it together throughout the readings, Byron and T. S. Eliot and a passage from Alice's childhood favorite, *The Little Prince*. Now came the true test . . .

"Wesley Leyland Carpenter, do you take this woman to be your lawfully wedded wife, for better or worse, for richer or poorer, in sickness and in health, as long as you both shall live?"

Sam's gaze rested on Wes. He was a man's man like her father: tall and well built, with a full head of hair the color of case-hardened steel and a startling streak of white down the center of his neatly trimmed black beard. The CEO of a multibillion-dollar cable network, he would provide for her daughter . . . never mind that Alice would bristle at the idea. More importantly, he would be good to her. That much was obvious just looking at them.

He was also fifty-four — six years older

than Sam, and twenty-eight years his bride's senior.

Because Wes was so perfect in every other way, Sam had swallowed her reservations. Even so, a voice cried in protest, *He's old enough to be her father!* When Alice was a baby, he had been on his second tour of duty in Vietnam. When he was old she'd be a young woman still. If they had children — and Sam certainly hoped they would — Alice might very well end up raising them on her own, or with the added burden of an ailing husband.

Age isn't everything, she reminded herself. And Alice wasn't exactly a simpering handmaiden. She was an accomplished woman in her own right, a TV producer with a successful talk show to her credit. She stood gazing up at Wes not as if he'd hung the moon, but as if they'd done so together.

Even so, Martin wouldn't have approved of the match, she knew. At the very least he'd have done his best to stall it. And who knows? He might have succeeded. Alice, both girls in fact, had idolized their father. And he, in turn, had lavished on them . . .

. . . *everything he withheld from you.*

The thought was startling, like a rude noise breaking the hushed stillness. Where had it come from? Hadn't Martin been as devoted a husband as he had been father?

Sam forced the thought from her mind. At the moment her daughter's happiness was all that counted. And just look at her! Alice seemed to glow like the bank of votive candles lighting the painted wooden Madonna to her right, the only hint of nervousness the faintly discernible quivering of her hands. Behind her veil, her smile was like sunshine finding its way through a morning mist. Her blue eyes fixed on Wes as he responded in a clear baritone: "I do."

Sam blinked hard, the sturdy oak pew, polished by generations of Delarosas, like a firm hand holding her upright. So far, so good. She'd managed to keep the waterworks at bay. Her gaze strayed to her eldest, who wasn't having nearly as much success. Laura, standing alongside her sister, was holding the bouquet tilted askew in one hand while dabbing at her eyes with the other.

Dear Laura. Anything could set her off: sentimental songs and movies, old photos in family albums. No wonder her door was Mecca to every poor, starved creature for miles around. It probably hadn't occurred to her — she was the least vain person Sam knew — that she didn't exactly fit the part of dying swan. Tears had left her olive skin blotchy, and pills of Kleenex dotted the front of her dusty-rose chiffon sheath, a dress chosen by Alice that was as stylish as it was spectacularly unsuited to Laura's less than willowy figure.

Sam's heart went out to her. Not in pity. How could you feel sorry for someone as smart and talented as Laura? Certainly, she wouldn't have been able to manage Delarosa's without her. If only Laura's husband had seen her for who she was, not for what she hadn't been able to give him. Peter's walking out on her had been a crushing blow; a year and a half since the divorce and she still wasn't over it. Sam could only hope she would one day fall in love again and be as happy as . . . well, Alice and Wes.

The priest turned his gaze to Alice. "Do you, Alice Imogene Kiley, take this man . . ."

Moments later Wes was slipping the ring onto her finger, its four-carat diamond catching the light in a wink of such brilliance Sam didn't have to dab at her eyes to know they were wet. Alice, in turn, slipped onto Wes's finger the plain gold band that had been her father's.

Father Reardon closed his book. "I now

pronounce you man and wife. And what God hath joined let no man put asunder." The light from above seemed to radiate from the billowing sleeves of his surplice as he lifted his arms in benediction. With the wry twinkle that, along with his Black-Irish good looks, had inspired some decidedly un-Catholic thoughts in a number of the female parishioners, he turned to Wes. "You may kiss the bride."

A knot formed in Sam's throat as she watched her new son-in-law lift Alice's veil. Their kiss, though chaste, hinted at a passion she could only wonder at. On her own long-ago wedding day had she felt about Martin as her daughter clearly did about Wes? Her most vivid memory of that time was how young they'd been, still in college; young enough for her friends to joke that there must be a baby on the way. Three months later, when she actually *did* get pregnant, all she could remember was feeling sick to her stomach most of the time. Then when Laura came, over-whelmed.

It's hard to stay in love, she thought, with a baby crying and the PG&E meter ticking and *Joy of Cooking* wedged between *Logic I* and *Poets of the Romantic Age*. A different kind of flame that burns, low and steady like a pilot light, when you've slept alongside the same man for years.

But all that was behind her now. Life without Martin had settled into a pattern. She had her house and business, the music festival committee. There wasn't room for the kind of passion she'd yearned for when young.

The realization brought a trace of melancholy that was quickly dispelled by the Bach cantata now echoing through the church, accompanied by the joyous pealing of *campanario* bells. As she rose to her feet, Sam felt as if she were being literally borne upward. She caught the eye of the best man, Wes's son, with his blond hair to his shoulders and silver stud in one ear, and thought she saw a touch of irony in the glance he shot her. Ian was only a few years older than Alice. What must he think of all this?

Sam fell into step behind him. Laura and the three bridesmaids, old friends of Alice's, marched ahead of them in a rose-colored column with the bride and groom leading the way. Sam smiled into the blur of beaming faces on either side of her. The church, eternally cool, its hand-hewn timbers imbued over the ages with the scent of smoke and incense, seemed to fold about her like a pair of tired wings.

The church doors swung open, flooding the aisle with sunshine. There was a moment, a single moment before anyone caught up to them, when Alice and Wes stood poised on the steps outside, a fairy-tale prince and princess framed by the arched doorway as if by the gilt edges of a book. Sam's throat tightened. She thought, *Is there really such a thing as happily ever after?*

Then she was outside, taking her place in the receiving line, extending her hand and cheek to the guests who spilled from the church like excited children from school. Her sister and brother-in-law, Audrey and Grant, with their two college-age sons, Joey and Craig. Her brother, Ray, and his wife, Dolores, all the way from Dallas. Ray and Dolores's two married daughters, followed by elderly Uncle Pernell and Aunt Florine, clutching as tightly to each other as to their respective canes.

Wes's parents, both hale and hearty, with the deep tans of avid golfers, stood to her right — an uncomfortable reminder that her own hadn't lived to see this day. She pictured them as they'd looked in the photo taken on their last anniversary: a tall, thickset man with a balding crown stooping into the camera's range, his cheek pressed to that of his petite, white-haired wife. What would they have thought of this unlikely match?

Sam's best friend stepped up to give her a Chanel-scented squeeze. In her wide-brimmed straw hat and fitted emerald suit Gerry Fitzgerald seemed straight out of a forties movie. No one who didn't know her would ever have guessed she was a former nun.

"You're holding up well," she said.

"Am I?" Sam drew back with a self-conscious little laugh.

"When it's my turn, they'll have to issue a flood warning." That wouldn't be for a while, they both knew. Gerry's daughter, the oldest of her two children, was only fifteen.

Sam's gaze was strayed toward Alice, warmly embracing her bridegroom's much stouter older brother, who could have passed for Wes's father. "She's beautiful, isn't she?"

"I could swear I was looking at you on your wedding day."

A long-ago image flashed through Sam's head: a pretty, dark-haired college girl, much too young to be getting married, wearing her mother's satin wedding gown taken in at the waist. She smiled. "I'm glad one of us remembers that far back."

"We're not *that* old." Gerry shook her head, green eyes sparkling with laughter. With her ex-husband and string of lovers, she liked to joke that she was *dis*gracefully aging.

"Old," Sam said with a wry, downward glance, "is a corsage without a man to pin it on."

Gerry cast a meaningful look at Tom Kemp, in line behind her. "I can think of someone who'd be more than happy to take on the job," she murmured.

Sam felt her face grow warm, then her husband's former partner was stepping up to kiss her cheek. He stood at least a head taller than Sam, who was tall herself, his shoulders slightly stooped from accommodating to a world that wasn't custom-built. A nice-looking man smelling faintly of aftershave, with twin crescents of newly shorn scalp where his square black glasses hooked over his ears. Sunlight skated off their lenses as he drew back to smile at her.

"Congratulations, Sam. You know the saying, you're not losing a daughter . . ."

"I'm gaining a son-in-law." She winced

inwardly at the triteness of it. But Tom meant well, she knew. "I'm glad you could make it," she said with sincerity. "It wouldn't have been the same without you."

"I just wish it could've been Martin walking her down that aisle." Ray had filled in, but it hadn't been the same.

"So do I."

As if sensing her discomfort, he was quick to add, "You look lovely, Sam." He reddened slightly, as if unused to giving such compliments. "I like your dress. It suits you."

"Thanks, I'm glad you think so."

Secretly, she didn't care for it. She'd been thinking mainly of Alice when she'd picked it out, wanting the spotlight to be on her. Now she wished she'd chosen something a little less . . . well, matronly.

Tom looked as if he wanted to linger, but feared he was holding up the line. He touched her elbow, his tall frame curved like a question mark. "Catch up with you later, okay?"

She felt a tiny stab of guilt. What would she have done without Tom these past few years? Holding her hand through the worst of Martin's illness. Guiding her through the blizzard of paperwork after his death. If she'd been avoiding him recently it was only because she was afraid of hurting him. He'd made it clear he wanted more than friendship. Unfortunately, she didn't feel the same way.

Sam turned to find the newlyweds dashing down the steps amid a hail of bird-seed — rice, Laura had pointed out, was harmful to birds — Alice with her hem hitched daintily to her ankles to avoid tripping on it and her white veil trailing like vapor in the breeze. A black limousine waited at the curb.

Guests began drifting off to the parking lot. If she didn't leave soon, Sam thought, they would arrive at the house ahead of her. She began to fret. Had Guillermo hung the wedding piñatas? Had Lupe remembered to put lemon slices in the punch?

Relax, a voice soothed. Her live-in housekeeper and gardener had been at Isla Verde almost as long as Saint Peter had been at heaven's gates. They would look after everything. And if a few details got overlooked what difference would it make? Nothing short of an earthquake could spoil this day.

"See you at the house!" Laura called to Sam.

She was helping her elderly housemate down the steps. Maude wore a snugly fitting satin gown nearly the same vintage as she that had left her somewhat hobbled. She paused to lift her hem, revealing matching blue pumps. "Wore my dancing shoes," she said with an impish wink, poking at her nest of ivory hair, in imminent danger of slipping from its pins.

Before Sam could make her own exit, several more people stopped to congratulate her, Father Reardon among them. He clasped her hand warmly. "Will we be seeing you on Sunday?"

Until last night's rehearsal she hadn't set foot in St. Xavier's since her husband's death. Too busy, she told herself. But wasn't there more to it than that? Maybe, she thought uneasily, she was afraid of what too much soul-searching might bring.

"If I'm not too worn out," she hedged with a laugh.

"I promise not to put you to sleep with my sermon." His gray-blue eyes sparkled, but she caught the glint of gentle reproach.

"You never do." Who could fall asleep looking at Father Reardon? "It's just not the same somehow."

His fingers tightened about hers. "All the more reason to come. To quote Robert

Browning, 'Earth changes, but thy soul and God stand sure.' " He let go of her hand, smiling the crooked little smile of a man well versed in matters other than religion. She could see why Gerry and he were such great friends. "End of sermon. Now off with you."

Sam made her way around the back of the church, where her little red Honda was one of the few cars remaining in the lot. She climbed in and turned the key in the ignition, but the engine gave only a brief groan. She waited a minute, then tried again. Nothing.

With a cry of frustration she clambered out, bumping her head on the door frame. A flash of pain, followed by a dull throbbing. Wincing, she reached up to massage her scalp.

"You okay?"

Sam wheeled about to find Ian Carpenter loping toward her. She cast him the somewhat abashed smile of a woman who hadn't been as scrupulous as she ought to in getting her car serviced.

"I've heard of brides being left high and dry," she said with a laugh, feeling more than a little foolish as she stood there rubbing her head, "but never the *mother* of the bride."

"Why don't I have a look?"

"Oh, I couldn't —"

But he was already peeling off his jacket. He lifted the hood, and after several minutes of poking about, straightened to announce, "Looks like you're going to need a new fuel pump."

"Oh, dear." She tried not to think how much it would cost. "I'd better phone the garage."

"You can do it from the house." He slammed the hood down, fishing a handkerchief from his pocket to wipe the grease from his hands. "Come on, I'll give you a lift." He gestured toward a white Chevy van at the other end of the lot.

"I don't suppose it would do to be late to my own party," she said, falling in step beside him.

Ian laughed. "No offense, but I don't think anyone will notice." With his blond hair tucked behind one ear, in which the tiniest crescent of an earring glittered, he reminded her of the boys who used to hang about when Laura and Alice were teenagers.

As she climbed into the van a wave of déjà vu swept over her. Wasn't it only yesterday she'd been a teenager herself, piling with her friends into similar vans on her way to black-light dances and protest rallies? Back then life had seemed an open door just waiting for her to step through it. And though the path she'd chosen suited her in most ways, it wasn't without a small measure of regret that she looked back now, slightly chagrined to realize that to this young lion of a man with eyes the color of a summer twilight and a smile that ought to be outlawed — the kind who once would have inspired sleepless nights and dreamy doodling in margins — she was nothing other than a nice older woman in need of a ride.

"Thanks," she said, as Ian slid in behind the wheel. "I don't know what I would have done. Can you see me hitchhiking in this dress?"

He flashed her a grin. *Son of the father,* she thought. That same smile, which seemed to promise the moon and then some, must have been what captivated Alice in Wes. "You'd be the only one in a pink dress and corsage."

"Actually, it's peach."

"What?"

"My dress. It's mother-of-the-bride peach. Did you know they have special racks in bridal shops? Everything strictly below the knee in shades that won't clash with the floral arrangements." She indulged in a rueful little smile at her own expense.

He cast her a coolly appraising glance as he turned out of the lot. "If I were doing your portrait I'd put you in something with a little more life to it. Venetian red."

She remembered that he was an artist. "That's all I'd need, to be hanging in some museum." She felt herself grow warm, and was more than a little aghast to realize she was flirting with this man young enough to be her son. "Turn left at the intersection." She pointed toward the post. Its quaint bell tower bordered in decorative tiles, featured regularly in travel pieces, cast a shadow over the old Park Rio opposite it.

"I know the way." Ian braked to let a group of giggling teenagers in shorts and T-shirts cross. "I was at the engagement party, remember?"

"Were you? I'm sorry. There were so many people . . ."

A lame excuse, she knew. The truth was she hadn't bothered to get to know Wes's son. She told herself it was because she'd been too caught up in the wedding. But wasn't there more to it than that? Wasn't Ian just one more reminder of how much older Wes was?

"I didn't stay long," he said. "I'm not

much of a party animal."

"Me neither. Most of the time, I'd rather be curled up with a good book."

Sam smiled at the irony. As the daughter of Jack and Cora Delarosa, she'd been dealing with people since she was old enough to see above the counter. They liked that she knew their children's names and remembered their various aches and pains. In turn, they often confided in her. Like head librarian Vivienne Hicks letting it drop just yesterday that she was thinking of seeing a therapist. And Edie Gringsby, the Presbyterian minister's wife, who feared her son might be on drugs. How many of those to whom she'd lent an ear or a shoulder would have guessed what a solitary creature she was at heart?

She gazed out at the tree-lined sidewalks bustling with shoppers. A chalkboard sign in front of the Wicker Basket listed today's specials. A table of marked-down books stood outside Between the Covers, where its owner, Peter McBride, was attacking the front window with a roll of paper towels and bottle of Windex. Across the street, at the rival bookshop owned by Peter's ex-wife, appropriately named The Last Word, Miranda McBride could be seen watering her potted kumquats.

Ian slipped a CD into the player — Charlie Parker — and tossed the case onto a floor littered with coins, crumpled straw wrappers, a paint-smeared rag. "You like jazz?"

"I love every kind of music," she said. "Especially classical."

He nodded. "You mentioned something last night about a music festival."

"I'm chairing this year's committee." She was surprised that he'd remembered. At the rehearsal dinner they'd been seated at opposite ends of the table. "If you're going to be around then, you should come. We have a terrific lineup."

"When is it?"

"Third week in October."

"I may be in London."

"I'll save you a ticket just in case."

"Thanks, I'd like that."

"Are you on the road much?" she asked after a moment.

"More than I'd like. If I could get away with it, I'd spend all my time in the studio."

"Why can't you?"

He shrugged. "Murals pay the rent. Luckily, most of it's done on canvas. I only travel for installations."

"I envy you."

"How so?"

"I always wanted to travel."

"What stopped you?"

They passed the town hall and court-house, a pair of Victorians that stood out like lacy pink valentines in a sea of stolid, white-washed adobe. He turned onto Grove Avenue, where the road began to climb.

"Too busy raising a family and running a business, I guess," she said.

"It's not too late." He flicked her a glance that seemed to challenge her in some way.

"You make it sound as if I could pick up and go any time I felt like it."

"Can't you?"

"It's not as easy as you think."

"You have help, don't you?"

"My daughter Laura. But she has enough to handle as it is."

He shrugged. "It was just a thought."

"When you get to be my age, you'll see. Nothing's easy."

"You talk as if you're an old lady."

"I'm forty-eight."

"That's hardly old. Besides, you look at least ten years younger." Ian shot her another grin, sending an electrical surge through her that definitely wasn't a hot flash. "If I didn't know better I'd have guessed you were Alice's sister." His mouth hooked down in a wry grimace. "Oldest line in the world, I know, but I swear it's true."

"Thanks. I appreciate the compliment." She spoke lightly even as the heat rushed up into her cheeks.

He's flirting with me. She stared at the layers of peach chiffon draped decorously over her knees. Yes, she could still fit comfortably into a size eight, and except for a few silver strands her hair was the same deep auburn it had always been. But these days, when she looked in the mirror, it was at a woman with fine lines about eyes that had seen as much tribulation as triumph. A woman who had come to depend on reading glasses, and whose medicine chest was stocked with several types of moisturizing cream. What could he possibly see in her?

Ian, for his part, wished there was a way to put her fears to rest without scaring her off. He'd had his eye on her for some time now — at the engagement party and at last night's rehearsal dinner. What had struck him even more than her long-necked beauty was how gracefully she moved, like a dancer: tall, forthright, ageless, her skirt barely rippling at her knees. Her clear gaze was equally direct, that of a woman with no games to play. If she wanted something, she would ask for it. If she wanted a man, he would know it.

Girls? He was tired of their endless attempts to mold him, of their patently obvious ploys garnered from books and magazine articles. When his last girlfriend, Emily, had started cutting phone calls short, he hadn't caught on at first . . . until he happened to see a female author on TV stressing the importance of ending a phone conversation after fifteen minutes. The idea being to leave the man wanting more, he supposed. After that, he'd begun timing Emily, clocking her in each call at just over fourteen and a half minutes. When he confronted her, she hadn't even had the decency to be embarrassed.

"Why should you be the one calling all the shots?" she'd huffed. "Maybe I have better things to do than always being at your beck and call."

He'd broken off with her then and there. What he wanted was a woman who'd laugh at the idea of timing a conversation as if it were an egg, a woman more interested in art and music and books than in finding some man to marry her. A woman very much like the one sitting beside him now . . .

"My studio's just up the coast." He spoke casually, knowing this, too, must sound like the oldest line in the world. "If you're interested in seeing some of my work."

Sam was flooded with shame. Did he see her as some pathetic older woman who'd fall into bed with the first man who showed the slightest interest? No, she told herself, he wasn't like that. *He's just being nice.* "Sure," she said, struggling to keep her voice even. "I'd like that."

They fell into an uneasy silence. The neatly trimmed oleander hedges that lined the roads near town had given way to live oaks and pepper trees. Wildflowers spilled from ditches and poked between fence slats: snowberry and jimson weed, daisy-like coreopsis, and her favorite, the white Matilija poppy. Road signs bearing the universal symbol of horse and rider marked trails that wandered off into the woods.

They wound their way uphill past Avery Lewellyn's antiques barn. Avery, who dressed up in a red suit every year at Christmastime and kept a herd of white-tailed deer corralled out back. Just around the bend was La Serenisa, a handful of rustic-looking cabins tucked amid a eucalyptus grove where at any given time one

Hollywood celebrity or another was usually holed up.

All this wild beauty wasn't by accident, Sam knew. The draconian zoning laws that drove developers to distraction had ensured that large parcels of rural land remain intact. The worst threat wasn't from man, but from the elements: earthquakes and floods, frosts that could decimate an entire orange crop, the dreaded brushfires that swept in with the Santa Ana winds in late summer and early fall.

"Ever been married?" she asked.

He tensed visibly. "No."

"I'm sorry, I didn't mean to pry."

"It's okay." He cast her an apologetic glance. "It's just that I get asked that a lot. Usually by people trying to fix me up."

"It was the furthest thing from my mind, believe me."

He laughed. "Good, let's keep it that way." She didn't dare ask if he was seeing anyone. He might take it the wrong way. "What about you? You must have been pretty young when you got married."

"Nineteen. It seemed like a good idea at the time." She gave in to a little smile. "The truth is we were too young to know any better."

"You must have been doing something

right. You stayed together all those years."

She felt a sharp tug of loss coupled with a guilty sense of release. "I guess that's more than most couples can say."

"How long since your husband passed away?"

"Two years."

"Alice talks about him a lot."

"She's still not over it."

"It must have been tough on you, too."

"It was."

She felt suddenly impatient. What did he know? Death wasn't just the final curtain going down; it was a hundred little indignities. Hospital rooms billed as private that were anything but. Doctors and nurses bustling in and out at all hours of the day and night. Tests, tests, and more tests to tell you what you already knew.

"My mother died when I was thirteen," he said.

"I'm sorry. I didn't know." She'd known only that Wes had been a widower for some time. "It must seem strange," she said, "your father getting married again after all this time." *To a woman young enough to be your sister,* she refrained from adding.

He shrugged. "I like Alice."

"That's not what I meant."

"I know." Ian slowed to keep from hitting a squirrel that had scampered into the road. "But it's not my opinion that counts."

"You're still entitled to one, aren't you?"

He laughed. "Honestly? I think they make a great couple. Better than he and my mom in a lot of ways."

She didn't comment. It would have paved the way for a discussion she wasn't prepared to have. At the same time, she couldn't help thinking of Martin and what a perverse custom it was to speak only in reverential terms of the dead. To bury your feelings along with your loved one, robbing yourself of the one chance you might have had to sort through all the odds and ends.

A scuffling sound caused Sam to twist around in her seat. She thought she saw a flash of movement amid the jumble of tarps and boxes in back. Probably just something that had been jostled loose. "You don't happen to have a dog, do you?"

"No. Why?"

"I thought I heard something."

"The engine knocks."

She thought of her own car. "You should have it looked at."

"I will. One of these days."

He'd sounded like Martin just then. Why

worry today when there's always to-morrow? But Ian was young, with no family to support. He could, and should, do exactly as he pleased.

She lapsed once more into silence. She'd been traveling this road all her life, but never grew tired of it. The walnut orchard where she and her brother and sister used to scavenge for windfall. The creek where generations of Delarosa children had captured minnows and frogs in jars. Just beyond it was a towering loquat tree, the ground below littered with fallen fruit. Sam remembered collecting it in bags and bringing it home to Lupe, who'd made it into jam.

They passed the little roadside reliquary, with its statue of St. Francis draped in cheap plastic rosaries, which marked the turnoff to Isla Verde. Minutes later Ian was pulling to a stop behind the long line of cars overflowing from her driveway.

She turned to him. "Thanks. Not just for the ride. It was nice getting to know you."

"Same here." He grinned, a brilliant flash that left her ashamed of the weakness that spread through her.

What was it? The way he'd spoken to her, not as a contemporary of his father's but as a peer? Or was it simply the day itself, one of happy beginnings and sad reminders? Either way, it left her feeling as if she'd been turned inside out, every nerve ending exposed. She was acutely aware of the layers of chiffon sliding coolly against her thighs as she stepped down from the van.

Together they strolled up the steep drive. As they neared the top, Isla Verde rose into view, the twin silo towers flanking the gated courtyard at its entrance, the steeply pitched terra-cotta roof and high, arched windows beyond. After all these years — a lifetime — its clean beauty still brought a small measure of wonderment. The house her grandfather had built, much of it with his own hands. The house she and her brother and sister had grown up in.

The pergola sheltering the front walk was ablaze with climbing black Susan, and the coral bells along the path glistened from recent watering. She was glad to see that Guillermo had trimmed the rosemary and cleared the grass under the grapefruit trees.

On the lawn in back groups of people stood chatting, their champagne glasses catching the sunlight in bright, heliographic flashes. A mariachi band played under the striped tent. Even the piñatas had been hung. They swayed from the arches along the columned porch, bright splashes of color against the cream-colored limestone.

Her sister caught up with her as she was heading inside. "There you are. I've been looking all over for you." Audrey looked more relaxed than usual, maybe from the champagne.

She caught hold of Sam's hand, pulling her over to the bench under the huge old sycamore they'd climbed as children. Sam sank down reluctantly, hoping to be spared the usual veiled barbs.

"Everyone seems to be having a good time," she remarked pleasantly.

Her sister smiled. "It's a lovely party."

Sam's gaze wandered to the circle that had formed about the newlyweds, Wes's and Alice's friends mostly. Alice, in her gown, appeared to float, cloudlike, against the scarlet cascade of bougainvillea at her back. Wes, an arm draped loosely about her shoulders, had his head thrown back in laughter at something funny one of their friends had said.

With an effort she brought her gaze back to her sister. If Sam favored their mother in looks, Audrey, with her high forehead and pronounced chin, her sallow complexion and crinkly Delarosa hair, took after their father. Unfortunately, she hadn't inherited his sweet nature. For her sister life's glass was forever half empty. It was cosmic irony that her married name was Payne.

"Between you and me, Alice would have been just as happy eloping," Sam confided with a laugh.

Audrey looked appalled. "I'm glad she came to her senses. Think what she'd have missed!" Her sister ought to know; both Audrey and Sam had celebrated their weddings on this lawn.

Sam, adept from years of practice, was quick to sidestep an argument. "I just wish Mami and Poppi were here."

"They wouldn't recognize the place. Honestly, Sam, I don't know how you keep it up. Even the orchard. But," here came the barb, "I suppose that's why Mami left it to you instead."

"It wasn't exactly a gift," Sam reminded her.

"Oh yes, I know." Audrey cut her off with an airy little wave. As if their parent's decision to move into something smaller might have been coerced somehow. As if the hard-earned money for the down payment had been nothing but a token offering. The truth was, Sam had been as surprised as Audrey, when their mother's will was read, to find the remainder of the debt forgiven. "Look, don't get me wrong. I don't envy you one bit. It's more than Grant and I could manage."

"I have help," she said.

Her sister gave a dry little laugh. "You mean Lupe and Guillermo? God, they must be a hundred years old. They were ancient when *we* were growing up."

Sam focused on Audrey's moving lips while trying to block out her voice. Her sister wasn't completely to blame, she thought. In some ways Mami and Poppi *had* favored Ray and her. Though, let's face it, Audrey hadn't been the most lovable child. Sam felt lucky her own two had been such a joy, that she hadn't had to choose.

She sat listening to her sister rant for a few more minutes, until she could escape without risking offense. When she ran into Gerry on her way into the house, it was a blessed reprieve. Her best friend fell into step with her, slipping an arm through hers.

"Looked like you were getting an earful back there," she observed dryly. "Your sister still reminding you of everything you got that she was robbed of?" She'd removed her hat, as extravagant as Gerry herself; it swung loosely at her side as she walked. Sunlight glinted on the strands of silver in her black curls.

"And then some." Sam rolled her eyes.

"Jealousy is like a weed," Gerry observed. "You have to yank it out by its roots, or it keeps growing back."

"I'm afraid this weed is sunk too deep."

"You don't know until you try." They stepped through the back door into the coolness of the kitchen, with its copper pots hanging from hooks over the blackened adobe fireplace. A small army bustled about arranging platters under the fierce-eyed direction of Lupe, the world's smallest general. Ignoring the crab *flautas* and prosciutto-wrapped asparagus, Gerry fished an apricot from the wooden bowl on the counter and bit into it lustily.

Growing up, Sam was considered the prettier of the two. Ironically, it wasn't until Gerry had been accepted by the convent that she'd suddenly blossomed, and the boys who'd ignored her began looking at her in an entirely different way. More than one, Sam suspected, had harbored the fantasy of rescuing her from a life of celibacy.

Now, thirty years later, Gerry had truly

come into her own. Her tomboyish lope had given way to a confident stride, and the green eyes that had once seemed too bold were softened with feathery lines. Even her current vocation suited her. As lay manager for Our Lady of the Wayside, it was her job to see that store shelves, including Delarosa's, were well stocked with the honey, cleverly marketed under the name Blessed Bee.

Satisfied that everything was running smoothly, Sam strolled with Gerry back outside. It was almost time for lunch. Platters whisked past on their way to the buffet table under the tent. At the dining tables, rolls and butter were being set out, water glasses filled.

For a moment, she allowed herself to see it all through her guests' eyes. Isla Verde, green island, where the sun shone brightly and flowers bloomed year round. From where she stood she had an unfettered view of wind-swept chaparral and oak-dotted hills rolling like a great tide toward mountains that millions of years ago the ocean had lapped.

Yet heaven, as she'd learned in catechism, didn't come without a price. Her sister was right about the upkeep. The roof leaked in a dozen places, and repairs to the elderly plumbing and electricity were endless. A variety of fungi and insects regularly afflicted the orchard, and the swimming pool was a constant battle against black algae. Even with Lupe and Guillermo it was overwhelming at times.

Her gaze strayed to Ian, chatting with Laura on the lawn. Her daughter looked happy, almost girlish. Ian appeared to be hanging on every word. Sam felt an unexpected pang, but was quick to brush it away, telling herself firmly, *Why not? They'd make a good match.*

Gerry leaned close to whisper, "He's adorable."

"Not to mention young enough to be my son," Sam shot back, knowing where this was leading.

Gerry was undaunted. "All that hair. Reminds me of the boys we used to date in high school. Most of whom are bald now." Her laugh was that of a woman who'd sampled her share of men. "I understand he's an artist."

"A fairly successful one."

"It sounds as if you two have gotten to know each other pretty well."

"We rode up together in his car. Mine died."

"Ah. A knight in shining armor to boot."

Gerry wore a sly expression that was all too familiar.

Sam wheeled to face her. "I know what you're thinking," she said in a low, warning voice, "and you can put it right out of your mind. I'm old enough to be his mother."

"You said that already."

"Well, it's a fact."

"I don't see why age should matter." Gerry arched an eyebrow, her gaze straying to the newlyweds. "It didn't stop Wes from dating Alice."

"You're terrible, you know that?" Sam, who could have strangled her friend just then, laughed in spite of herself. "Honestly, one would expect more from a former nun."

"Are you kidding? We're the worst."

Gerry made no secret of the fact that she enjoyed a healthy sex life. The only time Sam could remember her cutting herself off from the world was that terrible year just after leaving the convent. A time when nothing could console her . . .

Sam's thoughts were interrupted by a flash of movement inside the tent: a shadowy figure that materialized into a slender, dark-haired girl in torn jeans and a navy windbreaker. Glancing about furtively, she snatched something from the buffet table and stuffed it in her pocket.

"Hey! You there!" Sam set off in a brisk jog across the lawn.

The girl shot her a startled look, like a doe at the oiled click of a shotgun, then bolted. She might have escaped, too, if at that moment a figure hadn't hurtled past Sam in pursuit: a tall, jacketless man in a tuxedo shirt rolled up over his elbows, long blond hair flying.

The girl was almost too quick even for Ian. At the bottom of the slope she veered off abruptly in the direction of the orchard, diving headlong into the oleander hedge that bordered it. She'd nearly wriggled free when her windbreaker snagged on a branch. The hedge rustled violently as she fought to free herself. By now a number of guests had hurried over to see what all the commotion was about.

The girl stopped thrashing and shoved a hand into her pocket. Prompting Sam's brother to bellow, "Watch out! She's got a gun!"

Several people screamed, and there was a flurry of movement as everyone scrambled for cover. At that precise moment Ian dove like a linebacker blocking a pass, grabbing the girl about the waist and slamming her to the ground. They struggled briefly, dirt and leaves flying. A high-pitched wail skirled up into the cloudless blue sky.

"Get the fuck off me!"

He hauled the girl to her feet. She was panting, bits of leaves and twigs caught in her tangled brown hair. Her eyes were dark glints in the flushed redness of her face. She took a wild swing, but Ian leaped nimbly out of reach without letting go of her wrist. She swung again, weakly this time.

"Easy now," he soothed. "No one's going to hurt you."

"Leggo!"

"I will as soon as you promise not to run off."

"Fuck you!"

Sam trotted over, catching only a brief glimpse of the bruised-looking hollows under her eyes before the girl dropped her head. "I wasn't stealing," she said in a low, ragged voice. "I was just . . . hungry."

In a single motion she pulled free of Ian and reached into her pocket, tossing something onto the grass. Not the gun they'd imagined, a bread roll. Sam didn't know whether to laugh or cry.

"What's your name?" she asked, not unkindly.

The girl's head jerked up. "What's it to *you?"*

Sam replied calmly, "For one thing, this is private property and you're trespassing."

"I didn't steal nothing," she insisted.

"I'm not accusing you."

The girl glared mutely at Sam. She looked and smelled as though she hadn't showered in days. It had probably been that long since she'd eaten a proper meal. A runaway, no question. The sooner she was shipped home to her parents, the better.

"Maybe this is a discussion you'd rather have with the police," Sam said.

The color drained from the girl's face. She began to shiver. "No. Please. I'll do anything you say. Just . . . no cops, okay?"

Ian's eyes met Sam's, and with a nearly imperceptible shake of his head — as if to say, *let me handle this* — he said, "Relax. No one's calling the cops." He stuck his hand out, this time in friendship. "Ian Carpenter."

The girl hesitated before taking it, mumbling, "Finch."

"That your first or last name?" he asked.

"Both." She narrowed her eyes as if daring him to make something of it.

"Fair enough." He took a step back. "How long since you've eaten?"

She shrugged, dropping her head again.

"All right," he said patiently, "let's try another one. How did you get here? It's a long way to walk."

Sam remembered the scuffling noise in the van. "That was *you*, wasn't it? In the van?"

The girl took a step back, glancing on either side of her as if preparing to bolt. "It wasn't locked."

Ian shrugged. "It's okay. No harm done."

She shot him a grateful, if guarded look. "Can I go now?"

"Not until you've eaten." The words were out of Sam's mouth before she realized she'd spoken. It was the only decent thing to do. The girl looked more starved kitten than cat burglar.

Sam turned and began strolling casually up the slope. A moment later, a shadow fell over the grass at her side. She didn't have to look around to see that it was Finch.

Watching Alice walk to meet them, she felt a twinge of anxiety. Would she object? It was her day, after all. And she'd always been so particular, wanting everything just so, even when she was little. Martin hadn't called her his little princess for nothing.

Then there was Alice, taking Finch by

the hand and saying as if nothing were out of the ordinary, "Come on, I'll get you a plate."

Watching the unlikely pair trail off toward the tent, the storybook bride in her snowy gown and the ragged urchin with leaves in her hair, Sam felt her throat catch. She'd never felt so proud of her daughter.

"That was nice, what you just did."

She turned to find Ian smiling at her. "What else could I do? She looks half starved, poor thing." She gave him a stern look. "You, on the other hand, could have been killed. How did you know that wasn't a gun?"

"I didn't." He grinned, smoothing a hand over the top of his head. In the bright sunlight his hair gleamed like polished oak.

Martin wouldn't have stuck his neck out like that, she thought.

If any one of his family had been kidnapped, he'd have begged, borrowed, or stolen the ransom. But risk life and limb jumping into a fray? No, that wasn't Martin's style.

"Are you always this impulsive?" she asked.

Ian gave a snort of laughter, brushing idly at the grass stains on his shirt. One of its studs was missing, she noticed. "My dad has another word for it. Ask him how many times he had to haul me up by the scruff of my neck when I was that age."

"You don't look any worse for it."

"Lucky for both of us I figured out pretty early on what I was good at." He cupped a hand over his eyes, shading them against the sun. "Speaking of which, I meant what I said before. I'd love to show you my work."

"Sure," she said lightly. "One of these days."

In the wedge of shadow slanting over his face, Ian's gaze was unnervingly frank. All at once she was intensely aware of sun beating down, warming her through her flimsy dress. She might have been naked, the way her skin burned, the way her insides quivered at the thought of his touch. What was happening to her? She'd never felt this way before, not even with Martin.

"What about tomorrow?" Ian asked. "I'm staying over in town. I could pick you up in the morning."

She stared at her shadow falling over the perfectly clipped grass with what she hoped was a pleasant, neutral expression. "I don't know. It's pretty short notice."

"Do you have other plans?"

"Well . . . no. Not exactly."

"Okay then. Around eleven?"

She shook her head. "Maybe another time."

"What are you afraid of?" His voice was low and intimate. And, oh God, the way he was smiling at her . . . as if their roles were reversed, as if *he* were older and wiser somehow.

"Nothing," she lied, her heart racing.

"I'll be honest," he said. "I want to see you again."

She felt suddenly exposed. As if she'd been turned inside out like a pocket, every shameful thought spilling out into the open like loose change. Dear God. What must he think? A lonely older woman only too grateful for a younger man's attention?

"I don't think we should be having this conversation," she said stiffly.

She'd started to walk away when she felt his hand close over her arm. She didn't pull away, just stood there, rooted to the spot, the hot sun burning her through her dress. Gerry would have known how to handle this, she thought. Gerry would have known what to say.

"I didn't mean to upset you," he said.

Anger rose in her, anger at no one in particular. She eyed him coldly. "I'm afraid you have the wrong idea about me."

He cocked his head. "What idea would that be?"

"I don't think I need to spell it out."

Ian nodded slowly in comprehension, smiling that crooked little smile of his. "Oh, I get it. The age thing, right? You're not going to believe this, but it was the furthest thing from my mind."

"You're right, I don't believe you." A sliver of uncertainty crept in nonetheless. Was it possible he didn't see what *she* saw in the mirror?

He dropped his hand from her arm, but she remained motionless. "I enjoy your company. That's it, I swear."

"That doesn't change the fact," she said, "that I'm old enough to be your mother."

"But you're *not* my mother."

"Okay then, your stepmother's mother then." Spoken out loud it sounded so absurd she found herself breaking into a smile.

"Now *that* is weird." Ian regarded her with amusement, his blue eyes crinking. Then he jerked his head in the direction of the tent. "Come on, let's grab a bite. We can talk about it tomorrow."

"Tomorrow?"

"On the way to my place."

He made it sound natural, if not entirely

innocent. She met his smiling gaze. The sun winked off the silver stud in his ear, and she had to fight to keep from brushing a leaf from his hair.

"All right," she said. "As long as it's not a date."

"How about a promise kept?"

"I suppose that'll do."

As they made their way toward the tent Sam found herself wondering uneasily if the promise wasn't to Ian, but to some younger version of herself, the girl in her mind's eye looking back wistfully at the path not taken.

Chapter 2

Laura eyed the unkempt girl seated cross-legged on the grass, hunched over her plate of food. Finch, if that was her real name, which Laura doubted, was eating like someone starved, yet not without a modicum of manners. It was almost touching to see how she struggled with her knife and fork while attempting to hold her plate balanced on her lap. Every so often she'd glance up to see if anyone was watching, then quick as a hummingbird snatch up another morsel and pop it into her mouth.

Laura guessed her to be about sixteen. A runaway, but one with plenty of experience fending for herself. Scared, too. As if she were running from something . . . or someone. Laura didn't doubt that if fate hadn't intervened, she'd have kept right on going.

She strolled over, plate in hand. "May I join you?"

The girl's head shot up like a startled bird's. She was clearly unaccustomed to taking friendly gestures at face value. At the same time it was obvious she didn't want to appear rude. In that sense, too, she'd been taught a modicum of manners. Her young old face engaged in a brief tug of war before rewarding Laura with a nod.

Laura lowered herself onto the grass under the live oak where her grandmother used to make special picnics for Alice and her, with sandwiches and cookies on little flowered plates. A few yards away, in the rose bed off the porch, a tiny skeleton lay buried, a pet canary named Winkie. She remembered the mock funeral they'd staged, with Grammy bearing the tiny cardboard box as solemnly as a casket, while Alice brought up the rear, her small hand cupped about a guttering candle.

"You should try the guacamole," she said, pointing at the girl's plate, on which the dip sat untouched.

Finch nudged it dubiously with her fork. "It doesn't look like the kind you get at Taco Bell."

"That's because it's the real thing. Made with avocados from our own trees."

Finch brought a tiny forkful to her lips. "It's pretty spicy."

"In this part of the world everything is spicy. You'll get used to it." Laura nibbled on an empanada. Ever so casually she asked, "Where did you say you were from?"

"I didn't." The girl's face closed as abruptly as a door slamming shut.

Careful, a voice in Laura's head warned. She tried a different tack. "I was just thinking that if you needed a place to stay I could put you up for a day or two. My ranch is just a few miles down the road." She knew she ought to have her head examined — didn't she have enough to juggle as it was? — but the girl looked so damn . . . bruised. Like a horse that's been mistreated and is letting you know not to even think of getting near it with a saddle. How could she *not* offer?

Finch perked up a bit. "You have a ranch?"

"I guess you could call it that. I keep a couple of horses. Do you ride?"

"I . . . I've always wanted to," she confessed shyly.

"Well, here's your chance." Laura kept her voice light, remembering how skittish her Appaloosa had been when she'd first taken him in, all oozing sores and exposed ribs. She flashed the girl what she hoped was a reassuring smile. "I think you and Punch would get along just fine."

"That's a funny name."

No more so than Finch. "My mare's named Judy. Get it? Punch and Judy." No, she thought, Finch wouldn't get it. That was way too dated for someone her age.

But the girl surprised her by saying, "Oh, yeah. Like the puppets. I saw this show on the street once." She caught herself, as if fearing she'd revealed too much.

Laura's gaze wandered to the tent, where nearly every seat was filled. Wes's friends and relatives mostly — he seemed to have quite a few — with a respectable showing from her own family. Uncle Ray, fat and bald as ever, and Aunt Dolores, trim as in their wedding photos, only a little blonder. Seated on either side were Laura's married cousins, Jen and Kristy, both coincidentally pregnant. Jen just beginning to show, while Kristy looked about to give birth.

Laura felt a twinge of guilt. She'd been avoiding her cousins all morning. It was simply too hard, having to act excited for them when she was eaten up with jealousy inside. If she'd been able to have children of her own maybe Peter wouldn't have left.

"I could sleep in the barn if you have one." The voice beside her was soft and tentative, not that of the tough girl who'd been cursing a blue streak just minutes before.

Laura turned to Finch, her heart constricting at the hesitance in those bruised-looking eyes: that of someone used to second best. "Don't be silly," she said. "There's an extra bed in Maude's room."

"Is she your daughter?"

Laura laughed. "Lord, no. She's . . . well, that's Maude over there." She pointed her out at one of the tables. Maude was going on and on about something to Uncle Pernell and Aunt Florine, who wore slightly dazed looks, as if they didn't quite know what had hit them.

"Oh." Finch nodded, as if needing no further explanation. Clearly, she was used to homes that were anything but traditional.

"Believe me, she won't mind," Laura said. "Anyway, it's only for a couple of days, right?"

Finch fell silent.

Laura watched her awkwardly bring a forkful of food to her mouth, noting that her fingernails were bitten to the quick. She felt a tug inside, like a muscle giving way. As gently as possible, she said, "If you're worried I'm going to go behind your back, don't be."

The girl flicked her an apprehensive glance. "You won't call the cops?"

"You have my word on it."

For the longest moment Finch didn't speak. She just sat there, hunched over her plate, staring off into the distance. When at last she turned to Laura, it was with the clenched cautiousness of someone used to being lied to . . . or worse. "I guess it'd be okay." Almost as an afterthought, she muttered, "Uh, thanks."

"Listen, it's no big deal, okay?" Laura stood up, brushing the back of her dress, which was now hopelessly stained. But who cared? It wasn't as if she had any intention of ever wearing it again. A dress that made her look, she knew, like a rose-colored hitching post. "By the way, my name's Laura. Laura Kiley." She stuck out her hand.

After a moment of hesitation the girl reached up to take it. "Hi." Shy fingers slipped through Laura's like cool water.

"Listen, it'll be a couple more hours," she said. "If you don't feel like hanging around there's room in my car to curl up. The green Explorer."

The girl nodded distractedly, as if holding open her options. If she'd been a stray puppy or kitten, Laura would have tucked Finch under her arm to keep her from taking off.

The rest of the afternoon seemed to crawl by. Laura was glad to see her sister so happy, but the day had brought too many unwelcome reminders of Peter. She wanted nothing more than to be home, in her oldest pair of jeans, kicking back with Maude and Hector. When the cake was finally cut, and the bridal bouquet tossed pointedly in Laura's direction (which she just as pointedly ignored), she wasted no time rounding up Maude. The girl, on the other hand, was nowhere to be seen.

Laura found her fast asleep in the Explorer, curled up in back on a quilted saddle blanket, her filthy canvas backpack as a pillow.

Maude peered in the window. "Oh, the poor thing. She reminds me of Napoléon when we first got him. Do you think she'll let us keep her?"

Laura remembered how tenderly she'd nursed their tomcat back to health after he turned up on their doorstep, near dead and missing half an ear. *If only people were that uncomplicated,* she thought. "It's just for a day or two," she said firmly, more to convince herself than Maude. "I'm sure she has a family. They're probably looking for her as we speak."

"I wonder." Maude's blue eyes were

troubled. Was she thinking of her own family? The son and daughter-in-law who'd forced her to run off in the middle of the night, suitcase in hand. "Suppose she has good reason not to go back?"

"One step at a time, okay?" Laura dug into her purse, rummaging for her keys. "To start with, she could use a change of clothes. I'll check my closet when we get home." She'd kept a few things from when she'd been a size smaller, before lonely nights with only Ben & Jerry as consolation had gotten the better of her.

The girl didn't wake up when she started the car, and was still dead to the world when they pulled into the driveway fifteen minutes later. Crunching to a stop in the graveled yard, Laura saw the house as Finch would: in need of paint, the porch — onto which an old cat-scratched sofa had been dragged — listing slightly to starboard. Not exactly luxurious digs, though Laura wouldn't have had it any other way.

With Maude's help she managed to rouse the girl and steer her up the front path into the house, where Finch tottered groggily down the hall to Maude's room. Within seconds she was once again fast asleep. Laura covered her with the quilted afghan Maude had crocheted and tiptoed out into the hall, easing the door shut.

"I'll keep an eye on her," Maude whispered. "I know you're just itching to get out of that dress."

Laura thought longingly of a horseback ride. There was just enough daylight left. "I should turn the horses out." She hadn't seen them in the corral; Hector must not have gotten around to it.

"Take your time." Maude said. "From the looks of it she'll sleep straight through till morning."

The old woman slipped out of her satin pumps with a sigh of relief — all that dancing, no doubt; Laura had never seen old Uncle Pernell so red-faced — holding them out in front of her like a pair of naughty puppies by the scruffs of their necks.

Laura gave her a quick squeeze. "Thanks. You read my mind."

In her sun-splashed bedroom at the other end of the house, a rectangular patch stood out on the wall over the bureau, darker than the faded blue wallpaper around it, where a photo of Peter and her, taken six years ago at their own wedding, had been removed. She gazed at it as if through a window onto a bleak, wintry landscape.

Oh, Peter, was it just the baby I couldn't give you . . . or would we have drifted apart anyway?

What hurt even more was that his new wife was expecting. Six months along and reportedly big as a house. The only good thing was that they'd moved to Santa Barbara, so at least she didn't have to worry about bumping into them on the street. If only she could find a way to move on, too. Not from this house, but from all its memories. A tear slipped down her cheek. Laura brushed it away angrily. No more wallowing in self-pity. She'd done enough of that to last a lifetime.

She peeled her dress off and tossed it onto the bed. No sense hanging it up; it was going straight into the box of old clothes destined for Lupe's relatives in Ecuador. Pulling on worn Levis and an equally worn chambray shirt, she padded barefoot into the living room to retrieve her boots from the hearth. The room's scuffed floorboards and nicked walls, its chairs liberally sprinkled with pet hairs, seemed to leap out at her as she plopped onto the ottoman. An old chenille bedspread had been thrown over the sofa, clawed to bare wood in places, and the cattails in the painted milk can by the fireplace ought to have been replaced long ago. No place her sister would ever deign to live in, for sure, but it suited Laura like the well-worn boots she was tugging on.

In the kitchen, the dogs climbed from their boxes by the stove, yawning and stretching: Pearl, the golden Lab she'd had since she was a teenager, arthritic and blind in one eye, and the scruffy little black mutt named Rocky from Lost Paws. He trotted over to lick Laura's hand, his stub of tail flickering furiously, while Pearl's thumped like a kangaroo's against the cabinet behind her. Laura tossed them each a dog bone from the cookie jar.

"Behave yourselves, guys. We have company."

On the screened porch in back, a path had been carved through the jumble of mud-caked Wellingtons, old bicycles, folded lawn chairs, and chewed Frisbees. As she stepped down into the yard, she noticed yesterday's laundry still pinned to the clothesline. She smiled and shook her head in fond exasperation. The dryer worked just fine, but Maude insisted on doing things the old-fashioned way . . . even if it meant sleeping on sheets stiff as tarp.

Laura ambled toward the barn, thumbs hooked through the belt loops of her jeans.

The sun hung low in the sky, winking through the outstretched arms of the white oak ahead, and sending shadows trickling like runoff across the yard. In the far-off distance the mountains rose, dusky purple with paler stripes along their highest peaks. At sunset there'd be a brief spell, known as the pink moment, when the mountains to the east would glow with reflected light. If she hurried, she could make it to the top of the hill in time.

Inside the barn, she found the horses straining over their stalls, nickering at her approach: Punch, a seven-year-old Appaloosa, and Judy, the old mare she'd had since she was a child.

"Hi, guys. Miss me?" She reached into her shirt pocket for the lumps of sugar she was seldom without. Punch nuzzled her palm while Judy patiently waited her turn.

She heard a rustling in the hayloft, and looked up. A toe-sprung cowboy boot dropped onto the ladder, followed by a pair of sturdy, blue-jeaned legs. Then a muscled body leaped to the floor, agile as a cat.

"Didn't expect you back so soon." Hector grinned, brushing bits of hay from his T-shirt.

She offered him a crooked smile. "High heels make my feet hurt."

"Everything go okay?"

"The picture-perfect wedding. I'm sure they'll have the picture-perfect honeymoon as well." A note of sarcasm crept into her voice and she felt instantly ashamed. When had she become so bitter? Just because it hadn't worked out with Peter was no reason to take it out on her sister. She brought her cheek to rest against her Appaloosa's dappled neck, tilting her head to give Hector a sheepish look. "I'm happy for them. Really."

"That so?"

Hector approached her slowly, as he might have a skittish mare: a dark-haired man in dust-streaked Levis and a white T-shirt worn nearly transparent in spots. He was broad across the chest and arms, with a long waist that tapered into short, muscular legs slightly bowed from years in the saddle. The silver conch buckle on his belt glittered in the sunlight that fell in dusty slats across the barn's hay-littered floor. For a dreamy instant she thought about running her thumb over its polished surface, how cool and smooth it would feel.

Annoyed with herself, she straightened, pushing open the latch on Punch's stall.

"Okay, I'm feeling sorry for myself. But I should be over it by now. A year and a half is long enough." She tossed a halter over the horse's head and led him to the tacking area. "Besides, the wedding wasn't a complete wash. I met someone interesting."

She thought she saw something flicker in Hector's depthless eyes as he waited for her to fill him in. He never hurried such things, which was partly why she liked being around him, but which also drove her crazy at times. Watching him saunter over to fetch a blanket and saddle, she felt an urge to shake him like a piggy bank into coughing up his two cents.

"A girl crashed the wedding. A runaway." Laura grabbed a hoof pick from its peg on the wall and bent over to hoist one of Punch's hind legs. "I brought her home with me."

"Now why doesn't that surprise me?" Hector paused in the doorway to the tack room, a saddle slung over one arm.

"Why don't you saddle up Judy? I'll tell you all about it on the way."

Hector regarded her curiously, then nodded and said, "She could use the exercise. I didn't get around to it today. Fan belt went out again on the truck."

Through the open barn door she could

see his battered blue Chevy pickup in the yard. He was overdue for a new one, and God knew he'd be able to afford it working someplace else. The only reason he stuck around, she knew, was out of a sense of duty — two women all alone, who would look after them? *I ought to cut him loose,* she told herself. But Hector had been with her for years, and with her family before that. How *would* she manage without him?

She remembered the day he'd appeared at their house, broke and hungry, speaking only a few words of English. Not the first illegal alien to show up at their door . . . but there had been something different about Hector. When her mother brought him a bowl of stew he'd eyed it longingly, then shook his head, indicating mostly through gestures that it was work he was after, not a handout. An hour later he was at the door again, the grass raked and the driveway swept. Laura, sixteen at the time, would never forget watching him wolf down his food, long since gone cold. A familiar lesson brought home to her in a profound way: not everyone was as fortunate as she was. She had made up her mind then and there never to turn a blind eye to those in need.

Hector had been with her family ever since, working days and attending night school, where he'd learned to speak English before going on to earn his GED. Nowadays he juggled college courses with his part-time job here, occasionally lending Guillermo a hand with some of the heavier work at Isla Verde.

As they headed up the hill on horseback, Laura turned to him. "It wouldn't have hurt you to come, you know. I think Alice was a little offended that you didn't."

"Fan belts don't fix themselves," he said.

"That's not the reason, and you know it."

He shrugged. "I'm not against weddings. I just don't like going."

She couldn't tell if he was serious or not. Maybe the fact that he was thirty-two and still unmarried spoke for itself. Not, she reminded herself, that he hadn't had his share of opportunities. "Give me one good reason why not," she said, more to needle him than anything else.

"Maybe because most of them don't last."

A reference to Peter, no doubt. "Not everyone gets divorced," she said a bit huffily. "Look at my parents." The words brought a pang of sorrow. Her father should have been there to walk Alice down the aisle.

"Being together isn't always the same as

being happy." He drew ahead of her as the trail narrowed.

Watching his swaying back she wondered if he knew something she didn't. "What exactly are you implying?"

Hector twisted around in his saddle, the brim of his straw hat throwing a wedge of shadow over his face. "Nothing," he said. "Look, it's none of my business."

"My parents *adored* one other. In fact, I doubt Mom will ever remarry." Laura was brought up short by the conviction with which she spoke. Hector hadn't said anything to suggest otherwise, not really. Why was she so defensive? "Anyway what about yours?"

He flashed her a grin over his shoulder. "With ten kids I can't remember the last time those two sat down and had a conversation, much less argued."

Laura felt a pang of envy at the thought of all those children. Women, she thought, were divided into two groups: those who could have babies and those who couldn't. She'd go weeks without thinking about it . . . then there were days, like today, when she was constantly reminded of the fact.

The brush along the trail grew thicker as they climbed. The dry, brown grass fell away, replaced by a sea of sage and creosote punctuated by tall spears of yucca and agave. Bright splashes of color dotted the ground below — wildflowers flourishing against all odds. Johnny-jump-ups and shooting stars, Indian paintbrush and wild licorice; the air was fragrant with their scent. She caught a trace of old campfires as well: illegal aliens in search of the promised land, as Hector once had been. They usually found work in the orange groves, at half the wages paid to those with green cards.

The only sound was the hollow clocking of hooves against dirt worn to the smooth hardness of stone. Little gouts of dust spiraled up into the golden sunlight that slanted through the trees. Shadows had slipped out from under boulders and clumps of chaparral. Hector sat sharply etched against the deepening sky, a Remington bronze. She could see the muscles in his back straining against the worn fabric of his T-shirt.

At the top of the hill, they paused to let the horses rest. The sun had dipped below the distant mountaintops, crowning them in gold and painting those to the east a luminous rose — the elusive pink moment. Lion's Head and Sulphur Peak, Moon's Nest, and the snowcapped Sleeping Indian

Chief. On the neighboring hill, a moat of shadow had formed around the fortresslike walls of the convent. Laura could barely make out the dirt road to the apiary beyond, where the nuns of Our Lady of the Wayside had been harvesting honey for more than a century.

She sighed. "It's so peaceful." Coyotes and mountain lions still roamed these hills. She spotted rattlesnakes from time to time, even the occasional black bear. If you left them alone, she'd found, they didn't bother you. "Sometimes I think everything would be just fine if I could spend the rest of my life on horseback."

Hector chuckled. "You'd get awful saddle sore."

She thought of Peter. "I can think of worse things."

He frowned, and she saw a muscle flicker in his jaw. Laura thought of her mother's favorite expression: *If you can't say something nice about someone, don't say anything at all.* Hector had disliked her husband from the start, though she couldn't recall him ever uttering a single disparaging word. Peter, on the other hand, had been quick to criticize Hector behind his back for acting more like a family member than a hired hand.

A long moment passed, then he turned to her and said, "You're better off without him. You just don't know it yet."

She looked at him in surprise. Hector was seldom that blunt . . . ironically, because he didn't think it was his place. "Old habits die hard, I guess."

"Yeah, like smoking." He'd given it up last year.

Laura supposed getting over a divorce was the same in some ways — it got a little easier with each passing day. "I heard Peter and his wife are expecting." She was careful to strike a nonchalant tone in an effort to hold the pain, circling like a hungry jackal, at bay.

Hector nodded. "I ran into Farber last week. He mentioned something." Rich Farber, their family dentist, was an old friend of Peter's.

"I guess the ex-wife is always the last to know." Now the pain did strike, sinking its teeth to the bone. Laura squinted against the tears that welled. The bastard. Would it have hurt him to pick up the phone? Instead, she'd had to hear it from that old busybody, Gayle Warrington. "It shouldn't have surprised me," she said. "He wouldn't have married anyone who didn't want children."

"*You* wanted them."

"The difference is I couldn't have them."

"There were other choices." Hector's mouth was flat and unsmiling.

"Adoption, you mean?" She gave a short, bitter laugh. "I'd have gone for it in a heartbeat, but Peter wouldn't even consider it. Nothing but his own flesh and blood would do."

He shot her a keen glance. "I didn't know. You never said anything."

"I couldn't talk to anyone. Not even Alice." How to explain how inadequate she'd felt. Like factory goods marked down as irregular. Even now it was almost too painful to discuss.

He didn't say anything, but the compassion in his face eased the pain somehow. She told him then about the girl. How she'd appeared out of nowhere. How fiercely she'd fought back when Ian held her pinned and at the same time how oddly defenseless she'd seemed. Hector listened closely, nodding here and there as if in understanding.

When she was finished, he asked, "What about her parents?"

"I don't even know where she's from." Laura recalled Maude's words. "But from what I've seen so far, I'm betting her parents are the problem, not the solution."

"She might be in some kind of trouble."

"That, or she's running from it. I couldn't say for sure, but something tells me she's been abused."

"What makes you think that?"

"She's got the look," Laura said. "Like an animal that won't take food from your hand, no matter how hungry it is."

She ran her hand absently over the ropy scar on Punch's neck. Four years ago he'd been found cooped in a stall behind a derelict house, half starved and hock-deep in muck, the wound from a too-tight halter infected. The vet wasn't sure he'd pull through. It had taken months of careful nurturing before he was well enough to be ridden.

"I guess we'll just have to wait and see," Hector said. "Let me know if there's anything I can do."

She noted he'd said *we,* and was thankful that he saw this as a joint enterprise. "Thanks, I will."

Laura gave Punch a little nudge with her heels, and they started back down the trail. The sky was an ashy rose and a ghost moon sailed on a flimsy raft of cloud. A condor circled overhead in search of its evening meal. All quiet on the western front, she thought. For the moment, at least . . .

It was nearly dark by the time they got back. Laura dismounted and led her horse into the barn. As she flicked on the overhead light, its concrete floor was thrown into glaring relief. "I didn't realize it had gotten to be so late," she said, thinking of Maude all alone with the girl.

"You go on in," Hector said. "I'll take care of the horses."

She hesitated. "Don't you have class tonight?"

"I have time."

He plucked his hat from his head, tossing it onto a nail. In the stark light his face was sharply defined: his angular jaw and the lines bracketing his flared nose, his coffee-colored eyes narrowed in a more or less permanent squint. A band of sweat glistened faintly on his forehead, and his thick, black hair was pushed into damp little spikes. She looked away, not wanting him to catch her staring. Like when she was sixteen and had followed him around like a lovesick puppy. He must have known, though typically he'd pretended not to notice.

"Why do I always feel I'm taking advantage of you?" she asked.

He grinned, showing a chipped front tooth. "Don't flatter yourself." A reference, no doubt, to the women who'd tried, and failed, to get a handle on him.

"Okay then. Have it your way." She was halfway out the door when she turned and said softly, "Thanks, Hec. I really don't pay you enough, and you know it."

"Why don't you let me worry about that?" While Judy waited her turn, he replaced Punch's bridle with a halter and clipped it to the crossties. They both knew she couldn't afford more than a pittance, plus room and board. No use belaboring the point.

"I guess I have enough to worry about as it is," she conceded.

Hector grabbed a towel and began rubbing Punch down. "Just one thing: Don't get too attached." It was as if he'd read her mind. "Sooner or later you're going to have to turn her loose."

His words echoed in her mind as she made her way across the yard. Hector was right. Finch wasn't a horse or a dog she could take under her wing. *Whatever her problems it isn't my job to fix them.* She might even be biting off far more than she could chew. And yet there was something so vulnerable about the girl under that layer of callused toughness. A tiny spark of hope in those bruised eyes that had touched a chord. *I might not be able to fix what's wrong,* she thought, *but maybe I can keep that spark from going out.*

She found Maude at the kitchen table, sipping a mug of tea. She'd changed into her chenille robe and slippers. Her hair hung down her back in a loosely plaited braid the color of old piano keys. She glanced up at Laura. "Not a peep. Still out like a light."

Laura tugged her boots off, and tossed them onto the porch. "I'm not surprised," she said. "She looked as though she hadn't slept in days."

"Not to mention all that food on an empty stomach." Maude wore a distracted look as she brought her steaming mug to her lips. Her hand was trembling, sending hot tea sloshing over the rim.

Laura grabbed a napkin to mop the table, then sank down in the chair opposite her. "Maude, is everything all right?"

She was reminded of the state in which she'd first found Maude, around this time last year, stranded by the side of the road with her broken-down Impala. In the trunk was a suitcase and a Mason jar filled with old buttons collected over the years — the sum of her earthly possessions. Laura had given her a lift to the house so she could call for a tow truck. But it turned out the repairs would've been more than the old heap was worth, and besides, Maude was nearly penniless. Laura had invited her to stay for a few days, days that had stretched into months. Meanwhile, Maude, not one to sit idle, had taken over the cooking and laundry and all but the heaviest chores. Now she was as integral a part of the household as Hector.

"Elroy called while you were out," she said.

"Your son?" Laura tried to keep the disdain from her voice. The last time Elroy had phoned his mother was on her birthday, more than a month and a half ago.

Using both hands, Maude carefully lowered her mug to the table. "He wants me to move back in with Verna and him."

"*What?*" Laura sat back, stunned.

"I know, I know." Maude shook her head as if she didn't quite believe it, either. "It was the last thing I expected. You could've knocked me over with a feather."

"After the way they treated you? It's crazy!" And she only knew the half of it. Maude was far too loyal to paint her son and daughter-in-law as the monsters Laura was certain they were.

Maude sighed. "It doesn't make much sense, does it?"

"Elroy must feel guilty. I suppose this is his way of getting rid of it."

"I didn't think of it that way, but you could be right." Maude fell silent, lost in thought.

Laura began to worry. "That doesn't mean you have to do what he wants."

"Well, now, maybe it wasn't all that bad. I *was* a burden in a lot of ways. It's hard enough making ends meet without some old lady dragging you down. And Elroy has his father's quick temper."

There she went, making excuses for him again. "You're not dragging *me* down," Laura said. "Just the opposite."

"Bless your heart." Maude patted her hand, looking on the verge of tears. "Why, if I thought I was a burden to you I'd . . . I'd put myself down like an old dog."

"What did you tell him?"

"That I'd think about it." As if sensing her distress their little tabby leaped into Maude's lap. She stroked it tenderly while Napoléon, jealous of the attention Josie was getting, mewed pathetically at her feet — a big, fierce-looking tom with one torn ear and the disposition of a two-year-old.

"I didn't want to hurt his feelings. He said he was sorry for the way he treated me. He . . . he sounded as if he meant it."

"What about what *you* want?"

Maude smiled, as if the answer should have been obvious. "This past year has been the happiest of my life."

"Why didn't you tell that to Elroy?"

"He's my only child." Maude shook her head slowly, eyes bright with unshed tears. She was too kind to say it: *You don't know what it's like to be a mother.*

Laura winced inwardly nonetheless.

At that precise moment a piercing scream tore through the house, sending goose bumps swarming up the back of her neck. It was coming from the bedroom down the hall.

It was the same dream as always. A man chasing her down a dark street. She couldn't see his face, only the gun in his hand. If he caught her, he'd kill her. There was only one way out: She'd have to fly. She spread her arms, flapping with all her might, and felt herself lift up, toes hovering just above the pavement . . . but that was as high as she could go. And now the man was nearly upon her . . .

"Finch."

With a thump she spiraled up into consciousness, opening her eyes to a shadowy figure even more frightening than the one in her dream. Because this one was real. "*Whassat?*" She bolted upright, rubbing eyes coated in gray fuzz. Her throat felt thick and dry.

Firm hands gripped her shoulders, steadying her. "It's okay, honey. It's just me . . . Laura."

The girl began to shiver. It was cold, as cold as winter in New York. Then she remembered . . . the wedding . . . and falling asleep in the back of an SUV. She had no memory of coming here, and now looked about the strange room to get her bearings. In the light spilling in from the hallway she saw a dresser and overstuffed chair, and what looked like a quilt hanging on the wall. On the dresser was a jar that glittered as if with treasure; it was filled with buttons, she saw. She looked back at the woman.

"I must've been dreaming," she said groggily.

"Sounded more like a nightmare." The woman smiled. She'd changed into jeans and a chambray shirt, yet looked prettier somehow than at the wedding. Her brown hair pulled back in a ponytail, and her cheeks were flushed as if from the outdoors. "Do you want to tell me about it?"

"I don't remember." Someone had thought to cover her with a blanket, and now she pulled it up over her shoulders, holding it around her like a cape. She couldn't seem to stop shivering.

"I sometimes talk in my sleep," Laura confided, speaking as cozily as if she'd known her all her life. "That's what my husband used to say. Of course, I never had any idea until he told me."

"You're married?" Finch ventured.

"Divorced."

"Oh." To the girl this was normal. She knew hardly anyone whose parents were still together.

"Almost two years," Laura said.

Finch said the first thing that came to mind. "You don't seem old enough."

Laura laughed. "He was my high school sweetheart. We got married right out of college." She lifted a corner of the blanket, which was dragging on the floor, smoothing it over the bed. "Funny. I couldn't have imagined life without him, but I didn't curl up and die the way I thought I would."

The girl didn't know what to say. She was suspicious of all this niceness. At the same time she felt a strange yearning to trust this woman. She settled for a noncommittal shrug. "You didn't have a choice," she said.

"There's an old saying: God never gives us more than we can handle." Laura drifted into thought, the light from the hallway illuminating her square face that ought to have been plain but was somehow pretty. After a moment she roused herself and said brightly, "I'm not being a very good hostess, am I? What can I get you — a glass of water, something to eat?"

"Water would be nice." She'd never been so thirsty. At the same time, she felt strangely full . . . though she had no memory of having eaten. The events of the past few days had run together like colors on a finger painting.

Laura got up and left the room, returning moments later with a chilled glass in which ice cubes tinkled with a faint, musical sound. The girl gulped it down so quickly its coldness made her head ache.

Laura touched her shoulder. "You're shivering. Let's get you under the covers." She bent to pick up the backpack on the floor beside the bed.

"Don't touch that!" Finch cried.

The woman froze, clearly startled. "I didn't want you to trip over it," she said gently.

The girl's face flooded with heat. "Sorry," she muttered. "I just don't like people touching my things."

Laura straightened, planting her hands on her hips. "Look, you've got to trust *somebody*, so it might as well be me. I meant what I said. No snooping, and that goes for personal property, too. Scout's honor." Her voice was crisp, but not unkind.

Finch dropped her gaze, at a sudden loss for words. She didn't know how she was supposed to feel. Almost everyone she'd ever trusted had disappointed her in some way. Why should this woman be any different?

"Where's the bathroom?" she asked, realizing suddenly that she had to pee.

"Just down the hall." Laura pointed the way. "I left you a towel if you feel like taking a shower. Anything else you need just make yourself at home."

And that was it. Her first night in this strange place — walking as if in a dream down a hall lined with family pictures, its old boards creaking faintly beneath her bare feet. The woman eyed her from the bedroom doorway as anxiously as if she'd been a toddler taking her first steps. An odd feeling quivered in the girl's belly; a

feeling she couldn't recall ever having before — that of being watched over. She remembered her dream and all at once
seemed to grow weightless, as if flying.

# Chapter 3

Sam frowned at the clock on her nightstand. Six-thirty in the morning and she was as wide awake as if the alarm had gone off. Hadn't the wedding, followed by the lingering of her brother and sister and their respective spouses well into the evening, been enough to wear her out for a week? She ought to have slept until noon. But today wasn't just any Sunday. There was Ian. Picking her up for their date in just four and a half hours.

Not a date, she corrected.

So why hadn't she mentioned it to anyone? Laura, the least likely to jump to conclusions, or even her brother, Ray, who analyzed stock quotes and futures, not other people's lives. If it was all so innocent, a passing remark would have saved her from . . .

. . . *feeling like a teenager sneaking behind my parents' back.*

Sam rolled onto her stomach with a groan, burying her face in the pillow. Alice and Wes were in Maui by now, too far away to give their permission, if that's what she was looking for.

A vestige of teenage rebellion stirred in her now. Permission? *My God, I'm forty-eight years old!* She didn't need anyone's blessing to spend a pleasant afternoon with someone who was practically a member of the family. Never mind that he was a man, and an attractive one at that. Had Alice asked *her* permission before taking up with Wes?

Sam groaned anew at the comparison. Of course, it was flattering that Ian found her attractive; she was only human after all. And except for Tom Kemp, whom she'd never even kissed, there'd been no one since Martin. The idea of getting involved with someone young enough to be her — well, Ian's age — was ludicrous.

At the same time, it left her glowing as if she'd just stepped out of the bath. She felt both restless and strangely indolent, acutely aware of her nightgown twisted about her hips and the pale sunlight soaking into her bare limbs. She closed her eyes and imagined Ian running a hand up her leg. She could almost feel the light brush of his fingertips tickling the tiny hairs along the inside of her thigh, bringing to life what she'd believed dead.

She jumped out of bed as if goosed. It seemed disloyal to Martin's memory somehow . . . not so much as if she were cheating, but because she'd never felt that way with him; she'd never burned at his touch. What she'd fallen in love with were his quick mind and easy laugh, how he'd light up a room merely by walking into it. Martin had had a way of making her feel not just like the only woman in the world, but the only other *person*. Even his proposal had been one of a kind, as unique as Martin himself. They'd been sitting cross-legged on the bed in his dorm room surrounded by Chinese takeout cartons, when she cracked open her cookie to find a fortune that read, *Will you marry me?*

She hadn't known whether or not to take him seriously until Martin rose, wobbling, to his knees and slipped the paper ring from his chopsticks onto her finger, saying solemnly, "I'll buy you a real one soon as I can afford it."

What she hadn't realized at the time, looking into his broad Irish face flushed with impish delight, was that everything there was to know about Martin had been summed up in that single gesture: the wild romantic leaps with nothing to back them up, the grand gestures that were like the wedding ring he'd never gotten around to buying. It was her grandmother's gold band, given to her by her mother, that she'd worn her entire married life.

Her gaze fell on a photo of Martin in a pewter frame on the bureau, taken just before he became ill. He stood poised at the helm of his sailboat, squinting into the sunlight: a handsome, middle-aged man grown a bit soft about the middle, his curly silver hair blowing in the wind. Martin had always been happiest at sea. Their marriage, she thought, was just another version — with her the terra firma to his flights of fancy, the one who put the brakes on when things threatened to spin out of control. When he died she hadn't been utterly lost like many widows because all those years it had been *her*, not Martin, managing the household and paying the bills.

Sam tugged on her robe with something close to defiance. This room was her answer to all those years of excess. A few months after Martin's death, she'd had the carpet and wallpaper ripped out; she'd sold the ornate walnut bed and dresser and brought down from the attic her childhood bureau and bed frame, which she'd stripped to their original oak finish. Now the white stucco walls and polished heart-of-pine floor — accented by a simple Kazakh rug, a few framed watercolors, a vintage mica floor lamp — seemed to glow with an austere beauty.

Making her way downstairs, she could hear the faint clatter of her housekeeper in the kitchen. Lupe, no doubt rearranging things to her liking. Sam shook her head in exasperation. How many times had she urged the woman to slow down? She was in her seventies, after all, and not getting any younger.

Sam walked in to find Lupe teetering on tiptoe, trying to push a platter onto the top shelf of the old oak china cupboard. She darted over to help. "Here, let me." Taller than Lupe by at least eight inches, she had no trouble sliding it into place.

"*Gracias, mi hija.*" Lupe sank onto her heels with a sigh, casting Sam a look of mild reproach. "*Dios mío,* what are you doing up at this hour? Did you forget it was Sunday?"

"I could ask the same of you." Sam glanced about, frowning. "What's all this?" She gestured at the serving bowls and platters spread over the counter. "I thought everything was put away last night."

"It was." The stern lines of disapproval

in Lupe's face confirmed what Sam had already guessed: that the catering crew's cleanup hadn't been to her housekeeper's satisfaction. "Men," she scoffed. "What do they know about kitchens? It's a miracle nothing was broken."

"And even more of a miracle you aren't flat on your back," Sam chided. "Do me a favor, please, and take the rest of the day off."

Lupe dismissed her concerns with a snort. "I'd rather die on my feet than on my back." She gathered up an armload of bowls, a pint-sized woman in jeans and a red-checkered shirt, her face as brown and wrinkled as a walnut, her charcoal hair wound about her head in a tightly braided coronet.

Lupe's hair, only lightly threaded with gray, was her pride and joy. She washed it with special oils and dried it in the sun. Once, a few years back, Sam had come across her basking in the sunlight with her head in her husband's lap. Guillermo had only been combing her wet hair, but Sam had felt as if she'd stumbled upon something deeply intimate. Fifty years of marriage hadn't wiped away the small smile on Lupe's lips as she lay with her eyes closed and head tipped back, her hair spilling into her husband's knotted brown hands like a gift.

Sam caught the scent of something baking. "Do I smell corn bread?"

Lupe bent to stow the bowls and straightened. "Since you're up, it won't hurt you to eat something."

Sam groaned. "I'm still stuffed from yesterday."

"Men like meat on a woman's bones."

Sam reached for the coffeemaker by the stove, filling her favorite mug — one Laura had given her some years back, on which was printed THE WORLD'S GREATEST MOM. "I'm not looking for a man." This past year it had become a familiar refrain; Lupe wasn't going to give up until she remarried.

"A woman alone is no good to anyone. Now sit."

Lupe slid a skillet from the oven — corn bread, lightly golden on top and crispy around the edges. Sam surprised herself by devouring two thick wedges smothered in butter and Blessed Bee honey. Afterward, sipping her coffee at the table, she felt a contentment that eluded her most days. Maybe it was this kitchen, so rooted in memory: family meals about the oak harvest table, arriving home from school to find a pitcher of freshly squeezed lemonade in the fridge, Lupe teaching Audrey and her to pat out tortillas and prepare *masa* for tamales. There'd been popcorn popped in a long-handled wire basket over the open fire, birthday cakes decorated with marshmallows and gumdrops, and a gingerbread house each year at Christmastime.

She gazed about her, at the blackened fireplace and mantel hung with copper pots, the built-in cupboard with its hodgepodge of china she'd collected or inherited over the years. Sunlight fell in leafy patterns over the Mexican tiles at her feet. On the patio out back she could see a lemon tree, laden with fruit ready to be picked. An overlooked champagne glass from yesterday's festivities glittered on the wrought-iron bench by the pool.

The thought of Ian crept in, causing her heart to quicken.

"Oh, by the way," she said, "don't bother with lunch. I'm driving up the coast with a friend."

Lupe, washing dishes already spotless, turned from the sink. "Anyone I know?"

Sam felt her face grow warm. "Wes's son."

"The tall, blond one with hair to here?"

Lupe brought a soapy hand to her shoulder.

"His name's Ian. He's an artist. Quite talented from what I've heard." Sam spoke lightly, almost tripping over her words. "He offered to show me his paintings."

"*Dios mío.*" Lupe cranked off the tap with a groan of old pipes.

Sam stiffened. This was the price she paid for the woman having helped raise her: a housekeeper who acted more like a mother. "It's not what you think," she said.

"If you know what I'm thinking, you know it's wrong."

"Why? Because he's young and I'm . . ." Sam faltered. How could she expect Lupe, of all people, to understand? Weakly, she finished, "I'm not that old."

Lupe dried her hands with her apron — hands as tough as old shoe leather. "Not now," she said. "But one day you will be. You need a man who will look after you." A subtle reference, Sam knew, to Martin's shortcomings.

"I'm perfectly capable of looking after myself." She pushed herself to her feet and carried her plate and mug to the sink.

Lupe eyed her narrowly. "Will you be back in time for supper?"

"Don't count on it."

Her words had the desired effect. Lupe's lips drew in as tightly as a drawstring. And this was just the tip of the iceberg. Sam's daughters would be scandalized as well. To Alice, who'd worshipped her father, another man — never mind that it was Ian — would seem almost a sacrilege, while Laura would see it as one more cause to fret.

As she climbed the stairs, Sam thought of the girl who'd crashed the wedding. She wondered if Laura had made any headway with her. *I ought to phone —*

She hadn't finished the thought when it rang. Audrey calling to say what a wonderful time she'd had . . . and oh, by the way, had anyone reported getting sick? Grant was up half the night throwing up and thought it might have been something he ate.

Minutes later her brother called on his way to the airport. "Great party, Sis." Ray's voice boomed over the crackle of his cell phone. "Next time you're out our way we'll return the favor, Texas style."

She couldn't help smiling. Ray, a recent transplant to the Dallas area, had become more Texan than the Ewings of South Fork. When she'd visited last fall, her brother had greeted her at the airport wearing a ten-gallon hat and three-hundred-dollar Tony Lama boots. The barbecue in her honor had consisted of fifty of their "closest" friends, and enough ribs to feed a small third world nation.

After that several more people phoned to say what a beautiful wedding it had been and what a lovely time they'd had. By the time she hung up on the last caller it was nearly ten-thirty. She jumped into the shower and was tucking her shirt into her jeans when the doorbell rang. She dashed downstairs, but Lupe got there ahead of her, casting Ian a long, coolly assessing look before Sam could hustle him off.

"You're early," she said.

He glanced at his watch. "Actually, I'm right on time."

"Guess I'm used to being kept waiting." Martin had always been running late.

"My military school training," he joked as they made their way up the path.

Climbing into his van she was pleased to notice he'd tidied up except for a pair of binoculars resting on her seat. Ian stowed them in the glove compartment, explaining, "There's an osprey colony about a mile or so from my place. I thought we'd take a look."

Oh God, she thought. As a long-standing member of the land conservancy, her pet project, so to speak, had been the preservation of the golden eagle, now making a spectacular comeback. If Ian shared her passion, she was *really* in trouble.

"How far to your place?" she asked.

"Half an hour or so." He started the engine and coasted to the bottom of the drive, turning left onto Chumash. "We can stop for lunch along the way. I know this great little hole-in-the-wall."

"Sounds good."

She glanced at him out of the corner of her eye. Ian looked far more at home in chinos and a navy T-shirt than in a tuxedo. She could see the damp comb tracks in his hair. On his sockless feet were a pair of well-broken-in boating shoes. The silver stud glinted in his ear, and about his wrist was a braided leather band.

She felt herself grow warm. Did he have any idea of the effect he was having on her? It was as if time had taken a U-turn, and she was suddenly reliving the tumult of her teenage years: the wild crushes on boys, the intense yearning stirred by a lingering glance, the brush of a sleeve against bare arm, the scent of a certain aftershave.

She made small talk in an effort to appear no more interested than she would be in any member of Wes's family. They talked about Ian's growing up in Malibu and his years at UC Berkeley earning a master's in art. Sam, in turn, tried to convey to him what it was like living in the same place her entire life.

At the overlook on Pratt Bluff, off Highway 33, she asked to pull over. "See that?" She pointed out the old highway that twisted up through the foothills above Sorrento Creek. "My great-grandfather owned one of the valley's first orange groves. He built that road with the help of Chinese laborers. It was the only way he could truck his crops out."

"I thought he was a shopkeeper," Ian said.

"That came later; after a frost killed off most of one year's crop. He figured it'd be more profitable to import dry goods."

"Sounds like a sensible guy. You must take after him." Ian's voice was deep and musical, a voice she could never grow tired of hearing. He reached to brush a strand of hair from her face, his fingertips igniting a trail of fire along her cheek. As she stood rooted to the spot, her heart pounding, she wondered how sensible she was right now.

Sensible people aren't the ones having fun, a voice whispered.

Fifteen minutes later they were turning

onto the coast highway. Fog had left the ocean a tarnished silver that glittered in patches where polished by the sun. As they traveled farther north, the dockyards and eateries that clung like barnacles to the shoreline began giving way to sandstone cliffs and wind-scoured dunes. A few miles east of Purisima Point, Ian pulled onto an unpaved road where they got out to peer through his binoculars at giant osprey nests perched like wicker baskets atop a row of telephone poles. As Sam watched, a female osprey circled about, crying her shrill *tewp-tewp-teeaaa* before settling onto her nest.

By the time they reached Pinon, a tiny Portuguese fishing village just south of Santa Maria, she was starving. Ian drew to a stop in front of a funky-looking tavern sided in weather-beaten tongue and groove. Inside, a fisherman's net studded with Styrofoam floats drooped from the ceiling. The diners, families mostly, appeared to be locals. Sam didn't feel terribly inspired.

Ian squeezed her hand. "Trust me. I won't lead you astray."

Martin's words. Yet he *had* led her astray. In the end, all she'd had left was a stack of bills and a life insurance policy that had barely covered funeral expenses. She hoped she wasn't heading down a similar path.

Surprisingly, the food turned out to be every bit as good as advertised: tender mussels steamed in butter and white wine; mounds of sweet bay shrimp; flounder that melted at the touch of a fork, with chunks of warm sourdough bread to mop their plates. When dessert arrived — thick wedges of olallie berry pie topped with vanilla ice cream — Sam groaned that she couldn't eat another bite. She ended up polishing off her entire slice.

Ian's studio was at the end of a dirt road — a tiny cottage sided in shingles the weathered gray of driftwood. It sat on a long, sandy spit of land that looked out over a harbor. A small fleet of fishing boats bobbed from moorings along the pier. A bait shack leaned into the wind. Gulls wheeled and cried overhead.

"As you can see, it's not exactly Malibu." The gate to the yard gave a squeal as he pushed it open. "On the plus side, nobody around here ever locks up. It's like something out of a time warp."

"I'll take privacy over trendy any day."

Sam stepped into a large room with windows on all sides and skylights through which sunshine poured. The walls were paneled in pale wood and hung with an assortment of unframed canvases. Off to the right was a kitchen area no bigger than a ship's galley; at the other end a ladder led up to a loft bed. She paused for a moment, taking it all in.

"Oh Ian, it's lovely."

"Glad you approve." He looked pleased.

"I don't see how you could ever bear to leave it."

He shrugged, tossing his keys onto the small carved table by the door. "I have to earn a living somehow." With all his father's wealth, he was clearly no trust-fund kid.

She wandered over to a section of the wall covered in corkboard. Three partially completed canvases were tacked to it: the mural he was working on. The workbench below was littered with rolled-up tubes, palettes crusted with paint, brushes soaking in jars. An easel and drafting table were cluttered with more of the same. Unframed canvases, three and four deep, were stacked along the baseboard.

Her gaze was drawn to one in particular: an almost surreal portrait of a bare-chested black sailor roped to a halyard in Christlike crucifixion — as skillfully rendered as it was evocative.

"I had no idea," she said.

"Not what you were expecting?"

"I was picturing seascapes, boatyards — that kind of thing."

"The stuff they sell in tourist shops, you mean." He cocked a brow, eyeing her with amusement.

She thought of the pretty little seascape she and Martin had bought in a gallery some years back. "Not all of it's bad."

"I'd make more money, that's for sure." His gaze fell on a rough pencil sketch pinned to the drafting table. "On the other hand, I've never been one to color inside the lines."

She studied several more canvases: an alley cat nosing the strewn contents of a garbage can, an almost photographic portrait of an elderly Portuguese fisherman, flamenco dancers who seemed almost alive. Each more vivid than the next.

"I'm impressed," she said. "And I don't impress easily."

"I gather you haven't exactly gone the tourist route, either."

"Oh, we get our share," she said with a small laugh. "Usually, they take one look at the price tags and head right back out the door. Most of our trade is local."

"You must do a pretty good business."

He was referring, of course, to the fact that Carson Springs had its share of wealthy homes, with his father's among the most eye-catching.

"We do all right, though it's a little more competitive now than in my great-grandparents' day." She didn't add that receipts were down 20 percent from last year, a sign not only of the times but of playing catch-up. The years of Martin's illness had taken their toll.

"Ever get tired of it?" he asked.

"Sometimes," she confessed. "Back in college it certainly wasn't how I imagined spending the rest of my life. I suppose one of these days I'll retire, then I'll get to do what *I* want . . . as soon as I figure out what that is."

Ian smiled as if he found the whole idea amusing, a lazy smile that funneled through her like sand through an hourglass. "I hate to disappoint you," he said, "but right now you look about sixteen."

He knew Sam thought he was just flattering her, but at this moment, with her hair pulled back in a ponytail and the light falling over her face, smoothing out its fine lines, he could see how she must have looked as a teenager. Did she have any idea how much more beautiful she was now?

He took in the coppery highlights in her hair, the clean lines of her jaw, the thumbprint of shadow at the base of her throat. She wasn't wearing any makeup, and he loved the frankness of her unadorned face, the light that seemed to shine from her gray-green eyes. Even the way she was looking at him: as if she wanted to trust him, but wasn't quite ready.

Sam grew uncomfortable beneath his gaze. Why was he looking at her like that? She stared at his T-shirt, which was bleached in spots. Clearly, no one had taught him the proper way to do laundry. If she'd been his mother . . .

But you're not, whispered the voice in her head. A slow warmth traveled up from her toes, curling through her like sweet wood smoke, invading every hidden crevice. She felt weak all over, like after a long illness. This wasn't supposed to be happening, she told herself. There was no room in her life for this *thing* — desire, lust, whatever you wanted to call it — that seemed to have a mind of its own.

She felt a sudden need to set the record straight. "Look, Ian, if I've given you the wrong impression . . ."

He continued to regard her steadily. Oh, those eyes. Like the ocean that lulled you into a trance if you stared at it too long. "You haven't given me the wrong impression at all."

She flushed at the frankness of his reply. He knew what she was feeling . . . yes, in the face of every instinct telling her to run. "Are you always this direct?" she asked, trembling in the warm sunshine.

"When I'm interested in someone, yes."

Her mouth went dry, and she was distinctly aware of a pulse at the base of her throat. It was all she could do to maintain her composure. "Okay, I'll admit I'm flattered, but that still doesn't change the fact that I'm old enough to . . . know better."

"To know better — or know what you want?"

Sam's heart began to beat in great, lurching thuds. She brought a hand to her cheek; it felt hot. "Oh dear, I'm not very good at this, am I?" How ironic that she, the older of the two, was nervous as a schoolgirl.

He smiled encouragingly. "You're doing just fine."

He was standing so close she could see the fine, golden stubble dusting his jaw, and the tiny scar that curved in a crescent over one brow. His eyes were clear and guileless. He wasn't mocking her.

When he drew her into his arms and kissed her, lightly at first, then more insistently, it was as if she'd tumbled from a high perch — a feeling of weightlessness that brought a heady sense of release. She wasn't aware of kissing him back until her hands floated up to touch the back of his neck. Smooth, so smooth. Oh Lord, she'd forgotten the lovely suppleness of youth.

He smelled of clothes dried on the line, and tasted faintly of the sea. All at once she was flooded with memories of her teenage years — steamy car windows, hands fumbling with buttons in the dark, weak murmurs of protest. All of it new, exciting, forbidden.

A single thought beat like a pulse: *Don't stop.*

He untucked her shirt from her jeans. Then he was undoing her buttons, reaching around to unfasten her bra. Panic set in. Would he find her ugly? Her breasts that had nursed two children, her skin that was no longer firm. Standing before him, shivering, she had to resist the urge to cross her arms over her chest.

Ian bent to kiss first one breast, then the other, cupping them reverently in his palms. If she was less than perfect, he didn't seem to notice. Sam exhaled in a rush of breath that left her dizzy. Oh, his tongue. His touch. As if he knew exactly what she needed . . .

He unzipped her jeans, tugging them down over her hips. Then he knelt and began gently kissing her *there,* his breath warm and thrilling through the thin cotton of her panties.

"No." She pulled away.

He rocked back on his heels, peering up at her. "What's wrong?"

"I've never —" A flood of embarrassment choked off the words.

Ian seemed to understand. Wordlessly he rose and took her by the hand, leading her up the ladder to the bed. God, what must he be thinking? A woman her age who'd never — but it was Martin, who hadn't wanted to do . . . certain things, who'd made her feel dirty for even suggesting them.

And Ian wasn't Martin. She closed her eyes, listening to him undress. Then he was stretching out alongside her, his long limbs sliding cool against her skin.

"Don't worry. We'll take it slow." He began to stroke her while lightly kissing her mouth and neck.

The warm air atop the platform seemed to wrap about them like a cocoon. She felt herself begin to relax. His body was a marvel, all muscle and bone, smooth except where covered in fine golden down like the pelt of some lean, fleet-footed animal. When, at last, he gently pushed a hand between her legs they parted easily. It seemed as natural as breathing.

Ian moved lower, his mouth brushing her navel, the ends of his hair trailing over her belly. Then he was kissing her. Down there. Oh, sweet Lord. How did he know? Who had given him the map to her body? The pleasure was almost more than she could bear. Brazenly, she raised her hips to meet his mouth, biting down on her lip to keep from crying out.

When she came it was like being turned inside out, so exquisite it was almost painful. Wave after intoxicating wave. Light rushing at her behind closed eyelids. She cried out, and immediately afterward burst into tears.

Ian sat up, pulling her into his arms. "Shh. It's okay."

"I'm s-sorry," she gulped.

"Don't be."

"I feel so —" She broke off, not knowing how to put it into words.

"You don't have to explain."

"Was it . . . did you enjoy it, too?" she asked timidly.

He drew back in surprise. "Jesus. Someone really did a number on you."

"The only man I've ever been with was my husband." She felt a stab of guilt, as if she were betraying Martin's memory. "I assumed he was like most men."

"I don't know about other guys," he said, "but I find it incredibly sexy."

"I guess things were different in my day."

He smiled. "In that case, I'd say you have some catching up to do."

He kissed her, the scent of her on his lips like some exotic new fruit. Sam surprised herself by responding just as greedily as before. She ran her hands over him, *all* of him. Ian seemed to revel in her appetite, in each timid exploration that grew bolder. When he pushed her away it was only to whisper huskily, "No. I want to be inside you when I come."

He reached up, groping for a condom on the narrow shelf overhead. She thought: *In my day, too, it would've been me getting up to put in my diaphragm.*

She smiled at the idea. The last time she'd had a period was . . . well, she'd lost count. Pregnancy was the least of her worries. "You don't have to," she said, putting a hand over his and feeling the sharp edges of a foil packet.

He hesitated even so. "You're sure?"

"I'm sure."

Then he was straddling her, and she was opening her legs to take him in. Rocking to an age-old rhythm, their sweaty bodies making small sucking sounds as they came together and apart, heat flashing like summer lightning through her belly and thighs.

She teetered deliciously on the edge of release. When it finally came it was longer and deeper than the first time. As if her blood had been replaced by a warm elixir coursing through her. Ian held back as long as he could then with a single, hard thrust let go. He climaxed with a yell that was almost savage.

He collapsed atop her, panting. Sweat trickled into the crevices between their joined limbs. She could feel his heart racing . . . or was it hers?

After a minute or so, she eased out from under him. "My God," she breathed. "I had no idea. All those years, innocently going about my business, and the whole sexual revolution passed me by somehow." She shook her head, and began to laugh giddily.

He smiled lazily, reaching up to tuck a hank of hair behind her ear. "You're a quick study."

"I have an excellent teacher."

Sam realized that this was okay, too. Bantering. Making light of something so momentous . . . for her, at least. Sex didn't have to be spoken of only in sacred whispers.

"Does this mean we'll see each other again?"

He spoke lightly, teasingly almost, but his eyes studied her in the half light. What he was really asking, she knew, was whether or not she had the guts.

"I'd like that," she hedged.

"That's not exactly a yes."

"It's not a no, either."

"Are you afraid of what people might say?"

"I *know* what they'll say." She sighed. "Oh, Ian. It's easy for you. I've lived in Carson Springs all my life. People know me as Mrs. Kiley, the nice lady who runs Delarosa's. I've raised two lovely daughters, and buried a husband everyone thought was a saint. I subscribe to *Sunset* magazine, for heaven's sake. Are you beginning to get the picture?"

He brought a hand to her cheek. "If those people are your friends, wouldn't they want you to be happy?"

"I *am* happy," she said a bit defensively.

"There must be something more you want."

His eyes gleamed in the muted light. *He could have anyone,* she thought. *What does he see in me?* Even as she wondered, she found herself wrapping her arms about his neck and pulling him close to whisper, "There *is*. Make love to me again. Once more before we go."

They spent the remainder of the day in bed, until hunger forced them down into the world. Ian unearthed bread and cheese from the refrigerator, and made toasted cheese sandwiches — which tasted heavenly — chased by strong coffee in anticipation of the ride home. When it was finally time to go, she felt as if she were waking from a lovely dream.

It was after eleven by the time they pulled up in front of her house. She noticed the lights still on in the guest house. No sooner had he driven off than the windows went dark — Lupe ending her watch. It seemed a bellwether of things to come. If she couldn't escape scrutiny in her own home, what would it be like with the whole town watching?

After a restless night, Monday morning dawned clear and cool. The mechanic at the garage informed her that her Honda wouldn't be ready until Wednesday, so she rode into town with Guillermo. They sat in companionable silence, the windows of his old Ford pickup rolled down, the smoke from his Camel blowing across her in a thin, bluish stream: an old man with a mustache stained yellow from nicotine — as taciturn as his wife was talkative — and a middle-aged woman reflecting unhappily on the choice she was about to make.

She didn't regret what had happened with Ian — it had been so long, even God would have to agree she was owed. But her life was too complicated; there would be repercussions. Her daughters, for one. Her friends, too, all except Gerry.

Then there was Ian, mature in the ways that had thrilled her in bed, but what did he know about a real relationship? About *life,* for that matter? A life of marriage and motherhood, community activities and clubs. He couldn't begin to understand what this would do to her . . . or what he'd be getting into.

No, what she regretted was not being entirely honest with him, not closing the door all the way.

Guillermo, on his way to the hardware store, dropped her off a few blocks from

Delarosa Plaza. Sam didn't mind the walk; it would help clear her head. She strolled past the photo store, remembering the film she'd meant to drop off, still in a drawer at home. In light of yesterday, her daughter's wedding seemed a distant memory. At the Bow-Meow pet shop, she paused to peer in the window at the puppies — probably from the puppy mills that Laura, as a charter member of Lost Paws, campaigned against religiously. Sam indulged in a smile nonetheless; they were so cute.

She passed Françoise's Creperie, from which the delicious smells wafted. Inside she could see the owner bustling about behind the counter, a petite woman with cheeks flushed almost as red as her hair. Anyone expecting a French accent would have been disappointed, though. Françoise's real name was Fran O'Brien, and she spoke a thick Brooklynese. Sam recalled when she'd first moved to the area, seven years ago. Her husband had walked out, leaving her with two young children to raise on a secretary's salary. With help from her parents she'd pulled up stakes and moved three thousand miles to fulfill a lifelong dream. Now her little eatery was one of the most popular in town. Sam often spotted Fran's kids, teenagers now, helping out after school.

At Ragtime she caught sight of Marguerite Moore, on her way out the door. Sam arranged her face in what she hoped was a cheerful expression. "Morning, Marguerite." It didn't hurt to be nice. The thrift shop raised money for the music festival, and as much as Sam might dislike her, the woman put in more hours than anyone . . . even if she ignored the efforts of those, like Sam, who worked for a living as well.

Marguerite pinned a smile in place, a heavyset woman dressed to the nines, sporting a diamond ring that could have put an eye out. "Sam, I was just thinking of you." She brandished a manila envelope. "I finished typing up the minutes from our last meeting. I was just running out to make copies." Sam knew it stuck in her craw that she was forced to play second banana. Not an opportunity passed without Marguerite letting everyone know how tirelessly she toiled.

Sam plucked the envelope from her plump, bejeweled hand. "Why don't you let me take care of it? I have a copier at the store."

Marguerite's face fell. "Well, if it's no trouble —"

"No trouble at all. Bye, Marguerite."

Sam smiled as she sailed past.

Rounding the corner onto Old Mission, she saw that the Tree House Café was packed as usual, with a line of people spilling onto the sidewalk. Children clambered in and out of the tree house in the century-old live oak at the center of its large screened patio, while their parents enjoyed the opportunity to sip coffee and thumb through one of the dog-eared paperbacks from the bookcases in back. Waitresses scurried in and out of the small building housing the kitchen and gift shop.

Sam waved to its owner, David Ryback, making a run to Ingersoll's — for more of its buttermilk crullers, no doubt. David, the star of the football team when he and Laura were in high school together, waved back distractedly. She'd heard his son Davey was in the hospital again, and made a mental note to send a card.

Crossing the street, she stopped at Higher Ground for coffee and muffins. Minutes later she was strolling through the arch onto the plaza. Delarosa's stood at the farthest edge of the half-moon-shaped courtyard, flanked by shops on either side. The buildings were identical — Spanish-style adobe trimmed in colorful tiles and wrought-iron grilles. A terra-cotta overhang provided shade against the sun, and carved wooden benches respite for weary shoppers. Bougainvillea flowed in crimson waves down the high stone walls, and at the center of the courtyard, a tiered Moroccan fountain splashed in three-part harmony.

She pushed open the door to the shop. Laura was bent over the counter in back, arranging something inside the display case. Sam held up the paper sack in her hand. "They were all out of blueberry. I got you banana-nut instead."

"Fine." Laura flashed her a distracted smile.

Sam walked over to see what she was putting out. "I don't remember ordering these."

Laura arranged a necklace on the top shelf, and then straightened. "You were so busy with the wedding," she said. "I didn't want to bother you. Unusual, aren't they?"

Sam stooped to peer at the jewelry. Unusual? More like bizarre. Each piece with a bug cast in epoxy as its centerpiece — ladybugs, beetles, crickets, bees. Strangely beautiful in their own way, but at the same time . . .

"I'm not sure our customers are ready for this," she said, frowning. "Isn't it a bit too —" She searched for the word.

"Funky?" Laura put in. "That's the whole *point*, Mom. We need to attract a younger crowd. Remember those Japanese hair sticks? They sold out in just two days. The kids loved them."

It had been her daughter's idea to carry smaller, less expensive items like jewelry and key rings. Sam had worried it would detract from the high-end goods for which Delarosa's was known.

One brooch in particular caught her eye: an iridescent beetle framed in silver leaves. She fingered it thoughtfully. "Speaking of which, how's our runaway? I meant to call you yesterday. I just never got around to it." She thought of Ian, which had the effect of a drug, causing her to grow warm and heavy limbed.

Laura sighed. "She seems healthy, and God knows she eats enough, but you'd think she materialized out of thin air. I don't know any more than you."

"No word on her parents?"

"If they're even in the picture. Poor kid. She tiptoes around like she's scared of getting hit."

"Or the police getting involved." Sam recalled the girl's terror at the wedding. "What are you going to do with her?"

"Give it a few days, see what happens." Laura shrugged, but there was no hiding her concern. *The patron saint of lost souls,* Sam thought. "In the meantime, I have my hands full with Maude. Would you believe her son had a sudden change of heart and wants her to move back in with him?"

"I'd forgotten she even had a son."

"I think Maude was starting to forget, too."

"Can't she tell him she's happy where she is?"

"She tried." Flags of indignation stood out on Laura's cheeks. "I told her she's got to stand up to him. *Make* him listen."

"What's stopping her?"

"Misplaced loyalty." A corner of Laura's mouth hooked down in a wry smile. "She seems convinced he has a heart."

She was sliding the door to the display case shut when Sam impulsively reached inside and snatched up the brooch. She fastened it to her lapel, and stepped back to admire it in the mirror. The ancient Egyptians believed scarabs brought luck; maybe it would do the same for her.

Laura gave a nod of approval. "I wouldn't have thought so . . . but, yes, it's you. Definitely. Keep it up, Mom, and you might start a trend."

Sam smiled. "If I don't scare our customers off first."

She did a quick walk-through to make sure everything was in order, marveling, as she often did, at the elegant emporium that had evolved from her great-grandparents' cramped general store. Even in her parents' day it had been a hodgepodge — bolts of fabric, kitchen utensils, crockery in every shape and size. She recalled her petite mother forever climbing onto a wooden stepladder to reach the highest shelves, and her father rolling up his sleeve to scoop butterscotch and peppermints from the jars on the counter.

In the years since, housewares had gradually given way to high-end arts and crafts: hand-loomed textiles and Native-American baskets, imported glassware, one-of-a-kind ceramics. She fingered an embroidered tablecloth. A hinged box fashioned from layers of glass, in which tiny beads shifted and flowed, sat on the small pine table beside it. The one remaining vestige of her grandparents' day was the punched-tin pie safe in which jars of honey bearing the distinctive Blessed Bee label were displayed.

The bell tinkled. She looked up to see Anna Vincenzi pushing her sister's wheelchair through the door. Monica, in a yellow silk tunic top and matching trousers, her auburn hair twisted into a loose knot, might have been an empress on her throne.

"Samantha, darling, you're just the one I wanted to see," she trilled. "My agent's birthday is coming up, and he's been so very, very good to me. I need something special to show my appreciation." She coyly fingered a curl. Her career as an actress might have ended with the accident that left her paralyzed, but Monica was still playing the part of femme fatale.

Sam put on her warmest smile, directing it briefly at Monica before allowing it to settle on Anna, as plain and mousy as her sister was ravishing. "I know just the thing."

She led the way to a display of art glass against the wall. "This is our most popular executive gift." She picked up a paperweight layered with blues and whites swirled to resemble a world globe.

Monica gave it only a cursory glance. "Perfect. I'll take it. Oh, and don't bother with gift wrapping." She waved a crimson-nailed hand at her sister. "Anna takes care of all that."

Poor Anna. Any sympathy Sam might

have felt for Monica was eclipsed by the disgraceful way she treated her sister. It wasn't just today; Sam had witnessed it on other occasions. It was almost as if Anna were being punished for some reason.

Why did she put up with it? Sam wondered. Did she need the money, or like Maude, was it just a misplaced sense of loyalty? God knew Anna had enough on her hands as it was caring for their elderly mother. If only she'd lose weight, and stop wearing those awful jumpers and cardigans, maybe she'd find the confidence to break loose.

"Why don't you look around while I find a box for this?" Sam gestured toward the counter. "We have a new line of jewelry that just came in." A black widow spider would be ideal for Monica, she thought.

It wasn't until they were heading out the door, Delarosa's signature red-and-white striped shopping bag hooked over a handle of Monica's wheelchair, that Sam noticed a familiar black-garbed figure among the handful of customers in back: Sister Agnes.

Her heart sank. The plump, rosy-cheeked little nun looked as guileless as a child in a Nativity play, but lately Sam had noticed that something was always missing in her wake. Usually the items were small and fairly inexpensive: a pewter letter opener, a key ring, a miniature porcelain box. The question was, what to do about it? Sam didn't want to make a fuss. How would it look to the other customers, accusing a nun of shoplifting? Even more upsetting was the thought of having to pay a visit to Mother Ignatius. The best plan of action, she'd decided, was to simply keep an eye out so it didn't happen again.

"Good morning, Sister." Sam strolled over. "Is there anything I can help you with?"

"Ah, no, Mrs. Kiley, would that you could." The little nun, as Irish as the Blarney Stone, shook her head in regret. "But 'tis no sin to look, is it? You have such lovely things."

Sam smiled. "I'm glad you think so." Try as she might, she found it impossible to dislike Sister Agnes. She might be a thief, but she was a charming one.

"These, for instance." Sister Agnes fingered a delicate lace table scarf. "They remind me of home."

"We just got them in." Sam smoothed the scarf, tucking it back into the pile.

"Excuse me, I was wondering if you had another one of these."

Sam turned to find a nicely dressed gray-haired woman holding out a fluted bud vase with a chip in its base. "Oh, dear. I'm afraid it's the last one. Is there something else I can show you?"

"Let me poke around a bit." The woman reluctantly handed her the vase.

The exchange hadn't taken more than a few seconds, but when Sam turned around Sister Agnes was gone — along with the scarf. She heard the bell tinkle, and caught a flash of black serge as the little nun disappeared through the door.

She sighed. There was no avoiding it now. Like it or not, she'd have to speak to Mother Ignatius. Not over the phone, though. She'd have to make a special trip.

"Sam." A familiar voice, low and musical.

She turned around, startled to find Ian standing before her. How had he managed to sneak in without her noticing? Heat rushed up into her cheeks, and she darted a furtive glance over her shoulder. No one was looking their way. "What are you doing here?" she whispered.

He flashed her an easy grin. "I didn't realize I needed an invitation."

"You know what I mean."

He didn't appear the least bit fazed. In

the same unhurried voice he asked, "Is there somewhere we can talk? In private?"

She cast another glance over her shoulder. Laura was waiting on someone, and only one other customer was wandering about. "All right," she said, "but only for a minute."

She led the way to the tiny office in back, just large enough for a desk and file cabinet. There was no point offering him a seat. She nudged the door shut with her heel. The pounding of her heart seemed to fill the tiny, windowless space.

She didn't wait for him to speak. "Ian, listen, yesterday was . . . unbelievable. I don't regret it for a moment. But it can't go any further." She closed her eyes, leaning against the file cabinet. The metal felt cool against her burning skin.

"Because of the age thing?" He sounded more puzzled than anything.

"It's complicated."

"It doesn't have to be."

"For *you*."

"For either of us."

He stepped toward her, and suddenly she was in his arms. Oh God. How easy it was, like sliding into a warm bath. As if her mind had become separated from her body somehow. A body with a will of its own.

She felt his mouth on hers, his sly tongue . . .

Just this once, she pleaded, as if to some higher authority. After that, no more. If she was to have any chance of resisting him in the days to come she'd have to end it. Here. Now.

The question was *how?*

Wrapped in Ian's arms, lost in a kiss with no beginning and therefore no end, Sam wasn't aware of the door easing open behind her. She didn't hear her daughter gasp.

"Oh God, I'm sorry. I didn't realize."

Sam broke away from Ian. Her daughter stood in the doorway, gaping as if at a car wreck, her cheeks flushed and eyes wide with horror, a corner of her mouth flickering in an interrupted smile. Then, with a tiny cry, Laura scurried off.

Chapter 4

"Slow down," Alice said. "I don't want it to end."

As the Mercedes twisted up the steep road to their house she felt a sudden desire to retreat, burrow into the cocoon of these past three weeks. Maui had been a heaven in which they were lulled to sleep each night by the sound of the surf after lolling on the beach and making love all day. Now life back on earth — messy and unpredictable — was just around the bend, waiting to pounce.

In her mind she could see the red light on her answering machine, blinking like a reptilian eye, the stack of mail by the door, the pile of wedding presents to be unwrapped. Tomorrow there would be suitcases to unpack, calls to return, bills to pay. And then back to work on Monday, where a whole new mountain awaited her. This coming week, with the president in town and the Israeli foreign affairs minister announcing peace talks, she and Wes would be lucky to squeeze in more than a meal or two together, never mind candle-light and roses.

"We still have an hour or so before dinner." Wes flashed her a grin, miniature twin suns wheeling across the dark green lenses of his Vuarnets. "Enough time for a swim . . . or whatever else you have in mind."

"Our bathing suits are packed." She curled a hand about his neck. "We'd have to go naked."

He laughed his wonderful, booming laugh. "Alice honey, you're the only woman I know who doesn't feel the urge to unpack the minute she walks through the door. I think that's why I married you."

"The *only* reason?" She arched a brow.

"Much is contained therein," he replied cryptically.

The sun had set, and the mountaintops were awash in crimson light. The air blowing through the vents smelled faintly and medicinally of eucalyptus. Wes swerved to avoid a fallen branch, nipping in and out of their lane with the skill of a race car driver. He drove the way he did everything: without a noticeable rise in blood pressure. He was the only man from whose hands she didn't physically itch to wrest the wheel, the only one with whom she felt completely and utterly relaxed.

She studied his profile — like those on ancient coins — high forehead and Roman nose, clipped beard and thatch of curly iron hair. She rarely thought about the difference in their ages, and when she did it was always with a small measure of amazement. Wes wasn't like other fifty-two-year-olds. He approached middle age like Teddy Roosevelt charging San Juan Hill — teeth bared and saber rattling. In his seventies, he'd still be pressing down on the gas pedal, juggling four phone lines, and negotiating the sky in his Bell 430. And, she thought, swimming naked with his wife under the stars.

She remembered the day he walked into her life and changed it forever. Twenty-one and fresh out of UCLA, she'd just been hired as assistant producer on the *Marty Milnik Show*. Wes Carpenter, whom she had yet to meet — his office was on the executive floor above — might as well have been the Wizard of Oz for all the talk of his legendary feats. She'd heard the stories of his humble beginnings. How, as owner of a small TV station in Oxnard, he'd had the balls — in the days before licensing prohibited such practices — to beam syndicated network programs, via satellite, to local cable stations across the country. Then there was the one about the overdue bank loan being called: how he'd strriden into First National's boardroom like a figure out of the Wild West and gotten them not only to extend the deadline but also to up the ante.

She'd been at CTN about six weeks before she came face-to-face with Wes. She was on her way up to the newsroom on the sixth floor when the elevator stopped and a tall, broad-shouldered man with the largest hands she'd ever seen got in. He was wearing twill slacks, an open-necked shirt, and a corduroy blazer that, quite frankly, had seen better days. His cheeks were windburned above the dark line of his beard. *It's him,* she thought. Their eyes met and she looked down. Peeking out from under the cuffs of his slacks she saw something that made her giggle: one sock was brown, and the other navy.

When he caught her staring, she said, "I'm sorry. It's just . . . I couldn't help noticing." She pointed at his feet.

He looked down in surprise, and a slow grin spread across his face. "What can I say? Occasionally, I like to mix it up." He regarded her with interest. His eyes were an unusual brownish green, and he seemed to have more than the usual number of teeth. "And you are?"

"Alice Kiley." She put out her hand.

It was swallowed by his huge, warm grip. She'd never met a chief executive quite like him, one with the air of a truant schoolboy. "Who are you with?"

In that first dazed moment she mistook his inquiry for something far more personal, replying, "No one." She hadn't meant to bare her single status to this perfect stranger — boss, or no — it had just slipped out. One look at his puzzled expression and she realized her error. She felt herself flush. "Actually, I'm with you. I mean . . . I work for you."

Wes appeared to take it all in stride, as if accustomed to women making fools of themselves over him. But Alice couldn't quite believe this was happening. In school she'd always been the sought-after one — the girl voted in her senior poll as the one boys would most like to be marooned on a desert island with. She'd grown used to men stammering in her presence, and could have compiled an encyclopedia of pickup lines. This, though, was a new one on her: a man who made *her* blush.

"Well, I'll be damned." His eyes sparkled

as if she'd just told him something remarkable. "Never thought there'd come a day
when I didn't know everyone here. How
long you been with us?" He spoke with a
faint Texas accent, and she remembered
hearing that he'd grown up in Austin.

"Two months," she said, her blush deepening.

"That long? Well then, it's high time we
got to know one another. You free for
lunch?"

"As a matter of fact, I am."

"Twelve-thirty? I'll meet you in the
lobby." He winked. "I'll be the guy with
one brown sock."

The elevator stopped at her floor, and
Alice stepped out. She might have been
landing on the moon for the sudden loss of
gravity that sent her floating down the corridor. She knew what love was — with
Bruce Kitteredge, her college sweetheart, it
had been serious enough for talk of marriage — but this was the first time she'd
been infatuated. It was, she thought, exactly as depicted in cartoons: like being hit
over the head by a giant mallet.

She hadn't looked back since.

"I love you," she said now, with more
feeling than usual.

"Same to you, Mrs. Carpenter." He

groped for her hand and brought it to his mouth. Her ring — four carats of emerald-cut diamond — caught the light in a brilliant flash. She was reminded of the deep sense of certainty when he'd slipped it on. Nothing would ever come between them, she'd felt sure.

He shifted gears as the road grew steeper. They wound their way past sandstone bluffs to which scrub pines and manzanita clung precariously. To the right was a sheer drop-off affording a nearly panoramic view of the valley below: sunstrewn pastures and neat rows of orange trees, the green baize of Dos Palmas Country Club. After a seemingly endless climb, their house rose into view. Custom-built in Wes's bachelor days, it occupied the highest point on Fox Canyon Road: split levels of cedar and glass that, from a distance, seemed to jut from the hillside like some fantastic rock formation.

Alice felt a tiny beat of anxiety. They'd been living together more than a year, but it would be different now. Would marriage be everything she'd hoped for? Everything her parents' had been?

They started up the driveway — a nearly vertical incline that dipped into a circular turnabout where Wes coasted to a smooth stop. Alice climbed out, stretching to release the kinks from the long drive and even longer flight. The air, though not as warm as on Maui, was wonderfully dry. In the garden the birds of paradise were in bloom, the agapanthus bursting from their stalks. She watched a bird alight on the granite fountain nestled amid pillows of ornamental grass. It reminded her of something; she couldn't think what. Then she remembered: the girl at the wedding. Was she still with Laura, or had she been packed off to home? Alice would know soon enough.

She started up the path, feeling a vague sense of apprehension. The moment she set foot inside the honeymoon would be officially over, the world that had been left to fend for itself once again knocking at her door.

The first thing she noticed when she walked in was the pile of presents by the door — thoughtfully dropped off by her mother, no doubt. Ignoring it, she stepped down into the living room: a soaring anthem to the outdoors with its cathedral ceiling and skylights, its fieldstone fireplace and floor-to-ceiling glass. She pushed open the sliding glass door onto the deck. The last rays of sunlight glanced in Morse-like flashes off Monica Vincent's LoreiLinda, atop the neighboring hill. In the canyons below, shadows were creeping out from under boulders and pointing in long witchy fingers from clumps of silver cholla and ocotillo. Digger pines rustled in the mild evening breeze. Directly below, the pool beckoned, and she thought how nice a cool swim would feel.

A pair of strong arms wrapped about her from behind. She snuggled into them, dropping her head onto Wes's shoulder and pulling his arms more tightly about her.

"Still wish we were in Hawaii?" he asked.

"Mmm," she murmured with her eyes half closed.

At this moment, she wanted only this: to be alone with Wes, the outside world at bay. If only she could preserve it somehow, like a flower pressed between the pages of a book.

The phone began to ring inside the house. She made an effort to tune out its faint bleating, but when the machine didn't pick up after several rings it occurred to her that the message tape must be full. With a sigh, she reluctantly withdrew from her husband's arms and stepped inside.

She picked up the phone on the small lacquered cabinet by the sofa. "Hello?"

"I don't believe it — I actually got you. I've been calling for hours." Laura, sounding slightly out of breath. "Did you just get in?"

"A few minutes ago. I haven't checked my messages yet."

There was a pause, then Laura asked, "How was Maui?"

It was obvious she was champing at the bit with important news of some kind. Wasn't it just like Laura to make forced small talk before cutting to the chase?

"Perfect, except for having to leave." Alice decided to put her sister out of her misery. "Is everything okay?"

Another pause, then, "Are you sitting down?"

Alice had the sinking feeling the news wasn't going to be good. She lowered herself onto the sofa, its buttery calfskin cool against the backs of her sunburned thighs. "I am now."

"It's Mom."

Alice felt her heart lurch. With her dad's death, she'd lost more than a father; she'd lost her sense of complacency as well. She knew now what she hadn't as a child: that parents are mortal. She dragged a throw

148

cushion onto her lap, holding it pressed to her belly, which had gone hollow all of a sudden. "She's all right, isn't she?"

"She's fine. Unless you count temporary insanity as an illness."

Alice pictured her sister seated at her kitchen table, the sprung cord from the phone on the wall stretching halfway across the room. She felt suddenly impatient. "Laura, for God's sake, what *is* it?"

"She's seeing someone."

"Tom?" Okay. She could live with that. Tom Kemp was safe, even a little boring. If worse came to worse and her mother ended up marrying him, it would only be out of companionship.

There was a sharp intake of breath at the other end. "Not Tom. *Ian.*"

Laura's words trickled away, harmless as rain down a windowpane. Ian? *Wes's* Ian? Impossible. "You must be imagining things," she said. "You know Mom. Now that Wes and I are married she probably sees us all as one, big extended family — including Ian."

"I saw them." Laura pushed on grimly. "They were kissing . . . and believe me, it was more than friendly."

Alice tried to picture it, but the image kept dissolving. At the same time she was distinctly aware of the blood draining from her face and hands. She swallowed thickly.

"Is it . . . I mean, have they . . ."

"Slept together?" Her sister gave a dry little laugh. "I'm afraid to ask. Let's just say they've been seeing a lot of each other these past few weeks."

Alice groaned. "I get the picture."

"I'm partly to blame." Laura sounded miserable. "I let it slip to Aunt Audrey. I think Mom was sort of on the fence, but once the cat was out of the bag she got her hackles up. She said she was sorry I had to find out the way I did, but that maybe it was for the best. I think her exact words were, 'I'm sick and tired of pleasing others, and think it's high time I did as I pleased.' "

"Oh God. This is worse than I imagined."

In the brief silence that fell, she could hear her sister breathing. As a child, Laura had suffered from allergies, and Alice remembered being kept awake at night by her loud, snuffling snores. She wished suddenly that she were back in her old room now, in the house on Blossom Road, a little girl with her pillow mashed down around her ears.

"What do you think we should do?" Laura asked timidly.

This is for real, Alice thought. *It's really happening.*

The room began to revolve, like the baggage carousel at which she'd stood just hours ago, hours that felt more like days. "Let me talk to Wes," she heard herself say quite rationally, as if this were just a minor matter in need of sorting out. "I'll call you back, okay?"

She was staring sightlessly at the phone in her hand when she heard the sliding door thump shut. She looked up to find Wes walking toward her. His relaxed look changed instantly to one of concern, and he sank down beside her, draping an arm about her shoulders. "What's wrong? You look like someone just died."

"That was my sister. She . . ." The words wouldn't come. Alice chewed on a thumbnail, wishing it were a cigarette. She'd given up smoking when she met Wes, but suddenly she'd have given anything for a Parliament. At last she pivoted around to face Wes. "My mother's having an affair. With your son."

He looked stunned. "Well, I'll be damned."

"Can you believe it?"

He shook his head, whistling softly. "I'll admit, I didn't see it coming. How long has this been going on?"

"Since the wedding."

"A real whirlwind courtship."

"Don't joke."

"I'm not."

She covered her face with her hands. "This is a nightmare."

"I wouldn't call it that exactly."

"What *would* you call it then?"

Wes's face creased in a mirthless smile. "Let's just say we're not exactly in a position to be throwing stones."

Alice glared at him. "It's not the same."

"Close enough."

"She's old enough to be his mother!"

"And I, my darling," he squeezed her shoulders, "am old enough to be your father."

"It's different with us," she insisted.

"Because I'm a man?" He wasn't goading her; he seemed to genuinely want to know.

"I can't believe this," she said, shaking her head. "I can't believe you're not as outraged as I am."

"For your sake, I wish I were." He regarded her tenderly. "But it'd be more than a little hypocritical, don't you think? Anyway, I'm sure your mother had her doubts about us."

"She never said anything."

"Maybe we should extend her the same courtesy."

Alice pulled away and scooted to the other end of the sofa, from where she eyed him as she might have a stranger — a possibly untrustworthy one at that. "You sound as if you actually *approve*."

"I didn't say that. I was merely pointing out that there's a flip side to every coin." Wes, always so logical. It was one of the things she loved about him; it also drove her a little crazy at times. He held a hand out, as if beseeching her in some way. "Alice, what's *really* going on here? Is it just that Ian's so much younger?"

"What more do you need?"

She hugged herself, staring at the little teepee of kindling in the oversize slate fireplace. Up here it could get quite chilly after sundown, even in July. Tonight, she thought, was going to be one of those nights. The temperature seemed to have dropped at least ten degrees.

"I was thinking of your dad."

His words hit home. In a low, trembling voice she spoke aloud the thought tunneling into her like a newly hatched insect. "You'd think all those years together would *mean* something. You'd think his memory alone . . ." A lump rose in her throat, choking off her words.

"It's been two years," he said.

153

"What difference does that make? If she'd really loved him . . ." She turned to Wes. "She wouldn't be doing this. Making a mockery of everything they had with a man young enough to be her . . . it's obscene."

"Don't you think you're overreacting a bit?" Wes spoke gently. "She's only human, after all. Just because she's sleeping with Ian it doesn't mean she didn't love your father."

Alice's eyes felt raw and swollen though she hadn't shed a tear. "You don't understand. He was . . ." She searched for the proper word to describe him. Saint? No, anything but. More like a mischievous boy at times. When she and Laura were left in his care, it had been like *three* children misbehaving in their mother's absence: dining on cake and ice cream while the nutritious suppers Sam had prepared, carefully wrapped in plastic in the refrigerator, remained untouched; pillow fights; and on one memorable occasion a game of indoor hockey that had ended with her mother's favorite Lalique vase in shards. She'd been furious at him that time, but he'd charmed his way back into her good graces — like always.

Another memory surfaced — her father

drawing her onto the dance floor at their silver anniversary party. "For old times' sake?" he'd said with a wink, reminding her of when she was little and used to climb onto his shoes in her stocking feet. That night, swaying in her father's arms, she'd felt as she once had gliding over the living room floor atop his oxfords to the "Tennessee Waltz." As if nothing bad could happen to her as long as he never let go.

"He used to wake me up in the middle of the night sometimes when he couldn't sleep," she went on. "It was our special time, just him and me. He'd make hot cocoa and we'd watch an old movie on TV." She turned a mournful face to Wes. "How could she do this to him? How *could* she?"

She didn't need Wes to remind her that her dad was gone; she knew it from the hole in her heart, through which a cold wind seemed to rush.

"Is this about your mother, or you?" he asked.

She stood up, suddenly too weary to argue. "This isn't getting us anywhere," she said. Wes and his first wife had been on the verge of separating when she became ill. How could he understand the kind of marriage her parents had had?

She looked at him as if seeing him for the first time. Wes's cheeks were scoured red from the wind and sun, his muscular arm the deep tan of the leather sofa back on which it rested. His expression was that of a sympathetic bystander. Why couldn't he see how awful this was?

He rose and walked over to her, rubbing her arms as if to warm them. "What about that swim? It'll take your mind off all this."

She drew back, folding her arms over her chest. "I don't feel like it anymore."

Wes cocked his head, eyeing her as he might a petulant child. She found herself remembering the incident at the Ritz Carlton in Kapalua. She'd booked the reservation in her maiden name, and there'd been a misunderstanding when they were checking in. Before she could straighten it out, Wes had stepped in front of her, booming to the clerk, "Get the manager, please."

She hadn't really minded at the time, but winced now at the memory. Why couldn't he have let her handle it? *Because it wasn't the first time,* a small voice whispered back.

Alice marched stiffly to where her suitcase sat parked alongside Wes's like a large, obedient dog. With as much dignity as she could muster, she grabbed its leash and began dragging it down the hall. She'd gotten no more than halfway when he stepped up alongside her and lifted it easily, carrying it into the bedroom before going back for the rest of the luggage.

A moment later he returned with his own suitcase, which he heaved onto the bed. "You want to unpack? We'll unpack," he said cheerfully.

She felt herself thaw a bit. "Don't forget all those presents, too."

"We'll do those next."

"Let's just hope there isn't another espresso maker in that pile."

"That'd make three, right?" He unzipped his suitcase and turned to smile at her. In the once masculine bedroom she'd done over in muted yellow and cream, he stood out like an exclamation point.

She nodded. "It appears to be the wedding gift du jour."

"Back in my day, it was chafing dishes." He winced at the unfortunate reference to his first marriage. "Sorry, darling."

But it only served to remind her of how considerate he was normally. She found herself softening further. "What exactly *is* a chafing dish? I'm not sure I'd know what to do with one."

Wes tossed a handful of dirty laundry onto the floor, and walked over to where she stood. Pulling her into his arms, he murmured, "It's easy. Just light a match."

She drew back with a mock scowl. "I hope this isn't your idea of buttering me up. No pun intended."

He laughed, a deep laugh that rumbled up through his chest like a drum roll. "It's not too late for a swim," he said. "On the other hand, we could always skip that part."

He nuzzled her neck. Before Wes she'd always imagined beards to be coarse, but his was soft and springy. He smelled faintly of sunblock — hers — from when they'd made love this morning. Wes never bothered with the stuff. If two tours in Vietnam hadn't done him in, he liked to joke, he'd survive a few holes in the ozone.

She held herself stiff. "This isn't just some little thing that'll blow over," she said. "I'm really upset."

"Let me make it better." He pushed his hands under her top, stroking her back in slow circles until she began to relax.

Alice felt helpless to resist. How could you stay away from a man whose mere touch was like a spark to dry leaves? She lifted her arms obediently over her head as he peeled off her top. She wasn't wearing a bra; Wes didn't like them, and she was small breasted enough to get away with it. She moaned softly as he ran his thumbs over her nipples.

An image rose in her mind: the warm tide lapping their toes, and the starry sky turning slow cartwheels overhead as they made love on the beach in Wailua. She closed her eyes, letting the familiar sensations wash over her. Wes's mouth tracing the hollow between her breasts. The soft brush of his beard against her skin. His hands, at once rough and tender.

Alice arched against him and heard him groan in response. Then he was thrusting his hand under her skirt. "You're wet." He stripped her panties to her knees, and pushed a finger up inside her. "Jesus. I've wanted you all day." His voice was low and husky. "On the plane. On the drive home. It was all I could think about."

Alice parted her thighs, rocking against the heel of his hand. Delicious shivers coursed through her. She felt the last little grain of resistance dissolve. Oh God. Another minute of this, and she'd come . . .

Wes withdrew his hand and seized her by the waist, lowering her onto the carpet. Their second date, over too many martinis at Spago, when he'd asked what she was looking for in a relationship, she'd joked tipsily, "Rug burns." Another man might have looked at her oddly; Wes had merely raised his glass to her and replied, "My dear lady, I can't promise you the moon, but I can promise you that."

She unbuckled his belt and pushed his pants down over his hips, frantic with desire. He was just as eager. She felt his belt buckle graze the inside of her knee as he pushed into her with a hard thrust. All at once, she was filled with a delirious sense of wonder. The perfect lover, and he was all hers. Sweet Lord in heaven, it didn't get any better than this.

Wes wasn't rushing it. He knew when to pause . . . and how to move in ways that brought her maximum pleasure. It wasn't until she'd come several times, surprising herself — this morning hadn't she had her fill? — that he drew back to look at her.

"Should I use something?" Wes kept a supply of condoms on hand just in case.

Alice felt a familiar flutter of . . . regret? No, nothing as strong as that. "My diaphragm's in," she murmured.

It was all he needed. A moment later he was rearing back with a hoarse yell. She felt the warm pulse of his seed, and suddenly she wanted . . . she wanted . . . what *did* she want?

He collapsed onto the carpet with a breathless laugh. "Woman, you never cease to amaze me."

"Beats opening presents any day." She rolled onto her side, propping her head on her elbow. "Unless, of course, you plan on exchanging one of those espresso makers for something a little more risqué."

He cast a meaningful glance at the panties crumpled at her feet. "Careful," he growled. "That kind of talk could get you into trouble."

Wes, she knew, was entirely capable of going a second round. He was the only man she'd ever been with who could match her appetite, bite for bite. At times like this it was easy to forget he was so much older, that he had a grown son . . .

. . . *who happens to be sleeping with my mother.*

Alice sat up abruptly, hugging her knees. "It's getting late."

"Why don't I warm up something from the fridge while you finish unpacking?" he offered.

"That'd be nice." Their housekeeper, Rosa, was sure to have stocked it in their absence.

Alice unpacked while he showered, waiting until she could hear him banging about in the kitchen, whistling as if he hadn't a care in the world, before she collapsed onto the bed.

She stared up at the ceiling, more miserable than she had any right to be, more miserable than she'd have believed possible. All at once the prewedding jitters she'd been told to expect — of which she'd had none — descended with the force of an avalanche.

Wes's reaction to the news about her mother had been one of surprise . . . even sympathy. But he hadn't understood how she felt. He didn't know what it was like to lose a father; if his dad was anything to go by, Wes would still be wearing her out in his eighties. And there was more, a great deal they would never share. Starting with the fact that he'd had his family, and she . . .

It was a mutual decision, she told herself firmly. *No one's preventing me from having children.*

She pushed the thought from her mind and concentrated on the problem at hand. Wes wasn't going to be much help; it was obvious he had no intention of speaking to his son. That left it to her to try and talk some sense into Sam. Tomorrow morning, first thing, she would drive over there.

Alice pulled herself upright, eyeing the heap of clothing on the floor beside the bed. Wes's idea of unpacking was to leave his dirty laundry for Rosa to pick up, knowing full well that Alice wouldn't be able to abide looking at it until then.

She groaned and flopped back onto the mattress. From the kitchen she could hear the faint rattling of dishes and the sound of the refrigerator opening and closing. How could she be resentful of a man who would cheerfully make dinner after an eight-hour flight? Maybe the problem wasn't Wes, but her. Maybe *she* was flawed in some deep, fundamental way.

The long, exhausting day and prospect of an even longer one ahead caught up with her in full. She promptly fell asleep.

The following morning Alice was showered and dressed before Wes was even up. Breakfast was a slice of buttered toast washed down with black coffee strong enough to jump-start a battery. Then she was out the door, leaving her husband to weed through three weeks' worth of mail. She hadn't driven more than a hundred yards when she fished her cell phone from her purse and punched in Laura's number.

"It's me. I'm on my way over." The top was down on her Porsche Carrera, a gift from Wes, and she had to raise her voice to be heard.

"I'll make another pot of coffee." Laura sounded anything but glum. Alice heard the sound of running water and faint judder of old pipes. "You had breakfast yet?"

"I'm not coming over to eat."

"Let me guess? You're on your way to Mom's."

"Not me. *Us.*"

"Count me out." Her sister groaned. "I'm up to my ears in . . . you don't even want to know."

"Hey, you're the one who called *me*, remember?"

Laura sighed. "I know, but I've thought about it — I was up most of last night, as a matter of fact — and I'm not sure it's our place to be telling her how to run her life."

"We're not *telling* her anything," Alice said. "Just reminding her of what's at stake here."

There was a pause. In the background, she could hear a blend of voices, one deep and masculine — that would be Hector's — the other soft and tentative. Then Laura said, "I'm sure Mom's given it a lot of thought, too. She's not exactly the impulsive type."

"*Wasn't.* We're talking past tense here."

"Okay, but suppose she isn't interested in hearing what we have to say? What then?"

"She owes it to Dad to at least listen."

"What's Dad got to do with it?"

"How's it going to look?" Alice went on as if she hadn't spoken. "Mom gallivanting around town with her lover to all the places Dad and she . . ." She bit down on her lower lip, feeling as if she was going to cry.

"Oh, Al. I feel terrible. I shouldn't have made such a big deal of it." Laura beating herself up again. Why did she always think everything was her fault? "Look, maybe it'll all blow over in a week or two."

There was a surge of static and Laura's voice faded. "We'll talk about it when I get there!" Alice yelled. She thumbed the End button, and flipped the phone shut.

The sky was a cloudless sprawl overhead, the warm wind rushing at her a reminder of Kapalua, with its frangipani-scented breeze and mimosa sunsets . . . and the certainty she'd felt about Wes. Her hands tightened about the wheel. *Was* she making too big a deal of this? In the world of television, people had affairs all the time. Older men with younger women; older women with younger men. No one had batted so much as an eyelash when Lainie Bacheler, widow of CBS mogul Marvin Bacheler, who admitted to being sixty — which meant she was older — showed up at last year's Emmys on the arm of a man young enough to be her grandson.

But this wasn't L.A., and her mother was anything but the usual fodder for wagging tongues. And oh, how they would wag!

The poor dear, I had no idea she was so desperate.

It's obvious what this is about. What else could she want from a man young enough to be her son?

Martin will be rolling over in his grave.

Alice made the turn onto Grove, distracted at that moment by the tumbledown building on her right — the town's original one-room schoolhouse, where both her great-grandfather and grandfather had gone to school. Its windows were boarded over and its paint coming away in curly strips; litter lay in a small drift against the padlocked door. In her day it had been a prime high school make-out spot. Her boyfriend, Bif Holloway, used to park under that tree over there, where they'd kiss until her mouth was raw. But it had another distinction as well; in the fifties a scene in *Stranger in Paradise,* referred to locally as The Movie, was filmed here.

Alice's favorite story of her grandmother's was of the time she'd sneaked off to visit the set one Sunday while the rest of the family was at church. The biggest surprise, she'd said, was that the stars who'd looked ten feet tall on screen were short — practically midgets. It wasn't like watching a play, either. There'd been take after take, with a lumpy woman in a cardigan scurrying over with a hairbrush and hair spray between each one. Not very glamorous, to be sure, though her grandmother always grew misty-eyed when speaking of its director, Hank Montgomery. "Handsomest man I ever saw," she'd sigh. "Oh, he was quite the ladies' man!" It was Alice's first peek — if only vicariously — behind the plush curtain, and the lure of show business had been with her ever since.

Her sister's house was in full swing when she arrived, the kitchen a jumble of boots, jackets slung over the backs of chairs, dogs and cats nosing at bowls of kibble lined up along the baseboard. There was Hector, hunched over his plate at the table, and

Maude at the sink washing up. Laura stood at the counter, a mug of coffee in one hand and a tattered recipe card in the other.

"I can't remember if Grandma's banana cake calls for one cup of flour or two. That part is smudged." She peered at the card. "Or maybe I need reading glasses."

"Don't ask me. I wouldn't have a clue." Alice nodded hello to Hector. "Hey, Hec. Missed you at the wedding."

She tried not to sound offended. It wasn't personal, she knew. As long as she'd known him Hector had been this way: a genial loner. With one exception — he'd always taken his meals with the family. Her mother had insisted on it, and from the start he'd put up little resistance. Not until years later, after a number of his brothers and sisters had migrated north as well, did she realize how hard it had to have been leaving his own family behind. Proof lay in the fact that Hector remembered each and every one of his twenty-two nieces' and nephews' birthdays, even the ones he'd never met. His room in back of the barn was a gallery of family photos tilting from push pins.

He flashed her a disarming smile, revealing the tooth chipped in a fist fight back in his rowdier days. "Heard all about it from your sister." There wasn't a hint of apology in his voice. "Me? I'm holding out for the pictures."

"Such a beautiful wedding." Maude turned from the sink, beaming at Alice as she wiped her soapy hands on her apron. "And such a beautiful bride."

"You were quite the belle of the ball yourself." Alice recalled Maude's unusual, but oddly fashionable getup. "By the way, Maude, thanks for the . . . um . . ." What *had* she given them? "The letter organizer. I'm sure it'll come in handy."

The old woman smiled sweetly. "Actually, dear, it's a toast caddy."

Alice winced at her blunder. On the other hand, who in this century, on this side of the Atlantic, would give someone a silver-plated toast caddy? "Well," she said brightly, "since we usually eat breakfast on the run, we'll get more use out of it this way."

"That's how she stays so thin," Laura groused good-naturedly. With a sigh she tucked the recipe card back into its box. "I give up. I'll make devil's food instead."

"What's the occasion?" Alice asked.

"Finch," she said. "It's her birthday. Would you believe she's never had a birthday cake, not even the store-bought kind? What kind of parents would —" The thump of boots on the porch caused her to break off. Pearl and Rocky dashed to the door, barking excitedly.

It was the girl. "I cleaned out the stalls like you asked, and —" She caught sight of Alice, halting abruptly. "Hi." Her eyes were dark glints behind the screen door's buckled mesh. Then with a look of resolve she pushed it open and stepped inside.

Alice hardly recognized her. In just three weeks she'd filled out; in an old pair of jeans and clean white T-shirt, her dark hair was pulled back in a ponytail, she looked like any teenager. "Happy birthday, Finch." Alice struck a casual tone. "I hope you plan to celebrate by doing something a little more exciting than mucking out stalls."

The girl's cheeks reddened, and she dropped her gaze.

Laura stepped in quickly. "I thought we'd take a ride later on," she said. "You haven't seen anything until you've seen the view from the hill."

Finch shrugged. "Sure, whatever."

"The poppies are in bloom. You won't believe how beautiful they are." She turned to Alice brightly, as if she hadn't noticed how Finch had withdrawn. "I've been giving her lessons. Wait till you see her — she's a natural."

Some of the stiffness went out of the girl's shoulders. She flashed Laura a look that seemed to say, *I know you mean well, but I'm not ready to open up just yet.* "I'd better take a shower," she muttered, sidling past them.

Alice waited until she heard the thud of the door down the hall. "Any word on her parents?"

"Not a peep." Maude sighed, tucking a stray wisp into her bun. She might have been Auntie Em fretting over Dorothy. "Poor child. To think what she must have gone through . . ."

"I'm not pushing it for now." Laura spoke with unaccustomed firmness. "She'll come around when she's ready. Meanwhile, she's welcome to stay as long as she likes."

Alice wondered if her sister was getting in over her head. "Don't let it drag out too long. She has a home . . . somewhere. I'm sure her parents will want to know where she is."

Hector rose, and carried his plate over to the sink. "Excuse me, ladies, but I have work to do." The abruptness of his tone spoke louder than any words; he might just as well have told Alice to mind her own business.

She tried not to feel hurt. Hector, though polite and friendly to everyone, had always been closest to Laura — maybe because he thought she needed someone to stick up for her. It was a special bond that went both ways. Even now, Alice couldn't help noticing the way her sister's gaze followed Hector onto the porch, where he retrieved his hat from a rusty nail and slapped it against his thigh. For several long seconds after he stepped down into the yard, Laura's eyes remained fixed on the motes of dust swirling lazily in the shaft of sunlight where he'd stood.

She's in love with him, Alice thought. She recalled Laura's long-ago crush that only a blind man could have missed. Hector wasn't blind, just discreet. Laura had been just a teenager, after all, even if he hadn't been much older. Then there was Peter. She wondered if Hector would be so discreet now.

Alice was distracted by the newspaper on the table. A headline jumped out at her: SLAIN MAN'S IDENTITY REMAINS UNKNOWN. She scanned the article. Something about a transient found stabbed to death in the hills above Horse Creek. How ghastly. The last murder she could recall was that old booze hound, Anson Grundig, battering his poor wife to death, but that had to have been eight or nine years ago. Carson Springs wasn't exactly a hotbed of crime.

"What do you know about this?" she asked.

"It happened last Friday," Laura said. "No suspects yet, as far as I know. The police are still looking."

"I can hardly sleep nights just thinking of it." Maude's soft little cushion of a face seemed to fold in on itself. "A stranger on the loose, out to murder innocent people."

"It could be someone we know," Alice said.

Maude grew visibly pale.

Laura shot Alice a warning look, saying pointedly, "Don't you have to be somewhere?"

Alice glanced at her watch. "You're right. We should be going."

Laura looked about to protest, then sighed, forking a hand through hair already scrambled. "Okay, okay. Just give me a minute to throw something on." She glanced down at her rumpled shorts and T-shirt as if just now noticing what she was wearing. "God knows what Mom would do without us to keep her in line, right?"

In the car, traveling east along Old Sorrento Road past houses much like Laura's — most with barns and the requisite horse trailer out front — it occurred to Alice that she had no idea how serious this was. What if it was more than just sex? What if they were actually *in love?* She couldn't picture her mother moving in with Ian. That would leave only one other option: Ian would have to move into Isla Verde.

He'd be sleeping in their bed. Sitting in Dad's place at the table . . .

Alice felt slightly sick.

The road began to slope downward as they neared Sorrento Creek. They rattled over a cattle grid, past a sunny pasture dotted with oaks and in which cows grazed peacefully. Rising over the next hill were the vine-shrouded walls of Our Lady of the Wayside.

Alice recalled the time she and her sister had sneaked into the convent. She'd been ten and Laura twelve. All they knew of the nuns' sequestered existence was what their mother's friend, Gerry, had told them. Nothing could have prepared them for what lay behind those forbidden walls: the lush garden and quaint storybook buildings, the chapel from which sweet voices floated like a chorus of angels. It was just after dawn — they'd slipped away while their parents were asleep, riding their bicycles two miles in the near dark — and they were ravenous. Alice was reaching to pluck an orange from a tree when a voice rang out.

"Don't touch that."

A tall, stern-faced nun strode from the shadows of the chapel, a prayer book in one hand and rosary beads in the other. She cast a long blade of shadow in the rising sun.

"We . . . we were just looking," Alice managed to squeak.

"Where are your parents?"

"They don't know we're here." Laura, white with terror, stepped in front of Alice as if to protect her.

"I see." The tall nun appeared to be pondering what sort of punishment they should receive. "Come with me." She turned and began making her way down the path.

They'd had no choice but to follow her, trembling all the way, down a winding path and up a short flight of steps. After what seemed an eternity they reached a building with a cross carved in the stone arch above its stout wooden door and a statue of the Virgin Mary out front.

Inside it was cool and dark, and smelled like church. They walked down a long corridor, their reflections shimmering ghost-like on the waxed tiles, into a large, open-beamed kitchen filled with light. A wooden table stretched along one wall. The nun sat them down, giving them each a bowl of oatmeal from the pot on the stove.

"I'm Mother Ignatius," she said, not unkindly. She set out milk and honey. Alice saw that she was old — older than their parents — her face wreathed in lines, her blue eyes nested in crinkles. "When you're finished with your breakfast, I'll take you home."

Alice shot her a startled look. "How?" Nuns, to the best of her knowledge, didn't drive.

Mother Ignatius frowned in puzzlement, then the creases in her forehead smoothed. "Oh, the usual way. On angels' wings."

Alice wished they were on angels' wings now. For she had the uneasy feeling this mission — much as it might ultimately be for their mother's benefit — was anything but merciful. Wes's words came back to her. *Your mother's only human.*

Yet how could she sit still while her

mother dragged her father's memory through the mud? Long after Ian was gone, the taint would remain. Alice frowned and pressed down a little harder on the gas pedal.

They turned south onto Chumash, where pastures gave way to citrus and avocado groves. Through the trees Alice caught a glimpse of a ramshackle farmhouse — the old Truesdale place. No one had seen Dick Truesdale since his wife's death more than five years ago. It was rumored he'd taken to his bed and was now almost an invalid.

Minutes later they were pulling to a stop in front of her mother's house — the house Alice would always think of as her grandparents'. As she climbed from the car a familiar sound greeted her: the swishing of Lupe's broom. Alice could see her mother's elderly housekeeper through the wrought-iron gates to the courtyard: a rawhide strip of a woman attacking its tiles with her broom as if beating a snake to death.

"Lupe! For heaven's sake come in out of that heat," called an exasperated voice from inside.

Alice and Laura exchanged a glance. Their mother had been nagging Lupe to slow down as long as they could re-member. Nothing ever changed. Which, in light of their own task, provided little comfort. Laura lingered in the driveway.

"Are you sure we should go through with this?"

"We don't have a choice," Alice said.

"Remember those embarrassing talks about the birds and the bees?" Her sister groaned. "Who'd have thought we'd be having the same conversation with *her?*"

They made their way up the path, the pergola, ablaze in climbing black-eyed Susan, a cool tunnel after the hot drive. A wind chime tinkled softly amid the stubborn swishing of Lupe's broom.

She didn't see them at first, so intent was she on her task. Leaves from the potted citrus trees had been swept into neat little piles. A dustpan heaped with bougainvillea blossoms sat on the edge of the lily pond. Then she looked up, her wrinkled brown face breaking into a delighted grin.

"*Ay, mis hijitas.* No one told me you were coming."

"It was sort of spur of the moment." Laura glanced uneasily at Alice.

Lupe propped her broom against a pillar and walked over to hug them.

She playfully pinched Alice's waist.

"Marriage must agree with you. You've put on a few pounds." Her brown eyes sparkled. "Unless it's a baby on the way."

Heat rose in Alice's cheeks. *You'd better get used to it. You'll be hearing it for the next ten or fifteen years.* But something kept her from setting the record straight. Never mind Lupe, how would her family take it? Her poor sister, for whom motherhood wasn't an option. And her mother, who'd be devastated to learn there'd be no grandchildren.

"More like too many piña coladas." Alice managed a weak laugh.

"Lupe!" Sam called once more.

The old woman sighed as if to say, *You see what I have to put up with?* Shaking her head and muttering something in Spanish under her breath, she retrieved her broom and went on sweeping.

Just as they so often had in childhood, the two sisters wordlessly joined hands, stepping up onto the low porch and letting themselves in the door. The house was little changed from their grandparents' day. Worn Navajo rugs were scattered over the terra-cotta-tiled floor, and in the sunny, white-walled living room the Mission oak furniture stood out in stark relief. The only real difference was the bright Mexican folk

179

art that had replaced the gloomy old paintings of the previous era.

Sam must have heard them for she appeared just then, wearing a look of pleasant surprise. "Alice! When did you get back? You should have called to let me know you were coming."

Alice eyed her in disbelief. Could this be their mother? Sam's auburn hair was pulled back in a ponytail that revealed a pair of dangly, silver-and-turquoise earrings. Her cheeks were aglow and her gray-green eyes sparkled. Even the outfit she was wearing was new — a silky teal top and matching trousers that rippled like water about her slender frame.

A knot formed in Alice's stomach. *A woman only looks that way when she's in love.* Clearly, they had their work cut out for them.

She kissed her mother's cheek, catching the light scent of jasmine — a scent she couldn't remember Sam ever wearing. "Sorry," she said. "We only got back last night."

"Never mind. You're here now." Sam smiled and stepped back to look at her. "My goodness, I don't think I've ever seen you so brown. Was Maui as wonderful as everyone says?"

"It only rained once." Alice was eager to get off the subject. "Did you get my post-card?"

"Yesterday." Sam fingered a pretty silver pendant on a cord around her neck. A gift from Ian? "I can't believe it's been three weeks. It seems like you just left."

"I feel like I've been gone forever." *In more ways than one*, Alice thought.

"No need to rub it in," Laura grumbled good-naturedly. "I haven't been anywhere since that jewelry fair in Santa Fe last summer." With a weary sigh, she plopped down on the sofa.

"I've been pestering her for months to take some time off," Sam told Alice. "She always claims she's too busy."

Not half as busy as you've *been*, Alice thought.

She took a deep breath. "Mom . . ."

Laura beat her to it, blurting, "She knows about Ian."

Sam grew very still, her eyes flashing with an emotion Alice couldn't read. But when she spoke, her voice was steady. "You'd have found out sooner or later, I suppose."

Alice couldn't hold back a second longer. "I couldn't believe it when I heard. Mom, please tell me this isn't happening!"

Once again that flash of emotion, then Sam sighed. "I suppose I owe you some sort of an explanation. All right then." She waited until Alice was seated alongside Laura. "It wasn't something either of us planned. It just . . . happened. Ian's the first man since . . ." She caught herself, and said, "We enjoy each other's company. He makes me laugh." She shrugged. "That's about all there is to tell."

"Are you sleeping with him?" Under ordinary circumstances, Alice wouldn't have dreamed of speaking so rudely to her mother.

Sam stiffened noticeably, her eyes the cool color of slate. In an equally cool voice, she said, "I'm not even going to dignify that with an answer."

Alice couldn't believe it. How could her mother act as if it were no big deal? "This is my husband's *son* we're talking about," she cried. "It's beyond bizarre. It's . . . it's practically indecent!"

"No more so than your marrying a man twice your age."

Alice's cheeks burned. "If you think there's any comparison between —"

"Mom has a point," Laura put in.

Alice turned to glare at her. "Whose side are you on?"

"Nobody's." Laura's chin tilted up. "I'm just saying that people in glass houses shouldn't throw stones."

"Okay," Alice said, "maybe it *is* hypocritical. But I'm not the one making the rules. People aren't going to be as open-minded as they were about Wes and me." She looked pleadingly at her mother, standing there in her teal pantsuit like a blade of grass stubbornly pushing its way up through a sidewalk. "Is that what you want? To have everyone whispering behind your back? To be the butt of every joke?"

Flags of red stood out on her mother's cheeks. "If that were the case," she said quietly, "I think it would say more about the people in this town than it does about me."

Alice began to tremble. In some distant part of her brain she realized that perhaps she was being a bit hysterical, but she couldn't seem to stop herself. She was like a train hurtling down the tracks, screaming toward its destination.

"I can't believe you'd do this to Dad," she said.

The color drained from her mother's face. Slowly, she walked over to the ottoman by the fireplace and sank down. In a carefully measured voice, she said, "This has nothing to do with your father."

"It has *everything* to do with him." Alice shot to her feet, trembling. "It's like a slap in his face!"

"Your father's dead, but in case you haven't noticed I'm not." Sam rose, too, and walked over to the window, where she stood staring sightlessly out at the garden.

An uncomfortable silence fell, which ended with Laura saying miserably, "I never should have opened my big mouth."

Sam turned to cast her a stern, but not unloving look. "You're right, you shouldn't have. Not," she added with a small, wry smile, "that your Aunt Audrey wouldn't have gotten wind of it eventually. She seems to have a sixth sense about such things."

"Does this mean you plan to go on seeing him?" Alice asked in horror.

"For now," Sam said evenly. "I don't know about down the road."

"So it doesn't matter what *we* think?"

Her expression softened. "Of course, it does. You're my daughters. But I shouldn't have to ask your permission," she added firmly.

Alice's head was spinning. "I guess this means Tom is out of the picture." Her father's slightly boring partner seemed far more attractive all of a sudden.

Sam flashed her a keen look. "Would you be happier if he weren't?"

Alice didn't have an answer; anything she said would have sounded contradictory.

"Okay then, end of discussion." Sam put on a determinedly bright smile, saying briskly, "What do you say we head into the kitchen? I have a coffee cake just out of the oven. Oatmeal pecan — your favorite." She cast a hopeful look at her daughters.

But for Alice, who could barely breathe, food was unthinkable. "No thanks." She spoke coldly, shooting a meaningful glance at Laura, who rose reluctantly. "I'm sure you have other plans. I wouldn't dream of interfering."

Chapter 5

Sam stood motionless until the sound of the car engine had faded to a distant mutter, then sank onto the sofa. She'd known this was coming; she'd thought she was prepared. Why had it been so awful?

She'd expected Alice, of all people, to understand. But her daughter's face had told her everything she needed to know: Alice would never understand. It wasn't just that Ian was younger, or that he was Wes's son. Somehow, it had gotten tangled up in her feelings about her father. *I should have predicted it,* she thought. Alice had idolized Martin, her every achievement measured by the yardstick of his approval. There were times, Sam hated to admit, when she'd been jealous.

Yet wasn't she partly to blame? Hadn't she shielded the girls? They hadn't been privy to the tense discussions behind closed doors. They'd be shocked to learn how many times Martin had come to her, hat in hand, begging forgiveness for yet another foolish scheme gone south. Ian, on the other hand, they probably saw as feckless and irresponsible, a ne'er-do-well artist with no intention of settling down. A small, ironic smile surfaced.

For the short time they'd been lovers, Ian seemed to know her in a way her husband never had. The night before last, out of the blue, he'd presented her with a first edition she'd secretly coveted — Virginia Woolf's *A Room of One's Own*. It was as if he could read not only her mind, but also her heart and soul. They never ran out of things to talk about, yet he seemed equally comfortable with silence, as if sensing that beneath her ready smile and easy patter she was, like him, an essentially solitary creature. Best of all, he'd brought back the girl who'd once galloped bareback through pastures and skinny-dipped in the creek under a summer moon, a girl who'd dreamed of a man who would touch her in ways no one ever had.

How could she expect her daughters to understand? Laura and Alice knew her only as the mother who'd packed their school lunches and bandaged their scraped knees, who'd sent them off to college with six warm sweaters and fifty dollars in emergency money tucked into the lining of their suitcases. How much simpler for them if she'd been content to stay home every evening, with only the occasional night out with a friend. They wouldn't have to think of her having sex — or worry about some other man taking Martin's place.

They're not the only ones. The whole family will be up in arms. Elderly Uncle Pernell and Aunt Florine, both staunchly religious as well as set in their ways. Martin's mother, in a nursing home but still lighting candles at her son's makeshift shrine. And Audrey, most of all. Sam winced at the memory of her sister storming into the store like a Christian temperance zealot into a saloon.

"Sam, have you lost your *mind?*" Audrey cornered her in the storeroom as she was unpacking a crate of candlesticks. "Please tell me your daughter is imagining things, that there's nothing going on between you and that . . . that *boy.*"

Sam was too stunned at first to reply. The day before, when Laura had walked in on her and Ian, she'd been mortified, as if caught committing a crime. But now, faced with the furnace blast of her sister's outrage, she dug her heels in.

"I take it you're referring to Ian," she

said. "Don't worry, he's legal. I checked his driver's license."

"Joke about it all you want," her sister snapped. "You won't be laughing when this gets out."

Which will be sooner rather than later if you have anything to do with it. Sam straightened, brushing bits of straw from her slacks. She'd be damned if she'd let her sister see how rattled she was. "Aren't you making too big a deal of this?"

"You'll see." Audrey's mouth stretched in a humorless smile. "Then maybe you'll appreciate what I'm trying to do for you."

"Which is *what,* exactly?" Sam leveled a cool gaze at her sister. "Other than to make me feel ridiculous and over the hill."

"I'm only looking out for you." Audrey's voice became wheedling.

"Thanks, but I'm perfectly capable of looking out for myself."

"So I see."

"What exactly are you insinuating?"

"Oh, come on, we're both adults." Audrey gave a snort of laughter, reminding Sam of their high school days, when her sister used to grill her at the end of every date. Audrey, who'd spent most of *her* Saturday nights at home, had seemed to relish

189

every detail. "It's obvious what this is all about."

"Since you know so much, why don't you tell me?"

"Sex." Audrey said it as if it were something nasty she was spitting out.

Looking into her sister's flushed, self-righteous face Sam realized she could either retreat, and spend the rest of her life bowing to small minds like Audrey's, or throw all caution to the winds. There was no in-between.

The decision came with surprising ease. "I'm not only sleeping with him," she said, "I'm enjoying every minute of it."

It was like a kite soaring up, up into the blue, bringing a heady sense of release. Then the kite came crashing back to earth. Oh Lord, had she really said that? Knowing Audrey, it would be all over town by the end of the day.

In the weeks since, Sam had become aware of eyes following her down the sidewalk, and of customers inquiring a bit too curiously about her summer plans. Just the other day Althea Wormley, blue-haired president of St. Xavier's altar guild, had accosted her in line at the grocery store.

"Sam, I was just on my way over to see you. I want to officially invite you to our new-members' meeting. It's this Thursday, and we're *so* hoping you'll join us." Althea, who'd never paid much attention to her before, was clearly on a mission to save her tarnished soul. There was no mistaking her superior expression, or the way her hyperthyroidal eyes (she reminded Sam of an oversize pug) had darted over her grocery basket as if expecting to see something out of the ordinary — a bottle of champagne, perhaps? Or, God forbid, a spare toothbrush.

Sam had politely declined, reminding her that she was chairing the music festival committee this year. When would she find the time? Oh yes, she could handle the Althea Wormleys of the world. She would survive even Audrey. What was harder to take was her daughters' reactions. Laura would come around in time, she thought. She wasn't so sure about Alice.

From outside came the sound of Lupe hosing down the courtyard. Sam shook her head in exasperation. The woman would collapse from heat stroke before giving an inch. Sam was getting up to scold her one more time when a voice mocked: *Look who's being willful.*

Was it true? Was she risking everything? The respect of family and friends, a business that had been in the family for generations? She didn't even know if she was in love with Ian . . . and she didn't *want* to know. The prospect was too terrifying.

She reached for the phone. They'd made plans for a picnic on the beach, but though the day promised to be warm and sunny her heart was no longer in it. Before she could change her mind, she quickly punched in Ian's number.

"Hi. It's me."

"Hey, you."

"You sound out of breath."

"I was out jogging. I just walked in."

Sam pictured him in shorts and a tank top, slick with sweat. A familiar warmth spread through her . . . as unwelcome at this moment as a heat rash. She took a deep breath. "Listen, I'm going to have to take a rain check on that picnic. Something's come up."

"Anything I should know about?"

"Alice is back."

There was a brief silence at the other end. "I guess this means the honeymoon is over." His tone made it clear he wasn't referring to just Wes and Alice. "Did you tell her?"

"I didn't have to."

"I gather she wasn't too thrilled." Ian

clearly didn't need to have it spelled out.

"Something along those lines."

"What about my dad . . . did he weigh in?"

Sam had assumed Wes felt the same as Alice, but now she wondered. "He wasn't with her, that's all I know."

"Typical."

The note of bitterness in his voice made her wince. It had sounded so . . . adolescent. Like Alice's a minute ago. "I should go," she said. "I have something in the oven." A small lie, significant only in the fact that it was the first she'd told him.

"When will I see you again?"

She closed her eyes. "I need a few days. Just to let the dust settle. I'll let you know."

She could sense him wanting to object, but he said casually, "No sweat. I'll be around till Thursday."

Of course. She'd forgotten — the mural he was installing. Some office building in New York. He'd only be gone a few weeks, but she felt a sudden keen sense of loss that was entirely out of proportion.

On impulse, she offered, "Why don't I drive you to the airport? We'd get to say goodbye at least."

"I'm a sucker for goodbyes."

"What time's your flight?"

"Around five. How about I meet you at the shop around noon? We can stop for lunch along the way."

"Great." Her timing couldn't be worse she thought. Laura wouldn't exactly be thrilled that she'd be taking the afternoon off to be with Ian.

She felt a little better after hanging up. It was like that with Ian; just talking to him on the phone, her second thoughts seemed to vanish into thin air. He made her forget all the reasons their being together made no sense; all that she stood to lose.

Sam glanced at her watch with a sigh. It wasn't even half over and already the day that had seemed so rich with promise was settling into something pedestrian. There would be chores and errands, letters to catch up on, maybe later on an old movie on AMC. She felt unreasonably denied, though hadn't *she* been the one to cancel?

It seemed monumentally unfair all of a sudden. That she should have to go on protecting Martin's image beyond the grave, that she had to spare her daughters' feelings by once more putting her own on hold.

She recalled the one and only time she'd come close to leaving Martin. Eight years ago, yet all at once the memory was as fresh as if she were standing on the threshold now, suitcase in hand. Not because of an affair — oddly, that would have been easier to forgive — but because Martin had betrayed her in a way that was, to her, even more profound. That morning she'd intercepted a call from their accountant. Martin, she'd learned quite by accident, had withdrawn a portion of their savings by forging her name on a check.

Like always, he had an explanation. A deal for which he'd needed cash in a hurry. Since he'd planned on replacing it before she'd noticed, what would have been the point of worrying her? It wasn't as if he'd stolen anything.

But he *had* stolen something: her trust.

In the end, though, what kept her from leaving wasn't Martin. It wasn't even the girls, both away in college then. It was this house: the almost certain knowledge that she'd have had to sell it.

She was glad now that she hadn't left. A few years later, Martin had been diagnosed with cancer — ironically, his finest hour. His illness had been the one obstacle he couldn't charm or hoodwink his way out of; he'd battled it with a strength and dignity Sam hadn't known he possessed. When the end came, her tears had been genuine; she'd truly mourned him.

No, she'd made the right decision then. *The question is, am I making the right decision now?*

The following Thursday, when Ian arrived at the store, she was no closer to an answer. Watching him breeze through the door, his suede jacket slung casually over one shoulder, she was struck by how perfectly he fit the role of footloose young lover: a man with no real overhead and no family to support. Even the green canvas duffel he was carrying seemed absurdly small for the length of time he'd be away.

Laura looked up from the display she was arranging in the window. It had come in yesterday, a shipment of art glass from a studio up the coast. One item in particular, a deep blue vase patterned in stars, Sam had been tempted to keep for herself.

"So, you're off to New York." Laura's overly hearty greeting fell painfully flat. "I hear it's pretty muggy this time of year."

"I'll be indoors most of the time," he said.

"Well, have a safe trip."

"Thanks." He smiled as if he hadn't noticed her discomfort.

Sam finished with her customer, a henna-haired woman dithering over a

Nantucket lighthouse basket she'd claimed was beyond her budget . . . never mind the expensive-looking outfit she had on. She couldn't wait to get away, even if it meant abandoning poor Laura. The prospect of a few hours alone with Ian was simply too alluring.

Then they were outside, strolling across the plaza, elbows bumping in a conscious effort not to reach for each other's hands. She waved to Olive Miller, clearing a table in front of the Blue Moon Café. Olive and her identical twin, Rose, who resembled a pair of chunky bookends, had inherited the café from their father. Now widowed and in their eighties, they managed it on their own with the help of Olive's teenage granddaughters, identical twins as well.

One of them — Dawn? — waved to Sam. "Hey, Mrs. Kiley! Who's your boyfriend? He's cute!"

She was only teasing — to a teenager someone Sam's age was practically ancient; she probably joked with her grandmother the same way. Even so Sam blushed, which she disguised with a laugh, calling back, "I ordered you that necklace. It should be in sometime next week."

Dawn strolled over, tucking her order pad in the pocket of her apron. She was slender and fair, with a sprinkling of freckles, her flaxen hair pulled back in a ponytail that did nothing to hide ears that stuck out like handles on a jug. "With the ladybug?" Her twin sister had bought the last one in stock, and she'd been coveting it ever since. "Great! You know where to find me."

As they continued on, Sam gave Ian the fill. "One is Eve, the other Dawn. Their parents are old hippies from way back when. I think they grow a little pot on the side. It's a miracle their girls turned out so straight-arrow."

"Ever tried it?" he asked.

"What, marijuana? You've got to be kidding."

"Not even in college?"

"I was busy changing diapers, remember?"

"It's not too late."

She glanced at him to see if he was joking. She hoped so; she didn't need any more reasons to rethink this relationship. Wasn't it bad enough she was so much older, more concerned about her SEP-IRA than in any fun she might have missed in college?

But Ian's smile was so infectious she couldn't help smiling back. The sun shone on his oak-colored hair, and his shadow bounced jauntily over the plaza's uneven tiles. He paused to pluck a scarlet blossom from the bougainvillea that cascaded down the arch. Holding it to her cheek, he said playfully, "I was right. Red *is* your color."

"I'll remember that next time I'm picking out wallpaper."

Would he miss her in New York? She pictured him on the plane, seated next to some pretty young woman. In the close quarters, he'd notice the softness of her skin, the absence of wrinkles, and re-member when he'd taken such things for granted. They'd exchange numbers. The woman, of course, lived in New York and would be only too happy to show him around. And he —

"You mind grabbing a bite to eat here in town?"

Sam shook herself from her reverie. Was she up for it? People would stare. They'd be the main topic of conversation — for the first few minutes, at least. On the other hand, it wasn't exactly news that she was seeing a younger man. Her sister had made sure of that.

"Why not?" she said, putting on a bright smile. "It's early enough. We can probably snag a table at the Tree House." *In for a penny, in for a pound.*

The café was crowded when they arrived. As they made their way to a table dappled in shade, Sam glanced about apprehensively. No one seemed to be looking their way. Maybe it would be all right after all.

She sat down cautiously, her chair teetering on the uneven bricks. In the tree house overhead, two little boys were aiming pretend pistols at each other. At the table next to theirs Reverend Grigsby, pastor of the Presbyterian church, was tossing a scrap to his long-haired dachshund, Lily. Sam smiled. No one who'd ever seen her would forget the little dog, her paralyzed hind legs strapped to a pair of pint-sized wheels. Her portly owner caught Sam's gaze and straightened.

"Shh, don't tell." He placed a finger to his lips, brown eyes twinkling behind thick bifocals. "Doc Henry's been after me to stop. He says she's fat enough as it is."

"Your secret's safe with me." Sam silently blessed him for taking no notice of Ian.

She spotted Clem Woolley seated by the row of bookshelves marked R–T. The old man was smiling beatifically to no one in particular, his wispy white hair floating about his head like smoke. On the table in front of him was a stack of his own slim self-published volume, *My Life with Jesus*, available to anyone who might be interested. It was meant literally — as evidenced by the untouched burger on the plate across from his. For Clem, Jesus was as real as the man at the next table.

Sam waved to Gerry's daughter, Andie, sitting with a group of friends. She was clerking at Rusk's for the summer; she must be on her lunch break. Andie, the image of Gerry with her green eyes and curly black hair, playfully waggled her straw in return.

Moments later Sam glanced up from her menu to find two women in tennis whites eyeing her across the patio — both former classmates. Becky Spurlock, voted Most Likely to Succeed, now a plump housewife, and tightly packaged Gayle Warrington, owner of a travel agency. Gayle caught her eye and waved before leaning to whisper something to Becky.

Sam tried not to let it bother her. She wouldn't have traded places with either of those women, their lives as predictable as the check they were now divvying up. She knew because, until Ian, hadn't hers been just as predictable?

She watched a little girl in pigtails dart in and out between the tables, chasing her little brother while their frazzled mother attempted to round them up. A young couple in rubber flip flops and raggedy jeans, with at least five hundred dollars' worth of camera equipment slung about their necks, was busy snapping pictures of the tree, with its array of birdhouses donated by local artists.

Bleached-blond Melodie Wycoff sidled past them balancing a tray on which steaming bowls tilted precariously — never mind that it was the middle of July, the Tree House was famous for its cream of chili soup. "Be with you in a jiffy!" she called.

As Melodie was serving the young couple at the next table, Sam overheard her remark, "Awful, isn't it?" She jerked her head toward the newspaper in the man's hands. "Hasn't been anything like it since — well, I don't know when." Sam remembered that Melodie was married to a cop. She must be referring to the murder.

The woman, sallow and nervous looking, murmured, "They'll find whoever did it, I'm sure."

"Oh, they been beatin' the bushes all right," Melodie volunteered blithely.

"Trouble is, they got nothing to go on but a bloody knife with no fingerprints." She shook her head. "Poor guy. I hear his guts was spread up one side of the hill and down the other."

"Could you bring us some butter? We seem to have run out." The woman looked as if she'd suddenly lost her appetite.

"Sure thing." As she hurried off Sam caught a glimpse of leopard-print bra through Melodie's clingy white T-shirt. She'd heard a rumor that Melodie was sleeping with her husband's best friend — a fellow cop. It wouldn't surprise her to learn it was true. Hadn't there been some sort of a scandal back when Melodie was in Laura's high school class? Something involving the driver's-ed teacher?

I'm not the only one living in a glass house, she thought.

She smiled at Ian. "I wish you weren't going."

He placed a hand over hers. "Come visit me." She met his clear gaze and felt a flutter of excitement.

Then reality took hold, and she shook her head. "I can't."

"It's the perfect opportunity," he urged. "You've always wanted to see New York. Come for a long weekend."

"It's our busiest season."

"Can't Laura manage on her own for a few days?"

"I don't think she'd be too keen on it right now."

"Because of us, right?"

"That's part of it." Sam saw no reason to gild the lily.

He withdrew his hand and sat back, frowning as if he'd had something to say on that subject but had thought better of it. "I spoke with my dad. Apparently, Alice is still pretty upset."

She sighed. "I know."

"You talked to her since Sunday?"

"She won't return my calls." Sam felt her fledgling optimism slip away. "I think — *know* — it has something to do with Martin. They were very close."

"I guess we all have our own shit to deal with." Once again, she had the sense of Ian holding back. He brushed a leaf from the table, a silver ring glinting on his middle finger.

She traced the ring with her finger, its crude Celtic lettering making her think of rune stones. What would their future hold? "I'll think about New York," she said.

He smiled. "Don't take long, okay?"

How long was too long? "I won't."

She glanced up to find a familiar face eyeing them across the patio. Marguerite Moore. Her heart sank as Marguerite, who appeared to be alone, pried her considerable bulk from her chair and set sail in their direction. For someone so heavy she carried herself with surprising grace: the perfect matron in her cream-colored linen suit and chunky gold jewelry, her champagne hair coiffed to withstand a tornado.

"Sam, what a nice surprise." She turned to Ian. "I don't believe we've met. I'm Marguerite Moore."

Ian rose to take her hand. "Ian Carpenter."

"I'm on the music festival committee with your mother-in-law," she said.

Sam felt the blood drain from her face. Marguerite knew perfectly well Ian wasn't her son-in-law. She was nonetheless forced to reply, "Ian's father is married to my daughter. You remember Alice, don't you?"

"Yes, of course, forgive me. A senior moment." Marguerite tapped her temple, casting Sam a wry look that served only to remind her they were the same age. "I remember you mentioning it. Congratulations." She smiled disingenuously, eyeing the empty seat at their table. "Mind if I join you?"

Marguerite was famous for her chutzpah — useful when recruiting musicians if deadly to fellow committee members. But Ian wasn't the least bit thrown. "Actually, we were just leaving," he said. There was nothing in his tone to suggest he was being anything but truthful.

As she rose, Sam was gratified to see Marguerite flush. She couldn't have helped but notice that they'd only just arrived. "Well . . . it was nice meeting you," she said stiffly.

Outside, Sam turned to grin at Ian. "You were wonderful," she said. "I don't know what I would've done if I'd had to sit through an entire meal with that woman."

He shrugged. "It's not as if she had a gun to our heads."

"No, but I don't have your guts," she said. "I'd have stayed put and choked on every bite."

He flashed her a teasing look. "At least we'd have gotten fed."

"Poor Ian." She laughed and slipped her arm through his. "We'll pick up something along the way."

On the outskirts of Santa Barbara, they stopped at a taco stand where they sat at a picnic table and ate off paper plates, ordering dish after dish, each spicier than the next. When Ian suggested a walk on the beach, Sam didn't object. So what if she was wearing her good slacks? It hadn't stopped J. Alfred Prufrock. She rolled up her cuffs and kicked off her shoes. They raced each other to the shore, laughing breathlessly all the way.

Two hours later, they were pulling into the terminal at LAX.

She parked at the curb and got out to hug him. "Don't paint the whole town red." She smiled, blinking back tears. Why was she crying? It was only for a few weeks.

He pulled her against him, holding her tight. "I'll miss you." He smelled of the ocean, and maybe a tad too much Clorox in the wash. "Promise you'll do more than think about coming out to see me."

"I promise." She clung to him for a moment, then let go.

The people around them dissolved into a blur. Sam watched him disappear into the terminal, a silvery flash on the revolving door as it wheeled inward. She felt a sharp thrust of longing, a sudden wish to be unencumbered — by her past, by her children, by everything that held her anchored. Then she wouldn't have hesitated to run after him.

An hour and a half later she was winding her way through familiar dun-colored hills toward home. The sun was low in the sky, and stray clouds drifted overhead like errant sheep. She found herself slowing as she approached the dirt road to the convent. She'd put off speaking to the mother superior about Sister Agnes. Wasn't now as good a time as any?

Before she knew it, she was making the turn. The unpaved road was as bumpy as it was steep, and the rattling of the Honda's undercarriage ominous. She hoped this wasn't a mistake in more ways than one. The last thing she needed was another sky-high repair bill.

Luckily, she made it to the top of the hill, where she pulled to a stop and climbed out. A graveled path lined with rosebushes led to a wrought-iron gate set in an ivy-covered wall. She pressed the buzzer on the intercom — the only visible sign of present-day life in a setting that might have been from another era.

Several minutes passed before she heard the crunch of gravel on the other side and caught sight of one of the novices hurrying toward her down a shrub-lined path. A round, pink face framed in a starched white veil peered through the gate.

"I'm here to see Mother Ignatius," Sam told her.

"Do you have an appointment?" The girl sounded apprehensive.

"No, but I'm an old friend. Tell her it's Mrs. Kiley." Sam hoped it wasn't too late in the day. Evening prayers were at six, followed immediately by supper. The routine never varied.

The novice broke into a shy smile, unlocking the gate to let Sam in. "Sorry. The intercom's broken — I only heard you buzz. I thought you were from the magazine."

"What magazine?"

"*People*. Reverend Mother agreed to an interview but drew the line at photographs," she explained. "The woman has been calling and calling. Either she won't take no for an answer, or —" her smile widened, "she doesn't know Reverend Mother."

"A little of both, I suspect."

"I'm Sister Catherine, by the way." She put out a small hand surprisingly callused in one so young. "Come with me. I'll tell Reverend Mother you're here."

Sam followed her down the path into a walled sanctum out of a book of hours. At the center was a medieval knot garden over which a statue of Saint John presided. Paths wound through grassy areas lined with flower beds and fruit trees, disappearing under bowers and around tall hedges where secluded nooks provided areas for meditation and prayer. Roses were everywhere: in neatly tended beds, climbing up trellises and walls, draped over pergolas. All of it lovingly tended by the nuns. She passed one of the sisters, kneeling in the grass by a flower bed, her sleeves rolled up and her skirt tucked up into her belt. Farther down the path another sister was vigorously attacking an overgrown hibiscus with a pair of clippers.

Sam remembered her first visit years ago when she was little. Her mother had brought her along on a visit to the then mother superior, a kindly older woman named Mother Hortense, who'd instructed one of the novices to take her on a tour of the grounds while she and Mami spoke in private. It wasn't until the ride home, when Sam noticed her mother's red-rimmed eyes, that she realized Mami had come to ask for the sisters' prayers. Poppi, ill with pneumonia, had just that morning been hospitalized. The prayers must have worked, for that night her father's fever broke. A week later he was well enough to go home.

Sam followed Sister Catherine along a sheltered walkway lined with bas reliefs representing the twelve Stations of the Cross. Moments later she was stepping through an arched doorway into the main building.

Sunlight sifted through mullioned windows, casting pale diamonds over the tiled floor of the starkly furnished reception hall. She caught the smell of beeswax candles and lemon oil, just like all those years ago. From down the hall came the unexpected sound of a Chopin waltz being played on the piano.

"Wait here." Sister Catherine touched her elbow, then vanished down a narrower hall. She reappeared several minutes later to announce in a hushed voice, "Reverend Mother will see you now."

Mother Ignatius rose to greet Sam as she entered, a woman as plain and spare as her office. "Samantha, what a lovely surprise." A firm, dry hand gripped hers.

"I hope I'm not interrupting anything."

"I was just going over the monthly budget, and I can't think of a more welcome intrusion." She gestured toward the straight-backed chair facing her desk. "Sit down, please. What can I do for you?"

Sam sank into the chair, which was as

uncomfortable as it looked. She felt sick with what she was about to report. "I'm afraid this isn't a social call."

Mother Ignatius cast her a curious glance before settling back in behind her desk. "Well, I'm delighted to see you in any event. I'll have Sister Catherine bring us some tea." She pressed the intercom on her phone.

"Tea would be lovely," Sam said.

"Chamomile. Good for the nerves."

The older woman smiled, a smile that lent her plain, some might say homely face — a cross between Eleanor and Franklin Roosevelt — a kind of stark dignity. Sam remembered when they'd first met. Her daughters had been caught trespassing, and Mother Ignatius, newly appointed as mother superior, had personally escorted them home.

"I'm told *People* is knocking at your door," Sam began in an effort to put off the inevitable. "You won't be able to hide out much longer, you know. You're too good a story."

The older woman rolled her eyes. "Your friend Gerry has other ideas, I know, but I have a morbid fear of us becoming just another novelty act. Like Sister Wendy, or the singing nuns."

Sam smiled. "I don't think there's much danger of that."

Mother Ignatius withdrew a box of chocolates from a deep drawer in her desk and offered it to Sam. "Perugina. My sister sends them."

"I didn't know you were allowed," Sam teased, helping herself to one.

"Oh, we have our vices." She tipped Sam a wink as she settled back in her chair, folding her hands in front of her on the desk. "Now, what was it you wanted to see me about?"

Sam cleared her throat. "I'm here about Sister Agnes."

The mother superior sat silent, waiting.

"She comes into the shop from time to time," Sam went on, her face warming.

"Yes, I know." Mother Ignatius wore a look of weary patience. "She loves looking at beautiful things. Always has."

"I hate being the one to tell you this . . ." Sam felt as if she were confessing to a crime of her own, "but she does more than look."

Mother Ignatius's expression grew puzzled. "What are you saying?"

"She . . . takes things."

There was a long silence, broken only by the faint buzzing of a fly against the window. At last, Mother Ignatius asked softly, "How long has this been going on?"

"A few months. I didn't want to say anything at first . . . until I was absolutely sure." Sam felt terrible. "I was hoping it would go away on its own."

"I take it you haven't said anything to Sister Agnes."

"No." Sam fixed her gaze on the plain wooden crucifix on the wall above the desk. Like many of the ones at Our Lady of the Wayside, it bore no corpus — a reminder that Christ's burden wasn't to be borne by Him alone. "I thought it would be best if you spoke with her instead."

They were interrupted by a timid knock at the door. "Come in," Mother Ignatius called somewhat abruptly.

Sister Catherine's anxious pink face appeared in the doorway. "I'm sorry to disturb you, Reverend Mother. It's Sister Beatrice. She says it's urgent."

The older woman frowned. "It's always urgent with Sister Beatrice." She sounded irritated. "Tell her I'll speak with her after evening prayers."

The young novice bowed her head. "Yes, Reverend Mother."

She was easing the door shut when Mother Ignatius asked pointedly, "Aren't you forgetting something, Sister?"

Sister Catherine stared at her blankly a moment before squeaking, "Your tea! Oh yes . . . it's ready."

"We'll take it in the parlor."

When they were once more alone, Sam asked nervously, "What will happen to Sister Agnes?"

All at once Mother Ignatius looked every bit her age: an old woman long past retirement. "Send me a list of the stolen items and I'll see that they're returned." Her face creased in a weary smile. "As for the state of Sister Agnes's soul, I'm afraid that's for a higher authority than me to decide."

She led the way to the sitting room, furnished in simple but blessedly comfortable chairs and a heavy Jacobean-style breakfront. Over tea and honey cakes, they spoke of ordinary things: repairs to the chapel roof, the parish's newly appointed bishop — an old friend of Mother Ignatius's — and the recent media interest in their honey. When the bell signaling evening prayers began to peal, Sam rose to her feet.

They were making their way along the sheltered walkway outside when a nun came hurrying toward them. She was thin and pale, and appeared to glide an inch or so off the ground. Rosary beads clattered softly at her waist. As she drew closer, Sam noticed the prayer book in one hand — so worn its gilt lettering was unreadable.

"Sister Beatrice." The reverend mother's greeting was tinged with a note of resignation. It seemed appropriate somehow that they stood before the bas relief depicting the seventh Station of the Cross: Christ stumbling under the weight of his burden. "I'm sorry we didn't get a chance to speak earlier."

Sister Beatrice glanced briefly at Sam. "Forgive me. I didn't realize you had company."

"Can it wait until after prayers?" Mother Ignatius asked.

"Certainly."

"Is this about Sister Ruth again?"

Color crept into Sister Beatrice's pale cheeks. "She was late again for choir practice. And when I reprimanded her, she snapped that just because I was choir mistress —" She broke off suddenly, darting a look at Sam. "Forgive me, Reverend Mother. We'll speak at your convenience. Until then, I'll pray and meditate on the matter." She glided off, leaving Mother Ignatius to gaze wearily after her.

There's one in every bunch, Sam thought.

Sister Beatrice, despite the fact that they looked nothing alike, reminded her of Marguerite Moore.

When they reached the chapel, Mother Ignatius unexpectedly leaned forward and kissed Sam's cheek. "Take care, Samantha dear," she murmured. "I know it hasn't been easy for you these past few years. Don't make it any harder than it has to be." With that she disappeared inside, leaving Sam to wonder precisely what she'd meant.

She was setting off down the path when she caught sight of Gerry, walking briskly ahead of her, a package tucked under one arm. Sam called to her, and Gerry spun about with a delighted grin.

"Sam! What on earth are you doing here?"

Sam shot a meaningful glance over her shoulder. Gerry was the only one besides Laura who knew about Sister Agnes, and they'd been friends for so long the slightest gesture or facial expression was enough to communicate what was on their minds.

Gerry made a face, saying in a loud voice for the benefit of anyone who might be listening, "Come on. I have to drop this off at the honey house. You can keep me company while I tell you about the latest addition to our line."

"Which is?" Sam caught up with her, and they continued along the path.

"Blessed Bee moisturizer. It was Sister Paul's idea. Who'd have thought a degree in biochemistry would be so useful in a nun?" When they were well out of earshot, Gerry asked in a low voice, "Okay, how did it go?"

"Reverend Mother wasn't too happy when I told her."

"She'll survive. So will Sister Agnes." Gerry turned onto a narrower path that brought them to a gated side entrance. She pushed it open, and they stepped out onto a dirt road that sloped down to a wide meadow ringed with eucalyptus trees. "It's *you* I'm worried about. Andie told me what happened at the Tree House."

"Marguerite, you mean?"

Gerry nodded. "Apparently, she was furious. After you left Andie heard her going on and on to Reverend Grigsby about how sad it was that you'd sunk so low. And you know how that voice of hers carries." She cupped a hand around her mouth to bellow, *"Attention, everyone! Shuffleboard on the Lido deck in fifteen minutes!"*

Sam laughed in spite of herself. "Marguerite can stow it for the time being. I just saw him off at the airport."

"I see."

Gerry seemed to be waiting for her to say more, but Sam didn't know what to tell her. Nothing had been decided, yet she was as crazy about him as ever. She kept her eyes on the road ahead. The sun was setting, and the golden light had set fire to the meadow's tall grass, leaving the surrounding trees deep in shadow. Here and there Sam could make out the boxy white shape of a hive. There were dozens, she knew, each precisely placed to avoid confusion among the colonies.

Sam recalled the story of Blessed Bee's origins, one that had been told so often it was now legend. In the early thirties a nun of this order by the name of Sister Benedicta had been sent here to recuperate from a bout of tuberculosis. She thrived in the dry, sunny climate, and soon the other nuns began to notice her uncanny ability to commune with wildlife. It was said that sparrows would alight on her shoulders and deer would eat from her hand. But most astonishing of all were the bees: She could walk among them, even reach barehanded into their hives inside hollow tree trunks and not get stung. Soon the convent was in abundant supply of honey. Word of its delicate flavor and supposed curative powers quickly spread.

Requests began to pour in, and Sister Benedicta was put in charge of constructing an apiary. Within a few years Blessed Bee honey was being peddled throughout the valley, with the money going to a variety of charitable causes. All was prosperous and good until Sister Benedicta once again fell ill. This time, despite the doctor's best efforts, she didn't improve. Weeks later she was laid to rest in the tiny graveyard on the hill.

The handful of nuns still alive to tell of it always spoke in hushed tones about what happened next. The morning after Sister Benedicta was buried a swarm of bees gathered on her headstone. It was February, a time when bees normally hibernate. Even more unusual was that they resisted all efforts to dislodge them. As the weather grew colder they began to die off, one by one, dropping onto the grave like fallen blossoms. When spring came, all that was left of the hive was a sprinkling of dry husks from which a glorious burst of wildflowers had sprung. Those who came to pay their respects swore that if you listened closely you could hear a faint hum in the air.

Sam loved the tale. It embodied everything she cherished most about this valley

— its history and lore, at times interchangeable. Its people, too. A few bad apples — Marguerite Moore came to mind — weren't enough to spoil the whole barrel.

The road ended in a graveled turnabout, at the edge of which sat a long corrugated shed with a Ford pickup parked out front. Gerry unlocked the door, and they stepped into a large sunlit room. White canvas jumpsuits and netted hoods hung from pegs along one wall. On the opposite wall were shelves lined with jars of honey. A workbench stacked with boxes and packing supplies stood in the center.

Sam followed her friend into a larger room filled with stainless steel extractors, settling tanks, and metal troughs into which frames of uncapped honeycomb were draining. In the converted storeroom in back — Sister Paul's laboratory — Gerry dumped her package on a narrow workbench jumbled with vials and beakers. Jars of dried flowers and other, more mysterious-looking ingredients lined the shelf above it.

She unscrewed the lid from a small unlabeled jar and held it out for Sam to smell. "Get a whiff of this." Sam caught the scent of lavender and beeswax, maybe even a touch of honey. "Sister Paul would have been a world-class perfumer if the call to Jesus hadn't been greater."

"You're definitely on to something." Sam feigned an interest she didn't quite feel; her head was too filled with thoughts of Ian. "I'll take a dozen to start with. If it doesn't sell, I'll have the smoothest skin this side of the Rockies."

"Then Marguerite can hate you even more."

Sam indulged in a wicked smile. "You know, I think you're right. I think she *is* secretly jealous."

Gerry laughed lustily. "What she needs is a good *schtupping* of her own."

Sam shuddered at the thought. Marguerite, divorced for some years, probably hadn't had sex since Nixon was in office. "That wouldn't solve everything."

"I take it you're referring to your daughters."

Sam nodded. "They're pretty upset."

"Naturally. You're messing with the status quo." Gerry, who loved the girls like an aunt, didn't sound the least bit sympathetic. "Listen." She seized Sam by the shoulders, looking her squarely in the eye. "Ian Carpenter is cute, smart, and sexy as hell. He's also the best thing that's happened to you since —" She broke off.

She didn't have to say it: *since Martin died.*

Sam sighed. "Unfortunately, I'm a package deal."

"Your daughters are grown women with lives of their own. They'll come around." Gerry gave her a little shake. "It's *your* turn now."

"I feel as if I'm being selfish."

"It's about time!"

"It's worse than they think. I may be in love with him."

"Would that be so terrible?"

"Yes. No." She drew away from Gerry, turning toward the window. A dead bee lay on the sill. She picked it up, holding it delicately pinched between thumb and forefinger. "The truth is, I don't know. It's all so complicated." She stared at the bee, its wings glimmering like spun gold. "He wants me to visit him in New York."

"You told him yes, I hope."

"I said I'd think about it."

"Book the damned flight," Gerry growled. "If you don't, I'll book it for you." This was the same Gerry Fitzgerald who'd shamed old Father Kinney, their former parish priest, into rehab.

Sam felt a rush of affection as she turned

to smile at her friend. "Whatever comes of this, it's nice to know there'll be at least one person still speaking to me."

"How else am I supposed to give you a piece of my mind?" Gerry shook her head in affectionate despair. "I'm serious about that trip. It'll do you good to get away. You look a little worn out."

"Who wouldn't?"

"Seriously, are you okay?"

"I'm fine. Just the usual menopausal stuff." Sam shrugged. "You know, hot flashes, missed periods, that kind of thing."

"Do me a favor," Gerry said. "Make a doctor's appointment. *After* you've called your travel agent."

"If I go to New York, things will only get more complicated."

As if in echo of Sam's thoughts, she felt a sharp pinch on her thumb and looked down in horror to discover the bee wasn't dead after all. With the scant bit of life that was left in it, it had stung her.

Chapter 6

Ian hailed a cab at the corner of Twentieth and Eighth. Just a few short weeks and already New York had begun to seem like home. The tidal rush of traffic, the teeming sidewalks, the hot belch of sounds like a shot of epinephrine. In Chelsea, where he'd lucked into a brownstone apartment on loan from a friend, you could stay out all night and never be hungry, thirsty, or bored. He even had a favorite hangout, a funky little French café down the block where you could sit all morning nursing a grand crème and a *New York Times.*

There was only one thing missing: Sam.

Sam, who would be here in just five hours.

His pulse quickened at the thought. He still couldn't quite believe she was coming. A long weekend, that's all she could manage, but he'd make it count. There was so much to show her, so much *he* hadn't seen they could explore together. And far from home she might even forget, for a little while at least, all her reasons why this — *they* — could never work.

He leaned forward, directing the cabbie, "Lexington and Forty-seventh."

It was shortly before six, an hour when most people were heading home from work. Traffic was dense; he was used to that by now. It'd been three weeks already, with at least another week to go on a job that had been plagued with delays from the start. Starting with the painter improperly hanging two of the panels, which had taken days to correct, followed by a four-day hiatus while the building's new alarm system was installed. He was now in the final detailing phase when all his months of work came together in a perfectly realized whole.

The way he wished it could be with Sam.

Sam. These past weeks, however swamped, he'd thought of little else. With other women he'd loved it had always been a case of out of sight, out of mind. But Sam was special. Maybe it frightened him a little, or maybe he wasn't quite used to it. All he knew was that if she hadn't agreed to come he'd have gone a little crazy.

As the cab jounced its way up Eighth Avenue he thought of her refusing to let him meet her at the airport, insisting it made no sense. That was Sam for you — self-sufficient to a fault. She must have gotten into the habit with her husband, who struck Ian as having been the self-centered type. Not that she'd said anything against him; just the opposite, in fact. That was the tip-off — if the guy had been so great, why the need to constantly stick up for him? Sam's marriage clearly hadn't been as solid as she wanted everyone to believe.

He wondered if her husband had truly understood her. A man who'd preferred her made up and dressed to the nines, who couldn't see how much more beautiful she was without anything on. A man whose life seemed to have been a constant social swirl, with more room for friends and activities than his wife and kids.

He knew she was bothered by the age thing, but quite honestly he didn't think of her as older. She was just Sam. He wouldn't have traded her face — crow's feet and all — for any other woman's. In each one of those lines he saw a life honestly, if not always fully, lived. He saw a generous heart and curious mind. He saw a woman who, in her nearly five decades on this planet, hadn't been cherished nearly enough.

That was what he longed to do: cherish

her. Hold a mirror up to let her see what he saw, how unique and extraordinary she was. He couldn't predict the future. Hadn't he spent most of his adult life avoiding such thoughts (along with the women who'd pushed too hard in that direction)? The only thing he was sure of was that he didn't want to be apart from her.

The taxi lurched to a stop. They were at Lexington on Thirty-sixth, stuck in gridlock. The cabbie leaned on his horn, joining the blatting chorus. "Freakin' president," he muttered. "Last time he was in town, it was backed up all the way to Jersey."

Ian peered up at the Chrysler Building's spire, glittering above the boxy gray highrises around it. When he was four, his mother had shown him a photograph of it in a book, telling him it was one of the world's seven wonders — which for a long time he'd believed. Gigi, born and raised in New York, had spoken so wistfully of her native city he'd often wondered if she wasn't sorry to have married his father and moved away. Her passion had been the art scene, which even at a young age Ian, on the rare occasions he'd accompanied her to New York, had found to be more bullshit artists than the real thing.

He wondered what Sam, a woman for whom loving her children was as natural as breathing, would have made of Gigi. She was curious about his childhood, he knew, but he didn't quite know what to tell her. It wasn't that his mother hadn't shown him affection. But Georgina — Gigi to family and friends — had been mostly selfish and vain, a failed painter who'd turned to promoting young talent, invariably male.

He would never forget the day, sent home sick from school, that he'd walked in to find his mother posing nude on the living room couch for her current protégé, a coarse and pretentious young artist named Carlo. Ian was twelve. It was the first time he'd seen his mother naked.

Gigi had regarded him with mild annoyance, asking, "Darling, what on earth are you doing home this time of day?" There wasn't a hint of embarrassment in her voice. Nor did she reach for the yellow silk robe lying in a puddle at her feet.

"My stomach hurts," he'd said. It was true; he'd felt as if he might throw up.

"Well, for heaven's sake, go lie down." It was more than two hours before she finally tiptoed into his room, to see how he was doing. Ian pretended to be asleep while she felt his forehead. A few minutes later he heard the sound of the shower and the soft murmuring of Gigi's and Carlo's voices. He was certain his father wouldn't have approved, but Ian never said a word. What would have been the point? Wes was hardly ever around. It was as if Gigi and he led separate lives, with Ian, their only child, rattling about in the empty space between.

Ian was fourteen when his mother became ill. What he remembered most about that time was the pall that had hung over the house. All those protégés and fair-weather friends had vanished overnight. No one visited Gigi in the hospital, and only a few sent flowers. Her bitterness knew no bounds. Ian wasn't sure how much of it was because she was dying, and how much because she'd been brought face-to-face with the shallowness of her existence. She'd refused even the solace of her husband and son. When they came to see her she would turn her face to the wall, pretending to be asleep.

After she died, Ian turned away, too. He ran wild, staying out all night with friends, drinking too much. His junior year he flunked all but one course, and that was art. Wes laid down the law: If he didn't clean up his act, drastic measures would be taken. Ian didn't care; he was beyond caring. In a final fuck-you, he got wasted the night of his junior prom, and with a group of friends broke into a teacher's car. Hours later the cops caught them joyriding in West Hollywood, a trail of empty beer cans marking their trail. The following day, Ian was on a plane to New Mexico.

It was at Horizons, a wilderness program for wayward boys of wealthy parents, that he finally learned to cope. Not just with his mother's death, but from never really having had her in the first place. His counselor, a plainspoken black man named Leander Fisk, had provided the key.

"Ain't no such thing as accidents," he'd said one night as they sat huddled around a campfire, Leander and fifteen exhausted, mosquito-bitten boys. "Y'all were put here on this earth for a reason. Your job is to figure out what that reason is."

Leander was a living example. He'd grown up in the Deep South, hating and fearing whites. All that had changed one fateful day in 1969 when he was marching in a civil rights rally and a white man he didn't even know shoved him to the ground to take a bullet intended for Leander. Leander swore on the man's grave to devote the rest of his life to promoting racial tolerance.

Ian's destiny had been to seize upon the one thing of value that Gigi had given him: a love of art. From then on, he'd worked tirelessly, graduating from Berkeley in just three years before going on to earn his master's in fine art. In time the rift with his father began to heal. He would never quite forgive Wes, but he now saw his dad as someone who'd tried his best — even if he'd fallen short of the mark. Ian could only hope he'd be a better father to any kids Alice and he might have.

The taxi jerked free, and they were once more on the move. Minutes later it was pulling to a stop on the southeast corner of Forty-seventh and Lex. He paid the cabbie and got out. As he battled the tide of commuters spilling from the revolving glass door just ahead, Ian felt like the proverbial salmon swimming upstream. He didn't mind. While these people were jockeying for cabs and seats on the subway, he'd be settling in with his brushes and paint on the twenty-eighth floor, Johnny Coltrane on his Walkman, and all of Manhattan at his feet.

He stepped out of the elevator, using his keys to unlock the doors to the reception area. He paused just inside. The offices of Aaronson Asset Management always took a moment or two to get used to. In an era of sleek lines and minimalist decor they were a throwback to another century. Marble floor and walnut wainscoting, reproduction Sheraton desk and chairs, even a Waterford crystal chandelier. All in all, more suited to a Wall Street bank than a modern high-rise.

His mural spanned three walls above the wainscoting, depicting various vintage Manhattan scenes: the view from a boat docking at Ellis Island, circa 1900, the year Julius Aaronson, great-grandfather of the firm's present-day CEO, first arrived in this country; the Wall Street stock exchange just before the crash of 1929; steelworkers clambering over girders on the partially completed Empire State Building.

He was peeling the tarp from the scaffolding in one corner when the door to the office suites swung open. A petite, curly-haired young woman in a tailored charcoal pantsuit appeared: Julius Aaronson III's daughter, Marissa, or Markie, as she liked to be called.

She brought a hand to her chest with a breathless cry. "Ian! You scared me. For a second I thought you were my father."

He shrugged amiably. "What if I had been?"

"I'm supposed to be on my way to Amagansett," she explained. "Big family do. I told Dad I had a dentist's appointment. He doesn't approve of my working late. In fact, he doesn't approve of my working at all. Not in the hallowed halls of finance, that is. He'd have preferred it if I'd become . . . well, an artist." She smiled coquettishly, revealing a dimple in one cheek.

She was really quite pretty — in an Ivy-League-brat sort of way. Her eyes were a light toffee brown, her skin strikingly porcelain against the Sephardic blackness of her hair.

"You won't get rich that way," he said with a laugh.

"I'm rich already."

Ian was disarmed by her candor. "Why does that not surprise me?"

She eyed him closely. "You don't look as if you've missed too many meals yourself."

Ian thought of the early days, how noble he'd felt spurning his father's offer to help. He'd do it on his own, or not at all . . . which was basically a load of crap. He should have taken the money, as a loan if nothing else. It would've meant fewer commissions, and more time for what he enjoyed most.

"I get by," he said.

She stepped back to admire the mural. "I can see why. You're very good."

"Thanks."

"It reminds me a little of Diego Rivera's *La Creación*."

He was amused by her efforts to impress him, yet felt no need to encourage her by telling her that he, too, was a great admirer of Rivera.

She glanced at her watch — slim, expensive. "I was just about to call for takeout. Care to join me?"

"Maybe another time." He gestured toward the scaffolding. "I'm behind as it is."

She tried not to look disappointed. "Me too. I'll grab something to eat at my desk."

"Don't work too hard." Ian swung up onto the platform, where his paints and brushes were neatly laid out on a rag.

Markie flashed him a fetching smile on the way back to her office: at least ten thousand dollars' worth of orthodontics, all of it directed at him. Ian had no doubt she'd find plenty of takers, but could think of no polite way to let her know he wasn't interested.

Hours later he was dabbing with his

brush at the buttons on a stockbroker's greatcoat when he happened to glance up to see that it was a few minutes after eleven. Jesus. Where had the time gone? If he didn't hurry, Sam would get to the apartment ahead of him. He hastily cleaned and stowed his brushes.

He was waiting for the elevator when Markie slipped up alongside him. He didn't think it was a coincidence, but forced himself to ask pleasantly, "Off to Amagansett?"

She rolled her eyes. "Between you and me, I'd rather go home and crash."

The elevator doors thumped open, and they stepped in. "That's exactly what I plan on doing," he said.

As if she'd only just thought of it, Markie offered casually, "Listen, why don't I drop you off?"

"That's nice of you, but I'm all the way over on the West Side."

He could see that Markie Aaronson, only child of Julius Aaronson III, wasn't used to taking no for an answer. "It's no bother. This time of night everything is two minutes away."

Ian was left with no choice. "Well, in that case, thanks."

They rode the elevator down to the garage and minutes later were speeding south on Park Avenue in Markie's sporty little Mercedes convertible — a gift from her parents, no doubt. "Where to?" She raised her voice to be heard above the din of traffic.

"Twentieth and Ninth," he told her.

"Nice neighborhood. Very arty."

"The apartment's on loan from a friend." Ty, a former college roommate, was in Europe for the summer. A lucky break, since Sam was probably used to nicer digs than he could've afforded on his own.

"You're from California, aren't you?" She drove too fast, just as he suspected she did everything. A few blocks ahead, Grand Central's arch loomed like a finish line.

"Little town just north of Santa Barbara."

"I know the area. My grandparents have a house in Big Sur."

"You get out there much?"

"As a matter of fact, I'm flying out the end of the month."

From the exaggerated nonchalance with which she spoke, he suspected she'd only just decided. Why had he told her where he lived? She'd be all over him now. Suddenly, he felt impatient to be with Sam.

They were turning onto Twentieth when he spotted her climbing out of a cab. She looked up, squinting into the glare of the Mercedes's headlights, then broke into a wide grin.

"Anyone you know?" Markie pulled in behind the cab.

"A friend." Ian cast her a distracted smile as he climbed out. "Listen, thanks for the ride."

Then he was dashing to meet Sam, who stood with her arms out as if to embrace the whole world. He caught her, lifting her off her feet with the fury of his embrace. Her hair tickled his nose, and he could feel her buttons — small, cool circles pressing through the thin fabric of his T-shirt.

He drew away, holding her at arm's length. "You look wonderful."

"Liar. I look like hell."

"Rough trip?"

Her smile faded. "The worst. For a while there, I wasn't sure we'd make it." He could see now that she looked a little pale. Was it just the plane ride?

He touched her cheek. "Only a little further. Did I tell you it's a walk-up?"

"I've come this far, I think I can make it up a few flights of stairs." She bent to retrieve her suitcase, but he beat her to it.

There were some things she'd just have to get used to.

He led the way up a steep flight of steps. Ty had touted this a real find, but it looked more charming at night, when you couldn't see the chunks missing from the lintels and cracks plastered over with cement. He cast her an apologetic smile as they stepped into the small, dimly lit vestibule. "I warned you it wasn't the Ritz."

Sam gave the easy laugh of a woman who'd have been just as happy with peanut butter and crackers as caviar. "I don't intend to look a gift horse in the mouth. As long as there's running water, I'll be fine. Right now I'd kill for a shower."

"Right this way, Ma'am."

On the landing above, she paused to ask, "She someone I should know about?"

"Who?"

"That girl just now."

He caught the slight note of tension in her voice, and offered what he hoped was a reassuring smile. "Her? Just someone who works in the building. I ran into her as I was leaving." He wondered why he hadn't been more forthcoming. What difference did it make that Markie was the boss's daughter?

Moments later he was unlocking the

door to the apartment. They stepped into the living room, bathed only in the dim glow from the street lamp below. He set her suitcase down, and once more embraced her, burying his face in her hair. "I missed your smell."

She broke away with a little laugh. "Listen to you, anyone would think we've been separated for ages."

"It feels that way." He studied her face in the half light, its delicate planes and lucent, gray-green eyes. "I'm glad you came. I was afraid you'd change your mind."

She smiled. "I'm glad, too."

"I wish you could stay longer."

"I wish you were coming home with me."

"It's only for another week, if that. I'll be home before you know it." Ian switched on the overhead light. "I've got it all mapped out. Tomorrow, sight-seeing. You ain't seen nothing till you've been to the top of the Empire State. Then dinner in the neighborhood. There's a great little Japanese restaurant just around the corner. You like sushi?"

Sam wasn't even listening; she was gazing about the room, which was small, but long on charm with its wooden shutters and quaint marble fireplace. "I wasn't expecting anything this nice."

"The starving-artist garret was taken."

She looked faintly abashed. "I didn't mean it that way."

He grinned. "I know you didn't." He headed for the kitchen tucked off to one side — little more than a closet, really. "What can I get you? Water, wine, soda?"

"I'll take that shower if it's all right with you."

"Bathroom's all yours." He caught her loosely about the waist as she was sidling past, kissing her on the nose. "Don't be long." He'd never wanted to make love to a woman so badly.

Down the hall he heard the shower crank on, and a few minutes later she was poking her head out the door, her head wrapped in a towel. Another thing he loved about Sam: She was the only woman he'd ever known who didn't spend hours in the bathroom.

"Can I borrow your robe?" she asked. "I forgot to pack mine."

"Let me look at you first." Ian nudged his way inside.

Sam looked a bit startled, but didn't pro-test when he drew her into his arms, holding her gently pinned against the sink. Steam settled over him like a warm hand.

In the medicine chest over the sink, their reflections were a pale blur. He slipped a hand under her towel, and it dropped to the floor in a dark blue puddle.

Sam's eyes searched his, and he saw what he always did, that tiny flicker of insecurity, the voice of the uncherished wife asking, *Is it true, can he possibly want me?* Ian wouldn't have known where to start. It wasn't just that he wanted her; she was *everything* he'd ever wanted.

He let his hands and mouth tell her instead.

Sam's head tipped back, her hair falling in wet tangles about her shoulders. Water dribbled down the slope of her breasts. Ian bent to catch it with his tongue. It tasted sweet, like rainwater. He pressed his face against her neck. She smelled of shampoo and soap . . . and her own womanly scent. God, how could he ever give this up?

"I want you," he murmured.

"Here?"

She pretended to be scandalized, but when he pushed a hand between her legs she was wet. She moaned, parting them further. Ian, on fire, reached to unbuckle his belt, fumbling like a teenager. Later would come the long, slow hours of lovemaking. But if he couldn't have her right now, this very minute, he'd go crazy.

Tell him, a voice whispered. *Tell him now.*
But the words wouldn't come. She could scarcely breathe. Sam hiked herself onto the sink, wrapping her legs about his hips. It was awkward, but they managed. She could feel the cool porcelain pressing against her bottom as he thrust into her. Oh God . . .

Now there was only this: his warm breath mingling with the steam, his arms and chest slick with moisture, his body driving into hers. She gripped him about the waist. His damp hair stuck to her cheek. She could see their reflections shimmering on the wet tiles at his back. She squeezed her eyes shut, and forced her mind to go blank.

They came within seconds of one another, the force of it shoving her back hard. She felt the cold bite of the faucet in the small of her back, and would've slipped and fallen if he hadn't caught her. He held her tightly for a moment before gently releasing her.

They eyed one another, gasping for breath amid the lazily swirling steam. Something warm trickled down the inside of her thigh. Suddenly she knew it couldn't wait another moment. She had to tell *now.*

"Ian," she said. "I'm pregnant."

She'd only just found out. Even as she said it, it didn't seem real.

She saw the same disbelief mirrored in Ian's face. He took a step back, and incredibly, broke into a grin — the goofy grin of a man in shock.

"You're kidding, right?"

"I'm afraid not."

The goofy grin dropped away. "I don't get it. I thought —"

"So did I. Apparently, I was wrong."

"Jesus." He scrubbed his face with an open hand.

Sam felt a sudden chill. "Is that all you can say?"

Ian held his hands out, entreating her. "I'm sorry. Look, we'll . . . we'll figure something out."

She shook her head. "Abortion isn't an option." She'd considered it, of course — for all of two minutes. But how could she go through it, knowing what it was to be a mother? Thinking of her own two and what her life would've been without *them?*

A heavy silence fell. There was only the slow tick of water from the showerhead, and the faint throb of music from the apartment below. Ian wore the expression of someone sucker punched, and when he spoke it was with the cracked voice of a man who'd aged aeons in the space of a minute.

"We'll have it, then," he said.

"You don't sound too thrilled."

He closed his eyes. "Give me a break, Sam. I'm doing the best I can here."

"I know." Her voice softened. She wanted to say something to reassure him, but the words wouldn't come. This wasn't a setback — or even an illness. Those were reversible. This wasn't.

He's just a kid, whispered the voice in her head. *What did you expect?* She remembered the pretty young woman in the silver convertible. *She's who he should be with,* she thought. *Someone his own age, someone with all the time in the world to raise a family — or to wait.*

"Whatever happens," he said, "we're in this together."

It was the sort of remark she'd have expected from Martin: utterly useless. At the same time, she didn't know what he could have said that would have put her at ease. All she wanted was something, anything, that was firm, precise, like clear directions on the back of a box telling her how to proceed.

Too exhausted to continue, she pulled his robe from the hook on the door and slipped it on. When he reached to hug her, she gently pushed him away. "Not now," she told him. "What I need more than anything is a good night's sleep." She opened the door, and slipped out into the hall.

Ian stood motionless in her wake, staring at his foggy reflection in the mirror — that of someone he didn't know. He wanted to follow her, but the set of her shoulders had made it clear she wasn't interested in anything he had to say — at least not now. Somehow, he'd failed. He didn't know how, and maybe it didn't matter. The only thing that mattered, the only thing he knew, was that he had to find a way to make it right.

A baby.

Jesus.

Reality came crashing in. Was he ready for this?

In that instant, Ian saw himself as Sam must: young, unfettered, and about as far from father material as a man could be. But he wasn't his dad. He wasn't the sum of his childhood, either.

We need to talk, he thought. *Not tomorrow, or next week. Now.*

He had to make her see that it could work . . . as soon as he figured out *how*.

A minute passed, then two. He stood there, his eyes squeezed shut, gripping the edge of the sink like a man in pain. At last, he stepped out into the hallway and called softly, "Sam?"

No answer.

The bedroom door was closed. He knocked, and when she didn't answer, eased it open.

She lay sprawled across the bed in his robe, fast asleep.

 Chapter 7

"You need boots, for one thing," Laura said firmly.

"You don't have to go to all this trouble," Finch said. "I'm fine with what I've got." Her voice carried a note of defiance that Laura recognized for what it was: abject fear.

"You sound like Maude."

The girl's hard mouth flickered in a tiny smile. "I *could* use some new underwear."

Well, that's some progress at least, Laura thought. It had taken most of the morning, and practically an act of Congress, to talk Finch into this shopping expedition. She claimed she needed nothing more than what she had and the few castoffs Laura had given her. But both knew that this represented far more than new clothes and a pair of boots that fit; it was a turning point of some kind, an unspoken commitment.

As they strolled along Old Mission on their way to Rusk's, Laura made a mental list. The girl could use several pairs of jeans, some T-shirts and tank tops, a dress for special occasions, and sweaters for when the weather grew cooler. Assuming, of course, she'd be around then.

That's the sixty-four-thousand-dollar question, isn't it?

Laura was no closer to an answer than she had been a month ago. She still knew next to nothing about Finch. The only information she'd volunteered was that she was from New York and that both her parents were dead. When Maude had inquired gently about other family members, she'd clammed up. Further efforts to pry her loose had proved useless.

Only one thing was certain: They couldn't go on this way indefinitely.

They were passing the bookstore when Laura ventured, "Have you given any thought to school clothes?"

It was as if a wild animal she'd been hand-feeding for months suddenly caught the scent of danger. Finch's reaction was immediate and visceral; Laura could almost see her shrinking as her muscles contracted and her neck disappeared into her shoulders. "No," she said, staring at the ground.

"You'll have to enroll, you know." Laura spoke with studied casualness. "It doesn't have to be permanent. Just . . . well, until you decide what you want to do."

"I don't have to do anything I don't want to." Finch reminding her that she was sixteen now and could do as she pleased.

"What about college?"

Finch cast her a guarded look. Clearly, college had never been part of the equation. "What about it?"

"If you get good grades there are scholarships."

"Yeah, right." Finch was wearing that look again: the look of someone who finds it easier not to hope rather than risk having her hopes dashed.

"I'm serious," Laura went on. "If your grades and test scores are good, there'd be any number of colleges that'd be thrilled to have you."

Finch shrugged. "My grades suck."

"We could work on that," Laura said. "I was always good at math. And Maude . . . well, did you know she used to teach high school English?"

That got her. "How come she never said anything?"

"Oh, you know Maude, always hiding her light under a bushel." *Like someone else I know.*

Something long buried flickered to life

in Finch's eyes. "I got a B minus in English my sophomore year."

"That's encouraging."

"I didn't get all the homework in on time, but then I wrote this paper on *Silas Marner* my teacher must've liked. She gave me an A."

Laura smiled. She didn't remember the first thing about the book she, too, had slogged through in high school, but was all of a sudden grateful to good old Silas.

That reminded her of something else: transfer records. Finch would need them to enroll.

I'll cross that bridge when I get to it. For now it was enough that the sun was shining, the sky hadn't fallen, and on this beautiful Saturday in July they could have been mistaken for any mother and daughter setting out on a shopping expedition.

In front of Lickety-Split she nodded hello to a couple she knew from Lost Paws. Inez and Sue were herding their children out the door — two little boys, each with a dripping cone. One adopted, the other Sue's by artificial insemination. *It takes all kinds,* Peter used to scoff. But Laura marveled at the endless invention of families — like pictures that appear to be one thing until you look at them closely and see something entirely different. Sue and Inez's children, aside from being adorable, seemed as well adjusted as any.

"They're gay, right?" Finch asked when they were out of earshot.

"As far as I know," Laura said. "They don't advertise it."

"And that's okay?"

"Okay in what sense?"

"I mean . . . people around here are okay with it?"

Laura shrugged. "Sure. Why do you ask?"

"Just wondering."

Laura glanced at Finch out the corner of her eye. Was this her way of asking if she'd fit in, too? A girl all alone in the world, with no past and seemingly no future, who might not have been welcome elsewhere. Laura longed to reassure her but didn't want to scare her off. *One step at a time . . .*

They rounded the corner onto Espina Lane. Rusk's — the closest thing in Carson Springs to a department store — occupied what had at one time been several adjacent storefronts. In business nearly as long as Delarosa's, it was still owned and operated by the Rusk family. Laura pushed the door open, and they stepped into its air-conditioned coolness.

The interior was basically unchanged from when she'd been a child: menswear and ladies apparel at either end; shoes, belts, handbags, and jewelry forming the center aisles. In the children's department upstairs there was an old-fashioned scale for determining sizes, and on Tuesdays and Saturdays you could bring your kitchen knives to be sharpened in the housewares section downstairs. In the toy department at Christmastime, old Avery Lewellyn, dressed in his Santa suit, welcomed children onto his ample lap.

"Why don't we start with boots?" Laura suggested.

The shoe section was in back. Sturdy-looking lace ups and loafers lined wooden racks along the wall. A foot measurer — a relic out of Laura's childhood — sat on a floor scuffed by generations of children's feet. There was even a full selection of riding boots, ranging from English to cowboy.

"Can I help you?" Laura looked around to find Andie Fitzgerald walking toward them. Andie broke into a grin. "Laura, hi! I didn't know it was you." She glanced curiously at Finch.

Laura remembered when she used to

baby-sit for Gerry's kids. Andie had been a handful, not because she was spoiled but because the questions never stopped. Why is grass green? What makes stars shine? How do fish breathe? Seeing her now — her green eyes shining and black hair bouncing at her shoulders — Laura felt a rush of affection.

"I didn't know you were working here," she said.

"Neither did I, until Mom told me she was cutting off my allowance." Andie rolled her eyes, but didn't seem too bent out of shape. "I guess she figures when the going gets tough, the tough get going." She smiled at Finch. "Hi, I'm Andie."

"Hi." Finch idly examined a shoe, making an elaborate pretense of not looking her way. Andie, in her neatly ironed skirt and blouse, the St. Ann's medal from her confirmation hanging from a silver chain about her neck, might easily have given her the wrong idea — that she was from another planet — if not for the four tiny earrings in each ear.

"Finch is staying with me," Laura said.

Andie didn't probe. "Lucky you."

Finch seemed to relax a bit. "Laura's teaching me how to ride," she said shyly.

"Really? Cool."

Laura had given Andie lessons, too. Like Finch, she'd been a natural. "As a matter of fact, that's why we're here," she said. "We're looking for a pair of riding boots."

"What size?" Andie was suddenly all business.

"Eight and a half," Finch told her.

Andie disappeared into the back room, returning several minutes later with an armful of boxes. She lowered them onto the floor, and pried the lid from the top-most one. "Here, try these first. They're my favorite." Finch was seated in one of the chairs, unlacing a grubby sneaker when Andie said offhandedly, "Listen, I'm off to-morrow. If you're not doing anything, maybe we could go riding."

Finch frowned, staring at a point just past her shoulder. Laura held her breath. Then Finch said, "Yeah, sure. That'd be cool." She glanced uncertainly at Laura. "If it's okay with you."

It was all Laura could do not to cheer. "Are you kidding? You'd be doing me a favor — not to mention the horses."

And that was it. When Laura returned from a preliminary exploration of the ladies' sportswear section, the two girls were chatting easily. She sent up a silent little prayer of thanks.

An hour later, shopping bag in hand, Laura and Finch set off for the Tree House. They were strolling past the Quill Pen when they bumped into Tom Kemp on his way out the door. He was carrying a shopping bag containing a gift-wrapped box.

He held it aloft. "My secretary's birthday. I got her a box of stationery. How's that for originality?"

"I'm sure she'll love it," Laura said.

"Let's hope so." He smiled. "How've you been, Laura?"

"Working too hard, as usual," she said. "You remember Finch?"

"Sure. From the wedding." He spoke as if Finch having crashed it were no big deal. In that instant Laura caught a glimpse of what he must have been like as a kid — the kind who volunteered to take out the trash and mow elderly neighbors' lawns. He gestured toward their shopping bags. "Looks like you two have been busy cleaning out the stores."

"We worked up an appetite, that's all I know," Laura said with a laugh.

"How's your mom? I haven't seen her around lately."

Laura felt her mood shift as if a cloud had passed in front of the sun. "She's fine."

"Give her my best, will you?" He seemed

suddenly ill at ease. Had he caught wind of the gossip? Tom glanced at his watch. "Well, I'd better be going. Pressing date with the barber." He winked, heading off up the street.

Laura watched him go, feeling oddly wistful. If Sam had fallen for Tom instead, none of this would be happening. She thought of the bombshell her mother had dropped on them last night, which Laura was still struggling, unsuccessfully for the most part, to absorb.

Sam had asked them over for dinner — Laura and Alice and Wes — waiting until the table was cleared and the dishes stacked in the dishwasher before gathering them all together in the living room. "I have something to tell you," she'd said. Though she'd looked drawn, her eyes had been clear with purpose. "But first, I want you to know this isn't a topic that's open to discussion. However you feel about it, you'll just have to adjust."

Laura had braced for the worst. *They're engaged.* What else? Ever since New York, her mother had seemed withdrawn and preoccupied. Not exactly the blushing bride to be, but given the circumstances what could you expect?

Laura glanced about. Her sister wore a

dawning look of horror, while Wes merely looked concerned and maybe a little apprehensive. No one could have predicted what came next.

"I'm having a baby," Sam said.

Laura recalled only bits and pieces of the ensuing uproar. She was dimly aware of Alice weeping, and Wes doing his best to calm her. While Laura merely sat there, numb.

Then something had stirred in her. A monstrous envy, green and dripping, rising from the blackest jungle of her heart. *This is all wrong,* she thought. God had gotten it wrong somehow. *She* ought to have been the one making such an announcement. Hadn't she spent years trying? Subjecting herself to countless doctor's visits and one painful procedure after another. Only to be told, in the end, that she'd never have children of her own. Wasn't that why Peter had left? Now he and his new wife were having a baby . . . and her mother . . . *oh God* . . . it was too awful.

Laura had been sick about it ever since, but this morning had managed to push it from her head. Determined not to let anything spoil this day, she'd eaten breakfast, gone about her chores, even stopped next door to lend a hand to her neighbor, Anna

Vincenzi, whose mother had fallen and couldn't get up. Until her chance encounter with Tom Kemp had brought it rushing back.

Finch, seeming to sense the shift in mood, touched Laura's elbow. "Thanks," she said. "You didn't need to buy me all that stuff."

Laura roused herself, smiling. "No need to thank me. You earned it."

"What do you mean?"

"You help out around the house. You feed and water the horses and muck out stalls," Laura went on in the same matter-of-fact tone. "If anything, I owe you."

A corner of Finch's mouth hooked down. "I'm a lousy cook."

"You're trying. That's the important thing."

Laura didn't belabor that particular point. The girl's culinary disasters were the joke of the household. The night before last she'd attempted creamed tuna over rice, only had run out of rice and used instant mashed potatoes instead. Hector had teased that they could've hung wallpaper with the resulting mess. Even Finch had had to laugh.

Now she said, "I think I'll stick to reheating pizza."

Laura winked. "Don't worry. Maude secretly loves that she's the only decent cook we've got."

They were at the Tree House, sipping ice tea in the shade of the live oak, when Finch asked cautiously, "Um, Laura? If something was wrong with Maude, you'd tell me, wouldn't you?"

"What makes you think something's wrong?"

"I hear her crying in the night sometimes."

Laura hesitated. She hadn't meant to exclude Finch, only to shield her. Didn't she have enough of her own to deal with? "I gather she hasn't said anything to you about Elroy."

"Who's Elroy?"

"Her son."

"I didn't know his name. I only saw the picture of him on her dresser." Finch, folding her straw wrapper into tiny squares, glanced up with a frown. "He doesn't look anything like her."

"He doesn't seem to have inherited her nature, either."

"Is he the reason Maude's upset?"

Laura sipped her tea thoughtfully. On the far side of the patio, the café's owner, David Ryback, was deep in conversation with Delilah Sims. Delilah, beautiful in a wan sort of way with her pale skin and soulful eyes, her long black hair draped about her shoulders, was nodding as if in sympathy. Laura wondered if it had anything to do with David's son, eight-year-old Davey, in the hospital for the umpteenth time. If what Laura had heard rumored was true, the strain had left some cracks in David's marriage as well. Noting the cozy familiarity with which Delilah laid a hand on his arm, Laura wondered if she'd played — or was about to play — a part in it.

She looked back at Finch. "He's been after Maude to move in with him."

"Is she going to?"

"I hope not." Laura shook her head. "She lived with him before she came here. And from what little Maude's told me, I gather it wasn't exactly a bed of roses."

Finch's expression hardened. "A real asshole, right?"

"I haven't met him — but yeah, that about sums it up."

Laura grinned, feeling her mood lift somewhat. Her mother was pregnant, and she might be on the verge of losing Maude, but here she was on this fine summer day sitting down to a meal, and a moment of candor, with this girl who'd been so unexpectedly dropped into her life.

"I hope she decides to stay." Finch spoke with fierce conviction. "She belongs with us."

Us? Did that mean Finch intended to stay as well? Laura hoped so, for she'd come to the same conclusion: The girl belonged with her. At first she'd resisted it — not wanting to leave herself open to yet another hurt — but now something rose in her, something so fragile a mere breath could scatter it.

"I couldn't agree with you more," she said.

Hector was hosing the corral down when Laura pulled into the yard. He dropped the hose and pushed open the gate, ambling over to greet them.

He ran a finger over the Explorer's dusty hood. "How'd it go?"

"We got everything we needed."

Finch had darted off into the house, laden with shopping bags. It wasn't just Hector; she was skittish around men in general. Like the other day with Doc Henry. The crusty old vet had been out to look at Punch, and when he'd spoken a bit too abruptly, she'd jumped as if spooked.

"So I noticed. From what I could see it looks like she plans on staying a while." He peered at Laura from under the brim of his hat. "You sure you know what you're doing?"

"I'm not sure of anything." She sighed, nudging the car door shut. "The only thing I know is she needs a home, and at the moment this is the only one available."

"That you know of." He spoke mildly, but she caught the note of caution in his voice.

She told him about Andie, and how the two girls had clicked. And about touring the museum after lunch, where Finch had been fascinated by the wooden plow on display, one that had been used by Laura's great-grandfather to till the field for the valley's first orange grove.

"It's like she can't get enough," Laura said. "I know how it seems like she's pushing us away. But I have a feeling she wants to belong." She gave a crooked half smile. "If you're right, and I'm biting off more than I can chew, it wouldn't be the first time."

"Or the last."

He grinned. Dust had collected in the creases at the corners of his eyes, and half moons of sweat stood out under the arms of his tank top. She had a sudden, insane urge to scoop the battered straw cowboy hat from his head and plop it down on her own.

Once, when she was sixteen, she'd sneaked into his room over the garage at their old house on Blossom Drive. She could vividly recall the guilty flush she'd felt trying on his hat and boots, burying her face in his sweater. As though she'd crawled inside him somehow. At the time Hector had at least one girlfriend that she knew of; she'd spotted him in town once, an arm looped casually around her shoulders — a pretty young woman named Theresa. And as she'd stood there in his room, the thought of them together naked on his bed had burned in a part of her that'd never before known fire. She'd imagined being naked with him, too. His blunt, brown hands stroking her skin. His mouth on hers . . .

Laura found herself blushing now at the memory. "I'd better check on Punch," she said, starting toward the barn. "Is he still limping?"

"Not too bad." Hector fell into step with her. "Doc Henry stopped by again while you were out."

She could hear the horses nickering in

the barn. They knew the sound of her car and always waited a polite minute or two for her to appear, but they were growing impatient. Laura scooped a handful of alfalfa sweetened with molasses from the bucket by the door — their favorite treat.

The barn's hay-scented coolness was blessed relief from the heat. She could see Punch and Judy dancing in their stalls, and called, "Relax, guys. The marines have landed." She gave them each a small handful of alfalfa. Wouldn't it be nice, she thought, if her life were as uncomplicated as theirs? No ex-husband. No pregnant mother.

Her throat tightened, and her eyes filled with tears. Hector, coming up alongside her, shot her a curious look, then wordlessly drew her into his arms. She didn't pull away. *He's always been there for me,* she thought, burying her face in his shoulder, taking in his smell of horses and dust and hard-earned sweat. Would her neediness one day drive him away?

But if Hector was fed up, he showed no sign of it. He drew back to pull a clean, folded handkerchief from his pocket. Handing it to her, he rocked back on his heels to study her, waiting for her to tell him what was wrong.

"I'm sorry," she said with an embarrassed little laugh.

"No need to apologize."

She blew into the handkerchief with an unladylike honk. "It's my mother."

"You two have a fight?"

"It's worse than that." Laura drew in a deep breath. "She's having a baby."

Hector let out a long, low whistle. "That *is* something."

"Needless to say, none of us is too thrilled about it." She didn't know if Aunt Audrey had been told yet. When she got the word the shit would *really* hit the fan.

"What about the father?"

"Ian?" She gave a disdainful little laugh. "I'm not even sure he knows. He's still in New York. When he finds out maybe he'll decide to stay there permanently."

Hector frowned. "What makes you say that?"

"I don't exactly see him as father material."

"You don't know."

"I know enough."

He looked as if he wanted to defend Ian but all he said was, "It's the baby, isn't it? That's what's really bothering you."

"I wish it were mine." The words slipped out, a sob rising in her throat.

Hector drew her into his arms once more, stroking her head, and murmuring, *"Ay, pobrecita. Está bien."*

His voice was like the Spanish music she often heard drifting across the yard. "You don't know," she said thickly.

"I know what it's like to want something."

Do you have any idea how much I've wanted you? The thought seemed to come out of nowhere. A low, trembling excitement swept through her . . . only to be met by a bruising wall of despair. What good would come of it? If Hector had been remotely interested, wouldn't she know by now?

She lifted her head. "What do you want, Hec?"

"What everyone does, I guess — to be happy." He regarded her tenderly, squinting slightly in the half light. Motes of dust spun lazily in the rays of sunlight that had found their way through the barn's uneven slats.

Laura closed her eyes and felt her heart turn a slow cartwheel. If this were a dream he would kiss her — as he so often had in dreams. A kiss that would tell her she was special — not like the women she'd occasionally seen slipping from his room in the wee hours of the morning. Her eyes shut, swaying slightly on the balls of her feet, she leaned into him, bringing her forehead to rest against his. Hector didn't move.

They stood that way for an interminable second or two, Laura scarcely breathing, her heart lodged like a dry-swallowed aspirin in her throat. Then just when she thought she'd die if he didn't kiss her, she felt his hand under her chin and the gentle pressure of his mouth against hers. A quick brush of lips, no more. He drew back to smile at her. They didn't speak. The moment was endless, a seesaw hovering between earth and sky. She searched his face, yearning for him to say something, *do* something, to tip the balance. How could she could go on not knowing what it had meant? Suppose Hector only felt sorry for her?

Then the moment passed and he was turning away, going about his business as if nothing were out of the ordinary. She watched him fork hay into the horse's stalls, whistling as he worked. Clearly, he wasn't thinking about her — not *that* way. Laura felt unreasonably let down.

She started toward the door, her heart beating much too fast. Addressing the barn wall hung with tack, much of it old and worn but well oiled with Need's, she said softly, "Thanks, Hec."

"Anytime," he replied pleasantly.

She was crossing the yard when she heard the crunch of tires on the drive. The dogs must have heard it, too; she could hear them barking inside the house. She looked around to see a light blue Pontiac Seville pull to a stop behind her Explorer. Its dusty vanity plate read: IM4NRA.

A heavyset man in khaki trousers and a short-sleeved plaid shirt climbed from the driver's seat, hitching up his belt. Laura put him in his midfifties, with gray hair shorn like a marine's through which patches of pink scalp shone. He glanced about, not seeing her, then set off along the front path.

Tiny hairs prickled on the back of Laura's neck. Occasionally a lost traveler would pull in to ask for directions, but some instinct told her this man was no stranger. She was about to call out to him when he bounded onto the porch and began hammering on the door.

"Mama! It's me, Elroy!"

Laura broke into a run, Hector bringing up the rear. They were nearing the house when the front door swung open. Maude appeared in the doorway, looking distraught.

"I can hear perfectly well without your shouting," she said.

Elroy backed off, glowering. In his rounded chin and cupid's bow mouth, ridiculously dainty in a man his size, Laura could see the faint ghost of a resemblance. "Then why the hell haven't you returned my calls?"

Maude eyed him sternly. "You came all this way to ask me that?"

"You know damn well why I'm here." Elroy looked more than put out; he looked like a man whose entire life was a frayed thread about to snap. His hands curled into fists. "Go pack up your things, Mama. Verna's waiting back at the house."

But Maude only shook her head, and said firmly, "I'm afraid I can't do that, son. I'm sure you mean well, but I'm happy where I am."

His eyes narrowed. "You're just doing this to get back at me, aren't you?"

She shook her head sadly. "Is that what you think? Well then, I'm sorry for you."

She'd clearly struck a nerve. Elroy's shoulders drooped, and his fists unfurled. "Oh hell, Mama," he wheedled. "You belong with me, and you know it. Your own flesh and blood."

"No one would know it from the way

you act." Maude began to tremble, a tiny woman who seemed to teeter beneath her untidy bundle of hair.

Elroy shifted from one foot to the other like a guilty schoolboy. "Now, Mama, nobody asked you to leave."

"With you and Verna lording it over me every minute of the day, what choice did I have?"

Elroy had the decency to look ashamed. "Well, now, Mama, I'm not gonna pretend it was all hunky-dory. We're family, after all. Families have their differences."

"It was more than just differences."

"Mama, if you'd just let me make it up to you —"

"Thank you, I've had quite enough."

Laura climbed onto the porch. "So have I."

Elroy swung around clumsily, a hectic flush swimming up into his jowly cheeks. He bared his teeth in a cold grin. "Well, well, if it isn't the famous Laura Kiley I've heard so much about."

Hector, standing just below, hoisted a boot onto the steps. "I think you'd better be on your way, mister." Laura had seen that expression only once before — when Peter was leaving.

Elroy looked at him as if Hector were

something nasty that had just crawled out from under the porch. "I wasn't talking to *you*."

Before Hector could make a move, Maude said wearily, "Go home, son. Just . . . go."

It was more than Elroy could take. He lunged at her with a growl, meaty fingers curled. "You crazy old woman —"

A slender figure darted past Maude onto the porch. Finch. In her hand was a butcher knife that caught the sunlight, flaring like a struck match.

"Get away from her." Her dark eyes were fixed on Elroy, but they appeared to be not so much looking at him as through him. The knife quivered in her grasp.

Elroy's face went slack, and he took a jerky step back. A foot shod in a cheap tan loafer skidded onto the step below. His arms pinwheeled before he lost his balance, coming down hard on his hands and knees. The sight of him with his hind end sticking up like Pearl's when she wanted it scratched, an inch or so of hairy crack showing above the straining seat of his trousers, was so comical that a startled laugh escaped Laura.

The moment hung suspended.

After what seemed an eternity the girl's

hand sank to her side. She blinked, staring down at the knife as if not quite sure how it had gotten there, then with a low cry flung it into the bushes below, and fled past them down the steps.

 Chapter 8

She hadn't gotten very far when she heard the car engine. The girl dove into a tangle of greenery along the shoulder peering out just as Laura's dark green Explorer flashed by. Her heart was knocking in her chest; she felt almost sick with fear. Not so much that she'd be caught — but that she wouldn't. Maybe worse than jail would be years of hiding, of looking over her shoulder. It would be so easy to turn back. All she had to do was re-trace her steps — a few dozen yards at most. She eyed the road longingly where it curved like a beckoning finger toward Laura's. A pale cloud of dust from the Explorer hovered like a held breath.

You can trust her. She'll help you.

But what if she didn't? What if Laura turned her over to the police instead? *They'll think* I'm *the killer on the loose.* No, she couldn't take that risk. If the cops didn't arrest her, there'd be questions, phone calls, a trail leading back to Brooklyn — and to Lyle.

Fragmented images flashed through her head in bright, strobelike flashes. Red lines creeping down a ribbed undershirt. Eyes rolling to white. A foot stuttering against the floor in the final throes of death. She brought her hands to her temples, squeezing until it hurt, trying to force the images from her head. Another car, a big blue Pontiac, swooshed past in a sputter of gravel. She caught a glimpse of Maude's son at the wheel, face red and clenched like a fist. She waited until she could no longer hear its engine then crept cautiously out into the open.

Where to now?

She looked about. Grassy hills — hills she'd come to know on horseback — stretched as far as she could see on either side. She wouldn't be so easy to track up there. There was just one problem: She didn't know which direction to go in. The road to the highway was that way, wasn't it? She looked to the west, shading her eyes against the setting sun. Either way she supposed she'd get to it eventually.

A short distance up the road she found a spot where a fairly large animal had burrowed under the fence. Just enough room for her to crawl under. She tasted dust, and felt the back of her T-shirt catch on the wire — then she was home free.

She emerged into a rolling pasture dotted with oaks and scrub, and started up the slope, wincing as rocks and twigs dug into her soles through her rubber flip-flops. Halfway up the hill she brought her foot down on something sharp. With a cry, she stumbled and fell, landing on all fours amid the tall stickery grass. For several long seconds she remained where she was, a dry sob caught in her throat, until the throbbing in her hands and knees subsided. Trembling, she drew herself upright. Now a heavy despair set in.

Don't think about it.

If she let herself think about what she was doing she wouldn't be able to go on. It was all her fault anyway. She'd screwed up. Let her guard down, let herself care. About Laura and Maude. Even Hector. She'd begun to think of them as . . .

Home.

Oh, she'd known plenty of the other kind. Placements, they were called, which was just a fancy word for when no one wanted you. They never lasted very long. People like the St. Clairs, who happily cashed the county's checks but begrudged you an extra chicken wing. Shirlee and Lyle hadn't been the worst. Just the last.

With Laura she'd found something she'd known only from longing glances into lighted windows: a place where people wanted you just *because*. She would miss the creak of Maude's bed as she rolled over in her sleep. Laura in the center of the ring, calling, *"Heels down, toes out! Thattagirl!"* She saw them seated around the table in the big, sunny kitchen, reaching across each other for the salt and pepper, everyone talking at once.

Right about now she'd be treating the horses to their evening carrots. Punch first; he was the greediest. Then Judy, more ladylike, nickering softly as she waited her turn. She thought of their velvety noses against her palm, the earthy coolness of the barn. She would miss riding, too — the snug curve of the saddle, the reins in her hand, the wonderful knowledge that here, finally, was something she was *good* at. Tears welled, spilling down the girl's cheeks.

She remembered Andie, the girl at Rusk's — her first almost-friend. They were to have gone riding tomorrow. Now that, too, was blown.

If she thought about it too much she wouldn't be able to go on. Laura's kindness. Maude's unspoken understanding.

They'd known exactly how far to extend themselves without making her feel uncomfortable. For the first time in her life she'd had the feeling she *belonged.*

The grassy slope blurred. The girl blinked hard, and it swam back into focus. She found herself thinking of Mrs. Keyes, her foster mom when she was twelve. Once she'd come home from school with a bloody nose after having been attacked by three sixth-grade boys, and Mrs. Keyes, a big brassy-haired woman with a smile that never quite reached her eyes, had merely handed her a tissue and ordered her to stop bawling. *No use crying over spilled milk,* she'd said, her favorite expression along with *Feeling sorry for yourself isn't going to help.*

The girl was pierced with a sorrow so keen it was almost palpable. She lifted her face to the distant mountains — Sleeping Indian Chief, Moon's Nest, Toyon Ridge — shouldering their way into the orangeade sky. She'd wished for it for so long it was as much a part of her as the color of her hair, or the crooked little toe on her right foot: a home of her own. And now, just when she could almost feel it in her grasp, it was gone.

She pushed the thought away, wiping the

tears from her cheeks. *Feeling sorry for myself isn't going to help.* She had to look ahead now; watch where she was going so she didn't get caught.

She reached the top of the hill, sweating and out of breath. But all she saw were more hills, rolling off into the distance. The only sign of habitation was the walled convent on the other side of a thickly wooded grove. Our Lady of the Wayside. Its nuns were famous for their honey, Laura had said. They also kept pretty much to themselves; they wouldn't bother with her.

She heard the faint rushing of a stream, and her gaze was drawn to the grove below. She could lie low there until after dark, when there'd be less chance of getting caught. Cautiously, she started down the slope. The sun was nearly touching the horizon, leaving the hillside tiger-striped with shadow — an hour when she'd have been setting the table for dinner while Maude stirred something on the stove. Her throat clenched, and she had to stop more than once to catch her breath.

When she reached the grove, the girl sank down beneath a live oak with branches nearly as thick as its trunk. She was surprised at how tired she was; she hadn't come that far. On hikes with Laura she could walk for miles without feeling winded.

She closed her eyes. She would rest only until dark. Then head west, toward the highway. Once she got there she could thumb a ride.

As she drifted to sleep she imagined herself in the deep, clawfoot tub at Laura's. Tears floated up behind her closed lids, and in her half-conscious state the past weeks seemed nothing more than a dream — a beautiful one from which she never wanted to awake.

She slept for hours curled on her side on the ground, her head resting in the crook of her arm and her thumb lightly grazing her mouth. She didn't see the sun slip below the mountaintops, or hear the peep of nightjars in the branches overhead. The raccoon that stopped to drink from the stream lifted its head to sniff the air before slipping off undisturbed.

Somewhere around midnight she was startled awake by the sharp snap of a twig. She bolted upright, groggy and disoriented, her heart thudding. She couldn't see anything at first, only darkness. Then shapes around her began to materialize. A fallen branch, the glistening boulders of the stream. In the bushes along the opposite bank a flicker of movement caught her eye.

She froze, her breath catching in her throat.

A bear? Laura had warned her to be on the lookout, but the girl hadn't taken her all that seriously. She'd seen possums and raccoons, once even a rattlesnake. But the likelihood of coming across a bear in these hills had seemed as remote as a flying saucer.

Then she remembered the homeless guy who'd been found stabbed to death. Suppose his killer was out there? Goose bumps swarmed up her arms and legs, each thud of her heart like the whack of a baseball bat.

Another loud snap. She dropped to her belly, holding herself flat against the ground. If she kept very, very still he — or *it* — wouldn't notice her.

Probably a deer. A harmless little Bambi.

But the crackling in the underbrush was too loud. She squeezed her eyes shut, holding as still as humanly possible. She almost hoped it *was* a bear. If you left them alone, Laura had said, they usually went away. Her chances would be better than with —

Memories of Lyle came rushing back. She moaned low in her throat, struggling to block them out. Several more minutes crawled past, and now there was only the sound of the stream and dry rattle of leaves overhead. She remained perfectly still until her arms and legs began to grow numb, then lifted her head and looked around. No sign of anyone . . . or anything.

The pounding in her chest slowed. She held her head cocked, but when several more minutes passed without a sound, she lowered her head to the ground. She wouldn't sleep, she told herself. Just lie here until it was safe to get up and move around.

Hours later she woke from a familiar dream. She was running through a house in which blind corridors appeared everywhere she turned. Parts of the house were familiar — the living room was Lyle's and Shirlee's, the stairs those of a half-remembered elementary school, the hallway with its dour faces in frames along the wall that of the Keyes's Ditmus Avenue apartment. She felt a keen sense of urgency; she had to get out before something terrible happened — she didn't know what, only that her life depended on it. She was reaching for a doorknob when —

Wake up child wake up

She drifted up to consciousness, her eyes opening to a ghostly face that seemed to float as if disembodied in the darkness overhead. She let out a startled yelp, and lurched upright.

A hand patted her arm gently. "Easy, child," spoke a lilting female voice. Not a ghost after all. "You look as though you've had a bit of a shock. Did you see her then?"

"Who?" she croaked.

"Why, Sister Benedicta, of course." The disembodied face materialized into a nun in a dark serge habit and veil. "Our resident ghost," she said. "I've never seen her myself, though there are those who swear they have." A merry note crept into her voice. They might have been chatting over tea and cookies. "I'm Sister Agnes, by the way. And who, dear child, might you be?"

The girl heard herself stammer, "I . . . I'm Finch."

"Well now, isn't this a fine way to start the day?" The little nun rocked back on her haunches, breaking into a smile of such warmth and goodwill the girl couldn't help smiling back.

Then she remembered why she was here, and her heart began to pound. "What . . .

what time is it?" Had she somehow slept the whole night away?

"O'dark in the morning, as me mam used to say." Sister Agnes chuckled at her own joke. "I like to get my morning walk in before chapel. I do my best thinking then, with the world a blank slate just waitin' to be written on. Plus, you never know what you'll find." She beamed at the girl as if at a rare flower or bird she'd stumbled across.

"I should be going." The girl had pulled herself onto one knee when a wave of lightheadedness caused her to sink back.

Sister Agnes scarcely seemed to notice. "Take you, for instance," she went on in the same tea-party voice. "When I came across you, lying there still as death, I confess I thought the worst. All that talk of a murderer." Her expression clouded over briefly. "And now here we are chattin' like old friends."

"I must have gotten lost." Could she trust this nun? She talked like the Irish cops back home, but there was definitely something odd about her.

A small pale hand floated up, mothlike, to alight on her cheek. "Lost? Well, I suppose that's one way of puttin' it." She rose, still smiling, and held out her hand.

"Come. Let's get you home."

The girl just sat there, hugging her knees.

"I thought so." Sister Agnes sank back down beside her. "Are you running away then? Is that it?"

"I guess you could call it that."

"May I ask where you're headin'?"

The girl hesitated before replying miserably, "I don't know."

Sister Agnes nodded thoughtfully. "I see. Well, that's a horse of a different color, isn't it?" Blue eyes peered from a face made up of a series of circles — moon face, round chin, apple cheeks. "Anything I can do to help?"

"I don't think so."

"Maybe there *is*, and you just don't know it."

The girl tensed. "I don't believe in God, if that's what you mean."

Sister Agnes didn't appear shocked. "Never mind, child," she said. "*He* believes in you." She fingered the silver cross on a chain about her neck. "Oh, I know it doesn't always seem that way. There's times we think God couldn't possibly love us. Take me, for instance. I seem to have a habit of stealing things. One minute I'll be lookin' at something . . . and the next thing

I know I'll be walking out the door with that very same thing in me pocket." She heaved a sigh. "So you see, none of us is perfect, but that's no cause for losing hope."

An owl hooted in mournful echo. "I . . . I've done things I'm not proud of," the girl said.

Sister Agnes patted her knee. "What kind of project would we be for God if we went around behavin' like saints all the time? He'd have to find another hobby, for sure."

The girl managed a tiny smile. "Like bird-watching?"

"More like beekeeping, I should think. Something with bite to it, if you'll pardon the pun." She chuckled softly. "That's what our dear, departed Sister Benedicta is famous for, by the way. If it hadn't been for her we'd never have found our second calling."

"Honey?"

"Yes. Which reminds me —" Sister Agnes rose to her feet, brushing leaves from her skirt. A stout little woman with a body as round as her face. "You must be hungry. Come, let's get you fed."

The girl glanced up at her doubtfully. "Are you sure it's okay?"

"And why wouldn't it be when there's more than enough to go around?" If Finch had been referring to something other than breakfast, Sister Agnes wasn't letting on. This time when she extended her hand the girl grasped hold. "From the looks of it you'll be wanting last night's supper as well."

Realizing suddenly that she was starving, the girl wordlessly fell into step behind her.

Laura was crawling out of bed, half asleep, when she heard a car in the driveway. She dashed to the living room window and peered out. Last night, when Finch still hadn't returned, she'd phoned an old friend in the police department. Ernie would be discreet, she knew. He'd keep an eye out without making a federal case of it. After the incident with Elroy (which she saw no reason to mention), she wasn't taking any chances.

But it wasn't a squad car pulling in. Laura stepped out onto the porch, shading her eyes against the morning glare. A nun behind the wheel of the VW van belonging to Our Lady of the Wayside. She was puzzled — hadn't the items stolen by Sister Agnes been returned? — until she saw who was getting out of the passenger's side: Finch.

A hand flew to her mouth, and she bit down on her palm to keep from crying out. Finch started toward the house, trudging like a weary soldier home from battle: a lanky girl in wrinkled blue shorts and a maroon T-shirt who'd filled out some in the past weeks, and whose once-pale skin was as brown as Hector's. She looked as though she'd spent the night outdoors; her clothes were dirty and her long hair tangled — like when Laura had first seen her. Except that then her expression had been wary; now it was as if she was hoping to be let back in.

Laura's heart went out to her. Last night, as she'd lain awake fearing the worst, Finch must have been doing the same. It was all she could do to keep from dashing to meet her. She waited instead, a hand on the doorknob, hardly daring to breathe.

Finch paused halfway up the steps. "I didn't think you'd be up this early." Her voice was flat, her gaze fixed on a point just past Laura's ear.

"Are you kidding? I was up half the night!" Laura raked a hand through her hair, struggling to remain calm. "You scared the hell out of us, you know. Running off like that."

Pearl chose that moment to trundle onto the porch, yawning. Finch crouched down, wrapping her arms about the dog's neck. The old yellow lab wagged her tail, welcoming Finch with a lick. When the girl brought her head up, her eyes were wet.

"I'm sorry," she said.

"Well, you should be. We were worried sick." Laura realized she was practically yelling, and lowered her voice. "You could have phoned at least — to let us know you were okay."

"I didn't think you'd want to hear from me after —" She bit her lip.

"What happened with Elroy was his own fault."

"What if I'd *killed* him?" A pair of wide, brown eyes searched hers over Pearl's silky yellow ear.

"You didn't."

Finch shook her head. "I don't know what happened. I heard him yelling at Maude . . . and the next thing I knew the knife was in my hand." The blood drained from her face. Slowly, she straightened and stood up.

"You were only defending Maude," Laura said softly. She stepped forward to slip an arm about Finch's shoulders.

"Look, why don't we go inside? Frankly, I'm so happy you're back I can't think of anything else right now."

The girl hesitated. "You mean you're not going to turn me in?"

"Why would I do a thing like that?"

"You don't know me. You don't know what I've done."

Laura drew back to eye her sternly. "Look, let's get one thing straight. No matter what, you'll always have a home here. But I can't help you unless you're willing to take a chance on us, too."

"You don't know what I've done," Finch repeated in a hoarse whisper.

"I know you're scared." Laura spoke gently. "I also know you well enough by now to feel reasonably certain that whatever it is you think you've done, it couldn't be all that terrible."

The girl dropped her head; Laura could feel her trembling, and felt suddenly afraid. A chill settled over her as well. She'd been thinking along the lines of abuse, possibly sexual. But if that wasn't all?

Then the girl lifted her head, and a pair of tortured eyes met Laura's. In a voice that sounded as if it were coming from the other end of a tunnel, she said, "I let someone die."

Chapter 9

At the precise moment Laura was learning about the untimely death of a certain Lyle Kruger, her younger sister, Alice, sat buckled beside her husband in his Bell 430 as it hovered over the CTN Building in downtown L.A. It was Tuesday, the third week in August, a little more than a month since they'd gotten back from their honeymoon.

It felt more like a year.

She couldn't talk to Wes about her mother, so they talked about everything else instead. On the drive to the airfield it had been the problem with Marty Milnik. Marty's drinking, to be precise. He always showed up on time, always pulled it off somehow, but behind the scenes it was a different story. He was abusive to staff members, and last week had even managed to offend a celebrity guest. As Stacey Fields, reigning queen of bubblegum pop, was standing up to have her mike unclipped he'd growled in mock jest, "Next time wear a dress that fits."

The strain, not to mention this ghastly business with her mother, was really getting to her. She'd even started smoking again. Just one or two cigarettes a day — no big deal — but it was a sign, a *bad* sign.

The bull's-eye loomed. Wes, buckled beside her in the pilot's seat, calmly working the controls, seemed utterly oblivious to the helicopter's roar, which even muffled by headphones was deafening.

It was the one thing she'd never get used to. In the car they'd have kicked around ideas, sounded off about various frustrations, but here they were limited to brief exchanges over headsets, mostly concerning weather and ETA. She missed the days when they used to drive. She missed their long conversations with only the cell phone to disturb them.

The helicopter rocked down to a perfect landing. Watching Wes ease back on the throttle, the back draft scuffing his silver hair into spikes, Alice experienced the same little thrill as when they'd first met. This was no ordinary man, she'd thought. Wes was the kind of boss employees emulated even while they groused, whose exploits were endlessly discussed, whose private life was fodder for constant speculation. Everyone at CTN had a Wes Carpenter story, told often and with great relish. Like the time magazine mogul Bryce Chesterton had unwisely attempted a hostile takeover. Wes, encountering him at a fund-raiser, in the men's room of the Regent Beverly Wilshire to be precise, was said to have warned, "You want to show me how far you can piss, fine. Just remember who you're dealing with, son."

She watched him leap nimbly onto the roof and circle around to help her down, keeping a firm grip on her elbow. Leaving the Bell to the crew-cut man in overalls jogging toward them, they made their way to the elevator.

All but six of the CTN Building's eighteen floors were leased to other companies. On the ground floor were a shopping mall and food court, complete with dry cleaner and shoe repair. The joke around CTN was that employees could go their whole lives without ever setting foot outside, which wasn't far from the truth. Wes expected nothing less from others than he was willing to give himself. If that meant an all-nighter on breaking news, so be it. He liked to say he hadn't built this network rushing home each night to dinner and the six o'clock news. At Cable Television Network they *were* the news.

The newsroom on the fourth floor was the usual madhouse. People dashing up and down between aisles that stretched the length of a football field, banked by desks on either side — each fitted with a computer and miniature TV. Over a chorus of voices, phones cheeped and keyboards rattled. The closed-circuit consoles over the control room flashed silent images from CTN broadcasts all over the world. In the glass-walled studio, the lights were on and the cameras rolling. From where she stood Alice had an unobstructed view of the back of Maureen McKinnon's perfectly coiffed blond head, with the coil to her earpiece that her randy coanchor, Scott Ballard, liked to joke was the only thing ever to kiss Maureen's lily-white neck.

Scott and Maureen, who anchored *Morning Headline*, would be followed by Lars Gunderson's brief roundup of current events: half an hour of mostly boring sound bites solicited by a ponderous old ass more interested in hearing himself talk. Unfortunately, Wes had a soft spot for Lars, who'd been with him since the parting of the Red Sea. One of these nights, after a glass of wine, she'd talk to him about Lars. Meanwhile, she had her own headaches to deal with. Namely, Marty.

She headed down the hall to her office, the source of her very first argument with Wes. He'd wanted her to move to a larger one with a view, but she'd insisted on staying put. Her favored status had caused enough resentment. Such a move would only make it worse. In the end, though, staying put had been the wrong decision. Except for a cadre of loyal friends her fellow workers didn't stop resenting her just because she wasn't quite as comfortable as she could have been. If anything, they resented her more.

As she breezed into the staff room, lost in thought, she was only peripherally aware of her senior production assistant, Christy Kim, crouched over her desk with the phone to her ear, signaling to her frantically. Whatever it was could damn well wait, she thought, until she was sitting down. Preferably with a cup of coffee and a cigarette.

She pushed open the door to her office, and stopped short. A woman sat huddled in the chair opposite her desk. Marty's much younger wife, Brandi — clearly the object of Christy's frenzied signaling. Her eyes were red from crying, and she clutched a wadded-up tissue in one hand.

"You've got to talk to him. He's really

gone off the deep end this time." Her little girl voice didn't match her hard-bitten blond looks.

Alice's heart sank. She didn't have to ask what the problem was; it was the same old story every time. She lowered herself into her chair. "Did you call that number I gave you?"

Brandi dabbed delicately at her reddened nose. "Sure, I did," she sniffed.

"What did she say?" Her old friend Carol Avery was in charge of admissions at Betty Ford. If anyone could deal with Marty, it was Carol.

Brandi began shredding the tissue into her lap. "She said I should get everybody together — all his, you know, well *everybody* — and we'd all take turns telling him how his drinking makes us feel." She smiled uncertainly. "But you know Marty — he *hates* surprises."

"That's the whole *point*."

"Still, it seems kinda mean. Ganging up on him like that."

Alice blew out a breath. Jesus. It was too early in the day for this. "What did he do this time?"

"Nothing much — just tossed every stick of furniture into the pool." A nasty edge crept into Brandi's voice. "That was *after* he almost pushed my friend Jack in, too."

Alice could see it as if she'd been there: Marty, bellowing from the balcony of his six-million-dollar spread as he heaved chairs and tables, lamps and sofa cushions over the railing into the pool. She chose her words carefully. "Sounds like a cry for help."

"Oh, he was crying all right. But it wasn't for help." Lines had appeared on either side of Brandi's mouth, making her look years older than the thirty-four she claimed to be.

Alice's phone was blinking. She ignored it. "Look, would you like *me* to talk to Carol?"

"I'd like it even more if you'd talk to Marty."

There was a foxy glint in her eye that Alice didn't much like. She recalled that Brandi, Marty's fourth wife, had been a Las Vegas blackjack dealer when they met. "It won't work." She toyed idly with the small plastic action figure on her desk: Xena, Warrior Princess, a gag gift from her sister. "I know, because I've tried. A number of times."

"He's *got* to listen. You're his producer."

"I won't be much longer if he doesn't sober up." Alice leaned forward, fixing a stern gaze on Brandi. "Look, do both of us a favor. Call Carol back. Tell her it's *urgent*. She'll walk you through the rest."

Marty's wife shot her a petulant look. She looked as if she wanted to argue, but all she said was "I'll see what I can do."

"I wouldn't waste any time, if I were you." Alice's tone was firm. "There's talk of Marty's show being cancelled."

Brandi snorted. "Yeah, like *that* would ever happen."

"It's not entirely up to me."

"Oh come on. " Brandi's gaze fell pointedly on a framed photo of Wes and Alice, arm in arm on the Pont-au-Change — last summer's trip to Paris. "You're married to the boss, aren't you?"

"That has nothing to do with it," Alice replied coolly.

"Yeah, sure. Like I don't know the score. Come on, who are you kidding?" The weepy little girl's voice had been replaced by that of the tough blackjack dealer.

Anger rose in Alice. "Look," she said, "I'm willing to help out here. I'll even take part in an intervention. But I am no longer in the business of covering Marty's ass."

"Yeah, I know. That's 'cause you're too busy covering your own."

Alice straightened, her hand tightening

about the figurine. She could feel it poking into her palm like small, sharp teeth. "I'm not going to respond to that," she said.

Brandi rose, bits of tissue drifting to the floor. Her eyes — too blue to be anything but contacts — glittered coldly. "You think you're smarter than me? Well, at least I know what gives." Her mouth curled in derision. "Guys like Marty and Wes, they can have anyone they want. The only way you know they're getting older is the wives keep getting younger."

Alice walked to the door, and held it open. "The offer is still open if you decide to take me up on it."

Brandi swept past her, her hard gaze taking in the stubbornly utilitarian little office the way it might have a hand of cards. "I'll think about it," she said. Then, with a twitch of her boyish behind and a toss of her platinum mane, she was gone.

"Have you talked to Marty?" Wes asked.

They were seated outdoors, sipping after-supper brandies. The light was on in the pool, casting the patio in a swimmy aqua glow and silhouetting the trees in the canyon below. Overhead, stars were strewn like dice from a bottomless cup. From the sliding glass doors to Wes's den drifted the sound of Placido Domingo singing the aria from *La Traviata*. The only thing missing, Alice thought, was a cigarette.

"Not yet," she said, groaning a little. "But I shouldn't have threatened his wife with canceling the show. Whatever he's done, it was . . . unprofessional."

Wes didn't disagree.

"Just for argument's sake," she ventured cautiously, "what would happen if we *did* cancel? Assuming we could buy Marty out of his contract, that is."

"He'd land on his feet. Even drunk as a skunk, he always does."

"I wasn't talking about Marty."

"I know." Wes set his glass on the table with a hard little clink. Lit from below, his face was an eyeless mask. "To be completely honest, Alice, I've been wondering if maybe you'd be happier somewhere else."

"You're joking, right?" A weak little laugh died on her lips.

"No, I'm not."

"Are you firing me?" she asked softly.

"Don't be silly, darling. Of course not." Wes's tone was mild, even faintly jocular. "You know how I feel about us working together. I don't like seeing you get hurt — either personally or professionally. And let's face it, it wasn't just today, and it's not just Marty."

He was right, of course, but that only made it worse. "Since when do you decide what's best for me?"

"I wouldn't have said anything if it weren't for Marty."

"I said *if* the show were cancelled."

"Ratings are down," Wes went on in that same infuriating tone. "I just think we should consider very carefully what your next move should be. With your résumé —"

She cut him off before he could dig any deeper. "Why is it," she wanted to know, "that whenever you talk about *us* deciding something, it's really just *you?*" As she wrapped her thickening tongue around the words, she realized that perhaps she was a little drunk.

She sipped her brandy carefully, struggling to regain control. The night was so warm she'd changed into a little silk dress she could have threaded through her wedding ring. Now, as she sat with her feet propped on Wes's chair, toes curled under a strap, she wondered how it had come to this. As a little girl she had envisioned married life to be sophisticated, adult, and never, ever boring. And life with Wes was surely that. What she hadn't counted on was what happened when two strong people went head to head.

Wes frowned. "You know that isn't true."

"Do I? Let's look at the facts." She dropped her feet to the patio and leaned forward, the slate cool against her soles. "I work for you. I live in your house. I spend your money."

He put a hand over hers. "Careful," he warned. "Don't say anything you'll be sorry for."

She snatched her hand away. "God, I'm so sick of this."

"Of what?" His voice remained even, but she caught a flicker of something hard in his expression.

"I don't *know*," she cried. "All I know is that unless you plan on firing me, there is no *we*. It's *my* decision."

"I see."

"You still don't get it, do you?" She stared at the unyielding mask that minutes before had been her husband's face. It seemed to ripple in the queer undersea light. Had she tried too hard to please him? Because God knew any one of the dozens of women in line behind her would have been only too happy to take her place. Maybe she'd only convinced herself the decisions they'd made were a two-way street, thinking how nice, how *convenient,* that her own wishes meshed so perfectly with his. "I *love* you, dammit. I'm just sick and tired of *you* making all the rules."

"I didn't know that's what I was doing."

"Men like you never do." She set her glass on the table, and dropped her head into her hands in a useless attempt to stop it from spinning. "God, I'm sorry. I didn't mean that. It's just . . . it seems like everything is coming apart all at once. My job. My mother."

"Your mother is perfectly capable of looking after herself."

Alice raised her head, struggling to hold his blurred face in focus. "Maybe. But it still affects me. She's having a *baby,* for God's sake. That's not just a little blip on the radar screen — it's a fucking *earthquake.* About eight-point-oh on the Richter scale, I'd say."

"However you look at it," he said, "there isn't a damn thing you, or I, or anyone can do about it."

She shook her head, scarcely hearing him. "I wish you could have known my dad. He was sweet and funny and . . ." A tiny sob escaped her. "God, I miss him so much."

"I know." Wes squeezed her shoulder.

"I guess what I'm trying to say is I have nothing against Ian, not really, though that doesn't take away from his part in it. I'm sure I'll grow to love the baby, too. I just can't help feeling that if my dad were alive . . ." She let the sentence trail off.

"Everything would be like it was?" Wes finished for her. She couldn't tell if he was being sarcastic.

"I'm not naive," she said. "I didn't think she'd be alone forever. She's an attractive woman and there is — *was* — Tom. It's just . . . I never imagined anything like this. And it worries me. Mainly, because I can't help thinking about what it's going to be like for *us* in five or ten years."

"I'm not sure I know what you are getting at," he said, frowning.

She took a deep breath, the formless fear in the back of her mind taking shape at last. "I might change my mind about having a baby."

His mouth stretched in a humorless smile. "I guess I should have seen this coming."

"I didn't say I wanted one. Just that I *might*."

He leaned forward abruptly, and a band of light fell across his face, causing his eyes to blaze with sudden brilliance. Placido Domingo had stopped singing. There was only the soft chirr of crickets and nightjars in the canyon below. "In ten years, I'll be sixty-four," he reminded her.

"And I'll be thirty-six."

He shook his head. "I never led you down the garden path."

"I didn't say you had."

He rose suddenly, his long shadow spilling out from under his chair onto the bone-white coping. He looked weary in a way she'd never seen him look before. "It's been a long day," he said. "We'll both be more clearheaded in the morning. Why don't we call it a night?"

The ground tilted as she stood up. She hugged herself, shivering. There'd be no use discussing it tomorrow . . . or the next day, or the day after that. What would be the point? No one, not even Wes, could predict what lay ahead.

Chapter 10

"You'll feel a little pressure. Just try to relax." Inez Rosario's face appeared in the triangle between Sam's sheet-draped knees: a pair of soft brown eyes and a forehead wrinkled, she imagined, from forever peering up at patients from this angle.

Sam squeezed her eyes shut as latex-gloved fingers probed inside her. Relax? How could she possibly relax with her whole life turned upside down? Since finding out she was pregnant, nothing, absolutely nothing, had been the same.

Audrey, par for the course, had had more than a few choice words to say on the subject, with her brother, after a stunned silence, booming heartily into the phone, "Hell, Sis. You're just crazy enough to pull it off." But she didn't care whether or not they approved, not really. It was her daughters she was most concerned with. Laura, who'd been avoiding her at work — not an easy thing to do. And Alice, standoffish to the point of chilliness. What if they didn't come around? What if this baby brought an end to more than the tranquil life she'd banked on?

"Everything looks fine." The doctor's face surfaced once more, this time with a smile. She patted Sam's knee. "Okay, all done. You can sit up now."

Sam lifted herself cautiously onto her elbows. "That's it? No stamping me FRAGILE, THIS END UP?"

Inez had been a friend for years, and could appreciate a joke, but right now she was all business. "I'm not going to pretend it's a piece of cake having a baby at your age," she said. "There *are* certain risks. But there's no reason you can't have a perfectly normal birth." She peeled off her gloves and tossed them into the trash. "Now, why don't you get dressed, and we'll talk about this in my office?"

Sam had known her since their children were in school together. She recalled one particular evening when she and Inez had stayed up late stitching costumes for the fifth-grade class play. It seemed ironic that her old friend would be shepherding this new baby into the world at a time when the two of them ought to be comparing snapshots of grandchildren.

In the cozy office, more like a sitting

room with its chintz-covered easy chairs and Queen Anne-style desk, Sam eased herself onto the sofa. It wasn't just that she was sore. She felt as if she were carrying an awkward bundle that at any moment could slip to the ground and shatter. Why was she so nervous? In the beginning, hadn't she *hoped* to miscarry?

"Okay, Sam, what's on your mind?" Inez settled in behind her desk, a handsome woman only a few years older than Sam, with graying black hair that fell in crisp waves about her ears. On the credenza behind her was an array of family photos: her son and daughters at various ages, all three with gleaming dark hair and wide smiles. "I'm sure it hasn't been easy for you. Your family must have been pretty taken aback."

"That's putting it mildly."

Inez smiled. "I remember when Essie was pregnant," she recalled, referring to her youngest, Esperanza, the same age as Laura. "You'd have thought single moms were unheard of. Her grandmother had calluses on her knees from all the praying."

"Essie's young," Sam said. "When people think of a widow pushing fifty, it's as a fourth for bridge, or the extra guest at a dinner party."

"They're not the ones having this baby, *you* are."

Hadn't Ian said the very same thing? Ian, coming home tomorrow. Sam's heart soared at the thought, then just as quickly plummeted. What now? They couldn't exactly pick up where they'd left off. It wouldn't be like in New York, either, when they'd both been too shell-shocked to make sense of it all.

What if this was more than Ian was equipped to handle? Her mind flew back to the time, a few years after Alice was born, when she and Martin had talked about having another child. She'd been reluctant, mostly because of Martin. With another man she might have been willing, but he was so . . . well, *Martin*. Sometimes she'd thought of him as the son they'd never had: a little boy who would play outside until all hours, and spend his last dollar of allowance on ice cream.

If Ian wasn't ready for this . . .

"The truth is, I'm scared stiff." She brought a hand to her belly. It was still flat, but in a few more weeks there'd be no getting around the fact that there was a baby on the way.

"I take it you're referring to more than just health risks."

Sam felt her fears come rushing up all at once. "How many of your patients know, really *know*, what's involved?" Women, she thought, who hadn't already raised a family.

"Not many," Inez acknowledged.

"I *loved* being a mother." Sam smiled, remembering when her girls had been little. "But I haven't forgotten how hard it was. I'm not sure I'm up to starting all over again from scratch."

Inez eyed her cautiously. "Are you thinking of ending this pregnancy?" It went against her Catholic beliefs, Sam knew, but Inez would have referred her to someone if need be.

Sam shook her head. "No."

Inez's gaze wandered to a framed eight-by-ten photo on her desk. Inez and her husband, Victor, standing in front of their house, flanked by their children, Esperanza cradling a baby in her arms. She said gently, "You haven't told me anything about the father."

Sam felt suddenly too warm. "His name is Ian," she said. "He's . . . quite a bit younger than me."

"So I've gathered." When Sam shot her a curious glance, Inez added with a wry smile, "You, of all people, should know

310

that O.B. offices are prime watering holes when it comes to gossip."

Sam smiled. "Like I said, it's been a while."

Inez regarded her seriously. "That still doesn't answer my question. Is this Ian going to be in the picture seven months from now?"

Sam's mind flew back to their weekend in New York — Ian reassuring her over and over that he loved her, that they'd make it work. He hadn't actually said the words, "I want this baby." By the same token, neither had she. They'd wandered about the city instead, pretending to be having a good time — even succeeding at it here and there. The Metropolitan Museum, where every painting of Madonna and Child seemed to leap out at her. Central Park, with its sea of strollers. Greenwich Village, where each new taste had been more tantalizing than the next — until the trip across the harbor on the Staten Island Ferry, when she'd been as nauseated as if on an ocean voyage.

Her gaze wandered to the antique vitrine in which Inez's collection of vintage patent medicines was displayed — bottles and jars like the large purple one bearing the faded label: DR. KREUGHER'S ALL-PURPOSE

TONIC FOR DYSPEPSIA, INSOMNIA, NEURASTHENIA, AND FAINTING SPELLS. A sly poke at the trade, no doubt. But she found herself wishing now for a pill or tonic that would fix everything.

"He might think twice," she said, "if he knew what was involved."

Inez sighed, smoothing an iron-colored wisp behind one ear. "Come to think of it, how equipped were *we?* With Raquel, I don't know which of us was more scared — Victor or me." She chuckled softly at the memory.

"You had each other, at least."

Sam was thinking of Martin. Raising a child on her own, she thought soberly, might be easier than constantly tripping over a set of false expectations.

At the same time, a voice cautioned, *Don't judge Ian by another man's stripes.* Nor should she lose sight of the fact that Martin had been a good father in most respects.

Inez scribbled something on a pad and handed it across the desk. "Here's a prescription for prenatal vitamins. I'm going to give you a little free advice as well." She eyed Sam sternly as she rose to her feet. "Don't write chapter six before you've finished chapter two."

Sam looked into Inez's kind, no-nonsense face, with its feathering of lines about the eyes and mouth. It seemed aeons since they'd sat side by side in her living room, stitching tails onto tiger costumes.

"I'll try to keep that in mind." She rose, too, putting out her hand. "Thanks, Inez. I don't know how I'd get through this without you."

"That's what I'm here for." Inez's handshake was warm, if brisk.

"See you in a month?"

"Make that two weeks." In response to Sam's questioning look, she said, "As you said, you're not in your twenties anymore. I'd feel more comfortable keeping a close eye on things."

Sam walked back through the park, taking her time, savoring the chance to be alone with her thoughts. Lunch hour had come and gone, leaving the paths deserted except for a handful of tourists toting guidebooks and old Clem Woolley seated on a bench with a bundle of tattered pamphlets bound in string. He was strumming "Oh, Susannah" on his guitar, not very well, his head with its flurry of white hair bent low, his lips moving soundlessly. Two open cans of Pepsi and two unwrapped sandwiches sat atop the battered case at his feet. He didn't see her, but she smiled at him anyway. It must be nice, she thought, to be familiar enough with Jesus to know he liked tunafish on wheat, pickles on the side.

Farther down the path, she ran into Reverend Grigsby with his constant companion Lily trotting along nicely on her little set of wheels. "Afternoon, Alex." She bent to pat the dachshund's head. "I hear you've found a new organist."

The plump, bespectacled pastor bobbed his head. "Congratulations aren't quite in order yet." He dropped his voice to confide, "She's auditioning for the congregation this Sunday."

"She?"

"Carrie Bramley."

"Ada Bramley's daughter? I thought she moved away."

"Well, she's back. And in fine form, I might add. She's been studying music abroad. Which reminds me —" He peered at Sam, eyes swimming behind his thick bifocals. "How's it going with the music festival?"

"This year's should be the best ever."

She saw no reason to mention that at last Thursday's meeting there'd been a definite chill in the air. Marguerite Moore, with whom Audrey played bridge, had obviously been given the scoop.

"Wonderful." He beamed as if she were single-handedly responsible. "Something else to look forward to."

"Pardon me?"

He winked, patting his rotund belly. "I think you know what I mean."

She felt herself blush. "How . . . how did you know?"

"Oh, I hear just about everything in my line of work," he said mildly, his gaze tracking Lily as she took off after a squirrel, wheels and all, only to be brought short by her leash. When he looked back at Sam, she saw the compassion in his gaze, compassion tempered by knowledge of what lay ahead. "Don't let anything spoil it for you, Sam. You just go on ahead and do as you please." He patted her arm, then tugged on his dog's leash, chiding affectionately, "Come, Lily, those squirrels have better things to do than play with an old cripple like you."

Sam wandered off in a kind of daze, her ears ringing with Reverend Grigsby's words. Suddenly everything looked a little brighter: the escallonia, bowed with bright pink blossoms, the cape honeysuckle climbing up the gazebo. Life is full of surprises, she thought. Maybe, just maybe, Ian would surprise her, too.

Exiting the park, she strolled along Old Mission, pausing in front of Ingersoll's, where the tantalizing scent of baked goods fresh from the oven wafted onto the sidewalk. Food hadn't held much appeal lately, even the delicate little tapas with which Lupe had been trying to tempt her. But her mouth watered as she peered in at the cookies and tarts, the high cakes on pedestals. Even on weekday mornings the line stretched out onto the sidewalk for Ingersoll's honey-glazed doughnuts, hot from the vat. She'd been coming here since she was little, and remembered when Helga Ingersoll would lean over the counter with a bag in one hand and a cookie folded in crinkly paper in the other, saying, "One for Mama, one for you." She'd done the same with Sam's girls. Only now it was Ulla, as thin and dark as her mother had been stout and flaxen, bustling about behind the counter.

No, she thought, it hadn't been all work. What would her life have been without crayon drawings stuck to her refrigerator? And all those priceless school projects: tiny handprints pressed into clay, mobiles fashioned from Popsicle sticks, pinecone turkeys at Thanksgiving?

And her children just out of the bath, pink and delicious, wriggling as she toweled them dry. Like round-limbed cherubim, so precious she'd wanted to spirit them off to a place where they would never get any older. She saw Alice at four, giggling as she covered her nakedness with the shower curtain. And Laura, with her wet hair that refused to lie flat, who'd have been content to run around all day without a stitch on.

Every year at Christmas, she and Martin would take the children out to Ed Claxon's tree farm, where they'd tramp around as if in the woods of Maine. On the way home, with a tree strapped to the roof of the station wagon, they'd sing carols. Then there were gingerbread cookies wrapped in cellophane and strung with yarn, small fingers struggling to separate clumps of tinsel, and for the grand finale, Martin lifting one of the girls up to place the straw angel atop the tree.

Sam felt a tightening in her throat. How could she not love this child? Not seize this chance to snatch back the chubby toddler in corduroy overalls who had somehow escaped her? She could almost feel its warm weight in her lap, its small pink toes wiggling as she chanted, "This little piggy went to market . . ."

Yes, but where does Ian fit in?

She pushed the thought from her mind. She'd know soon enough. For now, all she could do was take a deep breath and hope it would all work out somehow.

Sam was stepping onto Delarosa Plaza when she ran into Tom Kemp, whom she hadn't seen since the wedding. He'd called a couple of times, wanting to get together, but she'd put him off. The last thing she needed right now was another reason to feel guilty.

"Sam. I just came from the shop." Tom greeted her heartily — perhaps a bit too heartily.

She flushed. "Oh?"

Sam slid her sunglasses down her nose to better see him. Tom, she thought, would cut a fine figure on the golf course: tall and narrow-hipped, with long arms that looked good in a short-sleeved shirt. He was goodhearted, too. Hadn't he stuck by Martin at the end, working twice as hard to manage both client loads? Insisting she was owed a larger share of the firm's profits than she was sure she was entitled to.

"There's something I wanted to talk to you about," he said.

He's heard about Ian. The sun filtering through the trees overhead felt suddenly too warm. Oh God. Was he going to make a preemptive bid of some kind? Offer her what no sane woman in her position could refuse — a chance at a future with a solid, well-heeled man her age? She cringed inwardly, but at the same time couldn't help thinking: *would that be so terrible?*

She glanced at her watch. "I can spare a few minutes."

"Good." He took her arm. "I'll treat you to an ice cream."

They strolled down the arcade to Lickety-Split. The ice cream parlor was clogged with the usual jam of strollers and mothers with little children in tow, everyone jockeying for space at the marble counter, with its array of sprinkles: chocolate jimmies, crushed M&M's, toasted coconut, dried blueberries. The blackboard on the wall listed the day's flavors. Sam chose olallie berry; it reminded her of when she and the girls used to pick them in summer.

Miraculously, the wooden bench out front was theirs for the taking. Even better, it afforded a view of the bookshop across the way, where she could see Peter McBride on his front porch, peering across at his ex-wife's rival bookstore. A sandwich board in front announced: ASSUMPTION DAY DISCOUNT! ALL INSPIRATIONAL BOOKS 10% OFF! Miranda, as far as Sam knew, wasn't especially devout. She was only doing it to annoy Peter — and it looked as though it was working.

"I hear you may be getting Yo Yo Ma this year," Tom began in an obvious attempt to break the ice.

"We're working with his manager on dates," she told him. "The headline news is Aubrey Roellinger. Have you heard? He's looking to move here in the fall."

"*The* Aubrey Roellinger? The conductor?" Tom looked suitably impressed.

"He's this year's guest conductor," she told him, "but that could become permanent down the line."

"Wouldn't that be something? Our very own resident conductor."

Silence fell. She waited for Tom to tell her why he'd come to see her when he could just as easily have picked up the phone, but he just sat there, staring at the sidewalk tiles as if working up the nerve to say something. At last he cleared his throat.

"Listen, Sam, I came across something the other day — a file I'd overlooked." He held his cone away from his slacks, giving it a cautious lick. "A real estate transfer Martin was handling before he — about three years back. It seems the client defaulted on his payments, and the deed had reverted back to the original owner."

She waited, wondering what any of this had to do with her.

He straightened. "The original owner was Martin."

She frowned. "I don't understand."

"It's not much, a little ranch house on a quarter of an acre. A few miles down the road from you, as a matter of fact. Martin must have bought it as an investment. I'm sure he'd have gotten around to telling you if — well, if things hadn't gotten so confusing at the end." He looked down. "Apparently he'd been holding the mortgage, and when the buyer stopped making payments . . ." He spread his hands.

"Are you saying I *own* this house?"

"Don't get too excited," he cautioned. "I've been out to see it, and it's pretty rundown. There are back taxes, too. Two years' worth. In fact, that's what made me hunt for the file — the town was threatening to foreclose."

Everything became suddenly clear. How Martin, spotting an opportunity for quick profit, had scooped up the house for a song. And because he was Martin, with a reverse Midas touch, he'd taken the down payment in cash, holding paper on the balance.

She felt a rush of anger toward her husband. It didn't occur to her to be pleased by her windfall. She was too busy wishing Martin were here in Tom's place so she could give him a royal piece of her mind. How could he have kept this from her when they'd been so strapped?

"I can't imagine where he got the money in the first place," she said, struggling to keep her voice even.

Tom looked uncomfortable. They both knew how easy it would have been for Martin to have sweet-talked one of his banker buddies into a loan with nothing down, or even to have taken cash in lieu of a check from one of his high-rolling clients.

"I'm sorry, Sam, I wish you hadn't had to find out this way. But look at the bright side." He brought his head up, a smile pinned crookedly in place. "It's yours now. You can do whatever you want with it. Rent it, sell it. Hell, you could even move into it if you wanted." His smile broadened at the joke.

She stared at the cone in his hand, smiling a little at the dribble of Kahlúa fudge ice cream making its way down his knuckles. Oddly, it made her like him all the more.

"Thanks, Tom. I appreciate your telling me in person." She touched his knee, nodding in the direction of his cone. "By the way, your ice cream is melting."

He looked down as if surprised to see it in his hand. "I didn't really want it," he said. "It was just something to do." He stood up, dumping it in the wooden trash bin on the curb.

She handed him a napkin. Who, she wondered, had appointed women the keepers of napkins and tissues? Who had decreed that mothers, not fathers, be the ones armed, at all times, for wiping runny noses and sticky hands? "I suppose I should stop by the office at some point," she said. "I don't even know where this house is."

"If you'd like, I could take you out there. Maybe one day this weekend?" He wiped his hands with the napkin, taking his time, working it in between his fingers. When he looked up at her, his expression was carefully neutral. "If you're free, that is."

He knows, she thought. He'd have to have been deaf not to have heard. Yet he wasn't jumping to conclusions. She felt a rush of gratitude. "I'm free on Saturday," she told him.

She'd made no plans with Ian. And suddenly the prospect of Tom — good old Tom, steady as Plymouth Rock — guiding her through the thicket of paperwork ahead was the most reassuring thing imaginable.

"If you decide to sell it, I could help with that, too." He eyed the ice cream melting to purple soup in her cup, observing dryly, "I guess you weren't too hungry, either."

"I guess not." She stood up, feeling light-headed, the way she had with both her other pregnancies. She didn't protest when Tom gently took the cup and tossed it in the trash.

He offered her his arm. "Come on, I'll walk you back. Laura will be wondering what's kept you."

But Laura was waiting on a customer when she walked in: Gayle Warrington trying to decide between two hand-blocked silk scarves. Sam recalled when they'd gone to school together. Gayle was one of those girls whose lipstick had always matched her nail polish, and who was forever doing sit-ups to keep her stomach flat. Judging from her trim figure and perfectly manicured nails, nothing much had changed.

Laura, on the other hand, looked dreadful. Her face drawn and puffy, her eyes red rimmed from lack of sleep. Anyone could see how unhappy she was. Sam felt a stab of guilt. *My fault.*

"If it's a gift for your mother," Sam heard her say, "you might want to go with the plum. The crane design is very traditional, very elegant, don't you think?"

"I'm just not sure . . ." Gayle tapped her folded sunglasses against a mouth the same coral hue as her blazer. "You don't know my mother. Look up 'safe' in the dictionary, and you'll see her name. She'd probably go with this one." She fingered the plainer ecru scarf.

"It would certainly go with everything," Laura said.

"Don't give her anything new to learn, and for God's sake, don't send her anywhere she hasn't already been." Gayle went on as if Laura hadn't spoken. "Never mind her daughter the travel agent could get her a discount fare." Her voice took on a sarcastic edge. "Paris? They don't have proper toilets, much less speak English. London? They speak the language, but you can't understand a word. Rome? Heavens, you'd have to sew in your valuables to keep from being robbed."

"I . . . I've always wanted to see Paris." Laura made an attempt to steer the conversation away from Gayle's mother.

"Well, stop by the office sometime. I know a lovely little hotel off the Champs-Élysées. The clerks speak *English,* and wonder of all wonders, it even has flush toilets." She gave the harsh laugh of a life-long chain-smoker.

"Maybe I'll look into it." Laura smiled. "Now, about the scarf —"

Gayle settled on the ecru, and when Laura had gone off to gift wrap it, she turned to Sam. "Your daughter's so sweet. It must be wonderful having her work for you."

"We're partners more than anything," Sam told her.

"Like Doug and me," she said, referring to her husband. They owned Off-and-Away Travel, four blocks down on Chestnut. "But to tell the truth," she leaned close to confide, "most of the time we're at each other's throats. Can't agree on a damn thing except my mother. We'd both like to put her on a slow boat to China." She gave another harsh smoker's laugh.

"I envy you having a mother at all. I wish mine were still around."

Sam kept her voice light, but the message wasn't lost on Gayle. Something dark and not altogether friendly flickered in her eyes. "Only kidding, of course. We love Mom to death. It's just that she gets on our nerves sometimes. Don't they all?"

"I suppose." Sam felt distinctly uneasy, thinking of the recent drop in her own approval ratings.

"Like this birthday we're not supposed to make a fuss over. God forbid we should take her at her word, we'd never hear the end of it." Gayle reached into her handbag and pulled out a MasterCard, snapping it down as if it were the winning card in a poker game. But when Laura reappeared holding a gift-wrapped box, her expression all at once turned doubtful. "She can return it, can't she? If she doesn't like it?"

"Absolutely." Laura smiled. "Just be sure to save the receipt."

She waited until Gayle was out the door before saying, "Whew! I thought she'd never make up her mind." She eyed Sam with concern. "Everything okay? You were gone an awfully long time."

"Right as rain." Sam felt a rush of tenderness toward her daughter, who was making a brave attempt to put on a good face — even though it wasn't working. "I ran into Tom Kemp on the way back," she explained. "There was something he wanted to go over with me."

"Oh yeah, he was just in looking for you," Laura said distractedly as she sorted through the jumble of scarves on the counter. "Anything important?"

"Some paper to sign." Later, she would explain about the house — when she could think of a way to do so without putting a dent in Martin's halo.

"Well, it was nice of him to tell you in person."

"Tom's been wonderful," Sam agreed.

Noticing the scarf that kept slipping through her daughter's fingers, Sam stepped forward to take it from her. "Here, let me do that. Why don't you take care of Customs?" She vaguely recalled some confusion about a crate of Quimper pottery being held at LAX.

Laura looked at her as if she'd dropped in from another planet. "Oh, Mom. I was on the phone with them *half the morning.* And that was between waiting on customers, and chasing those baskets that never showed, and —" She broke off with a small, choked sob, glancing about in horror. Luckily, the shop was deserted. Her face, in all its misery, swung back to meet Sam's. "It's no good," she said. "I can't keep on pretending."

"I'm sorry, honey. I know I've been a little distracted lately."

"It's not just that."

Sam recalled Gayle's halfhearted offer. "You're absolutely right. You've been doing more than your fair share, and it's time you took a vacation. As a matter of fact, I *insist* on it. I can hold down the fort for a week or two."

"I don't need a vacation." Laura shook her head sorrowfully. "And it's not just that you haven't been yourself lately —" She paused to pull in a breath, her cheeks reddening. "The thing is . . . well, the thing is I can't work here any more." She put a hand out, as if to stave off Sam's protests. "Don't get me wrong. I still love you. But . . . but it's just too hard. Seeing you every day, and knowing —" She broke off, swallowing hard.

Sam shouldn't have been surprised. Hadn't she sensed it coming? At the same time she felt as if she'd been struck a blow.

"Oh, Laura. I can understand you feeling this way now, but in time . . ." She faltered. What did she want to say? That things would be better when the baby was here?

"You *don't* understand," Laura cried. "You don't understand one little bit. How could you? *You* had your turn to be a mother. And now . . . well, it isn't *fair*." Her eyes glittered with unshed tears. "There, I've said it. You probably think I'm mean and horrible, but I can't help how I feel."

Sam reached out to her, only to have Laura shrink away. "Oh, honey," she said, close to tears herself, "I don't think you're horrible. If it's any consolation, I wish it *had* been you."

"But it isn't." Laura regarded her forlornly. "And there's no use pretending I'll get over it because I won't."

Sam wanted to cry out in protest, but held her tongue. "What will you do?"

"I'll stay long enough to help you train someone if that's what you're worried about."

"That's not what I meant."

"I have a few possibilities lined up." Laura shrugged, her eyes not meeting Sam's; she'd always been a terrible liar.

When she looked up her face seemed to plead with Sam to understand. "I'm not doing this to punish you, Mom. Please don't think that. It's not like it is with Alice."

Sam sighed. "I know, honey."

"Think of it this way." Laura mustered a faint smile. "Think of all the money you'll save."

"How so?"

"We're down twenty percent from this time last year," she said — as if Sam needed reminding. "Face it, Mom, you can't afford me."

Sam stiffened. "Don't you think you're overreacting a bit? Just because things are a little slow right now —" She stopped, appalled to hear Martin's tired rationalizations coming out of her mouth. Turning away to compose herself, she asked softly, "Can we talk this over later? When I've had a chance to think it through?"

"Sure, absolutely."

In Laura's desperate eagerness to please, Sam could see the enormous courage it must have taken for her to make such a stand. She even admired her for it. But none of that made it any easier to swallow. It was like those old Saturday matinee serials where the footbridge is being blown up as the hero races to cross it. Everything she'd ever worked for, everything she'd held dear, was disintegrating at her heels. How had it come to this? She'd spent a lifetime looking to others' needs. All she'd asked in return was a little happiness of her own. She hadn't meant for it to destroy everyone she loved.

"It's all right, Laura. I understand." Her voice was weary.

"It doesn't have to be the end of the world." Laura was quick to respond. "We'll still see each other. Alice will come around, too, you'll see. And there's Ian. Remember, you still have Ian."

"Hi. Sorry to wake you. My flight was delayed." Ian's voice drifted toward her through a blizzard of static.

"What time is it?" She fumbled with her pillow, positioning it against the headboard as she pulled herself upright.

"A few minutes past two. You said to phone when I got in."

Sam squinted groggily at the clock on the nightstand. Ten past, to be exact. "It's okay. I'm glad you did." She smiled sleepily in the darkness. "I can't wait to see you."

"Me, too." He sounded tired, and much

too far away. In the background, airport sounds crackled and hummed. "But listen, Sam, there's been a slight change of plans."

She grew suddenly alert. "Oh?"

A static-filled pause, then, "Shit. Sorry. Wrong bag." She heard him breathing hard at the other end, then the garbled bleating of a PA system. "There. I've got it."

"Ian?" She was wide-awake now. "What is it?"

"Another commission. In Big Sur. Old Man Aaronson wants a portrait of his mother. I'm sure Markie put him up to it, but hell, the money is too good to turn down."

"Who's Markie?"

"His daughter."

"I didn't know he had a daughter."

There was an awkward beat before Ian replied, "Didn't I tell you?"

"No, I don't believe so."

She knew with sudden certainty that he'd kept it from her. She didn't know how she knew; she just did. She recalled the girl in the silver convertible the night she arrived: pretty, dark haired. Just someone from the office, he'd said. Why hadn't he told the truth?

All of a sudden she had trouble catching

her breath. "How long this time?"

"Two weeks, tops."

"Will I see you before you go?"

"Afraid not. They're sending a car."

"Why the rush?"

"The old lady leaves for Europe in a couple of weeks," he explained.

"I suppose you'll be staying at their house."

"Yeah, and here's the good part." Ian sounded excited. "I'll have the guest house, which means you can visit on weekends. I've already talked to the Aaronsons about it. They're cool with it."

Sam felt suddenly irritated. If he expected her to be equally delighted, he had another think coming. What did he imagine she was, some free-spirited twentysomething who could take off on a whim? Had he even remembered she was pregnant?

"I don't know," she sighed. "There's a lot going on right now."

"Is everything okay?" At once, his tone turned solicitous. "What did the doctor say?"

They'd agreed to put off any discussion of the baby until his return. She didn't want her future decided over the phone. Now she realized that that had been a mistake. The days and weeks of skirting the issue had given room to doubt.

"She gave me a clean bill of health." Sam aimed for an upbeat tone.

"And the baby?"

"The baby's fine."

She waited for him to say something. But there were only the distant sounds of horns honking and people bellowing. He was outside now, walking briskly. Then, "I see it — the limo. Listen, I'll call you when I get there. Will you be around in a few hours?"

"If I'm not here, try me at work." She said nothing about Laura's precipitous announcement.

There was a silence, and for a moment she thought they'd been cut off. Then, in a voice almost too low to hear, he said, "I miss you, babe. Just a little while longer. Can you hang on until then?"

"I'll try." She managed a little laugh.

"Sam . . ." His voice faded into the static, but not before she thought she heard a faint, *I love you*. Then the line went dead.

She wanted to weep with frustration. There was so much she longed to say, so much she needed to hear. Words that would reassure her, that would pave the way for the future. For the idea of his moving in with her was still unimaginable . . . as unimaginable as her moving in with him. And what about the baby? Only one thing was sure: They couldn't go on like this, like lovers in a Rohmer film.

Yet wasn't this the handwriting on the wall? The reason she felt like crying? In her mind she saw her old kindergarten teacher, Mrs. Ogilvie, bending over a drawing she'd done. "What's missing from this picture?" she'd asked. "I see a mommy and a daddy, but no Samantha." *Where is Samantha now?* Sam wondered. She no longer saw a place for herself, much less Ian, in the life she'd once imagined.

She would have to come to a decision. Soon. A decision that, whichever way she turned, would mean hurting someone she loved.

Sam flopped over in bed. Getting back to sleep would be impossible. She would simply lie here, counting the hours until daylight.

Ian didn't call until after she'd left for work. The message was on her machine when she got home; apparently he hadn't felt the need to track her down at the shop. That evening, when they finally spoke, their conversation was strained. She told him she'd see if she could arrange to drive up the following weekend since she'd already made plans for this one. She gave him a brief fill on the house, playing down Tom's role in the whole thing.

Saturday morning, when Tom arrived to pick her up, she was surprised by how glad she was to see him. They chatted easily along the way, though he seemed a bit subdued. They talked mainly about the house, Tom explaining it would need some painting and interior work, and possibly a new roof as well.

Sam was expecting the worst when, after several miles of back roads lined with citrus and avocado groves, they turned onto a rutted dirt lane. All she could see of the house was a weather vane in the shape of a rooster poking above the treetops.

"Like I said, it's not much," Tom warned. "Doesn't look as if the owner did much in the way of repairs." He pulled to a stop before a small frame house badly in need of paint. Pink fairy roses grew in a thick tangle around the porch, climbing up over the railing.

There was a flurry of movement as they got out: ground squirrels scampering across the weed-choked yard. Partially shading the front walk was a pomegranate tree. Badly overgrown, its branches bent so low they were brushing the ground, it was nevertheless hung like a Christmas tree with ruby-colored globes. It seemed an omen of some kind. When she was pregnant with Laura and Alice, pomegranates had been the only thing she'd craved.

Upon closer inspection, she found the house in better shape than she'd dared hope. Someone had taken the time and care to strip and varnish its wooden shutters and the front door was of solid oak with a beveled glass oval.

Tom produced a key and she followed him into a darkened living room smelling of dust and mice droppings. She threw open the shutters and light flooded in, revealing a shabby sofa and chairs, a braided rug marked with burns. The fireplace was clearly functional. A basket of kindling stood on the hearth alongside a set of blackened tools.

"I've seen worse," she said. "At least the roof is sound."

"How do you know?" he asked.

"The smell." Every winter during the brief rainy season, Isla Verde sprang dozens of leaks. For weeks the house always smelled of damp carpeting and must.

Tom bent to examine the chimney flu; he tapped the floorboards and moldings. When he flicked the switch and the light didn't come on, he tramped down to the basement to check the fuse box. He even looked to see what kind of shape the plumbing was in.

In the kitchen he pulled his head out from under the sink and stood up brushing bits of dirt from his slacks. "I'm no expert," he said, "but except for the living room floor everything looks to be in pretty solid shape. A few repairs, a coat of paint, and you should have no trouble selling it."

"How much do you think I could get?" She fingered a skeletal philodendron on the sill that miraculously showed signs of life.

"Sixty, seventy thousand. Maybe more, depending on how much work you want to do."

"In that case, the first place I'd start is this kitchen."

She looked around at the dated ranch-style cabinets; the ancient beige linoleum peeling away from the floor like an old Band-Aid; the stove and refrigerator in a particularly unappetizing shade, popular in the seventies, known as harvest gold. On the plus side, there was a sliding glass door off the breakfast nook, with a small patio and garden beyond. A jungle, of course. But with a couple of helpers and a few weeks' hard work . . .

"I know a contractor who doesn't charge an arm and a leg. I could give him a call if you'd like," Tom offered.

"I'd knock out the wall between those two back bedrooms, too," she went on, only half listening. "Make it one large room, and use the master bedroom as a guest room."

Tom nodded thoughtfully. "You'd certainly get more money that way. Look, I know a good realtor, too. I could —"

"I'm not going to sell it."

An idea was forming. One so revolutionary she hardly dared voice it. Why not rent out Isla Verde and live *here* instead? There was plenty of room for the baby, and the money she'd save would kill two birds with one stone: give her enough to pay off back taxes and make this place livable. Not only that . . . not only that . . . she could — well, of course, why hadn't she thought of it before? — she could put *Laura* in charge of Delarosa's. When the baby came she'd have to take time off anyway. If Laura were running things . . .

"I'm going to live here myself," she said. The prospect left her slightly breathless.

"Why on earth would you want to do that?" Tom stared at her in disbelief, his glasses, knocked slightly askew, giving him an endearingly befuddled look.

She didn't owe him an explanation, but there was something about the way he was looking at her — like a little boy peering out expectantly at the postman coming up the walk, hoping that *this* would be the day his official forest ranger walkie-talkie set would come.

"For one thing," she said, "Martin didn't exactly leave me well off." She took a deep breath and forced herself to hold his gaze. "For another, I'm going to have a baby."

If he'd looked befuddled before, Tom now looked positively poleaxed. "I see." He spoke softly, with the air of someone who didn't see at all, who might have been standing on the railroad tracks with a train whistling toward him, for all he knew.

She felt an odd sympathy for this man who'd been her husband's friend and partner, and who might have been something more to her if not for Ian. "It was a shock, as you can imagine. It's taken me a while to get used to the idea," she plowed on resolutely. "But now it's time to face facts. Isla Verde has gotten to be more than I can handle. At my age, with a baby . . ."

She saw no reason to spell it out.

Tom blinked, rousing from his trancelike state with what appeared to be an effort. "If it's a question of money, I'd be happy to lend you some."

She felt deeply touched, and not just by his generosity. She placed a hand on his arm. "Thanks, Tom, but you've done enough as it is."

"It's not just the money, Sam." He paused, his face reddening. "I know this is probably the world's worst timing, but I'd even thought, well, that you and I . . . that we might . . ." He let the sentence trail off.

"Oh, Tom." She shook her head in regret.

"Nothing's changed," he went on. "I mean, aside from the obvious. What I mean is . . . this doesn't affect how I feel."

"Baby and all?" She arched a teasing brow.

"I missed the boat when it came to children." He mustered a small smile. "Though it certainly wasn't for lack of trying." Tom had been divorced as long as she'd known him. It never occurred to her that he and his wife had wanted a family.

"I appreciate the offer, Tom." She spoke as gently as possibly. "More than you know."

His face fell. "Is it the father? Are you marrying him?"

"I don't know," she said. "The only thing I'm sure of right now is that I have some major changes to make. Starting with knocking down a few walls of my own."

Tom regarded her with what, amazingly, seemed to be renewed respect. "The offer is still open as far as my friendship is concerned," he said. "I'll help in any way I can. No strings attached." He grinned, the grin of the anxious boy she'd seen a minute ago peeking out from behind the man's sober face. "Now, about that contractor . . ."

Sam scarcely heard his next words. She was too busy turning over in her mind, like a precious found object, the rather amazing discovery that not everyone felt as her sister and Marguerite Moore did. There were those who accepted her, who would stand behind her. People like Gerry Fitzgerald and Reverend Grigsby . . . and yes, even Tom Kemp.

If only her daughters felt the same way.

Chapter 11

The following Saturday, Laura awoke, heart pounding, from a dream in which she'd gone to visit her mother, and Sam hadn't known who she was. Her heartbeat slowed as familiar surroundings materialized in the morning light: her oak dresser with its clutter of framed photos; the clunky old wardrobe that'd been her grandmother's with its one door that wouldn't stay shut; the padded rocker over which yesterday's clothes had been thrown — dusty jeans sprung at the knees, a plaid shirt rolled up at the sleeves, white cotton underwear as sexless and utilitarian as those worn, no doubt by the nuns on the hill. Then she remembered her dream.

I don't know my own mother anymore.

When she'd told Sam she was quitting, the only thing on her mind had been where she was going to find another job. In a million years she couldn't have predicted what came next: that *she'd* be put in sole charge of Delarosa's.

Her mother must have known this, for she'd said firmly, "This is *my* decision, so I don't want you feeling responsible. I couldn't bear it if I thought this was hurting you."

"How can I *not* feel responsible?" Laura had wanted to know. Her mother clearly saw this as the solution to everything: a way to save money as well as resolve the problem of the two of them working together.

Sam had been quick to set her straight. "All right, you may have jump-started it, but the truth is both of us will benefit. I have my own future to think of, and for lots of reasons this makes sense."

Incredibly, that wasn't all. It seemed her mother was moving out of Isla Verde into a small run-down house in the Flats bought by Laura's father as an investment — which Laura hadn't even known about until now. And Isla Verde — where every nick and stain had a story, where generations of pets were buried, and the yard was shaded by trees grown from avocado seeds sprouted on the kitchen sill — was to be rented out to a perfect stranger.

Laura still hadn't quite absorbed it all. Thoughts of last week's startling turn of events tiptoed about in her head, not quite daring to give way to the inevitable worries beyond. For if her mother was capable of reinventing her life to this degree — moving into a house needing more work than this one — rotten floorboards and old wiring wouldn't be the only things torn out. *Alice and I could be next.*

She waited a few more minutes before climbing out of bed. It was only barely light out, but further sleep would have been impossible. She knew because this wasn't the first morning she'd woken with her heart in high gear and the ghost of a dream riding shotgun in her head. But it was Saturday, at least. Two whole days before the madness of Monday. Laura sighed at the thought. Last week, while her mother met with real estate agents and contractors, she'd been stuck doing the job of two. Between waiting on customers and tracking orders, marking new inventory and going over receipts, there'd been sorting through responses to the ad she'd placed and interviewing prospective employees. Which hadn't left much time or energy for anything, or anyone, else.

Like Finch. Laura thought back to the girl's recent revelations. No wonder she had nightmares! What amazed Laura was how she'd managed to keep it a secret for so long. Even now she could see in her mind Finch's tortured face as she recounted the events of that night.

"They didn't know I was in the apartment," she'd said in an odd, halting voice. "There were two of them, two men talking to Lyle — I couldn't see their faces from down the hall. All I know is they wanted their money."

"Money for what?" Laura had asked.

"The coke."

"Did your foster mom know he was dealing drugs?"

"Shirlee? Yeah, I think so. But she worked nights, so she wasn't around much." Beads of sweat had broken out on Finch's brow; she looked ill. "I never said anything. Lyle would've gotten mad. And when he was mad —" She broke off, swallowing. "Anyway, I could hear them in the living room. Shouting at Lyle. Saying he was holding out on them. Lyle said something back. Then the next thing I knew, a gun went off. I ducked under the bed. I didn't know what else to do."

"You did the right thing." It was all Laura could do to keep from wrapping her arms around the poor, shivering girl.

"They didn't stick around. I guess they were scared of getting caught."

"Did you phone the police?"

"I thought he'd be dead," Finch went on as if she hadn't heard. "But when I got to him he . . . he was still breathing. He begged me to call an ambulance. But I just stood there. Watching him die. I could've saved him, but I . . . I didn't."

Laura pulled the girl into her arms, rocking her as she began to weep. She was staggered by the knowledge, not of what Finch had done — or *thought* she'd done — but of what she'd must have gone through. Where were the people who ought to have been looking out for her? County officials, social workers, teachers?

Now it was up to Laura to decide what was best. Finch remained adamant about not bringing in the police, and rather than betray her trust Laura had reluctantly agreed. At the same time, it was clear they couldn't go on like this. Jumping at every car that pulled into the driveway, hesitating to pick up the phone. Something had to give.

Tugging on jeans and a sweatshirt, Laura crept through the living room and down the hall. In the kitchen, Pearl's tail thumped against the side of her box while Rocky wandered over to see what was up. She sank onto her haunches to give his head a good scrub. "Don't *you* go giving me any grief now, you hear?" The terrier licked her face in response. His curly black face, with its ragged ear that flopped like a rabbit's, seemed to say, *We know you're doing your best even if it doesn't always look that way.*

She straightened with a sigh. The cats were making themselves known as well, winding in and out between her legs, mewing as if she hadn't fed them in ages. She shook kibble into their bowls, and was at the sink filling their water dishes when she caught a movement outside: a woman stepping from the shadow of the barn. Laura saw a flash of blond hair and pale legs before she disappeared around the other side.

She felt a surge of jealousy, though it shouldn't have surprised her. This wasn't the first woman to stay the night. Besides, Hector didn't owe her an explanation.

She thought of the kiss in the barn. Maybe he *had* felt something. Deep affection that had momentarily crossed over into another realm. But it clearly wasn't leading anywhere. Ever since then it had been business as usual as far as Hector was concerned, while *she* walked around like a moonstruck idiot: terrified he would guess how she felt, equally terrified he wouldn't.

Well, you can relax. She need look no further than out the window for proof that he wasn't interested.

Suddenly she felt stupid for ever having imagined he could want her — a one-woman Noah's ark who looked more like a page out of *Practical Horseman* than *Vogue.* Any sane man would run for the hills. Any true friend would let him go.

She heard a noise, and turned to find Finch in the kitchen doorway, dressed in navy shorts and a wrinkled Tour de France T-shirt, never mind the pretty flowered nighties Laura had bought her. "Isn't today Saturday?" she asked, yawning.

"Yup." Laura set out the cat's bowls, and reached for the coffee pot by the stove. "Hungry?"

"I should feed the horses first."

"Hector —" Laura broke off. "Come to think of it, I'm sure he'd appreciate the extra sleep. I heard him roll in pretty late last night."

Finch started for the door. This past week she'd seemed easier somehow, her step lighter, as if the burden that'd been weighing on her had been lifted. Abruptly she turned. "Uh, Laura? I was just wondering — you haven't changed your mind or anything, have you?"

"About what?" Laura scooped coffee from the canister.

"You know." Finch dropped her voice.

"I gave my word."

"You could get into trouble."

"Why don't you let me worry about that?" Laura tossed her a small crooked smile. "Look, one way or another we'll get this sorted out, but I promise I won't do anything without talking to you first. Okay?"

The girl was silent for a moment, and Laura caught a flicker of something in her eyes, something wanting desperately to believe that amid all those unkept promises and broken trusts there might, just might, be someone she could count on.

"My real name is Bethany," she said softly. "Bethany Wells."

Laura thought of an injured chipmunk she'd once nursed back to health. For weeks it had cowered in its cage, refusing to let her near it. But gradually it had grown to trust her, until one day she was able to hold it cupped in her palms — a warm silken ball quivering like the very essence of life itself.

She felt that same quickening now.

"Nice to meet you, Bethany." She

stepped away from the counter, hand extended, feeling the world shift a bit on its axis while the morning ticked on unaware: tap dripping, coffee burbling, dogs and cats rooting in their bowls.

Soft, shy fingers curled about hers. Brown eyes peered up at her hopefully. "Would it be okay if you still called me Finch?"

Laura nodded, swallowing against the lump in her throat. "Sure thing."

"You won't say anything to Maude, will you?" Finch didn't need to spell it out. They both knew how absentminded Maude could be. She might spill the beans without meaning to.

"My lips are sealed."

Finch hesitated, then said, "The other day she told me you got divorced because you couldn't have kids. Is that true?"

Laura felt a twinge of familiar pain, but it was muted somehow. "Partly," she said. "The truth is we probably would've broken up anyway."

Finch nodded in understanding, saying with unexpected fervency, "Well, if you ask me, any guy who couldn't see how great you are doesn't deserve you."

Laura grinned. "You know something? I'm starting to think so myself."

Then Finch was outside, the screen door wheezing shut behind her. It was a moment before Laura was able to fall back into step with the morning. She was putting away the dishes from the night before when Maude appeared, bundled in her robe as if the weatherman had predicted eighteen instead of eighty degrees.

"Coffee. How lovely," she exclaimed, as if Laura didn't make it every morning. "With toast and cinnamon butter, I think."

"I'll whip the butter," Laura said. "Do we have enough bread?"

"I should hope so. I took a loaf out of the freezer just last night." Maude reached into the bread bin, her smile fading as she stared in dismay at the soggy package in her hand: the rump roast meant for tonight's dinner. "Heavens." She raised a pair of stricken eyes to Laura. "I must be getting forgetful in my old age."

Laura knew what she was thinking. It was one thing to be living here when she, too, had been something of a runaway, but now that Elroy had made his intentions known, however crudely, Maude must be worried that she'd worn out her welcome.

Laura set her mug down. "Nonsense." She gently pried the soggy packet from Maude's hands. "We wouldn't be able to manage without you. Do you think it makes one bit of difference whether we eat roast beef or . . . or leftover macaroni and cheese?"

"Better make that spaghetti and meatballs. I got hungry in the middle of the night." Maude risked a tiny smile. With her frizzled braid draped over one shoulder, she resembled a fluffy white cat.

Laura hugged her, thinking of Elroy, which made her think of Sam and how complicated it all was with one's parents. How much easier it was with someone whose history wasn't all tangled up with yours. She didn't love Maude *in spite of* their not being related. She loved her all the more because of it.

"Never mind," she said. "We'll go out."

Maude drew back, frowning. "That's generous of you, dear, but can you afford it?"

"I don't see why not." She wouldn't think about the vet bill that was due, the ancient oil burner about to go, or the gutters in need of replacing. All that mattered was that her little makeshift family was all in one piece — if only for the moment.

She was setting the table when Maude asked cautiously, "Did you hear anything last night?"

"Like what?"

"I thought I heard someone scream."

Laura hadn't heard anything except Hector's truck. "It might have been a bobcat."

"No, it was definitely human. It sounded like a woman."

"Mrs. Vincenzi?" Their nearest neighbor, who suffered from Alzheimer's, was prone to occasional screaming fits. But the Vincenzi house was a quarter of a mile down the road, so it wasn't likely to have come from there. Even so, it wouldn't hurt to check. "I'll give Anna a call after breakfast to make sure everything's okay."

The sun was peeking over the roof of the barn by the time breakfast found its way onto the table. Maude had toasted the half loaf of bread that surfaced from the refrigerator, and Laura filled in with homemade granola and a bowl of sliced peaches from the orchard at Isla Verde.

Finch tramped in from the barn, and Hector appeared a few minutes later, yawning as if just out of bed. Laura glanced up at him, then away, struggling to maintain her composure. Didn't her heart know to stop pounding? Judging from last night's activities, she'd been the furthest thing from his mind.

"I wasn't sure you'd be joining us," she remarked mildly.

"Me neither." He yawned again, scrubbing his head.

In his jeans and sleeveless undershirt he seemed almost indecently exposed. She tried not to stare at the ridges on his chest and back, to which the thin cotton clung; at the tightly packed muscles in his arms, with their veins that would pulse warmly beneath her fingers. She was careful, too, not to meet his eyes, the color of the dark beans he was scooping into the grinder — his own private stash.

"I figured you'd want to sleep in. After getting in so late, and all." Laura kept her tone light.

He didn't even look up. "Did I wake you? Sorry. Muffler's going on the truck. I'll get it looked at next week." The whir of the coffee grinder saved her from having to reply.

When he was seated at the table, steaming mug in hand, Laura slid a piece of toast onto his plate. He shook his head when she passed the butter. "Better not. I'm taking it easy on my stomach."

Maude glanced at him in alarm. "I hope you're not coming down with something."

"More like the dog that bit me." He gave a low chuckle. "Used to be I could kick back with a few beers and not feel it the next morning. Must be getting old."

"I know the feeling," Maude sighed.

"I'll get you some Alka-Seltzer." Laura started to get up.

Hector reached out to lightly capture her wrist. Their eyes met briefly, and she felt a little current of electricity travel up her arm. "I know where to find it. You stay put."

His fingers burned against her skin. Could he feel her pulse racing? She waited a polite beat before slipping free to butter another slice of toast she didn't want or need. "I'm interviewing another person on Monday," she said to no one in particular.

She glanced up to find Hector regarding her thoughtfully over the rim of his mug. "You're sure your mom won't change her mind?"

"She won't."

"You sound as if you wish she would."

"It'd be better than feeling guilty all the time."

Maude patted her hand reassuringly. "Your mother has a mind of her own. I'm sure she's only doing what's best for her."

"She's been doing a lot of that lately," Laura muttered darkly.

"She's having a baby." Maude spoke as if it were the most natural thing in the world, never mind that Sam was old enough to be a grandmother. "When women are expecting they do all sorts of things they wouldn't normally." She was getting that far-off look again. "I remember when I was carrying Elroy. I took it into my head to visit my Aunt Ida. Didn't make a whit of difference that she lived all the way out in Providence, Rhode Island. I wouldn't rest until I was on that train." Maude smiled absently at the framed sampler on the wall: NO MATTER WHERE I PUT MY GUESTS, THEY ALWAYS LIKE MY KITCHEN BEST. "It was two days before I could keep anything down. By the time I stepped off that train, I was so faint I could barely stand up." She sighed. "There've been times I've wondered if that's why Elroy turned out the way he did."

"It's not your fault," Finch said.

Maude turned to her. "What? Elroy?"

"You didn't make him the way he is."

Out of the mouths of babes, Laura thought.

"Maybe not, but he's still my son." Maude shook her head sadly.

Finch shot her an apprehensive look. "That doesn't mean you have to live with him."

"Who said I was going anywhere? Goodness, I'd already made up my mind about that long before he came to see me. And after the way you chased him off, I'm fairly certain he won't be back any time soon. Though I would welcome an occasional visit —" she smiled naughtily, "as long as it didn't include Verna's cooking."

"I hope my mother doesn't see me the way you do Elroy — as someone trying to bully her," Laura fretted aloud. "I certainly never intended for it to turn out this way."

"I don't know about your mom quitting." Hector chewed thoughtfully on his toast. "But moving into a smaller place makes sense. That big house of hers is a lot to handle."

"At least she had Lupe and Guillermo. Out there, she'll be all alone." Laura didn't have to mention the murderer on the loose; it was all anyone could talk about these days.

"What if she's not alone?" Finch glanced innocently about the table.

Laura sighed. "You mean Ian? Nobody seems to know." She didn't add that no one had had the guts to ask, either. And with Ian off on some other project, it was anyone's guess. "All I know is that I'm going to have a hard time replacing her at the shop."

"*I* could work for you," Finch said tentatively.

You'll be in school, Laura almost said, but bit her tongue. "It certainly is a thought. Maybe you could start by lending me a hand until I work something else out."

Maude rose from the table. "Why don't I wash up? You must have other things to do." She cast a pointed look at Laura.

Laura remembered the scream Maude had heard.

"I should check up on the Vincenzis," she said, pushing herself to her feet. "You know Anna. When I phone, she always says everything's fine." The last time she'd dropped by, Laura had found poor Anna close to tears as she struggled to restrain her mother, who had her coat and hat on and was insisting she had to pick her children up from school.

"I'll keep you company. Bet she could use someone to trim that hedge." Hector's chair scraped over the worn linoleum. "Wait here, I'll get my clippers."

It wasn't until they were strolling side by side along the dusty road that Laura began to relax. It should have been just the opposite; she should have found it tougher being alone with Hector. God knows he wouldn't have noticed if she'd stripped off

360

her clothes and danced naked in the road. What was he thinking about as he ambled beside her, grass-stained clippers in hand? The woman he'd been with last night?

After a few minutes, he cast her a sidelong glance, observing mildly, "You're awful quiet. Everything okay?"

"I was just thinking about Finch," she lied.

"Still haven't figured out what to do with her?"

"It's not that," she said. "I just have to find a way of doing it." She wished she could confide in him, but a promise was a promise. "Listen, if I have to go to New York for a few days, you'll look after everything while I'm gone, won't you?"

"First your mom, now you," he teased. "What's so special about New York?"

"I can't tell you yet. Just trust me, I know what I'm doing."

He nodded. "No problem. Take as long as you like."

"I have to make some calls first. I'll let you know, okay?"

They walked in silence a little longer, then Hector touched her elbow. "Everything else okay? With you, I mean." His eyes glinted in the shadow cast by the brim of his hat.

She knew what he was referring to: the baby. "I'm fine." Laura kicked at a rock. Along the shoulder wildflowers heavy with dew — prickly poppy and golden yarrow, meadow rue and wild onion — nodded drowsily in the morning sunlight.

"That's good."

Laura squinted up at the hot blue August sky, where a scattering of clouds scudded over distant Sulphur Peak. "All right," she said at last, "I'm still not happy about it, but if my mom wants to screw up her life that's her business."

"Maybe it wasn't so great to begin with."

Laura shot him a narrow look. "What do you mean?"

He shrugged. "Look, it's not my place to say anything, but I had the impression your mom wasn't all that happy." He didn't have to say it: *before Ian.*

There was a time Laura would have told him he was crazy, but now she found herself asking, "Did she say anything to make you think that?"

"Just a hunch."

Laura sighed. "Nothing would surprise me at this point."

Around the next bend, the Vincenzi house came into view. Ranch style, like hers, with a long dirt drive. But that was where the comparison ended. Anna, her hands perpetually full with her mother and Monica, clearly had no time or energy left-over for upkeep. Paint peeled from the clapboard siding, and the roof was a checkerboard of missing shingles. In the yard, weeds had overtaken the lawn and the hedge, as Hector had predicted, was badly overgrown. It would take weeks to get this place in shape.

Laura felt angry all of a sudden. You'd think Monica, with all her money, would do more than simply employ Anna. Mrs. Vincenzi was *her* mother, too. The same was true of Anna's younger sister, Liz — not as rich as Monica, but successful enough. The least they could do was pitch in for full-time nursing care.

She knocked on the front door. Usually Anna rushed to answer it, looking flushed and a bit anxious, as if half expecting bad news. But when the creak of footsteps finally came, they sounded weary and defeated — as if bad news had already found Anna.

Laura barely recognized the woman who answered the door. Anna's mousy hair was disheveled, her skin blotchy as if from exertion. Even the robe she had on was buttoned up wrong. Maybe it wasn't Mrs.

Vincenzi who'd screamed, Laura thought, but Anna herself. Out of sheer frustration.

"Laura. Hector. What a nice — I wasn't expecting you." Anna's smile flickered like a faulty bulb. "Sorry, but this really isn't a good time. I don't mean to be rude, but —"

She broke off at the sound of a loud shriek: old Mrs. Vincenzi having one of her spells.

"Anything we can do to help?" Laura asked gently, not wanting to intrude. At the same time, it would have been inhumane to walk away.

"No. Thanks. I can handle it." Anna cast an anxious glance over her shoulder.

Laura was grateful when Hector pushed past her into the house, saying firmly, "We're here. Might as well pitch in." Anna must have been grateful, too. She didn't protest.

The living room was dark, as if there hadn't been a moment to so much as draw the curtains. It smelled, too. Like a house that had been shut up too long. There was something so tired and sad about it all. Like a tire with the air slowly leaking out of it.

They found Mrs. Vincenzi crouched inside the hall closet, arms over her head, and knees pulled in tightly against her chest. She lifted her head only long enough to let loose another shriek. "Joey, no! Not the face! *Please not the face.*"

Laura turned to Anna. "Who's Joey?"

"My father." Anna's shoulders slumped. Right now she looked closer to her mother's age than Laura's. "He died when I was little." She didn't need to elaborate.

Hector lowered into a crouch, the worn heels of his boots hovering an inch or so off the floor. "It's okay, Mrs. Vincenzi. Nobody's going to hurt you." He spoke soothingly, the way he did to horses.

"Please, no. *Noooooooooooooooo.*" The old woman began to sob, clutching her head as if to shield it from imaginary blows. Empty hangers clacked overhead.

"Mama. For God's sake, Mama." Anna sounded close to tears herself.

The old woman's head jerked up to reveal pale wet eyes staring in naked terror at something only she could see. "Don't you *dare* lay a hand on those children! Joey, don't you dare!"

"It's okay, Mrs. Vincenzi. He's not here. You can come out now." Hector went on in that low, gentle voice no horse or human had ever failed to respond to. He held out a blunt, work-hardened hand.

The old woman eyed it with suspicion. "Go 'way."

"Mama . . ." Anna pleaded.

The old woman dissolved once more into sobs, rocking back and forth as she keened, "No . . . not the children . . . *no . . . no . . . no . . .*"

Laura hunkered down beside Hector. "Would you like to see your children, Mrs. Vincenzi?"

This time, when she lifted her head, the expression on the old woman's pale, doughy face — which bore a disquieting resemblance to Anna's — was one of trembling expectancy. "They're all right?"

"They're fine. I'll take you to them if you like." Laura held out a hand.

A long moment passed. Then all at once, the old woman went as boneless as the old coat sagging from a hanger overhead. Bony fingers, more claw than hand, closed around Laura's. She couldn't help noticing, as Mrs. Vincenzi staggered to her feet, that her quilted pink robe was the twin to Anna's. She had a sudden image of Monica killing two birds with one stone at Christmas. Wouldn't that be just like her?

A short while later, with her mother settled on the sofa in front of the TV, peaceful as a baby, Anna turned to them. "I don't know how to thank you. If you hadn't come along when you did —" Her voice caught.

"What are neighbors for?" Laura was careful not to make too big a deal. It would only embarrass Anna.

She bit her lip. "You've done so much already."

"It goes both ways. You have no idea what a load off my mind it is knowing you're just down the road." One day, when she could, Anna would return the favor.

Anna smiled weakly, fingering a button on her robe. "Isn't this awful? I can't even offer you a cup of coffee."

"We've had ours. Why don't you sit while I make you some?"

Laura looked around to find that Hector had slipped out the door — no doubt to trim the hedge. She took Anna's arm, leading her into the cheerless kitchen with its wallpaper sporting a faded pattern of windmills. It was spotless except for the dirty dishes in the sink.

Anna followed her gaze and blushed. "I haven't had a chance to wash up. She kept me up half the night."

Laura wondered again about the scream Maude had heard. "Did she wander off again? Maude thought she heard —" She broke off at the sound of Hector yelling from the backyard. Lord, what now?

The two women raced to the back door.

The yard was as overgrown as the front, and it was a moment before Laura spotted him, standing under an acacia tree from which an old tire swing hung, staring fixedly at something on the ground.

She was halfway to him when she saw something sticking up from the tall weeds: a hand with long red fingernails. Below it, a pale belly over which flies swarmed thickly.

Her stomach rushed up into her throat.

Beside her, Anna screamed.

"I think," Hector's voice seemed to come from very far away, "we'd better call the police."

Chapter 12

Finch watched the cop out of the corner of her eye. He was young, with short brown hair and freckles, and looked a little like Potsie on that old show *Happy Days* on TV Land. Not like cops back home, with their hard eyes that missed nothing and had seen it all. This one, more than his partner, seemed nervous and unsure. He was writing something in his notepad, concentrating so hard the tip of his tongue stuck out. She shivered, pressing a throw cushion to her belly.

Now he was turning to Maude. "Mrs. Wickersham, this scream — when would you say you heard it?"

Maude, seated beside Finch on the couch, frowned at the rug, from which tufts of dog hair stuck up like cowlicks. "Well, let's see . . . it must have been around three."

"Are you certain of the time?" The older cop's eyes narrowed. He was as heavyset as his partner was lean, with long sideburns

369

and slicked-back hair like they wore in the seventies.

"Why, yes."

"Could it have been closer to midnight?" Potsie put in.

"No, it was three."

"You're sure?"

"If you must know, I felt the call of nature." Maude blushed a little. "I get up the same time every night."

Even Finch had to smile. She glanced over at Laura who sat on the easy chair opposite the couch, Hector perched on its arm, a hand resting on her shoulder. They both looked pretty shook up.

"Did you hear anything else unusual?" the older slick-haired cop asked.

"Just the scream. It was loud enough to wake the dead." Maude flushed at her unfortunate choice of words.

"Nothing else?" the young cop asked. "No gunshot?"

Maude shot Laura a confused look. "I thought you said she'd been stabbed."

Laura shook her head in disgust, as if at the dirty trick he was playing: trying to confuse Maude into revealing something she might've been holding back. She was very pale, and kept shifting in her chair, glancing up at Hector every so often. Obviously this was her first experience with a dead person. Finch felt an almost big-sisterly sympathy.

"We don't have the coroner's report yet." Mr. Mod Squad folded his arms over his chest, scanning the living room as if he half expected to see a bloody knife sticking out from under the couch.

"We've told you everything we know." Laura spoke politely, but it was clear she'd had enough. "Maude heard a scream. We thought it might have been our next-door neighbor, Mrs. Vincenzi. She sometimes wanders off, and gets . . . disoriented. When Hec — Mr. Navarro — and I went to check up on her . . . well, you know the rest."

Mr. Mod Squad's beady eyes fixed on Hector. "What is your relationship to Ms. Kiley, sir?"

Laura glanced up again at Hector, her cheeks coloring.

"I work for her," he said.

"Do you reside here as well?"

"I have a room off the barn."

"And you didn't hear this alleged scream?"

"I was out until late. Shooting pool at the Red Rooster with some of my buddies." Hector hadn't moved a muscle, but

Finch could feel his tension across the room.

"Can you give us the names of these friends, sir?"

Something flashed in Hector's eyes, and in an uncharacteristically sarcastic voice, he answered, "Sure. For a couple of beers, I'll bet they'd even vouch for me."

Mr. Mod Squad frowned, clearly not amused. "At some point we may need you to come down to the station for further questioning. Would you have a problem with that?"

"Depends."

"Sir?"

"On whether or not I'll need a lawyer."

The cops exchanged glances, and as if coming to a mutual decision backed off — for the moment, at least. Finch was just beginning to hope that maybe, just maybe, she was off the hook, too, when Potsie turned to her.

"And what exactly is *your* relationship to Ms. Kiley, Miss — ?"

"Finch." It came out more of a squeak.

"Miss Finch." He jotted it in his notepad.

"She's a friend of the family," Laura put in.

"Out for a visit?" Mr. Mod Squad eyed

Finch suspiciously.

"She lives with us."

Laura's clipped tone was enough to steer them away from that topic — clearly the cops had no interest in wading through unpleasant family business. When the younger one flipped his notebook shut, it was all Finch could do to keep from sagging with relief. There'd be more questions down the line. Every possible witness would be grilled, every piece of evidence examined. They might even run a check on her. But at least this would buy her time to figure out what her next move should be.

Laura walked the cops to the door. They all waited in silence until the patrol car had pulled out of the driveway. Maude was the first to speak. "Do you think they'll find the person who did it?"

"They'll arrest *somebody*." Hector lurched to his feet with a look of disgust and paced over to the fireplace. Finch recalled the story of how he'd slipped into the country illegally, and how even after he'd gotten his green card the cops were constantly on his tail, harassing him at every turn. Once even arresting him for loitering. Finch knew exactly what that was like; it had made her see him in a way she might not have otherwise.

"You have an alibi," Laura reminded him. "You were out with friends."

"Yeah, until a little after midnight. Then I was asleep in bed. Alone."

Laura shot him a startled look. "Alone?"

"That's what I said."

"What about the woman I saw?"

"What woman?"

Laura flushed. "Outside the barn. It must have been around six or so. I thought . . ." She bit her lip.

Hector shook his head, insisting, "I wasn't with anyone last night."

They shared a look. If Hector had been alone, then who was she?

"Well, one thing's for sure." Maude got up to straighten the afghan that had slipped off the back of the couch. "None of us will get a good night's sleep until whoever did it is behind bars."

For a long moment no one spoke. The only sounds were the ticking of the clock on the mantel and the faint skittering of a mouse behind the baseboard. Even the dogs and cats were quiet for a change. At last, Finch hauled herself to her feet.

"I'm going for a walk," she announced.

They all looked at her as if she'd said she was going to the moon.

"Stay close to home," Laura warned.

Finch knew she ought to have been as worried about the murderer on the loose as they were, but an odd sense of relief swept over her just then. She thought, *At least they don't think it's me.*

"It's my life's work."
Sister Agnes rocked back on her heels to survey the garden she'd been weeding. It followed the path that wound along the sunny side of the chapel, an odd assortment of bushes, trees, and flowering herbs, each with its own inscribed plaque. Finch bent to examine one.

Cinnamon
(Cinnamomum zeylanicum)
"I have perfumed my bed with myrrh, aloes, and <u>cinnamon</u>."
Proverbs 7:17

"I started it when I first came here as a novice," Sister Agnes went on. "Do you know how many plants and trees there are in the Bible? Eighteen. I remember thinking, wouldn't it be wonderful if they were out where we could see them? A biblical garden — just as it might have looked in the days of Christ."
"It must have taken a long time," Finch

said, noting how large some of the bushes and trees had grown.

"Thirty-eight years come spring." Sister Agnes set aside her trowel and rose awkwardly to her feet, wincing a bit at the stiffness in her limbs. "And don't me old bones know it."

"You're not so old."

"Old enough to remember when all this was but a few wee slips of green." She limped over to a tall bush bursting with bright pink blossoms. "This is one of my favorites, though perhaps the least rare."

Finch studied the plaque.

Rose
(Nerium oleander)
"Listen to me and blossom like the Rose that grows on the bank"
Ecclesiastes 39:13

"It doesn't look like any rosebush I've ever seen," she said.

"That's the beauty of it, don't you see?" Sister Agnes said. "Expecting one thing, and finding another. Like the good book itself. A great deal lies in the eye — or heart, as the case may be — of the beholder."

"What's that one over there?" Finch gestured toward a tall tree pointing like a finger toward heaven.

"Cedar of Lebanon." Sister Agnes quoted by heart, " 'The righteous shall flourish like the palm tree . . . he shall grow like a cedar in Lebanon. Those that flourish in the house of the Lord shall flourish in the courts of our Lord. They shall still bring forth fruit in old age . . .' " She broke off with a smile, staring down at her dirt-stained hands. When she looked up again, her smiling gaze fixed on Finch with a directness that was both comforting and a bit disquieting. "Now, what was it you came all this way to see me about?"

The girl glanced about, but there was no one to overhear. Only the sound of an organ drifting from the chapel, accompanied by a sweet, if somewhat thready soprano singing a hymn. *When Jesus wept, the falling tear in mercy flow'd . . .*

Cautiously, Finch said, "I want your opinion about something."

"You're surely welcome to it, though I'm afraid I'm not much of an authority in secular matters."

"It's . . . well, it's more of a religious question."

"Oh?" The little nun studied her with interest. "These days I'm not sure I'm much of an authority on that, either." She gave a rueful little smile, groping absently for her rosary beads.

"Would it be a sin for a nun to lie if it was for a good cause?"

Sister Agnes lifted a brow. "Now what cause would that be?"

Finch felt her cheeks grow warm. "Mine."

"I see." Sister Agnes's expression didn't alter. "And just why would this nun be lying for you?"

"They found another body," Finch blurted. "This morning, behind our neighbor's house."

"Jesus, Mary, and Joseph."

Sister Agnes rapidly made the sign of the cross, her face nearly as white as her wimple. Finch realized her mistake at once, and was quick to set her straight. "I had nothing to do with it."

"Now, why would I think such a thing?" But it was clear she had, if only for an instant.

"The cops came. They asked a bunch of questions."

"I should think so."

Finch recalled Hector's words. "They're not going to stop until they arrest someone."

"Let's just hope it's the right someone."

Finch dropped her gaze, staring at a

weed that had been overlooked. "I told you before I was running away, but I didn't tell you why. The thing is . . . I did something. I don't know if it was against the law, but I'm sure it's a sin. If I were Catholic, it would probably get me sent to hell."

"Shh, child." Sister Agnes brought a hand to her face. It smelled of the herbs Maude used in cooking. "Not another word. Whatever it is, the Lord knows I'm in enough trouble as it is without any of that lying we spoke of."

Finch raised a pair of burning eyes to Sister Agnes. "If it comes to that, would you hide me for a little while? If it was to keep me from going to jail?" There, it was out. She'd done the unspeakable: asking a nun, not just to break the law, but to commit a sin.

Before Sister Agnes could reply, the crunch of gravel caused Finch to wheel about. A tall nun with a face as narrow as a boot was gliding toward them along the path, hands folded in prayer. Her long fingers were pale against the dark fabric of her habit.

"There you are, Sister. I've been looking everywhere." She sounded impatient, as if Sister Agnes ought to have known some how.

"Sister Beatrice." Sister Agnes's expression clouded over briefly, but she quickly recovered her manners. "I don't believe you've met my young friend, Finch."

Finch put out a hand, which Sister Beatrice shook tepidly. She reminded Finch of a teacher she'd had in the sixth grade, Mrs. Friedlander, who if she caught you chewing gum in class forced you to wear it on your forehead the rest of the day.

"Sister Agnes is showing off her pet project, I see." Sister Beatrice smiled, exposing a row of small teeth below a pale expanse of gum.

"What did you want to see me about, Sister?" The older nun's voice took on a slight edge. She gazed, pointedly it seemed, at a bushy, silver-leafed shrub with a plaque that read:

Wormwood
(Artemisia Herba-Alta)
"*. . . bitter as <u>wormwood</u>*
sharp as a two-edged sword."
Proverbs 5:4

"Reverend Mother would like a word with you." Sister Beatrice made it sound as if some terrible punishment were in store.

Sister Agnes looked stricken. "What . . . what does she want?"

It was clearly the response Sister Beatrice had been after. She smiled with thinly veiled triumph. "I'm sure I couldn't say. I don't presume to know the mind of our esteemed mother."

Finch watched her turn, long skirt rustling over the path as she headed back in the direction of the chapel. How could a nun be so mean?

"Oh, glory, what have I done now?" Sister Agnes brought a trembling hand to her cheek.

Finch felt a rush of indignation. "She's just trying to cause trouble." She didn't know Sister Beatrice, but she knew the type.

The little nun cast her a gently reproving look. "You mustn't say such things, child. We're not allowed even to *think* them. All of us are equally blessed in the sight of our Lord. Even," she sighed, "if some of us feel a tad bit superior to others."

Silence fell. There was only the cheeping of baby birds in the fig tree overhead and the distant voice singing, *When Jesus groan'd . . . a trembling seiz'd all the guilty world a-round . . .*

Finch began to feel uncomfortable.

Sister Agnes still hadn't given her an answer. And why should she? Didn't she have enough on her mind as it was? *It was stupid of me to have asked.*

She was about to turn away when a soft hand lighted on her arm. She looked into a pair of blue eyes filled with kindness. "If there was ever any need of it, and I'm not saying there would, I'd not be above turnin' a blind eye to certain things. It wouldn't exactly be a lie now, would it?" The little nun reached into her pocket, and produced a ring of keys. Detaching one, she pressed it into Finch's palm. "It's to the honey house. No one, not even the police, would think to look for you there."

Chapter 13

The last weekend in August, when the hysteria surrounding the murder had settled into a quiet paranoia, Alice and Laura met for lunch at the Tree House. In the shade of its ancient live oak, over ice tea and shrimp salads, they discussed the latest development in what had become known, simply, as The Problem with Mother.

"I can't believe she's actually going *through* with it," Alice said.

Who in their right mind would trade Isla Verde for a poky little house in the Flats? She'd assumed her mother would come to her senses, but from what her sister was telling her — that construction had already begun — it didn't seem too likely.

"Believe it." Laura spoke grimly. "If everything goes according to schedule, she'll be moving in next month."

"Oh God, this is worse than I thought."

"That's not even the worst of it."

Alice groaned. How could it get any worse?

"She found someone to rent Isla Verde," Laura said. "He's signing the lease next week."

"Who?" Alice felt a twinge of guilt. She hadn't spoken to her mother in days. She was usually out when Sam called, and the messages had been piling up lately.

"Aubrey Roellinger."

"The conductor?" Alice had heard of him, of course. Who hadn't? She recalled, too, something in the news a while back about his wife's death in a car accident. "What about Lupe and Guillermo? What's going to happen to them?"

"Part of the deal is they get to stay in the guest house." Laura gave a small wry smile. "After all these years, Mom is finally getting her wish. She's forcing Lupe to retire."

Alice shook her head. "None of this makes any sense."

"Tell me about it." Laura picked at her salad, looking fretful. "For one thing, how safe will it be, Mom living all alone out there in the middle of nowhere?"

The thought of Ian surfaced. "Assuming she *will* be alone."

"I'd rather see her shacked up with Ian than . . ." Laura couldn't bring herself to say it.

384

The murder had left her deeply shaken, Alice knew. The victim, a young teacher at Portola High, was rumored to have had a drug problem, and there'd been some talk of a drug deal gone bad, but no one had any doubt that the homeless man's killer had struck again. Laura confessed that she now slept with a loaded shotgun by her bed.

"Any new developments on that front?" Alice was careful to speak in code. At the height of lunch hour, in the town's most popular eatery, an overheard remark could be like a match dropped into kerosene.

"The police kept Hector down at the station for hours." Laura dropped her voice, glancing about to make sure no one was listening. "It was like the Spanish Inquisition."

The indignant flush that rose in her cheeks said more about her feelings for him than anything. Alice wondered if Hector had caught on, or if he'd even noticed the change in her sister. She'd lost weight, for one thing, at least ten pounds. In the spaghetti-strapped shift she wore, a flattering yellow-and-red print, it really showed. She was wearing her hair differently, too, smoothed back over her ears with a pair of silver combs.

"They must be desperate to pin it on someone," Alice said.

Her gaze strayed to Melodie Wycoff loading a tray of drinks at the bar. She didn't seem to be in any particular hurry — too busy flirting with Denny the bartender. Everyone knew she was cheating on her husband. Jim Wycoff's quick temper was common knowledge as well. Alice had heard enough statistics on cops going berserk to wonder if Melodie might be next to land in the morgue. She shuddered at the thought.

Several people were browsing by the bookshelves in back, where sunlight filtered through the makeshift roof of corrugated plastic sheeting, throwing crisscross patterns over the patio below. It was said the Tree House had more titles than they could keep track of, and Alice knew that to be a fact. A couple of months ago she'd been lucky enough to come across a first edition of *The Pickwick Papers*, priced at a dollar fifty. For a glorious moment she'd thought about buying it, but knowing how much it would mean to the Rybacks, had brought it to their attention instead. Its value on the rare book market, she imagined, would cover a good portion of Davey's medical bills.

"They picked up a migrant worker the other day." Laura interrupted her reverie. "But he had an alibi. He was in jail at the time, on a drunk-driving charge."

Alice brought her gaze back to her sister. "Great, just great. So our mother will be at the mercy of any psycho who happens along? Just exactly where *is* this house, anyway?"

"Just off San Pedro, out by the old schoolhouse. It's not as bad as you think. In fact, it's kind of cute."

Alice felt another guilty twinge, stronger this time. She shouldn't be hearing about this from Laura; she should have driven out to see for herself. Even so, she found herself saying, "I'm sure this isn't what Dad had in mind when he bought it."

"I don't think Mom even knew about it until now."

"Why wouldn't he have told her?"

"I don't know. It doesn't make much sense, does it?"

"A lot got lost in the shuffle when he was sick."

Alice didn't like dwelling on that particular time; the memory was still too painful. The long days and nights standing vigil at his bedside, watching him waste away until there was almost nothing left. The awful agony of knowing there wasn't a damn thing she, or anyone, could do to prevent his suffering.

"I'm sure it was something like that." Laura nibbled halfheartedly at her salad.

"Whatever, it sounds as if she's got it all worked out." Alice felt suddenly lost. Sam was supposed to be the one off her rocker, but right now she seemed more certain of herself and what she wanted out of life than either of her daughters.

"There's just one wrinkle," Laura said. "We still don't know about Ian."

Alice choked a little, the thought of him like a bone in her throat. She reached for her glass, and over its tinkling rim flashed her sister an ironic smile. "I guess no news is good news."

Laura leaned close to confide, "All I know is that lately Mom's been seeing a lot of Tom Kemp."

Alice perked up. "Seriously?"

"Don't get too excited. It's not what you think. He's helping out with the house — permits, contractor, that kind of stuff."

"Maybe he'll grow on her."

"Maybe." Laura looked doubtful.

They shared an ironic smile. Time was their mother had been as predictable as the seasons. But all that had changed. Now she was like the Santa Ana winds that could sweep down out of nowhere, bringing sudden extremes in temperature and whipping small blazes into forest fires. It was anyone's guess what she'd do next.

"Wes tells me Ian's in Big Sur," Alice said.

"Really? If Mom told me I must have forgotten. These past few weeks, I've been running around like a chicken with my head cut off."

"How's it going?"

Alice glanced at David Ryback, greeting someone at the door. Like Laura, he'd taken over the family business when his dad retired. That had been — what? Eight, nine years ago. Since then, the Tree House, already popular among locals, had become a tourist destination as well. David had seen to it by assiduously courting the press, ensuring that mentions of the café appeared regularly in travel articles and best-in-the-region roundups. He'd also had the bright idea of bottling the olallie berry jam for which they were known. It was available in the gift shop along with T-shirts, mugs, and a Tree House cookbook. Would her sister have as much success with Delarosa's? Or be unable to keep up with its demands?

"I'm managing," Laura said. "Thanks to Finch. She's been a godsend."

The forced cheer in her voice made Alice ask, "Business still off?"

"Not so you'd notice, but we're down from last year."

"Pardon me for stating the obvious," Alice said, "but why aren't you online like everyone else?"

Laura rolled her eyes. "Believe me, it wasn't for lack of trying. Mom wouldn't hear of it. She'd always say it wasn't the kind of image she wanted for Delarosa's."

Once more, they shared an ironic smile.

"Mom's not running things anymore," Alice reminded her.

"Yeah, but I'm up to here." Laura held a hand to her chin. "This is the first Saturday in weeks I've been able to duck out for more than a sandwich. I can barely squeeze in bathroom breaks. Where would I find the time to put together a Web site?"

"I could help. I know a few people."

Laura eyed her the way a drowning woman might view a life preserver. "Oh, Alice, that'd be —" She broke off. "Would it cost much? I'm not sure I can afford it."

"I'll take care of everything, don't worry." Alice spoke lightly, knowing how sensitive her sister could be when it came to money. "You can pay me back in shares."

Laura reached across the table and squeezed her hand. "Thanks, Al. You have no idea how much I appreciate this."

"No problem."

"What about you? What's next?"

Alice's thoughts turned to her own plight. Her show was being canceled. A royal bender that had landed Marty in court-ordered rehab had proved the final straw. There'd been no talk yet of replacing him, but in the halls of CTN it was as if the air conditioner had suddenly been cranked up to near freezing. People who'd been nice to Alice were suddenly avoiding her. People who'd avoided her were suddenly being nice. They all knew the score: Wes wouldn't fire her, but one way or another she was dead meat.

"We're kicking around a few ideas." Alice affected a breezy tone. "Nothing definite yet."

"Well, at least you won't starve."

She was only teasing, but it struck a nerve. Alice didn't need any more reminders that she was living off the fat of the land — Wes's, to be exact. Eager to change the subject, she asked, "How's everything on the home front?"

"Maude's decided to stay."

"What about Finch?"

Laura brightened. "Oh Al, she's such a great kid. All she needed was a little time to come out of her shell. In fact, I've been thinking —" She broke off suddenly, the color draining from her face.

Alice followed her gaze. Standing by the door was Laura's ex-husband, Peter. He stood chatting with David, an arm about his very pregnant wife. Alice hadn't seen him since the divorce, but he looked the same. Still handsome in a watered-down, weak-chinned sort of way. His blond wife, bursting like a ripe peach, was far prettier than he deserved.

"Let's get out of here," Alice muttered, signaling for the check.

"No." Laura clutched her fork like a lifeline. "He got rid of me once before, he's not going to do it again. We're staying if it kills me." When Melodie arrived at their table, she announced brightly, "I'll have the olallie berry pie with a scoop of vanilla ice cream."

"Make that two." Alice couldn't remember the last time she'd splurged on anything so fattening, but it wouldn't kill her. Besides, it was in a worthy cause.

They were digging into their desserts

when Peter and his wife wandered by on the way to their table. He caught sight of them and started, then flashed his best salesman's grin.

"Laura. Alice. What a surprise."

What a schmuck, Alice thought.

Her sister smiled. "You're looking well, Peter." *Score one for Laura.* You'd never know by looking at her that she was dying inside. "I don't believe I've met your wife." She stood up to offer her hand. "Hi, I'm Laura. You must be Georgia."

Peter's wife, clearly desperate to avoid a scene, shook her hand with an enthusiasm that was almost embarrassing. "Laura, hi. Wow. This is amazing. I've heard so much about you."

Laura's eyes dropped to her stomach. "When's the baby due?" She managed to sound warm, even interested.

"Just one more week to go." Georgia patted her belly.

"Well, the best of luck." Laura's easy smile widened to include Peter as well. "And congratulations."

It wasn't until Peter and his wife were seated at the other end of the patio that she let out a ragged breath. She looked shaken and a bit pale, though as determined as ever to put up a good front. She even took her time with the check, insisting it was her turn to pick up the tab.

It wasn't until they were out on the sidewalk that she moaned, slumping onto the bench next to a rack of tattered paperbacks with a slotted box for paying on the honor system. "Oh God, why did I have to order the berry pie? Tell me my teeth aren't blue." She bared them, managing to look both comical and miserable.

Alice struggled not to smile. "Only a little." When Laura flashed her an evil look, she said, "Just kidding. They're fine."

"You're probably just saying that."

"Okay, then how about this? In a few years, he'll be bald and she'll have stretch marks from here to L.A."

"Is this supposed to make me feel better?"

Alice grabbed her hand and pulled her to her feet. "To hell with your ex-husband," she said, steering her sister down the sidewalk. "We have better things to do than listing all the reasons to hate him."

"Like what?"

"Like seeing this house of Mom's." Peter's wife had brought home the fact that their mother was two and a half months pregnant, a fact that Alice could no longer ignore.

But Laura was shaking her head. "Thanks, I've already seen it. I have to get back to the shop."

"I thought you said Finch could manage."

Laura glanced at her watch. "It's after two."

"We'll be back by three-thirty."

"I don't know . . ."

Alice tucked her arm through her sister's. "You can call from the car." As they made their way down the street, she was struck by the irony of where she'd parked her Porsche: in front of The Pea in the Pod maternity shop. It seemed an omen somehow . . . or maybe just a cruel cosmic joke.

The first thing Alice noticed when she pulled in was the yellow pickup parked alongside their mother's Honda, a stack of lumber jutting from its tailgate. She found a spot in the shade, under an acacia dripping with powdery yellow blossoms, and switched off the engine. Laura, who suffered from hay fever, promptly sneezed.

"Bless you." Alice handed her a Kleenex.

"Thanks." Laura sneezed again, then blew her nose.

They exchanged a solemn look. This

wasn't going to be easy, Alice thought. Not because she was here to give their mother a piece of her mind, but just the opposite. She'd come to listen and hopefully learn. Which might be the hardest thing of all.

They climbed from the car and started up the walk. From inside came the pounding of hammers and high whine of a power saw. The front door stood open, and sunlight lay in pale oblongs over the partially laid floor. From Laura's description of what it had looked like before, Alice couldn't believe how much had been accomplished in so short a time. Tom must be on intimate terms with half the town council to have gotten permits so quickly.

She stepped inside, her heart quickening. All around were signs of construction. Piles of sawdust and scrap ends of lumber, tools and sawhorses, a paper sack spilling nails. The living room was small but cozy, with double-hung windows and a brick fireplace. Alice had expected something a lot more rundown. But this . . . well, it was certainly livable.

She picked her way around a pile of lumber. "Is Mrs. Kiley around?" she yelled to one of the workers over the whine of the saw.

"*Allá, en la cocina!*" He yelled back, gesturing toward the doorway on her left.

In the kitchen she found their mother deep in conversation with the contractor, a bandy-legged little man in sawdust-speckled jeans with a carpenter's pencil stuck jauntily behind one sunburned ear. Sam glanced up with a look of surprised pleasure.

"Girls! I wasn't expecting you." There was nothing in her voice to suggest any tension between them. "Carl, these are my daughters, Laura and Alice." She gave Alice a small, tentative smile.

In the few weeks since Alice had last seen her, Sam had blossomed. It wasn't just that she was beginning to show, she looked younger, almost . . . luminous. Alice felt oddly excluded, which didn't make any sense. If anyone should feel shut out, it was her mother.

Laura glanced about, remarking, "I can't believe how much you've done."

"It looks like more work than it really is," Sam said. "Overall, the place is pretty sound. Come on, I'll give you the grand tour." They followed her down the hall into a large, sunny bedroom, originally two small ones with the adjoining wall knocked out. "This," she said with a sweeping gesture, "is mine."

Alice felt her stomach drop out from under her. It was all so surreal. Was she really here, in this strange house, being shown the bedroom her mother and Ian might be sharing?

"It certainly is . . . airy," she said.

She didn't dare ask which room was the nursery.

"It faces east, so I'll get the morning light. You know how much I love waking up to sunshine."

Sam stood at the window, gazing out at the yard with a secret little smile. Its grass and shrubs were a jungle, but the view of the mountains more than made up for it. Off in the distance Alice could see Toyon Ridge, with the snowcapped Two Sisters Peaks just beyond.

"Nice closet." Laura wandered over to peer into it. "You'll have plenty of room for all your stuff."

"I won't need much," Sam said. "Most of it's going into storage."

"The furniture, too?" Alice asked.

"The bulk of it stays put. I'm sure Mr. Roellinger will take good care of it." Sam turned away from the window to smile at her. "If he doesn't, he'll have Lupe to answer to." She didn't seem the least bit bothered that *she* wouldn't have the use of all those lovely antiques, most of which had been in the family for generations.

What about us? Alice wanted to cry. *Are we going to be left behind, too?* She thought of the family albums with photos of her and Laura growing up. They'd probably be put into storage as well . . . to make room for ones filled with snapshots of the baby.

"I can't imagine you anywhere but at Isla Verde," she said.

There wasn't a hint of regret in the look Sam gave her. "I *will* miss it in some ways. But you have no idea how much work it was. Now I'll be able to afford a full-time property manager. Believe me, it'll be a relief."

"You never said anything before."

"Why complain when you have so much else to be grateful for?"

"You could have prepared us, that's all."

"Prepared you for what?" Sam spoke lightly, but with a new firmness. "Did either of you ask how I felt when *you* moved out? Or when you got married?"

Alice eyed her in astonishment. She'd expected to find her mother overwhelmed, maybe even a little distraught. But standing before her was a straight-backed, clear-eyed woman who wasn't giving an inch. *My God,* she thought, *do I even know this person?*

She ran her finger along a sill coated with plaster dust. "You haven't said where Ian fits into all this." She spoke with the careful precision of the hammers pounding down the hall.

Sam's gaze slid away. "We haven't made any plans yet."

"Well, if I were you," Alice went on, "I wouldn't count on him for Thanksgiving." She didn't know where this meanness was coming from. Hadn't she come to make peace? "Wes can tell you what he's like — flaky and irresponsible. Why do you think he was sent away as a teenager?"

"Alice . . ." Laura spoke warningly at her back.

Sam stepped away from the window. A shadow fell over her face, and she looked all at once her age — a woman nearing fifty. "I think I know him a little better than you do."

"The way you knew Daddy? My God, you didn't even know about this *house*."

Sam regarded her intently. Her gray-green eyes were cool, her mouth curled faintly in irony. "I thought we were discussing Ian."

Alice felt the world shift a little, and she was suddenly unsure of her footing. "I just meant . . ." She faltered.

"If anyone was irresponsible, it was your father." Sam, wearing an odd, faraway expression, smoothed an edge of rose-patterned paper that was peeling away from the wall. "You didn't know, did you? All those hare-brained schemes and sure-fire investments that never amounted to a hill of beans. That was your dad, too."

There was a low buzzing in Alice's head, like a swarm of angry hornets. She edged back a step, her foot coming down on something wobbly — a loose board — and reached for the wall to keep from stumbling. "Dad wasn't like that. You're exaggerating."

"Why would I do that?" Sam shook her head sadly. "What would I possibly have to gain?"

"It's not fair." Alice began to tremble. "He isn't here to defend himself."

"No, he isn't," Sam said, not without a touch of regret.

Alice felt a sharp pain in her palm, and pulled her hand away to note dispassionately that it was bleeding. She must have scratched it with a nail, except oddly, she felt no pain. "Okay, maybe he made a few bad investments. That doesn't change the fact that he was a good father."

"Yes, and don't we have the pictures to

prove it?" A bitter note crept into her mother's voice.

Alice glanced at Laura, who looked as bewildered as she did. "What are you saying?"

Her mother's hard face was almost more than she could bear. "Did you ever wonder why your father is in every family photo and I'm in almost none? Who do you think was taking all those pictures?"

Alice had never thought of it one way or another. All she'd ever seen was what was *in* those photos: Dad cuddling them on his lap, helping build sand castles, holding them up to see into cages at the zoo. It had never occurred to her to wonder why her mother wasn't in them as well.

But that didn't prove anything. "If Daddy was really like that," she said with a casual cruelty that left her breathless, "why make the same mistake with Ian?"

"Appearances aren't everything."

"What do you *really* know about him?" Alice pushed on, her head ringing with the hammer blows from down the hall.

"I know he sees me for who I am, not for who he wants me to be."

Alice faltered. Was that what she'd been doing — holding her mother to an impossible set of standards? Maybe, but whose fault was that? All Alice's life hadn't she promoted the image of selfless wife and mother?

"How long do you think he'll stick around?" she asked in a voice that seemed to be coming from somewhere outside of her. "How many snapshots will *he* be in?"

Sam shook her head sadly. "Oh, Alice. What's made you so hard?" The house had fallen momentarily silent, and as she stepped toward them, Alice heard the faint crunch of plaster. "Is it Wes?"

Alice shot back, "This has nothing to do with Wes. Just because Ian is his son, the only son he'll ever have —" She broke off, then thought, *Sooner or later I'm going to have to tell them.* "All right, you might as well know. We're not having kids." She frowned at Laura, who was looking at her aghast. "It's not what you think. It was my decision as much as his."

But all at once that wasn't how it seemed. The looks on her mother's and sister's faces told a different story, that of a young bride coerced into giving in to her much older husband. Alice, feeling suddenly unsure of herself, abruptly wheeled. "I've seen enough," she said. "Come on, Laura, I'll drive you back into town."

★ ★ ★

Hours later she arrived home to find her husband tinkering with the grill. Master of the Universe meets Mr. Fix-It. She smiled at the picture he made, crouched on the patio in his shorts and T-shirt, one arm thrust up inside the barbecue — a brick behemoth big enough to roast a skewered pig — while blindly groping behind him for his wrench.

She picked it up and handed it to him. "Why not just call a repairman?"

"For one thing, we'd wait two weeks for what I can do in two minutes." He gave the loose nut a few turns with the wrench, grimacing the way men do: the universal male at work. "For another," he said through clenched teeth, "they'd charge two hundred for a two-dollar part."

"We can afford it," she said.

"The point," he gave a final twist, "isn't whether or not we can afford it." She knew what he was going to say even before he said it, "The point is not to get taken."

Alice's thoughts returned to her father. She'd known only his fun-loving side, but what if her mother was telling the truth? Was she supposed to think less of him now? She'd spent a good deal of the afternoon driving about aimlessly, pondering that very thought . . . only to conclude that, Rock of Gibraltar or no, her dad had been worth two of any other father.

"Are we barbecuing tonight?" She kept her voice light so Wes wouldn't know she'd been crying.

"I picked up some steaks while you were out." He brought his head up, wiping his greasy hands with a rag she recognized as an old pair of her panties.

"Oh God, I'm sorry. I forgot." It came back to her now: She'd promised to stop at the store on her way home.

He flashed her his just-left-of-center grin — the one she imagined the Red Baron had worn streaking across the sky in his World War I Fokker. "No big deal. I figured you had enough on your mind."

She felt tears just below the surface. How long since they'd sat down to a romantic dinner? Since they'd made love? As she gazed down at him, crouched on his heels with that damn pair of panties in one hand, a wave of longing swept through her.

"I'll make the salad." She'd started toward the house when she felt Wes's hand close about her ankle. He caressed it lightly with his thumb, smiling up at her lazily.

"All taken care of," he said.

"Wine?"

"Chilling in the fridge."

"Looks like you've thought of every-thing."

"Almost."

Wes slipped off her mule and began stroking her instep, sparking a flash of heat that left her trembling. Alice pulled her foot from his grasp and took a small back-ward hop, catching hold of the chaise longue. In the pool below, her reflection shimmered like the slow dissolve at a movie's end. She didn't know why she was so upset with Wes; what had he done to deserve it?

"I'm going inside." Her voice was small and tight.

Wes caught up with her as she was pushing open the sliding glass door. "Alice, what is it? What's wrong?" He caught hold of her, grabbing her by the shoulders and forcing her around.

Then they were in the den, Wes's den, all manly leather and inlaid teak, where the computer was always on and the fax ma-chine forever humming. She wrenched away so abruptly she lost her balance and plopped into the chair against the wall, an enormous leather club chair that reminded her of nothing so much as an oversize catcher's mitt.

She looked up at him. He seemed to tower over her. "I stopped at my mother's new house on the way home."

"And?"

"It wasn't what I expected."

They both knew the house was beside the point. Wes eyed her closely, crossing his arms over his chest. His faded gray T-shirt from the Iron Man Triathlon in which he'd competed back in 1976 — when she was only one year old — seemed to mock her.

"How did your mom seem?" he asked.

"Not what I expected, either. She . . ." Alice paused, struggling to put it into words. "She seems at peace. Like she doesn't give a damn what any of us thinks of all this."

"What about Ian? Where does he fit in?"

"I don't know. I'm not even sure she does."

Wes sighed, leaning back against his desk. Flying toasters floated across the computer screen at his back. "I guess we'll just have to wait and see how it all plays out."

Alice's head had begun to throb. Had he remembered to pick up Advil? "It's funny," she said, screwing a thumb into her temple. "My mother seems to be under the impression that *we're* not exactly rock solid."

Wes eyed her quizzically. "What would make her think that?"

"I told her there wouldn't be any grandchildren."

"I see." He looked tired all of a sudden. "I guess it always comes back to this, doesn't it?"

"Oh Wes." She swallowed against the lump in her throat. "When I said 'I do' I guess I wasn't thinking of all the 'I don'ts.'"

"Are you saying you're sorry we decided against kids?"

"No. Just . . . I'm not sure I knew what I was giving up."

Wes wore a cool, considering expression. What was he thinking? That she was no different from her mother, pretending all this time to be someone she wasn't? She wouldn't blame him if he felt tricked. *He* had never led her down the garden path.

"I didn't know you felt this strongly about it," he said.

"I didn't, either."

"Alice . . ." Wes straightened. She was shocked to see his dark eyes glittering with tears. She'd never seen him cry, not even when his mother had nearly died last year. "If it's that important to you, I don't want to stand in your way."

Alice jerked a little in surprise. "What are you saying?"

"We can have a baby if that's what you want."

"You mean it?"

"I don't say anything I don't mean." He smiled a little. "You, of all people, should know that."

"I wouldn't want it to be a burden."

"No child of ours would ever be a burden."

The tears that had been shimmering below the surface spilled over, dropping into her lap. "Oh Wes. I didn't think you would . . ." She rose unsteadily to her feet.

Wes drew her into his arms. "You mean more to me than anything in the world." She could feel his fingers trembling a little as he stroked her head. "Anything else is just the icing on the cake."

"I love you."

"If I've been unfair —"

"No." She shook her head, his soft shirt grazing her cheek. He smelled of bay rum and barbecue. "You've never been anything but honest."

"Which is more than I can say for you." He drew back to smile at her. "You've been smoking, haven't you?"

She blushed, feeling as guilty as a schoolgirl. "Just one. In the car."

"Not," he said, "that I don't find it sexy as hell. Reminds me of when we were first dating." He undid the top button of her blouse. "You wearing anything under this?"

"Why don't you find out for yourself?"

He reached in to cup a bare breast, stroking her nipple until it stiffened. It was like a bolt of lightning shooting down through her navel. "Promise me one thing." He nuzzled her neck. "If we ever get divorced, you'll take me as part of the settlement."

"That's not funny." She smiled anyway.

"It wasn't meant to be." When he finished unbuttoning her blouse, he worked a hand down the waistband of her skirt. "I could never let you go. You have this strange hold over me, you see."

"Never mind your damned settlement. We're not getting divorced."

"Is that a promise?"

"Guaranteed."

He pulled her against him. She could feel how excited he was, and that excited her even more. She pushed a hand up under his T-shirt, splaying her fingers over his back, feeling the dimple of scar tissue from when he'd been wounded in Vietnam. It reminded her of how brave he was . . . and how close she might have come to losing him.

"There's just one thing . . ." she whispered.

"What's that?"

"Promise *me* you won't always give in. I might get spoiled." She unzipped his shorts, grinning down at him. "See what I mean? We haven't had dinner, and I'm already thinking about dessert."

They usually took it slow, one button at a time, stopping to kiss and fondle along the way. But she felt suddenly impatient. Even the time it would take to climb the stairs was more than she could wait. She wanted it *now:* fast, furious, hot enough to curl her toes.

They stripped off their clothes, and Wes lowered her onto the sofa, straddling her while holding her arms pinned over her head. She cried out as he thrust into her, feeling a small, sweet ache at her core.

A minute later, when she felt him holding back, she cried, "No. Don't stop."

"I'll come," he whispered hoarsely.

"It's okay."

"What about — ?" He didn't have to say it. The condoms were upstairs.

"Wrong time of the month," she murmured. *The wrong time for what?* whispered a tiny voice in her head.

Then Wes was moving inside her again. Faster now, in quick, hard jabs. Muscles flexing, contracting, flexing. Shoulders glistening with sweat in the sunlight that slanted in through the blinds.

They came together in a burst that seemed to engulf her entire body. Greedily, she clung to Wes, biting him, biting *hard,* not caring if it hurt, just wanting to take as much of him into her as she could.

He collapsed onto her, spent.

At first, there was only the afterglow, the delicious sense of having had her fill. Then a flicker of anxiety took hold. It was unlikely, with her period due any minute, but suppose she *were* to get pregnant? Did she want a baby? A real live baby, with all it entailed? Or had it been just a case of wanting something she couldn't have?

Now that the decision was hers, and hers alone, it scared her.

A baby, she thought. A baby would change everything. No more rollicking on the sofa. No more candlelight dinners and midnight skinny-dipping in the pool. And that was just for starters. You had to want a child desperately — as desperately as Laura — to give up so much.

The question was, did *she?*

Alice drifted into a light doze, only vaguely aware of Wes easing away from her and gently covering her with a blanket. As if from a distance, she heard the soft click of a phone, then Wes's low voice, saying, "Ian? It's Dad."

 # Chapter 14

"Who was that?" Markie asked when he'd hung up.

"My dad."

"What did he want?"

"He was just calling to say hi. I guess it's been a while."

"Lucky you. If a whole day went by without one or the other of my parents checking up on me, I'd think they'd dropped off the planet." She laughed her high, girlish laugh and rolled onto her stomach.

They were lounging by the pool, Markie in a bikini consisting of little more than two strips of fabric no wider than his thumb, he in his Pacific Rim trunks. The deck, which jutted from the side of the cliff, looked out over an ocean so blue that if he'd tried to capture it on canvas it wouldn't have looked real. Waves churned on the rocks below, and in the cloudless sky overhead, seagulls floated nearly motionless, like pen strokes on pale blue parchment. *I could look out at this every day for the rest of my life and never get tired of it,* he thought.

With an effort, he drew his attention back to Markie. "Ready?" he asked, replacing the phone on the small glass table by the chaise, which held her Discman, an empty Coke can, the latest issue of *Forbes*, and an ashtray with several lipsticked butts. "We should try to squeeze in another hour while the light's still good."

"Let's go for another swim first." With a lazy smile she uncoiled from the chaise.

A few months ago he might have been tempted . . . but the only thing on his mind now was finishing this damn portrait. He'd known, of course, when asked to do the old lady's, that sooner or later Markie would appear on the scene. Hadn't that been the idea all along? What he couldn't have predicted was that she'd sweet talk dear old Dad out of another five grand for *hers*. And how convenient that the Aaronsons left for Europe two days after she arrived. Ian would have hightailed it, too, but the money was too good.

Ten grand in the bank would show Sam he was serious, not just about her, but the baby. She'd see that he wasn't like her husband. She'd know she could count on him.

They'd spoken over the phone last night, and she'd agreed to drive up next weekend — two whole days to sort things out, days in which the perfect moment would surely arise to . . .

Ask her to marry me.

Ian's pulse quickened at the thought. When had it first come to him that that was what he wanted? He couldn't have said. The process had been so gradual, it seemed he'd always known.

"You'll have all day tomorrow," he told Markie. Tomorrow, God willing, they'd be done with sittings, and he could devote the next few days to the finishing touches.

For once, she didn't argue. "Oh, all right. If you're going to be *that* way about it." She injected a teasing note, but he sensed her disappointment. None of this was working out the way she'd planned. A week of togetherness, with only the housekeeper to lend a thin veneer of respectability, had brought them no closer than before.

He pushed his way out the gate. Flagstone steps wound down the steep hillside to the guest house below. He hadn't gone more than halfway when he heard a splash. Ian felt a surge of irritation. That would mean another ten, fifteen minutes before she meandered down to meet him, still in her bikini. Then another fifteen to blow-dry her hair. Jesus. If it was like this now, what kind of tricks would she pull when he told her Sam was coming?

But when Markie finally appeared, damp and out of breath, her short dark hair standing up in kittenish tufts, he didn't have the heart to be angry. She looked adorable, and knew it. "Don't be mad, Ian. It was so hot. I needed to cool off." She crossed the living room and flopped down on the sofa.

The guest house was a miniature version of the main one, with post-and-beam ceilings and a redwood deck facing out over the ocean. What he liked best was the light; it poured in even on foggy days. He'd set his easel up by the sliding glass doors to the deck, using a rattan loveseat as a backdrop. Old Mrs. Aaronson, he recalled with something close to wistfulness, would sit for hour upon hour without moving or uttering a single complaint.

"It doesn't matter now. By the time you dry off and get dressed it'll be too late." He spoke evenly, carefully wiping his brushes clean. The room smelled faintly of linseed oil and turpentine. He preferred working with acrylic, but the old lady, a great admirer of Sargent, had insisted on oil.

He eyed the nearly finished portrait on the easel, seeing it less as a whole than as a checklist of things to correct. A little more cadmium around the eyes? A touch of blue highlight to the hair? The dimple would have to be flattened, too. It didn't show that much, except when she was laughing.

"We got *hours* in before lunch," she said, unperturbed.

Lunch. Back home, in his studio, that usually consisted of a sandwich tasting faintly of paint and gesso. But here it was a far more civilized affair. With old Mrs. Aaronson at least two hours had had to be allotted, starting precisely at noon, for a spread that would have rivaled a sultan's. Today's lunch had consisted of cold coconut soup, curried chicken salad, slices of mango wrapped in prosciutto, and rolls fresh from the oven. Not that he hadn't enjoyed every bite. The trouble was that one day had a tendency to melt into the next, whole afternoons dissolving in a wine-induced haze. Aided and abetted by the pool and the siren's call of the surf.

Ian slid open the door to the deck. It was low tide, and a flock of sandpipers was making its way along the glistening ribbon of sand below. Farther out to sea, a blue heron glided inches above the water as if tracing an invisible line. He followed its progress, so caught up in his thoughts he didn't notice Markie slipping up alongside him.

She leaned up against the railing. "Feel like a walk?"

"Not particularly." He brought his gaze back to the sandpipers, like miniature clowns on stilts jerking along the kelp-strewn tide line. But the scent of Coppertone on warmed skin was making it hard to concentrate.

"What *do* you feel like doing?"

"Actually," he said, "I was thinking of calling my girlfriend."

"Well, I'm sure you won't mind if I don't stick around." He didn't have to look at her to know she was sulking.

"Not in the least," he replied.

Markie didn't budge. "The older lady, right?"

"Sam."

"Just how old *is* she?"

Ian turned to her with the same pleasant smile he'd been wearing all week. "Not that it's any of your business," he said, "but she has kids your age."

She dropped her gaze, picking at a splinter on the railing. "Don't get me wrong. I'm not hung up about that kind of thing. It's just that personally I can't imagine dating anyone that much older." She flashed him a little smile. "But that's just me."

"I take it you've never been in love."

"Once or twice. It was no big deal, believe me."

"Like I said, you've never been in love."

She frowned. "You're not that much older than me, you know."

Old enough to know better, he thought. He noticed she was shivering, and said matter-of-factly, "You'd better throw something on. You'll catch cold."

"I left my robe by the pool."

"There's a shirt on my bed."

Markie shot him a faintly chastened look and did as she was told, returning moments later with his oldest chambray shirt, daubed with paint, draped about her shoulders. Its tails dangled to her knees, reminding him of Audrey Hepburn in *Roman Holiday.*

"Just for the record," she informed him, "I wasn't prying. It's just that you hardly ever talk about her. I was curious, that's all. What's she like?"

"You'll see for yourself," he said. "She's coming up next weekend."

Markie was clearly taken aback. "Oh? I thought . . ." She caught her lower lip between her teeth.

He knew what she'd thought — that it'd be just the two of them. "I ran it by your grandparents before they left," he said with a shrug, making it clear he didn't owe her an explanation. "They were cool with it."

Markie's charm school manners quickly rose to the occasion. "In that case, I'll tell Pilar to set an extra place for dinner on Friday. That is, if you haven't made other plans."

Friday he'd planned on taking Sam to dinner at Ventana, but he could see that Markie was trying. One night wouldn't hurt. "Thanks," he said. "That'd be nice."

"Sandra, right?"

"Sam," he corrected.

"Sam." She smiled. "I'm looking forward to meeting her."

By the time Friday rolled around, dinner with Markie was the last thing on Ian's mind. His head was too filled with thoughts of Sam. Would she want what he was offering? Over the phone she'd sounded excited, brimming with plans for the new house. Chattering on about kitchen cabinets, and whether or not to replace the old sash windows with double-glazed aluminum ones. Not a word to suggest she was thinking about anything other than her own immediate future.

It shouldn't have worried him, but it did. They'd agreed to hold off making a decision, sure, but he hadn't expected her to sound so . . . well, *cheerful.* As if she hadn't a care in the world. As if his being away were no big deal. He'd taken it for granted that she'd want to marry him. But what if she didn't? What if she had other ideas?

The instant he caught sight of her strolling down the drive those thoughts vanished like smoke from a doused fire. He watched her walk to meet him, her hair aglow with the setting sun, a silver bracelet glinting on the arm she lifted in greeting. A slender woman in a sleeveless yellow dress, carrying a small canvas bag. Beautiful, ageless. *His.*

She was slightly breathless when she reached him. "Sorry I'm late. I got caught in traffic."

"You're here now, that's all that counts." Ian pulled her into his arms, inhaling her fragrance: something delicate and flowery, with an underlying scent all her own. He felt her tense slightly, and drew back at once. "Are you okay?"

"I'm fine. Just a little tender." She

smiled that secret little smile he'd seen on other pregnant women, and he felt a sudden urge to scoop her up like the hero in an old black and white epic. He seized hold of her bag instead.

"We'll take it easy, I promise," he said.

When they reached the end of the drive, she paused to take in the house. "Lovely. Very Frank Lloyd Wright." She pointed to the guest house below. "Is that where you're staying?"

"Wait until you see the view."

"From here it's breathtaking." She laughed, looking at him as she said it.

This was the woman he'd fallen in love with, teasing and high-spirited . . . and not above the occasional cornball remark. He felt himself relax. Yes, it was going to be all right.

Inside, she headed straight for the bedroom, where she kicked off her shoes and flopped down on the bed. "Nice firm mattress," she said. "All the amenities, I see."

He didn't tell her that Pilar came each morning to tidy up. She'd think him spoiled. "I made room in the closet for your things."

"I'll unpack later."

Ian gazed down at her lying on her back with her eyes sparkling up at him and her hair spilled like copper ink over the pillow. She looked irresistible. He was about to stretch out alongside her when she leapt up off the bed and padded barefoot into the living room. She paused in front of the easel, where the portrait he'd stayed up half the night to finish was propped.

"I had no idea she was so pretty." Her voice seemed to hold a faintly accusatory note. "Is she around? I suppose I should pop in at some point and say hello."

"We're having dinner with her tonight."

"Oh?" Sam turned to him. She was better than Markie at disguising her feelings, but he caught the glint of disappointment in her eyes.

"I'm sorry," he said, walking over to wrap his arms around her. "I couldn't think of a way out without being impolite. I hope you don't mind too much."

"Don't be silly. Of course not." She drew away, drifting over to the table against the wall, scattered with shells and beach glass. She fingered a piece of driftwood in the shape of a dagger.

"There's a beach nearby. We could picnic there tomorrow." He grinned. "Just the two of us."

She looked as though she'd like nothing more than to go now. But it was too late.

They were expected for dinner in an hour. "Wonderful," she said. "I've been inhaling sawdust for so long I've almost forgotten what it's like to breathe fresh air."

"What did you decide about the windows?"

"Carl convinced me to go with aluminum. I'll save in the end."

"And the kitchen cabinets?"

"Didn't I tell you? I found the original ones from the thirties in the garage, under an old tarp. It means I can get rid of the ghastly seventies redo without breaking the bank."

Ian felt suddenly impatient. All this talk about the house, and she hadn't once mentioned the possibility of his living there. Was she waiting for him to say something first?

"When do you expect to move in?" he asked.

"In a few weeks if all goes well."

"I can't wait to see it." Ian looked out at the sun sinking into the ocean, transforming it into a galaxy of glittering pinpoint lights. Why couldn't he just come out with it? What was stopping him? Casually, he asked, "So what else is new?"

"Except for a murderer on the loose, not much." Her tone was dry.

He saw the worry in her eyes. "Still no leads?"

"The usual suspects have been picked up for questioning, but so far there's been no arrest."

It was the opening he'd been looking for. "I don't like the idea of your living out there all alone."

"I won't be alone. I'll have Max."

"Max?"

She laughed. "Relax, he's a dog."

This was the first he was hearing about it. "I didn't know you were getting a dog."

"I'm not. He's on loan from a friend, just until they catch this guy."

A male friend being chivalrous? The sense of unease grew stronger. "Speaking of the home front," he said. "I spoke to my dad the other day. He said Alice had been out to see you."

"She didn't stay long." Sam fingered a blue lozenge of beach glass, not meeting his eyes.

"How did she seem?"

"Still upset, but at least we're talking."

"And Laura?"

"Putting on a brave face."

He saw a corner of her mouth turn down, and wanted to take her in his arms, smooth away her worries the way the ocean had the sharp edges of the glass. Why couldn't she see what was so crystal clear to him — that they belonged together?

"Sam . . ." *I won't let you down the way your husband did.*

But she wasn't focusing on him. She was looking out the window. "You're right about the view. It *is* spectacular. A person could get spoiled pretty quickly around here."

"Believe me, Markie Aaronson is living proof." He gave a caustic little laugh and walked over to where she stood, slipping an arm about her waist. "Sorry it's not just the two of us tonight."

She relaxed against him, dropping her head onto his shoulder. "Never mind, we'll have the rest of the weekend to ourselves."

"Hungry?"

"I'm eating for two, remember?"

"How could I forget?" He brought a hand to her belly, feeling a secret little thrill as he gently traced its swell. He couldn't have put into words what he was feeling; it was beyond communicating. "Look, Sam, I know we agreed to hold off talking about this until I got back. But —" He broke off at the sound of a knock on the door.

Markie. Ian could have killed her. He marched to the door and wrenched it open. But it wasn't Markie, just Pilar, looking embarrassed. A small, plump woman who spoke almost no English, she had the sense to realize she'd come at a bad time.

"Miss Markie, she ask you and the *señora* —" she glanced nervously over his shoulder at Sam " — come now for drink."

Never mind that Markie could simply have picked up the phone. "Tell her we'll be there in half an hour." He tapped his watch, a battered Swiss Army, repeating, *"Media hora."*

Pilar glanced down shyly. "I make for you a . . . a . . ." She poked at her palm with a work-hardened finger, searching for the word.

"Hors d'oeuvres?" Hot, no doubt. His heart sank. Well, no sense taking it out on Pilar. "All right, tell her we'll be right up." On impulse, he reached out to take her hand. *"Gracias,* Pilar. For everything. I've known French-trained chefs who aren't fit to carry your saucepan."

"Perdoname?" She eyed him in confusion.

"Never mind. Just . . . *gracias por todo."*

No sooner had he shut the door than

428

Sam slipped up alongside him, wearing a pale green shawl. He glanced out to see that the fog had begun to roll in off the ocean in great, soft bales. "Look at the bright side," she said. "This way, we'll have an excuse to leave early."

She pulled him close abruptly, kissing him deeply. She tasted sweet and somehow forbidden, like berries out of season. God, what he wouldn't have given to carry her off to bed, right then and there. It had been too long. But no time now. Later . . .

He took her arm, guiding her outside onto the path. Fog scudded in thin patches over the hillside, partially obscuring the steps above. A damp chill had crept in as well. It seemed a bellwether for the evening ahead, which Ian had a bad feeling about all of a sudden.

But Markie was on her best behavior. Smiling warmly as she greeted them, dressed in something appropriate for a change: a slinky black dress that fell to her calves. She extended her hand to Sam. "Markie Aaronson. It's nice to finally meet you. Ian's been so mysterious, I was beginning to wonder if you really existed."

Sam smiled. "As you can see, I do. Slightly travel worn, but mostly intact. Thanks for having me." She glanced about, taking in the floor-to-ceiling windows and diagonal-cut redwood paneling, the spiral staircase of iodized copper and slate to the floor below. "What an absolutely amazing house."

"It's my grandparents', so I can't take any credit for it." Markie strolled over to the bar. "What can I get you to drink?"

"Club soda for me." Sam cast Ian a meaningful look.

He shook his head. No, he hadn't said anything about the baby. "I'll take a beer, if you have one," he called.

Markie returned moments later carrying their drinks. She handed Ian a chilled Heineken, saying with cozy familiarity, "I asked Pilar to make some of those delicious crab puffs you're so crazy about."

The evening, Ian could see, wasn't going to be as painless as he'd hoped. Still, it took two to tango. If he simply refused to play along . . .

He lifted his bottle. "To Pilar."

"I saw the portrait," Sam said, sipping her soda. "It really captures you."

"Really? I think it makes me look a little young." Markie smiled, casting a teasing sidelong glance at Ian. "On the other hand, when I'm old and gray I'll have something to look back on."

Sam gave a rueful little laugh. "Trust me, that day will come sooner than you think."

Markie eyed her speculatively, as if not quite sure what to make of Sam. "Ian tells me your children are grown. I find that hard to believe. You don't look old enough."

"My youngest was married in June." Sam didn't add that it was to Ian's father. "Laura, my eldest, runs the family business."

"And what do you do?" Markie sipped her wine.

"Me?" Sam hesitated, then said, "I guess you could say I'm retired."

The word seemed to hang in the air, heavy with import.

Pilar appeared just then with a platter of crab puffs, warm from the oven. Ian helped himself to one, though he hardly tasted it. The evening was shaping up to be a long one.

He couldn't have imagined just *how* long. All through dinner Markie chattered on and on. Mostly about herself. Her budding career at Aaronson Asset Management, and how much she adored her loft in Soho; the Fire Island house share lined up for next summer, and the trip to Nepal she was planning for next fall. All of it fun and interesting . . . and very much the province of youth. Sam might have been one of her grandmother's elderly friends with nothing to do but smile in wistful memory.

But what could you expect? Markie *was* just a kid, after all. At times, she made him feel old. The interminable meal was nearly over when he tuned in to hear her remark, "I was telling Ian just the other day that he ought to come with us." She cast him a look of bright innocence. "You haven't been to Nepal, have you?"

He choked down a bite of salmon. "Thanks, but I'll settle for a postcard."

"Don't be such a stick-in-the-mud. You'd love it." She flapped her napkin teasingly, and he was a little alarmed to see that the wineglass she'd only just refilled was once more empty. "Wouldn't he, Sam?" As if he were Sam's son, not her lover.

"That's for Ian to say," Sam replied evenly.

Markie turned to Ian, prattling on, "You'd *love* my friends, especially Lana. She's a riot. God, some of the crazy things we've done! You don't even want to know."

You're right. I don't. He shot Sam a look of solidarity.

"Oops. I almost forgot." Markie wobbled to her feet. "Pilar had to go home early. I was supposed to take the flan out of the oven. God, I hope it's not overdone."

"Need any help?" Sam started to get up.

Markie waved her down. "No, you sit. I've got it."

They could hear her clattering about in the kitchen, then the sound of something being dropped into the sink, followed by a sizzling noise and Markie yelling, "Shit!" A minute later, she stuck her head through the doorway to announce good-naturedly, "Dessert is DOA, and my dress is soaked. Hang tight, it won't take a minute to throw something else on."

When she reappeared a short while later, Ian scarcely noticed what she was wearing. It wasn't until Sam's expression grew tight that he saw what Markie had thrown on: jeans and a baggy chambray shirt dabbed with paint. *His* shirt.

"Sorry about the flan." Her face was innocent as a newborn's. "Would you settle for ice cream instead?"

"Thanks, but I'll pass." Sam looked a little pale, but managed to maintain her composure.

Ian rose abruptly, too angry to stay another minute. Only supreme willpower —

and the thought of the check he had yet to collect — kept him from showing it. "I'm sure Sam's tired after her drive. We should be going."

"So soon? It seems like you just got here." Markie didn't sound too disappointed. Why should she be? She'd already achieved what she'd set out to accomplish.

Ian glanced at Sam as they made their way to the door. Her expression was closed. Any attempt to explain, he sensed, would only make it worse. On the other hand, how could he *not?*

Outside, they descended the steps in silence. Fog swirled, the milky glow from the lights along the path casting a caul about Sam, making her seem untouchable somehow. A gull was crying somewhere, and it suddenly seemed the loneliest sound in the world.

When they reached the guest house, Sam stepped ahead of him through the door. She was groping for the switch when Ian placed a hand over hers. "It's not what you think."

"How do you know what I'm thinking?"

She slid her hand out from under his. The curtains weren't drawn, and he could see onto the deck, where fog drifted in ghostly tatters. In the half darkness of the living room, her face was cool and smooth as marble.

"I loaned her my shirt," he said. "That's all."

"I'm not accusing you of anything."

"You don't have to," he said. "I can see it on your face."

"Then you don't know me as well as you think." Her eyes were dark with shadow, making them seem bruised. "Oh, Ian, don't you see? I wouldn't blame you if you *had* slept with her. She's sexy. She's smart. And let's face it, *she's your age*."

"Are we back to that again?" Frustration rose in him. "What the fuck does age have to do with it?"

"Everything."

Ian could hear waves smashing against the rocks below. He wanted to smash something, too. He took a deep breath. "She was only trying to make you jealous."

"You could've warned me."

"I didn't think she'd go this far."

"Come on, Ian." She gave a weary smile. "Isn't that why you're here?"

"Whatever Markie's reasons are, it's not why *I'm* here."

"When I asked about her in New York, you didn't tell me she was Mr. Aaronson's daughter. Why?"

She had him there. "I don't know," he said. "I guess I didn't want you to worry." It sounded lame to his own ears, not quite the declaration of an innocent man.

But Sam just stood there, shaking her head. "It's not just Markie, Ian. There'll be other Markies. Dozens of them. And the older I get, the younger they'll seem."

She looked so sad, he longed to erase it. Brush, paint, canvas, these were his tools. The only way he knew to alter reality. How could he change this? "Sam." His voice cracked. "Sam, I want to *marry* you."

Something flared briefly in her eyes, then went out. Abruptly, she moved away from him and into the light that fell in a pale rectangle over the carpet. "You feel that way now," she said, crossing her arms over her chest. "But you won't in a few years."

"Christ, Sam. What can I say to convince you?"

"Nothing. Nothing at all."

The room blurred, the only thing that stood out Sam's elongated shadow stretching away from him. He brought his head to rest against the wall, and in a low, hoarse voice he hardly recognized as his own asked, "What are you telling me?"

"Oh, Ian, I just don't see how it can work."

"What about the baby?"

"Isn't it a little late for you to be asking that?"

"I thought we'd agreed to wait until I got back."

"That was weeks ago, and you're still not back."

"So it's not just the age thing, is that what you're telling me?"

She hesitated, then said softly, "I guess not."

"You think I'll let you down?" *Like your husband.*

"I'm not accusing you of anything." She sounded on the verge of tears. "It's no one's fault. It just *is.*"

"Sam, I love you. I want this baby. Maybe I didn't at first. But once I got used to the idea . . ." His voice trailed off. She wasn't buying it. He could see it on her face. "Look, I'm not Martin. I don't want to be damned for another man's sins."

"What do you know about Martin?"

"I know he hurt you. I see it in your eyes."

Something flashed in her eyes now. "Martin was *there* at least." She drew in a breath, as if to calm herself, saying in a queer, flat voice, "We'll work something out. You'll still see the baby." And in that one statement he saw his whole future mapped out: the brief visits with his child, the moments of awkwardness when he arrived to pick it up. His kid would feel exactly as *he* had growing up: forever missing his dad.

Ian's hands clenched and unclenched, hungry for something to grab hold of, something to stop this slow hemorrhaging. "This isn't what *I* want." He spoke through gritted teeth.

"I know."

"Did you drive all this way to tell me?"

"No." She gave a crooked little smile that was painful to look at. "I *was* hoping it would work out. And when I saw you . . ." Eyes glittering, she reached up as if to touch him before her hand fell heavily to her side. "But it's no good. It's not just my family, or Markie. It's you. Me. The baby. *Everything.*"

"So that's it? You're not even willing to take a chance?"

"I don't have that luxury."

She crossed the room and was reaching for her bag, still by the door where he'd left it, when his words to Markie rose to taunt him: *Trust me, you've never been in love.* He must have been talking about himself, too. No woman before Sam had ever made him hurt this way.

He wrested the bag from her grip, more roughly than he'd intended, and hurled it to the floor. "No," he said in that strange, choked voice that wasn't his. "Not tonight, not in this fog. I can't stop you from going, but I can keep you from killing yourself."

"I can't stay here," she said.

"I'm not giving you a choice." He switched on the overhead light, and the room seemed to rush up around him. He found his way into the bedroom, hand out to keep from bumping into walls. He dragged his duffel from the closet and began blindly stuffing in clothes.

"Ian, I can't let you do this."

He felt her hand on his arm, and wheeled about.

Whatever she saw in his eyes made her flinch and step back, perhaps recognizing that this was the only thing he *could* do, the only thing he had any control over.

"There's a motel a few miles up the road," he found himself saying in an eerily calm voice. "It's only for one night."

She sank down on the bed looking defeated. When he'd finished his packing, such as it was, she rose with tears in her eyes to kiss his cheek. "I guess this is good-bye."

"It doesn't have to be, Sam. If you change your mind —"

He stopped when he saw that she was crying, a hand over her belly as if to shield it. All of a sudden he had trouble catching his breath. Unable to meet her eyes, he stared at her throat instead: long and pale, with its collarbone that made him think of a gull in flight.

He knew that when he got back tomorrow morning she'd be gone.

Chapter 15

September in Carson Springs brought the kind of weather that made poor men rich and rich men content. Long days of Indian summer with temperatures in the seventies, followed by evenings crisp as apples from the orchards above Sorrento Creek. Birds grew fat on wild grapes and gooseberries and cactus pears. Even the bees of Our Lady of the Wayside seemed to move at a more leisurely pace, drunk with sunshine, bobbing and looping amid pastures golden as the honey itself.

At the Dos Palmas Country Club, golfers sprouted like groundsel, and the thwack of balls could be heard as far east as the hot springs, where the spa run by Monica Vincenzi's sister Liz was enjoying a flood of tourists in search of the latest seaweed wrap, volcanic mud massage, or bee-pollen facial. At Valley Inn, La Serenisa, and Horse Creek Lodge rooms were booked well into November. And downtown, at the old mission on Calle de Navidad, weekends brought the steady pealing of *campanario* bells as one newlywed couple after another dashed down the steps amid a hail of rice.

School, which weeks before had seemed as remote a prospect as old age, was all at once looming. At the Gap in Del Rey Plaza, traffic was thick and a welter of signs announcing sales on school supplies had sprouted at the Staples next door. Two days before the start of the fall semester, fifteen-year-old Joey Harbinson climbed the white oak by the courthouse, refusing to come down in protest of its slated removal. It was no small coincidence that Joey's parents had been threatening to pack him off to military school.

Talk at the Tree House ranged from the yield of apple and grape harvests to the new gym going up at Portola High, and whether or not the fire that was being battled in Los Padres National Forest would bring an influx of wildlife like last year's, when a rash of vandalism turned out to be the work of displaced bears. Few spoke of the murders. It made people too uneasy. Nor did they inquire too closely about the health of young Davey Ryback, on the waiting list for a kidney donor. They gossiped instead about such topics as the recent *Los Angeles Times* article extolling the virtues of Carson Springs, the old Cumberland Express refurbishment by dotcom billionaire Conrad Hirsch, and the rumored resurgence of the dreaded Mediterranean fruit fly in an orchard just north of Ventura.

Organizers of the music festival hadn't stopped buzzing about Aubrey Roellinger leasing Isla Verde and Sam Kiley moving to the Flats. Though no one had seen much of her lately. Except for committee meetings and the usual errands around town, she'd been keeping a low profile.

That did nothing to stop tongues from wagging.

Rumor had it her lover was in Europe, painting rich ladies' portraits and taking advantage of all the perks therein. But no one knew for sure because there hadn't been a sighting of Ian Carpenter since July. The only man with whom Sam had been seen keeping company was her husband's former partner, Tom Kemp. Althea Wormley had spotted them lunching at the Tree House, and Gayle Warrington reported that Tom had been in recently to inquire about an Alaskan cruise. Yet they appeared to be nothing more than friendly, which caused no end of aggravation. How much juicier a love triangle would have been!

But Sam had her share of supporters as well. Marguerite Moore had met with surprising resistance when she suggested that Sam step down as president. Reverend Grigsby's wife, Edie, argued that if Christ could forgive, who were they to judge? And mousy little Vivienne Hicks, who rarely expressed an opinion, surprised everyone by speaking quite heatedly on the subject of a woman's right to make her own reproductive decisions. Others, like Miranda McBride, from The Last Word, made a point of dropping by the new house, while elderly Rose Miller and her twin sister, Olive, presented Sam with a hand-knit baby blanket.

"I knitted this part," said Rose, proudly showing off the half that was blue, while Olive finished the sentence, as the twins were prone to do, with "And the pink half is mine."

Even more fiercely partisan were friends like Tom Kemp and Gerry Fitzgerald. Gerry, in particular, stalked about like a smoke jumper, stamping out sparks of gossip wherever they appeared. In Shear Delight she'd practically chased Althea Wormley into the street, blue hair still in curlers. Its proprietress, Norma Devane had showed her support by refusing to charge Gerry for her haircut.

Meanwhile, Sam went about her business the same as always, head held high. If she heard whispers, or noticed glances aimed at her thickening waist, she paid them no mind. Whatever she might have felt, it was as closely guarded as her plans. Mainly because Sam, who'd always been so sure of her direction, her calendar mapped out months in advance, didn't have a clue what this next phase of life would bring — except that while other women her age were planning graduations and weddings and retirement parties, she'd be changing diapers and walking the floor at two a.m. A prospect that six months ago would have horrified her, but which she now saw as a rich new opportunity.

The last Tuesday in September found Sam on her way to Audrey's for supper. She wasn't exactly looking forward to it but when Audrey had extended the olive branch Sam hadn't had the heart to refuse. They were sisters, after all, even if it sometimes felt more like a life sentence than a bond.

On the drive east across the valley her thoughts turned, as they always did on long drives, to Ian. The memory brought a dull throb, like a broken rib that hadn't quite healed. Winding her way up Norte Road, past sun-dappled pastures and rolling hills, she recalled the trip home from Big Sur. How she'd nearly turned back; how she'd had to pull over in Morro Bay, where a kindly waitress at a truck stop listened to her pour her heart out over endless cups of coffee. By the time she'd reached home, there were no more tears left and her heart was a hot cracked stone in her chest.

It didn't matter that she loved him and that he loved her. What was love in the face of everything that went into making a home? For the longest time she hadn't wanted to face it, but the truth was inescapable: Ian was no more equipped to be a husband and father than Martin. It wasn't just his age. It wasn't just that he traveled often and light. It was everything. Things Ian couldn't even know or anticipate. She needed a husband, a father to her child who would happily spend an afternoon assembling a tricycle or cheering himself hoarse at a Little League game. A man who would be there for her, too, content to curl up on the sofa in front of *Masterpiece Theatre* for no other reason than to keep her company, who wouldn't ask what there was to eat when what he really wanted was for her to fix him something. Passion played a part, yes, a *large* part, but she also needed someone to love her at her worst, and . . .

Be there. Always.

Oh, she didn't blame Ian. How could she when it was that spur-of-the-moment unpredictability with which she'd fallen in love? But trying to shoehorn him into her life, a life that suited her in more ways than not, would only end in them resenting each other.

Yes, she thought, breaking up had been the right thing to do. But knowing that hadn't made it any easier. She swallowed against the lump in her throat. No more tears. She was done with all that. Time to move on. And to look ahead. *The baby* . . .

She'd gone from accepting this pregnancy to seeing it for what it was: a gift. A magical, marvelous gift. To have a child again at her age! With all the time in the world to watch it grow. Yes, she tired more easily these days, but in some ways she'd be better equipped than with the girls. She was wiser and more patient. She would cherish each and every moment, for she knew now what she hadn't then: how fleeting they were. God might not have granted her every wish, but He'd given her this. And for that she was grateful.

Sam made the turn onto Agua Caliente, and the Asana Spa panned into view: a low cedar structure built in levels, like steps down a wooded rise. Below, wisps of steam rose from rock pools, fed by underground springs, that were shielded from view by thick clumps of bamboo. Heaven right now, she thought, would be a long soak in one of those pools.

A mile or so down the road she turned up another hill. Corral Estates, as it was grandly known, had once been vast tracts of ranch land where cattle grazed. It had since given rise to one of Carson Springs's few subdivisions. These days, cookie-cutter houses lined roads and culs-de-sac with horsey names like Roan Circle, Pinto Drive, and Bridle Path Lane. Her sister and brother-in-law's house, a modest split-level with a mailbox mounted on a wrought-iron lasso, was at 25 Mustang Place.

Audrey greeted her at the door wearing a purple dress, which flattered her for a change, and sporting the diamond tennis bracelet Grant had given her last year on their silver anniversary. She was wearing her hair differently, too, in a modified chip cut.

"I like your hair," Sam said.

Audrey fingered the ends self-consciously. "Norma talked me into it. I wasn't sure."

Norma Devane, proprietress of Shear Delight, had been one of Audrey's closest friends since high school. Every spring, Audrey raised money for Norma's annual wig drive for patients in chemotherapy. Last year alone she'd single-handedly brought in over two thousand dollars, a fact that helped Sam feel more charitable toward her now. She wondered if Norma, who'd sided with Gerry on her behalf, had had anything to do with the softening of Audrey's stance.

"It makes you look years younger," Sam said.

Audrey's eyes narrowed a bit, as if she weren't quite sure whether to take it as a compliment. Then, as if deciding to give Sam the benefit of the doubt, she smiled. "Dinner's almost ready. You can keep me company in the kitchen."

As Sam was walking past the living room, like a Macy's display with its flocked sofa and smoked-glass coffee table, she poked her head in to say hello to Grant. It was with an obvious effort that her brother-in-law, ensconced in his Naugahyde recliner in front of the TV, tore his gaze from the baseball game in progress.

"Sam. Hey, nice to see you."

"How have you been, Grant?"

"Can't complain. And you?"

No mention of the baby. Had he forgotten?

"Never better," she said.

Grant was the only member of the family who never seemed to change. He'd lost most of his hair in college, and what remained was combed over his bald pate exactly as it had been on his wedding day. He was even the same weight, give or take a few pounds, though she couldn't help noticing the roll of pudge creeping over his belt. Too many of those Snickers pies for which her sister was famous. Sam hoped it wasn't on the menu for tonight; her stomach wouldn't be able to take it.

"Glad to hear it." Her brother-in-law's gaze strayed back to the TV.

Sam tried not to take it personally. It wasn't so much rudeness, she thought, as years of tuning out Audrey.

She caught up with her sister in the kitchen, a gleaming shrine to Martha Stewart with its pickled pine and country checks, its hand-painted watering can stuffed with dried flowers. Saran-wrapped bowls lined the counter, ready to be reheated in the microwave. Roast chicken, brussels sprouts, creamed onions. In short, a menu more suited to a New England winter than Indian summer in Carson Springs.

She must feel guilty for the way she acted, Sam thought. Or maybe her sister had finally realized blood truly is thicker than water. Audrey wasn't a bad person, she thought, just terminally resentful.

"There's white wine and soda in the fridge. Help yourself." Audrey raised her voice to be heard above the whirring of the electric mixer.

Sam found an open bottle of Chardonnay and poured her sister a glass before helping herself to some milk. "Cheers," she said.

Audrey switched off the mixer, eyeing the tumbler in Sam's hand. "When I was pregnant, I mixed mine with Ovaltine. Grant says that's why both boys turned out so dark." She gave a wry, remembering smile. "Any cravings yet?"

"Pomegranates. Just like with the girls."

"Figures. You always were a little strange."

"I'm not the one who colored Grandma Delarosa's Easter lilies with my paint set,"

Sam was quick to remind her.

"I was five!"

"Well, I see you haven't lost your artistic touch. Did you make those?" She pointed to the stenciled linen tea towels hanging stiff as cardboard on the wooden rack over the sink.

"Last Christmas. Don't you remember? I gave you a set." Audrey popped the beaters with a practiced snap of her wrist. "By the way, how are you settling in over at the new house?"

When Sam had announced she was moving — and that their childhood home was being rented out — she'd expected Audrey to be up in arms. Instead, she'd seemed to take it in stride.

"It's different," Sam said cautiously. "But in some ways, nothing's changed. Lupe and Guillermo drop by at least once a day to see if I need anything."

"She still cooking for you?"

"Believe it or not, I'm perfectly capable of feeding myself." Sam reached for the sponge and wiped a smear of potatoes from the counter. Smiling, she added, "But you know Lupe. It's among her personal Ten Commandments never to show up empty-handed."

Audrey smiled knowingly in return.

"I even lugged Mami's old sewing machine down from the attic. I'm making curtains for the bedroom and for . . ." Sam hesitated before adding, "the nursery."

"Somehow I can't picture you sewing curtains." Audrey sounded vaguely disappointed for some reason. Peeling Saran Wrap from the chicken, she extracted a carving knife from the wooden holder by the range.

"It's a nice break from minding the store."

"You don't miss it?"

"Not in the least." The realization had come as a pleasant surprise. "Lately, between the house and the festival . . ." she shrugged. "In a few months, who knows?"

"You'll certainly have your hands full when the baby comes."

"In a nice way." Sam smiled dreamily and brought a hand to her belly, where only yesterday she'd felt the first flutter. "You know, Aud, I never would have believed it, but I'm really looking forward to this baby."

"You must have forgotten how much work it is."

"I won't mind."

"You say that now . . ."

Audrey's back was rigid, her shoulder

blades pinched into sharp little wings as she tugged apart the chicken. With sudden clarity, Sam understood what all this was about: Her sister *wanted* her to be miserable. That's why she hadn't minded about Isla Verde, and why she'd stopped treating her like Hester Prynne. Audrey was prepared to be forgiving, even magnanimous. But Sam, instead of being crouched in a corner with her head hung in shame, was making lemonade out of lemons and enjoying every drop.

"I know what's involved." She spoke evenly. "I raised two, after all."

"Exactly my point." Audrey turned to face her. "How long since you changed a diaper or wiped up spit up?"

"If that was all there was to having kids," Sam said, "there'd be a lot more only children in this world." She was determined not to let this spin out of control like so many other conversations, which invariably ended with Audrey taking pot shots and good old Sam being left to stew. "Anyway, I won't exactly be fending for myself. I'll have help."

"Ian?" Audrey's mouth curled in disdain.

"I was referring to Lupe." Sam felt her face grow warm. "But since you mentioned it, yes. Ian has every intention of being a father to this child."

"When he can fit it into his busy schedule, you mean."

"He'll make the time."

Audrey snorted. "He says that now, but just wait."

Sam's face was burning now. She walked over to the sink and rinsed her milk glass under the tap. "If there's a point to all this," she said coldly, "I wish you'd get to it."

"Aren't I allowed to be concerned about my own sister?" Audrey smiled ingratiatingly, but the glint in her eyes told a different story. "With the girls, at least you had Martin."

"Martin." As far as her sister knew her marriage had been ideal. Why give her a reason to gloat? But now Sam found herself saying, "If you'd asked who their pediatrician was, he wouldn't have been able to tell you. Or what sizes they wore, or that Laura is allergic to penicillin. I doubt he'd have remembered their birthdays if I hadn't been there to remind him."

Audrey looked stunned. "But I thought . . ."

"You thought wrong."

"Well, you certainly had *me* fooled."

Sam longed to put Audrey in her place, but something stopped her. Maybe it was hormones, or maybe now that she was finally living the life *she* wanted, lumps and all, she could allow herself to feel genuinely sorry for her sister. Poor Audrey, so blinded by resentment she couldn't see past her own nose — resentment that had its roots in childhood, with Audrey's belief that she'd been denied all the love and attention showered on her siblings.

She smiled, upending the dripping glass in the drainer. "You want to know the truth? I was always a little envious of you and Grant." That might've been a bit of a stretch — okay, *more* than a bit — but she was instantly rewarded by the color that bloomed in Audrey's cheeks.

"You were?" Her sister's voice rose on a note of incredulity.

"Grant was always so good with the boys. Always out in the yard, tossing a football or helping them build something."

"The girls adored Martin."

"He adored them."

"But —"

Sam shook her head. "They were more like dolls to him. Something to play with, then put back on the shelf. Cute and fun as long as *I* was the one shouldering all the responsibility. Maybe that's why they idolized him. When you're busy polishing someone's armor you don't always notice the flaws underneath."

Audrey surprised her by confiding, "Funny, ours are always complaining. Always a bone to pick."

"If they complain, it's because they can." Sam thought of her daughters and felt sad all of a sudden.

"Well, for heaven's sake, why didn't you say something?" Audrey cast her a faintly injured look as she arranged the chicken on its platter. "I'm your sister, for goodness sake."

Sam sighed. "It's complicated."

Audrey nodded in understanding. No one knew better just *how* complicated it was with sisters. But instead of offering some self-righteous comment as she might have in the past, Audrey merely dipped a spoon into a saucepan on the range, and held it out for Sam to taste. "What do you think? More salt?"

"Perfect. I wouldn't add a thing."

Dinner went smoothly. Audrey brought her up to date on the boys, both away in college. Grant went on and on about his plumbing supply business, which to hear him tell was growing in leaps and bounds.

It was all Sam could do to keep a straight face. Her brother-in-law had been saying that for the past twenty years, yet nothing ever changed. Audrey was still driving the same old Chevy station wagon with which she'd ferried the boys to school.

The only difference was that it no longer bothered Sam: her sister's little pretensions, her veiled references to the life they could've had. Like everyone, Audrey and Grant were merely getting by as best they could. If a little extra grease was needed now and then to keep the wheels turning, what real harm was there in that?

When the table had been cleared and the dishwasher loaded, she glanced discreetly at her watch. She wanted nothing more than to be home with a cup of tea, poring over her new gardening book — a housewarming gift from Miranda McBride. But when Audrey suggested a game of honeymoon bridge, she didn't rush to make an excuse. It wouldn't kill her to stay an extra hour, she thought.

They played two hands, both of which Audrey won. She was glowing with triumph as she walked Sam to the door. "It's only fair," she said. "You always beat me when we were kids."

Sam sensed her sister wanting to be reassured that she hadn't *let* her win. "Don't rub it in," she groaned.

But for once, Audrey was in a mood to be generous. "You're just out of practice, that's all. We ought to play more often."

They lingered in the foyer. In the dim light, her sister's face was soft, reminding Sam of when they'd been teenagers and would style each other's hair. Audrey stood with her hand on the knob, twisting it absently. "Well, if you need anything you know who to call." Moths flickered about the porch light, touching down then away with frantic little ticking sounds. "I haven't forgotten what I know about babies, either."

"I don't doubt it." Sam touched her arm. "Thanks for dinner, Aud. It was delicious."

"Drive safely," her sister called after her.

Sam was halfway down the drive when she remembered the gift-wrapped box in her car: their grandmother's sterling bud vase. She'd found it while cleaning out the china closet and had meant to give it to Audrey. Retrieving it from the front seat, she hesitated only a moment before popping it into the mailbox. Her sister would find it tomorrow, when she could enjoy it without having to give grudging thanks.

The rest of the week flew by. Sam spent

most of Wednesday pulling weeds and pre-paring the soil in the garden. On Thursday a trip to the nursery for fertilizer and flats of seedlings was followed by an emergency meeting of the festival committee. Their star violinist had broken her wrist, and they needed to find a replacement. A feat, with the festival just three weeks away, akin to a miracle. Marguerite Moore sug-gested tapping her dear old friend, Isaac Stern, which provoked a smile or two. Marguerite's brief one-on-one with the legendary violinist had to have taken place a good fifteen years ago. It was doubtful he'd even remember her.

On Friday she treated Tom to lunch at La Serenisa. It was the least she could offer after all he'd done. And if she felt a bit awk-ward around him still, he made it easier by keeping his feelings to himself. At their table by the window overlooking the stream, over chilled lobster salads and seared foie gras, they chatted like old friends.

"I don't know how to thank you," she told him as they were strolling back to their cars. "Lunch hardly seems enough."

Tom cast her a modest look. "As far as I'm concerned, the slate's been wiped clean. That was the best meal I've had in months."

She smiled. "You won't get very far as a

lawyer talking that way."

They were making their way along the fern-lined path that wound through deep shade to the parking area below, taking their time, in no particular hurry to get back to their respective lives. Along narrower paths that branched off from the main one, cedar-shingled guest cabins were tucked discreetly amid the trees, barely visible in places. In areas where sunlight had found its way through the dense canopy overhead, flowerbeds lush with bloom — bleeding heart, lady's slipper, trillium, gentian — made her think of her own garden, and how much she looked forward to watching it grow.

"Speaking of which, I had a word with Mr. Roellinger the other day," Tom said. "He loves the house and said to tell you that anytime you get homesick and want to stop in for a visit, you're more than welcome."

"Somehow I don't see that happening." She braced herself for a proprietary twinge, but none came. "I'm afraid the poor man doesn't stand a chance against Lupe, though. She'll be over there every chance she gets."

"I thought she was retiring."

"Tell *her* that."

"What about you? Ever think about

going back to work one day?"

She shrugged. "Maybe. When the baby's a little older. In the meantime, I'm perfectly happy with the way things are."

He shot her a sidelong glance. "It doesn't get lonely?"

"Max is all the company I need right now." These past weeks she'd grown truly fond of Tom's dog. She'd be sorry to see him go.

As if he'd read her mind, Tom said, "Keep him as long as you like. I wouldn't sleep nights, thinking of you all alone out there."

His eyes, behind their square black frames, were filled with concern, his broad shoulders angled downward as if in a conscious effort to keep from towering over her. Sam felt a twinge of regret. Why Ian? Why couldn't she have fallen in love with Tom Kemp instead?

In the parking lot she kissed his cheek before climbing into her car. "Honestly, Tom. I really *couldn't* have managed without you."

"What are friends for?"

"I can see now why Martin depended on you so much."

"We looked out for each other," he said, loyal to his partner even in death.

She glanced in the rearview mirror as she was pulling out. Tom was standing where she'd left him, watching her go, his expression reminding her of how Max looked whenever she headed for the door. Like his dog, Tom wouldn't be endlessly available. One day he'd have better things to do than wait for an invitation that might never come.

She was surprised to find a lump in her throat.

The following day, Gerry arrived on schedule to help paint the nursery. Saturdays were normally reserved for her children, so Sam was especially appreciative, until it became clear her friend was on a self-appointed mission that had less to do with lending a hand than doling out a piece of her mind.

They'd barely started on the trim, a pale gold that would go nicely with the yellowish cream for the walls, when Gerry said offhandedly, "I don't know why you didn't ask Ian's opinion. He's the artist, after all."

"This isn't exactly the Sistine Chapel," Sam said.

Gerry glanced at the ceiling. "Now that you mention it, a cherub or two wouldn't hurt."

"Very funny."

"I wasn't trying to be." Gerry settled back on her heels. In pleated khaki trousers, with a brightly patterned scarf knotted about her head, she was a glamorous Ethel Mertz, with a mouth to match. "Sam, you can't go on acting like he doesn't exist. Whatever cockamamy arrangement you two come up with, he's still the father of this child."

Sam dabbed furiously at the sill. "How do you know we haven't discussed it?"

"I'm your oldest and, I hope, dearest friend." Gerry was as relentless as the fly bumping against the windowpane. "Even if you didn't look the way you do, I'd know."

"Naturally, the way I look couldn't have anything to do with being pregnant."

"Pregnant, and blooming like a rose. That's not what I meant." Gerry set her brush aside, and rose to her feet with a crackling of joints. "You're miserable, and you know it."

"As a matter of fact, I've never been happier." Sam glared at her until a dribble of paint working its way down between her knuckles prompted her to lower her brush.

"Like you were with Martin?"

Sam looked at Gerry standing in a pane of sunlight, a headline from one of the newspapers spread over the floor spooling out from under her heel: FEDS JOIN SEARCH FOR KILLER. Old friends, she thought, could be dangerous, too. They knew too much.

"That's hitting below the belt," she said.

"Not when it's for your own good." Gerry walked over and pried the brush from her hand, propping it on the can. "It's one thing to *want* to be happy," she said, "another to make believe you are when you're not. Believe me, I'm a Purple Heart veteran of that war. If I had a dollar for every time I should have shot my mouth off at Mike, I wouldn't have to work for a living."

Sam recalled her friend's divorce, how messy it had been. But Gerry wasn't the type to wallow in self-pity. The only time Sam had seen her cry, *really* cry, was that terrible year after leaving the convent. A time Gerry hardly ever talked about, and Sam knew enough not to bring up.

"Okay, so I'm not *blissfully* happy," she admitted. "But I'm not exactly miserable, either. I'm . . ." she searched for the word "hanging in there."

Max wandered into the room just then, his plumed orange tail that acted like a magnet for every burr and foxtail within a five-mile radius wagging expectantly. He stood there looking at her until Sam patted his head. It wasn't until she noticed the feathery streak of paint on the wall behind him that she shooed him out into the hall.

When she turned back, her friend was standing by the window looking out. Sunlight streamed around her like in an illustrated Bible story: the Blessed Virgin Mary, infinitely knowing and wise.

"Why does it always seem nobler to soldier on? Mother Courage was probably a bitter old harpy with a bug up her ass." Gerry turned to eye Sam with fond exasperation, a smudge of yellow paint on one cheek. "So what if Ian's younger and knows nothing about babies? That didn't stop Wes from marrying Alice — or either of us from having kids."

"Can we please not discuss this?" Sam made it clear from her tone that it wasn't a request. "I've had about all I can take."

"Not from me, you haven't." Gerry stepped away from the window, not the Blessed Virgin but a gypsy with fierce eyes and corkscrews of black hair trailing from her scarf. "Remember the promise we made to each other when we were kids? We swore we'd never let each other get away with something we knew was wrong."

"We're not sixteen anymore," Sam said.

"And since you brought it up, I don't recall your taking my advice when I begged you not to go into the convent."

"I should have listened."

"Nobody could tell you anything in those days."

"I *was* pretty full of myself, wasn't I?" Gerry shook her head at the memory. "Not exactly ideal qualifications for a nun. It's a miracle I made it to my final vows. Just think what would have happened if I'd actually gone through with it instead of —" She broke off abruptly with a smile that didn't quite reach her eyes. "Listen to me, going on about myself when it's *you* we're discussing."

"Were we? I thought the subject was closed." Sam retrieved her brush.

Minutes later she looked up to find her friend staring out the window, wearing an odd, faraway look. When Gerry spoke, it was in a soft, almost dreamy voice. "Do you know what I regret the most? That I didn't hold her. Just once . . . before they took her away."

Sam felt a light chill tiptoe up her spine. They hadn't spoken of it in years, but she didn't have to ask what her friend was referring to. "I didn't know it was still bothering you," she said gently.

Gerry turned to her with a look that in the blink of an eye revealed everything. The heartbreak she'd kept hidden all these years, the tears shed into her pillow at night, the endless wondering about an infant daughter now grown.

"It never goes away," she said.

"Have you thought about looking for her?"

"No." Gerry spoke firmly.

"Are you afraid she'll want to know about her father?"

"Partly. If the diocese were ever to find out . . ." Gerry broke off with a sigh. "Mostly, though, it's just . . . well, it wouldn't be fair to either of us, stirring all that up again."

"What if she comes looking for you someday?"

"I'll cross that bridge if and when I get to it." Gerry hugged herself, trembling a little.

"You still haven't told the kids?" Andie would understand, she thought. Sam wasn't so sure about eleven-year-old Justin.

"What for? They'd only ask questions I couldn't answer."

"For your own sake then."

"Like penance, you mean?" Gerry shot her a smile that was painful to look at, like the jagged neck of a bottle that moments before had been whole. "Hail Mary, full of grace . . . twenty-five years ago I gave up my child and now I want her back?"

Sam caught the glint of tears, and regretted having snapped at her earlier. "I just hope," she said, walking over and laying a hand on her arm, "I was as good a friend to you then as you are to me now."

Gerry laughed a little, thumbing away her tears. "Does that mean I'm forgiven for butting in?"

"Not quite." Sam smiled. "But I'm working on it."

Gerry bent to pick up her brush, regarding it thoughtfully. "While you're working on it there's something else I'd like to know — why yellow? In a few weeks, you'll know whether it's going to be a boy or a girl." She was referring, of course, to the results of the amniocentesis.

"I asked Inez not to tell me the sex."

Gerry looked at her in disbelief. "How will you be able to stand not knowing?"

"I didn't know with the girls."

"You didn't have a choice back then."

"Maybe those days were better in some ways."

"We didn't have Huggies then. Or proper car seats."

Sam shook her head at the memory. "Can you believe it? Those awful things that hooked over the back of the seat. It's a wonder more babies weren't killed." She looked out the window, where the sun shone over freshly turned earth in which the newly planted perennials thrived. A garden was something she understood, something she could cope with. She sighed. "It's been so long, I feel like Rip Van Winkle."

"Watch it," Gerry growled.

Sam laughed. "*You're* not having a baby."

"Thank the Lord Jesus." Gerry simultaneously rolled her eyes and made the sign of the cross. "Which doesn't change the fact that I fully intend to support you any way I can."

"I could use a Lamaze coach." Sam hadn't thought of it until now, but it occurred to her that Gerry would be the ideal candidate: one who wouldn't cut her any slack.

"I'd be honored." Her friend gave a little curtsy.

Sam waited for her to bring up Ian, but for once Gerry kept her thoughts to herself. That ought to have satisfied her, but somehow it didn't. For without an argument there was no one to reason with, no way to rid herself of this yearning. Was she making a mistake? Was the happiness that had eluded her with Martin just within reach? The wrong size and shape and brand, but happiness all the same. Would she wake up one day, gray haired with a child in tow, to find she'd missed the boat? The thought was terrifying.

Chapter 16

"Do you think they'll ever catch him?"

"I read somewhere that ten percent of all homicides go unsolved." Laura held herself braced as they approached a sharp bend in the road. "Ease up now. Remember what I told you."

Finch tightened her grip on the wheel. "Slow going into a curve, speed up going out."

"Not *speed*. Accelerate. There's a difference."

The girl frowned in concentration. This was only her third driving lesson, and though she was as apt a pupil as on horseback, it was still nerve-racking. They were sticking to back roads until Laura could figure out what to do about a learner's permit.

"I heard Melodie Wycoff say they found some evidence." Finch eased nicely into the bend, and the old Truesdale place, ragged and unkempt, swung into view. An equally dejected-looking mutt sat by the mailbox canting at a drunken angle.

Laura shuddered at the memory. *Melodie and her big mouth,* she thought. "I thought that kind of thing was supposed to be confidential."

"The shoe prints around the body, for one thing — she says they're too small to have been made by a man." They passed a boarded-up fruit stand with a strawberry field beyond.

"I guess that rules out Hector."

"But not me." Finch shot her an uneasy glance.

Laura considered her answer carefully. It wouldn't do to make light of Finch's concerns. Being paranoid wasn't going to help, either. "I think," she said, "if the police were looking for you, they'd have caught up with you by now. Besides, you have an alibi. You were with Maude."

"For all they know, I might've sneaked off while she was asleep." Finch's knuckles were white against the wheel.

"Aren't we getting a little ahead of ourselves? If the killer *is* a woman, which I'm not convinced is the case, that would leave about nine thousand other suspects. As far as anyone knows it could be *me*. Or Anna Vincenzi. Or even Maude."

They were nearing a fork, where the

road branched off in the direction of Dos Palmas and on the left, toward Laura's: two miles of rutted blacktop and sagging fences, with the occasional holographic flash of eyes at night to remind you of just how far out in the boonies you were.

"I just wish they'd catch him," Finch said. "Or her."

Laura thought of the mystery blonde she'd glimpsed outside the barn that day. She'd given a statement to the police, but as far as she knew nothing had come of it. Could the woman be connected with the murder?

"You know what's really creepy?" she said. "At least once a day I'll be ringing somebody up and think, 'Is he the one?' Some ordinary guy who probably never even ran a red light."

It was the one sour note in what had been a series of pleasant surprises. Business was up — today had been their busiest day in weeks — with much of the credit going to Finch. Laura studied the girl out of the corner of her eye. Her long hair, glossy as a thoroughbred's coat, was tied back in a loose ponytail, and nails once bitten to the quick were painted a becoming shade of pink. In a new slim-fitting skirt and top, one of the outfits from

Rusk's, she bore little resemblance to the surly, gaunt-cheeked runaway of just three months ago.

The transformation didn't end there. At the shop, where her part-time position had quickly blossomed into full-time, Finch had proved to be a natural saleswoman. She seemed to know exactly what someone was looking for even when he or she didn't have a clue. She'd even made a few suggestions about inventory, one of which had been a runaway success: rune stone necklaces that were being snapped up by teenagers even faster than the bug jewelry. And hadn't it been her idea, too, to put a real pair of budgies in the brass bird cage by the door? What'd been gathering dust for ages had sold in a matter of days, birds and all, with two more on order.

Her sister had been indispensable as well, making good on the promise to set her up with a Web site designer. But the tectonic shift that had taken place was Laura's discovery that she *liked* being in charge. It was overwhelming at times, sure, but she no longer had to second-guess every decision; she could take a chance on items her mother would have raised an eyebrow at. Now all she had to do was hang on a little while longer, until the Web site was up and running and the recent boost in business translated into black ink.

There was a hard jounce, and Laura was flung forward against her seat belt.

"You want to keep an eye out for those potholes," she said, struggling to keep her voice even. "And for heaven's sake, *slow down*. This isn't the Indy 500."

Finch's driving wasn't her main worry. At some point they'd have to stop acting as if this were just a temporary living arrangement and start looking to the future. Like school, for instance, for which they'd need transcripts. Then there was the much larger, and far more complicated, question of who, if anyone, was her legal guardian.

Finch eased up on the accelerator. "Sorry. I didn't realize I was going so fast."

"It has a way of sneaking up on you." Laura waited a full minute before venturing casually, "You know, Finch, I've been thinking. You can't stick to back roads the rest of your life. At some point you're going to have to get a driver's license."

"That'd mean filling out forms and stuff." Finch frowned and shook her head. "No thanks. I'll stick to back roads." Laura watched her jaw harden and her mouth settle into its old stubborn lines.

She wanted to reassure her in some way, but resisted the temptation. This wasn't the right moment. Instead, she gazed out the window at the narrow road with grassy hills on either side and mountains rising in the distance. She thought, *No sane person could hold her responsible for that man's death*. Finch was a good kid. Smart, too, for how else could she have survived? And now the spark that a dozen plus years of institutional neglect hadn't extinguished had been fanned into something truly miraculous. *If I'd had a daughter . . .*

Lost in thought she didn't notice how far they'd come until they were turning into her driveway. Hector spotted them and waved. It had rained the night before, breaking the spell under which the valley had drowsed and turning the dusty corral into a sea of mud — a rare opportunity Laura's mare clearly hadn't been able to pass up. She was covered in mud from head to hoof, water running off her in brown rivulets as Hector hosed her down.

Laura climbed stiffly from the passenger's seat. *Remind me to take a Valium next time*. She remembered when it'd been Sam giving *her* driving lessons. Come to think of it, hadn't it always been her mother? Quietly, efficiently, and without fuss looking after her and her sister, making sure they had everything they needed, that homework was done, hems let down; that they didn't run out of tampons or shampoo or toilet paper.

The discovery that her father hadn't been as dependable saddened her, though deep down it had come as no surprise. Hadn't she always known he couldn't be counted on when push came to shove? Laura remembered the times she'd waited for him after school, how she'd been the only kid left, shadows lengthening across the school yard and tears in her eyes when he finally arrived to pick her up. He always had an excuse — he'd been caught up in something and had forgotten, or some appointment had run over. His biggest concern, she recalled, was that she not tell her mom.

Laura stretched to release the tenseness in her muscles. A light mist hung over the yard, where long shadows marked the shortening days. Judging from the size of the mud puddle in which Hector stood he'd been at it a while. She picked her way over, unmindful of her good navy pumps.

"Nothing like a bath to spoil the fun." She patted Judy, who stood meekly, head hung as if in shame. "Sorry you had to get stuck cleaning up the mess. She can be a real clown, can't she?"

Hector grinned. "She was just feeling her oats."

"What did the vet say about Punch?" Doc Henry had been out again today to check on his leg.

"That he could use more exercise."

"I know I haven't been around much —"

"I'll take care of it."

"I'm asking too much of you as it is."

He shrugged. "I've been thinking . . . maybe I should take a break from school. Place is starting to look a little run-down." He gestured in the direction of the corral, where the gate sagged from loops of baling wire.

She refused to even consider it. "You're already making up for the course you dropped last semester. No, it's out of the question."

"Too late. I already talked to my adviser." He used the edge of his hand to slice a sheet of muddy water from the mare's flank.

"Oh, Hector." She was pierced with guilt.

"Just two classes. I can make them up next semester."

Laura folded her arms over her chest, eyeing him sternly. "You can't keep doing this, you know. At the rate you're going you'll be an old man by the time you graduate."

"I'll be an old man no matter what."

"Hec . . ."

"Would you hand me that?" He gestured toward a raggedy towel draped over the wheelbarrow.

Laura fetched the towel and handed it to him, watching as he briskly rubbed Judy down. His movements were quick, like a boxer's, and at the same time oddly graceful.

She felt her face grow warm. These days, blushing had become a habit. She'd made peace with the fact that he would never see her as anything more than a friend. And that he wouldn't always be around. But like cacti that bloom but once a decade, and cicadas that rise from the earth every seven years, the blood that had rushed so readily to her cheeks at sixteen had come full circle.

"Listen, are you going to be around tonight?" she asked. "I thought maybe we'd take in a movie. My treat."

"Can't. My brother's in town," he replied without looking up.

"Which one?"

"Eddie."

Eddie rode bulls, she recalled. "Isn't the rodeo in Paso Robles?"

"Yeah, but what's another hundred miles?"

Eddie was his favorite brother. Maybe one reason they were so close was because they were both confirmed bachelors. A woman would have to be as gorgeous as Alice, she thought, for Hector to take the plunge. It would help, too, if he hadn't known her since she was a pudgy kid in braces.

"Well, don't stay out too late," she teased, starting toward the house, "And give my best to your brother."

"Hey, I forgot to tell you," Hector called after her. "Your mother phoned while you were out."

Laura stopped and retraced her steps. "What did she want?"

"To see how you're doing, I guess." He shrugged, taking hold of Judy's halter and leading her into the barn.

Laura felt guilty all of a sudden. Her widowed mother, three months pregnant, living all alone out in the middle of nowhere. *It should have been me checking up on her.* Was she still angry at her mother? Maybe. In the same utterly irrational way she'd been angry at her father for dying. Parents, she thought, weren't supposed to die.

Or fall in love. Or have babies.

As she trudged toward the house, she wondered if she was so different from Maude's son. He seemed to view his mother's newfound happiness as some sort of defection, proof that she no longer loved or needed him. Wasn't she just as bad, blaming her mother for living her life as she saw fit?

She glanced down at muddy shoes looking more like feet of clay than another pair of dress pumps she'd ruined. All of a sudden she felt small and mean-spirited.

Maude was at the stove when she walked in, stirring the contents of a sizzling pan. "Liver and onions," she announced.

Laura tried not to make a face. "Smells delicious."

"Finch said the very same thing. Glad you both like liver so much." Maude tipped her a knowing wink. "By the way, I hear you're teaching her how to drive."

"She's a quick learner."

"One of these days we might even teach her how to cook."

Laura smiled and went about setting the table. Plates, napkins, flatware, the glasses from Safeway that Peter used to complain about. There was comfort, she thought, in old habits and old things.

"She'll be needing a driver's license." Maude seemed to have read her mind.

"I know." Laura reached down to scratch Pearl, who lay stretched in the middle of the floor like a matted yellow rug. The dog's tail thumped against the worn linoleum. Not to be one-upped, Rocky wandered over to have his head scratched, too. "She's terrified . . . and not just of taking the test."

"I don't blame her."

Laura walked over to slip an arm around Maude's shoulders. She felt tiny and fragile, and smelled faintly of lavender. "We're a funny bunch, aren't we? Like left-over peas rolling around in a can."

"No two alike." Maude scooped liver onto a plate, her eyes unnaturally bright.

The time had come to put matters to rest. "You know you'll always have a home here, don't you? As long as you want." Some things, she thought, had to be said more than once for them to stick.

Maude shot her a timid look. "What if I get sick?"

"I'll take care of you."

"I'm eighty-four. A year or two from now I won't be able to get around like I used to."

"So?"

"I wouldn't want to be a burden."

"You could never be a burden. Anyway," Laura said, "who would make me liver and onions?"

Maude smiled up at Laura. "Something tells me you'd get along just fine without it."

Something sloughed away inside Laura, a weight she hadn't even known she was carrying. Maybe Hector needed to hear how she felt, too. She'd risk making a fool of herself, sure, but how much worse to spend the rest of her life wondering. She realized suddenly that the baby wasn't the only reason she was jealous of her mother. She envied Sam's courage — the courage to leap into the unknown.

Hours later, Laura sat curled on the seat-sprung sofa on the porch, waiting for Hector to return. The tension was almost more than she could bear and when his truck finally pulled in shortly before midnight, its headlights cutting a bright swath across the yard, she nearly jumped out of her skin. His tires crunched to a stop, and the engine died. She heard the thunk of a door, and saw a shadow angle up the side of the moonlit barn. She followed its progress, her heart thumping in her chest, until it had rounded the corner and was swallowed up by the deeper shadows beyond.

She rose on legs weak as a newborn's. A light wind had kicked up, and out in the darkness somewhere she could hear a loose gate banging against its latch. It seemed to scold her as she ran lightly down the steps. She'd never visited him at night; it was a line she hadn't dared cross. But now here she was, chasing her shadow across the moonlit yard, heart in throat, and her hopes pinned on the slenderest of chances — a chance that if dashed might forever cost her his friendship.

She caught up with him as he was letting himself in the door. Hector swung about with a startled look that was quickly replaced by relief. "Laura. For a second there I thought —" He took a step back, squinting at her in the light that spilled through the open door. "Hey, what's wrong? You look a little flushed."

"Can I come in?" she asked breathlessly.

"Sure." He held the door open. "Don't mind the mess. I haven't had a chance to clean up."

"Like I'm such a model housekeeper myself." She managed a weak laugh.

Laura stepped into a room as simple and uncluttered as Hector himself: a bed and dresser, a plain pine table and chair. The only sign of disarray was the clothing piled on the floor by the bed. She felt a sudden, perverse longing to gather them up, bury her face in them.

"I'll make coffee," he said.

She watched him move to the small counter in back, which held just enough space for a sink, coffeemaker, and microwave. He filled the coffee pot from a plastic jug in the fridge. The beans, whole from an unlabeled sack, were poured into the small Braun grinder she'd given him last Christmas. If Hector was fastidious about anything it was his coffee.

When it was ready, he filled a mug and handed it to her. "You want to tell me what's up?"

Laura sank into a chair, her heart still beating much too fast. "I was just lonely, that's all." *This was a terrible idea,* she thought, *I shouldn't have come.* Hector just stood there, sipping from his mug, wisps of steam curling up around his face. She opened her mouth to tell him the whole truth, but at the last second chickened out, asking, "Did you have a good time tonight?"

"We knocked back a few beers, had a few laughs." Hector grinned, showing his chipped front tooth.

"Any sign of your brother settling down?"

"You could say that. He's buying land out in Montana. That's what he drove all this way to talk to me about. He wants me to go in with him." Hector might have been discussing the weather.

Laura felt as if she'd been punched in the gut. "What did you tell him?"

"That I'd think about it."

She felt angry all of a sudden. "What's stopping you?"

"This place, for one thing."

"You shouldn't let that hold you back." She stopped short of saying what was on the tip of her tongue, *We'd manage just fine without you.* It wouldn't have been true; they'd be lost without Hector.

"You'd better give me that before you spill it." He reached for her mug.

Laura looked down and saw that her hands were trembling. She was flooded with shame. "I'm sorry," she said, not knowing why she was apologizing.

She handed him the mug and watched him place it on the table along with his. He wore what he jokingly called his uniform: jeans and T-shirt — tonight's was green with a denim jacket thrown over it — and a pair of toe-sprung cowboy boots. His shiny black hair fell in thick, straight layers to just below his ears. Even his smile was the same as always.

Yet everything had changed.

"Sorry for what?" he asked.

"That you're leaving."

"I didn't say I was."

"It's your life. Do what you want." Laura dropped her gaze, staring at the worn hooked rug on which he stood. "I'm sorry. I didn't mean it that way. It's just . . . well, after a while you get used to things being a certain way. It's selfish, I know. I have no right."

He sank onto his haunches before her. "Laura." Just that, her name. Yet she'd never heard him speak it so tenderly. He cupped her chin, lifting her head to meet his gaze.

She blinked, and felt the wet kiss of tears against her lower lashes. "Don't go." The words slipped out, soft as a sigh.

In a single motion he rose, pulling her to her feet and into his arms. He held her tightly, saying her name again, "Laura." Gently, as if consoling her.

She brought her head to rest against his shoulder, acutely aware of his muscles pressing against her ribs. He smelled of smoky taverns and aftershave. When they kissed it was as natural as taking the next breath. Hector's mouth, warm and sweet, tasting faintly of coffee. Her own parting in response. Not like before; this time for real. She could feel the edge of his teeth and the sharp point of his belt buckle. Hungry. Wanting her, *needing* her, as much as she wanted and needed him.

He slipped a hand up the back of her neck, pushing his fingers into her hair, gripping it hard. "How could I leave you?"

It was like music, the way he said it. "I thought —"

He drew back to place a finger against her lips. "We go from here."

Later, Laura wouldn't recall who undressed whom. It seemed one minute they were clothed . . . and the next naked, their bodies glowing in the moonlight. Hector led her over to the bed, which smelled of him and brought a wealth of images: his clothes drying on the line, his worn boots, his saddle polished to the smoothness of wood.

I'm dreaming, she thought. Like the dreams from which she awoke in a tangle of sheets, sweating and ashamed. Only now there was no shame. Just the quiet knowledge that he wanted her. She closed her eyes, letting her head fall back against the pillow. She could feel the calluses on his hands and shivered as he touched her there . . . and there. Then he was on his knees, straddling her. Not ashamed to let her see how aroused he was.

She wrapped her fingers around him and felt him shudder in response. He pulled her hand away and brought it to his mouth, running the tip of his tongue over her palm.

"Was I doing it wrong?" she asked.

"Just the opposite." He smiled lazily.

"Tell me what to do."

"Just relax."

He cupped her breast, running his thumb lightly over her nipple. The sensation brought a tug of pleasure that traveled all the way down between her legs. Laura let go, let herself sink as if into a warm bath. Had it ever been this good with Peter? She couldn't recall. There was only this: Hector's mouth taking up where his hands left off, his tongue raising goose bumps, his flesh gliding warm against hers.

She opened her legs, crying out a little as he entered her. Not just because it had been so long, but because it felt so good. So right.

Hector made love the way he rode — with the assuredness of someone born to it, pausing every so often to stroke her cheek, or run the tip of his tongue along her neck. Murmuring endearments as he rocked against her.

They came together. Crying out, arching into one another. As if there had never been any doubt that this would take place, as if the past twelve years had been but a prelude, an inevitable progression of events leading to this moment. She brought her legs up, wrapping them tightly about his hips, losing all sense of where he left off and she began. Aware only of the warm wave that rose, crested, then rose again.

When it was over, he rolled onto his side, and she felt a rush of cool air against her sweat-slick skin. Gently, he kissed her temple, then the moist hollow of her neck. "We'll take it slow next time."

"Will there be a next time?" She spoke lightly, but the uncertainty must have shown in her face.

Hector smiled. "That's up to you."

Laura felt giddy, a laugh bubbling to the surface. She pushed herself up onto her elbow so that they were facing one another. "Oh Hector. You still don't get it, do you? I'm crazy about you. I have been for years . . . even when I didn't know it."

He traced the slope of her breast. "I was sort of hoping you'd say that."

She didn't dare ask it: Did that mean he'd stay? The question trembled like a leaf about to fall. "There's just one thing," she said, "I'm not very good about writing."

He cocked his head, looking puzzled. "Is there something I'm not getting here?"

"Montana's a long way off."

He grinned. "That's what I told Eddie."

"You bastard." She took a playful swipe at him.

"If you'd known my mind was made up, you wouldn't have asked me to stay." His logic was, as always, irrefutable.

"You could've just told me how you felt."

He caught her wrist and held it to his mouth. She could feel his breath, warm against her palm. A sweet shiver coursed through her. "You had to trust me first."

"Trust was never an issue."

"Not just to look after this place. You had to know I'd never hurt you."

Laura smiled, shaking her head. "You're nothing like Peter."

He looked at her long and hard, then asked, "Does that mean you'd consider getting married again someday?"

She felt more than heard his words: an electrical jolt that shot straight down through the pit of her stomach. Then a strange calm descended over her. Like the time she'd been rear-ended and the woman who'd hit her had asked if she was okay, and she'd answered, "I'm fine," as if it'd been nothing more than a polite exchange in passing.

In exactly the same tone she said to Hector, "I haven't ruled it out."

He didn't say anything. He just smiled.

They made love again, and this time took it slowly. When they drew apart at last, Laura was glowing, not just with contentment, but with the sweet knowledge that this was only the beginning. There would be a next time, and a time after that — days and nights strung together like links on a chain.

She fell into a sound sleep with her head tucked into the warm curve of Hector's arm. For once she slept without dreaming, with only the occasional hoot of an owl or distant howl of a dog nipping at the outer edge of consciousness. She didn't hear a car pull into her driveway shortly before two or see a shadowy figure climb from it.

It wasn't until she was jerked from sleep by the dogs' frantic barking that she tumbled out of bed to peer out the window. All she could see was a corner of the house, where a red light pulsed in strobelike flashes, washing the weathered clapboard in crimson.

Chapter 17

This time it was for real. No going back.

There was just this: putting one foot in front of the other.

For weeks now her backpack had lain in readiness under the bed. Maude was the only one who'd known, but she hadn't said a word. It was an understanding they shared: that the world, like the moon, was divided into two halves. The sunny half where people like Laura lived and the dark half, where the sidewalks were cold and every escalator you went up was going down.

Like the cop she'd caught a glimpse of as she sneaked past the living room. She'd barely noticed what he looked like. What difference did it make? He was all cops rolled into one: short, tall, fat, thin, young, old. The cops taking her to a new mommy and daddy, or social worker, or judge. The cops responding to a domestic or searching for drugs. And worst of all: the ones who had her whole story written at a glance.

No notebook this time. Only the faint sizzle of a walkie-talkie over the anxious fluting of Maude's voice. The girl felt a burst of love that nearly eclipsed her fear. Maude would stall him. She would lie outright if she had to. *That's what people who love you do.* The thought was like something warm tucked inside her sweatshirt as she slipped out the back door, easing the screen door noiselessly shut.

The cruiser was parked in the driveway behind Hector's truck, its light flashing. Incredibly, the keys were still in the ignition and the door, when she tried it, unlocked. She reached in and snatched them, thinking, *The cops back home wouldn't be this stupid.* A flick of her arm and they went sailing out over the front path to land with a soft crackle amid the hydrangeas.

Then she was sprinting down the drive, the road ahead gleaming pale as bone in the moonlight, the hills beyond folded in shadow. Her backpack tugged at her shoulders as she ran, a cruel reminder of how unaccustomed to its weight she'd grown.

But this time she'd come prepared at least. She felt the pocket of her jeans, where it bulged slightly — Sister Agnes's key. She would lie low at the convent until first thing tomorrow. The search would have widened by then. The cops wouldn't think to look so close to home.

Home. The thought was like a sharp rock in the pit of her stomach. She pictured Maude, Laura, and Hector gathered about the kitchen table, the dogs in their boxes by the stove, the cats padding about underfoot. Only this time Laura would know better than to come looking for her.

Finch found the hole in the fence and crawled under, setting off up the hill. It was easier now because she knew the way, and with sneakers and long pants — not to mention a full moon — the going was fairly easy. Before long she spotted the convent, no longer strange and forbidding, but a place where she'd be safe from harm. Even the thought of its resident ghost didn't frighten her. If there *were* such things as ghosts, wouldn't they be like people? Some good, some bad?

As she started up the path she'd first walked with Sister Agnes — what seemed a thousand years ago — she heard only the soft tweep of nightjars. The tall grass whispered against her jeans, and the air was filled with the faint dry scent of sage. She allowed herself a last image of Laura and Maude, like a precious sip of water: Maude in her robe with one button dangling loose, and Laura in a rumpled T-shirt down to her knees.

The girl stumbled, and the stony path rose up to smack her. She picked herself up, brushing dirt from her stinging knees and swiping angrily at her eyes. No tears. That was for later, when she would have the luxury of feeling sorry for herself.

Hugging the shadows, she crept around back of the convent to where a dirt road sloped to the pasture below. The moon floated overhead, a ghostly galleon. Amid the meadow's tall grass tiny white flowers shone bright as stars. She could see the boxy outline of the beehives, quiet this time of night. Sister Agnes had told her that bees were like people in that way: They worked hard all day, each at its own assigned task, and rested at night.

She realized she would miss Sister Agnes, too. She'd always thought of nuns as set apart somehow; she hadn't known they could be so understanding. She dug the key from her pocket. Warm from her body's heat, it seemed to glow in the cup of her palm. In the moonlight the corrugated shed below was starkly outlined, its windows dark.

The lock opened easily, the door swinging open. The girl felt her heart lurch as she stepped into pitch darkness, easing the door shut behind her. A row of ghostly sentinels, floating above the floor, with gaping holes where their faces should have been, seemed to leap out at her. She let out a startled little squeak, gooseflesh crawling up her arms. But a closer look revealed them to be white canvas jumpsuits and netted hoods hanging from pegs along the wall. The nuns wore them when collecting honey, she recalled. She let out a breath and lowered her backpack to the floor.

Gradually her eyes adjusted to the darkness. Now she could make out rows of shelves lined with jars that glistened like gold. In the center of the room was a long table jumbled with boxes, and in the far corner a desk with a computer hooded in plastic. It made her smile, thinking of nuns browsing the Internet. It didn't go somehow with Sister Agnes's biblical garden.

She was looking for a place to curl up for the night when she heard the crunch of footsteps along the path. Instinct honed by a lifetime sent her diving under the desk. The pounding of her heart seemed to fill the tiny space.

A moment later the footsteps paused and she heard the soft click of the door. It swung open and a narrow avenue of moon-light flooded in, illuminating the floor just inches from where her backpack lay propped against a table leg. Oh God. Would it give her away? Then the figure stepped inside and she let out a tiny, inaudible sigh of relief. She couldn't see its face, only a pair of shoes peeking from under the hem of a long dark skirt.

Not a cop after all — a nun.

Her heart wouldn't stop pounding, even so. There was something strange about this nun. Why wasn't she turning on the light? Why was she creeping around in the dark like . . .

. . . *like a burglar.*

She glided past the girl, catlike, disappearing into the next room. A moment later Finch heard the scraping sound of something heavy, like a trunk or cabinet being dragged away from the wall. She could hear the woman muttering to herself. Then the sound of a match being struck. The doorway was illuminated and a long witchy shadow angled up the wall just inside.

The girl was swept by a sudden chill. All at once she felt deeply afraid, though she couldn't have said why. Fear that turned to bewilderment when the nun reappeared minutes later dressed in an ordinary skirt and blouse, high heels clicking against the floor, hair too perfect and blond to be real curling about her shoulders. Her back was turned and from where Finch crouched all she could see was the candle about which her hand was cupped and her long shadow swaying over the rows of glistening jars.

She'd almost passed beyond Finch's line of sight when she turned, as if hearing a noise. In the flickering candlelight her face, garishly lit from underneath, leaped suddenly and horrifyingly into view: long and horsey, with small deep-set eyes and slash of crimson mouth.

Laura eyed Mother Ignatius curiously. She'd never before seen a nun dressed in anything but a habit. The mother superior wore an ordinary white chenille bathrobe with a pair of blue terry slippers peeking from under its hem, her cropped gray hair proof that what the girls had whispered in catechism was untrue: Nuns didn't shave their heads.

They were gathered in the small sitting room where aeons ago Sam had taken tea: Laura, Finch, Sister Agnes, and Mother Ignatius. It was a quarter past three, with the other nuns asleep, presumably unaware of the worrisome situation just down the hall.

Mother Ignatius fixed her gaze on the girl, a pair of flinty gray-blue eyes shining from a face that all at once looked ancient — like those of mummified saints. *She must be close to ninety,* Laura thought with a small measure of surprise. Her mind flew back to the long ago morning when she'd caught her and her sister trespassing. That had to be — what? Almost twenty years. The woman had seemed old as the ages then, and yet here she was, still going strong.

"You're certain it was Sister Beatrice you saw?" she asked sternly.

Finch glanced nervously at Sister Agnes, in her robe, too, who nodded encouragingly.

"It was her, all right," Finch said.

"You're absolutely sure?" The question seemed superfluous, given that the mother superior had to have done a bed check.

"I'm sure." Finch's hands twisted in her lap.

"About what she was wearing, too?"

Finch nodded. In the muted glow of the table lamp, her eyes looked bruised, just as when Laura had first found her — a scrap of a girl looking as if she didn't have a friend in the world.

Laura felt a rush of love. *You're not alone,* she wanted to say.

Less than an hour ago, she'd been sure it was all over. Maude's stricken white face, and the cop barking into his walkie-talkie, had told her everything she needed to know: Finch was gone. She'd stood there, numb, struggling to answer the cop's questions while telling him next to nothing. No, she hadn't known the police in New York were looking for the girl. She had no idea, either, where Finch might have gone. Laura had seen no need to tell him what she *did* know, for she was as convinced of Finch's innocence as she was of her own. She'd even indulged in a secret little smile when the rookie discovered his car keys missing and had to radio for backup.

Shortly after, when Mother Ignatius phoned, it had seemed the answer to Laura's prayers. Her only thought as she raced to her car was that she'd sort it out somehow. Explain everything to the police, hire a lawyer if necessary. As awful as things might look right now, it'd be a relief, after all the tiptoeing around, for it to be out in the open.

Now she could see it wasn't going to be as clear-cut as she'd hoped. Finch, it seemed, had unwittingly stumbled into something far more serious than any trouble she herself might be in.

"Was she behaving strangely in any way?" Mother Ignatius, despite her advanced age, stood straight as a steeple.

"You mean, like, crazy?" Finch frowned, nibbling on a thumbnail. "No, not really. It was just weird, that's all, seeing her all dressed up like that. Like . . . like a normal person."

The mother superior's mouth flattened in a small, humorless smile. "It might surprise you to know, my dear, that underneath our habits we're all quite normal."

Finch reddened. "I didn't mean . . ."

"I know what you meant." Her smile softened. "And no, it's not our practice to traipse about in wigs and high heels."

Laura thought once more of the blond woman outside the barn. Could it have been Sister Beatrice? Prowling around in the middle of the night dressed in street clothes wasn't a crime, even for a nun. But suppose it hadn't stopped there.

Suddenly, she wished Hector were here.

Sister Agnes spoke up. "Temptation takes many forms." She bowed her head, fidgeting with the sash on her robe. "Perhaps if Sister Beatrice were to get help . . ." She let the sentence trail off.

Mother Ignatius cast her a sharp look. "I'm afraid this is more than any of us is equipped to handle, Sister." She didn't have to say what they all suspected: that dressing up in street clothes might be the least of Sister Beatrice's sins. When she reached for the phone on the table beside her, no one was surprised, least of all Laura.

What startled her was her own hand shooting out to cover Mother Ignatius's. "Wait." Laura looked at Finch slumped in her chair. She could only imagine the courage it must have taken for her to come forward, to risk her own safety for what might, in the end, amount to a false alarm. "Could we leave Finch out of this? She's been through enough as it is. If the police think she's involved in any way —"

Finch cut her off. "It's all right. Anything would be better than this. Always running. Always scared." She lifted her bruised eyes to Laura. Hope was the one thing they hadn't been able to take from her, and now it, too, was gone.

Laura's hand fell heavily to her side. She watched with weary resignation as Sister Agnes bowed her head and prayed, "Our soul waits for the Lord, who is our help and our shield. May your kindness, O

Lord, be upon us who have put our hope in you."

They all watched as the mother superior punched in the dreaded three digits. "This is Mother Ignatius of Our Lady of the Wayside," she spoke crisply into the phone. "We have an urgent matter requiring the police. Would you send someone at once?"

On the other side of town, oblivious to the drama taking place at Our Lady of the Wayside, Sam sat curled on her living room sofa, wallowing in an old weeper on AMC — a truly awful movie that nonetheless had her digging into the pocket of her robe for a tissue. She seemed to cry at the drop of a hat these days: Hallmark commercials, sentimental songs, couples in the park holding hands. The only thing she didn't dare cry about was Ian.

When she'd woken and couldn't get back to sleep, she'd thought about phoning Gerry, but four in the morning was too early even for best friends. Gerry, when she realized it wasn't an emergency, would kill her. Sam hauled herself to her feet with a sigh. She felt heavy, the flat stomach in which she'd always taken such pride replaced by a round little tummy.

I'm too old for this, she thought.

It'd be different when the baby was here. She'd have help. But for now it was just her. Like an old house, sagging a bit here and there, with room for one more.

It's not just that, a voice spoke clearly in her head, the way voices do in the wee hours of the morning. *You miss Ian.* She'd tried to push him from her mind by immersing herself in a flurry of activities. Decorating the house, gardening, endless committee meetings for the festival that had entered the military-operations stage. She'd even taken up crocheting again, with a half finished baby blanket to show for it. But each day was like swimming against the tide.

In the sleepless hours before dawn she had no defense against the loneliness. She would wake while it was still dark, an ache in her throat, picturing him asleep in his bed or perched on a scaffolding in some other time zone.

Was he thinking of her, too?

She thought of the one time she'd phoned, in a weak moment she'd regretted as soon as his voice came on the line. It had been clear and upbeat, not that of the wounded man she'd left behind in Big Sur.

"Did I catch you at a bad time?" she'd asked, her pulse racing.

"Just the usual. Boy genius at work." He gave an ironic chuckle that cut through her like a blade. "What's up?" As if she were an old friend checking in after a lengthy absence.

Sam hesitated. "I just . . ." What? Why *had* she called? "I just wanted to see how you were doing. And to let you know . . . Ian, I'm sorry I didn't return your calls." He must have left five, six messages.

There was a brief silence at the other end before he said, "I was calling to see if you were okay."

"I'm fine. The amnio . . ." She closed her eyes, remembering how scared she'd been when the results came in, how desperately she'd wanted him there. "Everything looks normal. Ten fingers, ten toes."

"That's good." He sounded relieved. "Boy or girl?"

"I don't want to know." It had never occurred to her that Ian might feel differently, and now, though he hadn't uttered a word, she could sense his displeasure. She was quick to add, "I'll let you know when . . . the time comes."

He gave a bitter laugh. "I guess I'm owed that much, right?"

Sam winced, closing her eyes against the image that rushed up at her — Ian peering through binoculars at an osprey nest, in which baby birds cheeped.

"I'm sorry," she choked.

"Me, too." He sucked in a breath. "Listen, I'm sort of in the middle of something. Call me if you need anything. I'll be around."

She hadn't spoken to him since.

She reached for the remote on the coffee table and switched off the TV. Amazingly, she felt no sleepier than before. She glanced a bit enviously at Max, sacked out on the rug. All he did was sleep and chase squirrels, though if he were ever to catch one he probably wouldn't know what to do with it. She smiled. Tom had meant well, but his dog was really just a big old chicken.

She padded barefoot into the kitchen. When her daughters were little and couldn't sleep she'd given them warm milk. Maybe it would work for her. She reached into the cupboard under the stove, rattling around until she found the smallest of her saucepans. She poured milk into it, and while waiting for it to heat found herself looking about in wonder at all she'd accomplished.

Finding the original cupboards had been the biggest bonanza. Restored to their rightful place, with a fresh coat of pale green paint, they went perfectly with the deep porcelain sink and built-in china cupboard. The old beige linoleum had been replaced with tiles, and the pine table from the sewing room at Isla Verde, though a snug fit, was perfect in the breakfast nook. The oak high chair she'd found at Avery Lewellyn's antique barn, in need only of refinishing, provided the finishing touch.

I won't feel so lonely when the baby comes.

She tested the milk with her finger and poured it into a mug, adding a teaspoon of honey. As she sank down at the table, idly stirring her mug, it occurred to her that this house wasn't the only thing that had been renovated. Her life, too, had been altered — drastically in some ways, more subtly in others. In addition to finding out who her true friends were, she'd discovered who *she* was: not just a mother, or a widow bravely carrying on, but a middle-aged woman capable of pulling up stakes, even reinventing herself. When you got right down to it, wasn't there something pretty remarkable about that?

She smiled at the irony. Wasn't it only a few months ago she'd looked upon this unexpected blessing as a curse? One that had disrupted her life and dumped a whole new set of responsibilities in her lap just as she was disentangling herself from old ones. And yet . . .

I wouldn't be here otherwise. Enjoying the kind of freedom she'd always dreamed of. At Isla Verde she'd have had to draw the curtains to keep the television's glow from Lupe, who'd have wanted to know what she was doing up so late. A light in the kitchen at this hour would have had her housekeeper poking her head in to see if Sam needed anything. And it wasn't just the lack of privacy. There'd have been end-less calls to the plumber and electrician, the pool man and roofer. Leaks to plug, cracks to plaster, bugs to be exterminated. Now the property manager took care of all that.

She didn't miss Delarosa's, either. It had been time to step down, leaving Laura to flourish in a way she couldn't have other-wise. The few times Sam had stopped by, she'd sensed a subtly different atmosphere, as if a window had been opened to let in fresh air and sunshine. Even Laura seemed happier.

Sam caught a movement outside the sliding glass door, and started. She seldom drew the curtains at night. What would have been the point? The only creatures out and about at this hour were the raccoons and possums that regularly raided her trash cans. It wasn't until Max began to growl in the next room that she felt a flicker of concern.

A minute later he padded in, still rumbling. She stroked his head. "Relax, boy. It's just our old friend Rocky Raccoon. If you're lucky he'll leave you a bone, though I wouldn't count on it."

Max continued to growl, wandering over to the door with his plumed tail rigid, staring out at the darkness. She'd never seen him like this, and the little hairs on the back of her neck stood up as well. What if it was something other than a raccoon?

Her thoughts turned to the murders the paper had been full of all summer. Daily warnings were issued against hitchhiking and going out unaccompanied at night. But while forensic experts were busy combing every shred of evidence, so far there'd been no arrest.

Sam hadn't given it much thought, other than to lock her doors and windows — more as a precaution than out of any real concern — probably because an intruder was the least of her fears.

She'd finished her milk and was rinsing

her mug at the sink when Max erupted into furious barking. "What is it, boy?" Her voice was thin and high pitched. Almost before she realized it, she was reaching into the drawer on her right, groping blindly for — what? She didn't know until her hand closed firmly about a knife handle. Even so, she was struck by the absurdity of it. She'd read too many newspaper stories, that's all.

Yet she couldn't stop the goose bumps that scurried up her arms like tiny biting insects. Her heart banged against her ribs and she was more wide-awake than ever. Sam walked over to the door, jiggling the handle to make sure it was locked. She was heading into the living room to double check the front door as well when it occurred to her that all anyone would have to do to get in was smash a window.

The room went a little gray, and she thought, *I should call the police.*

But what real cause was there for alarm? A dog barking? Dogs barked at everything. If she phoned the police every time Max barked, she'd be like the boy who'd cried wolf.

On legs gone suddenly rubbery, she walked down the hall to her bedroom. It was as spartan as her old one: a Shaker-style bed and dresser, the mica floor lamp from home, a pretty antique quilt from a trunk in the attic at Isla Verde. As she climbed onto the bed, shivering, she wanted nothing more than to wrap herself in the quilt and have all this turn out to be nothing more than a bad case of nerves. She looked down at the knife in her hand. Dull as all her others, no doubt. It would be no more protection than that silly dog.

She could hear Max barking in the next room, furiously and without letup. She reached for the phone on the nightstand. However foolish she'd feel when the police arrived, it was better than being scared out of her wits. She was punching in the numbers when the sound of breaking glass from down the hall went through her like a jolt from a downed power line.

She let out a strangled yelp, her heart slamming up into her throat. Someone *was* out there. Someone who was inside now.

She dove to the floor, the receiver to her ear.

But the line was dead.

Chapter 18

Alice had known this day would come. She'd braced herself against it the way she might have against some minor medical procedure. Ian was his son, after all. But when Wes had suggested they invite him for supper she'd been thrown for a loop nonetheless. Now that the dreaded evening was here, it was requiring every bit of her considerable willpower to keep her smile pinned in place. While a few miles away her sister was sitting down to her own supper, and at police headquarters downtown they were receiving notification of a sixteen-year-old runaway named Bethany Wells, Alice was passing her stepson a bowl of fingerling potatoes.

"Why don't you finish these?" She cast a bright look at Ian. The months of charting a smooth course through Hurricane Marty had trained her well.

He reached for the bowl wearing an equally shatterproof smile. "Sure, if no one else wants them. Great meal, Alice."

"I'm glad you liked it," she said.

"I didn't know Alice could cook until we were practically engaged." Wes, at the other end of the table, beamed proudly. "She didn't want to blow her cover as a hard-bitten career woman."

"A presently unemployed career woman," she amended with a dry laugh.

"How's the job search going?" Ian helped himself to the potatoes, though she had the feeling he was only doing it to be polite.

"I've gone on six interviews so far."

"Alice is being modest," Wes said. "She's gotten two offers already. Lifetime and Channel 2."

"I'm holding out for the networks," she explained. "I have an interview with CBS on Monday. They're looking for a new executive producer for the *Shannon O'Brien Show*. We'll see . . ." She shrugged as if her pulse weren't racing at the thought.

She could see that Ian was interested . . . and maybe a little perplexed. He probably couldn't imagine Wes firing her, and for good reason. In the end, it had been more of a mutual decision. Wes had been right about one thing — at CTN, where to many of her coworkers she'd never be anything other than the boss's wife, her effectiveness would always be undercut. What surprised her was how invigorated she'd felt since she left. No more Marty Milnik. No more cold shoulders and catty backstabbing. The professional camaraderie with Wes hadn't ended, either. They still bounced ideas off each other. In some ways it was *better* than before.

There was only one fly in the ointment: her mother. She'd tried hard not to blame Ian. The truth was she *liked* him. But the thought of him sleeping with Sam was like something she'd swallowed that wouldn't go down. The perfectly set table, with its bank of flickering candles, looked *too* perfect all of a sudden: a stage set for a play.

"Well, here's to success." Ian raised his wineglass.

If he was feeling the chill, he was doing a good job of hiding it. In his chinos and open-necked shirt he looked relaxed and tanned from a recent trip to Provence, where an old friend on the board of an art school had twisted his arm into giving a master class. She pictured him tooling around the French countryside, giving not a thought to his pregnant ex-girlfriend back home.

At the same time, it occurred to Alice that she'd gotten her wish. Hadn't she wanted — no, *campaigned* — for their breakup? But instead of feeling happy she had the awful sense of its being wrong somehow. Maybe that's why she was so uptight now. She couldn't decide whether she was angry at Ian for being with her mother in the first place or for *not* being with her now.

"Speaking of success, here's to the Giants." Wes lifted his own glass in honor of the plum commission Ian had just been awarded: a mural for the clubhouse at San Francisco's brand-new stadium — a commission that would mean the difference between relative obscurity and minor fame.

"It's quite an honor." Alice forced a smile.

"Don't think I'm not aware of it." Ian's humility seemed genuine.

She found herself wondering if maybe, just maybe, she'd misjudged him. Was he as cavalier as she'd painted him? Still, there was no excuse for the way he'd treated her mother. Alice didn't have to hear the whole sordid tale. It was the oldest story in the world: younger man dumps older woman.

For her husband's sake, though, she was going to have to find a way to get past it. Somehow. "Will you be spending much time in San Francisco?" she asked.

"Not if I can help it." Alice caught a

glint of something dark in his eyes.

She felt a sudden desire to goad him. "No more trips to Europe? A freewheeling bachelor like yourself?" She spoke lightly, but the hard look on Ian's face told her she'd hit her mark.

"A baby needs a father."

An uncomfortable silence fell. So far they'd avoided touching upon the subject. Their first evening as a family had been fashioned instead out of small, safe, biodegradable subjects. But it was a flimsy structure, a paper kite now impaled on a tree limb. How, she thought, could you *not* talk about something so huge?

Wes cleared his throat. "Well. That wasn't so bad, was it? Only about three-point-eight on the Richter scale." His joke didn't elicit a laugh, but it wasn't intended to. "More wine, anyone? I know I could use a refill." He poured some into his glass before passing the bottle to Ian.

Ignoring it, Ian looked from Wes to Alice. "I'd like to make one thing clear, then we can move on," he said evenly. "This is nobody's business but Sam's and mine. If it'd been that way from the beginning, things might have turned out differently."

Alice felt her face flush at the obvious insinuation that *she* was somehow to blame. "If you'd given any thought at all to my mother, *none* of this would be happening." Each carefully enunciated word was like an ice cube clinking into a chilled glass.

Ian eyed her curiously. "You really believe that, don't you?" His tone was mild, though once again she caught that flicker of something dark and unreadable in his eyes.

Alice placed her napkin on the table, cream linen with pale beige piping — part of a set that was a wedding present from Wes's Aunt Estelle — pressing it with the heel of her hand into a precise square. "What I *know*," she said, "is that right now my pregnant mother is sitting home alone."

She saw something twist in Ian's face, though he hadn't moved a muscle, something so deep and private Alice had the feeling of having intruded. In that moment, he resembled a fair-haired, clean-shaven version of his father. "I would think," he said, "you'd be thrilled. Isn't this what you wanted?"

Wes, observing all this from the head of the table, raised his voice at last. "Alice is right about one thing, son. Whether or not you meant it to be, this has been upsetting for the whole family."

Ian eyed him coolly. "This isn't a board-room, Dad. Something you can *negotiate*." The bitterness in his voice seemed to reach far back into something Alice had no part of. "I love Sam. I'd have married her if" — his gaze settled on Alice — "she'd felt it was an option."

Alice sat back, stunned. *Had* she misjudged him? Right now, she was too angry to care. "I'm sure she had her reasons."

"I can think of two offhand — you and Laura."

Alice leaped to her feet. "I won't sit here and let you insult me! *I'm* not the one who started all this. You —" She began to cough, literally choking on the affront.

Wes shot to his feet, looking alarmed. But Alice waved him down, managing to pull in a deep breath before sagging back into her chair. She took a gulp of water. When she looked up, Ian was on his way to the kitchen, plate in hand.

"Thanks for dinner," he said. "I'm sure you won't mind if I don't stick around for dessert."

"Ian, wait." Wes got up from the table and walked over to him, placing a conciliatory hand on his arm. "Can't we talk about this? Like civilized human beings?"

The plan had been for Ian to spend the night. It was a long drive, and the coast highway could be treacherous at night — especially with the wine he'd drunk at dinner. But Ian looked as if he'd rather take his chances on the road than stay another minute under their roof.

"If you ask me, we've all been a little *too* civilized." He looked at Alice, huddled in her chair, more miserable now than angry. "You have a problem with me, Alice? You should've aired it a long time ago."

Wes's hand fell heavily to his side. "You're right, son. But don't blame it on Alice. *I* should've said something." He shook his head. "I guess I kept thinking it would all blow over."

"The way it blew over when I was a kid?" Something ugly flared in Ian's eyes. Just as quickly, he averted his gaze. "Sorry. That was hitting below the belt."

All at once Wes looked every minute of his fifty-three years. "No, it's okay," he said. "You're right. I let things go on with your mother way too long."

"It wasn't just Mom. Last time I looked in the dictionary, 'parents' was plural." Ian's gaze cut over to Alice. "You think a father is just the guy who comes home at five and mows the lawn on Sunday? Then you don't know anything."

The anguish in his face was more eloquent than any words. It had never occurred to Alice that he might actually *want* this baby. She recalled Sam's revelations about her own father, the man against whom every other man in Alice's life had been measured — and usually fallen short. Until Wes. But even *he* had his limitations. Look at the grudge his son still held after all these years. Maybe her father hadn't been as perfect as she'd thought, either.

"Sit down, Ian." A weary note crept into her voice. "It's a long drive, and you're upset."

He shook his head. "I'll help wash up, then I'm off."

"*I'll* do the dishes." Wes was already rolling up his sleeves.

"We'll all pitch in," Alice said, pushing herself to her feet.

In the kitchen, while Wes was clearing the table, she turned to Ian. "I'm sorry if I seemed a little harsh."

He shrugged. "You're married to my dad, not me. You don't have to worry about my feelings."

"It's not that simple. We're family now."

"Yeah? Well, I sure hope it's an improvement on my last one." He set his plate down on the counter. "Look, I don't mean to be rude, but aren't we a little old for *The Brady Bunch* routine?"

The corners of Alice's mouth turned up in a little smile. "I've only seen it in re-runs." Suddenly she was seeing the role she'd played in all this. If her mother and Ian truly *did* belong together, she'd done them a terrible disservice. She put out her hand. "Truce?"

He shook it, solemnly if somewhat stiffly, saying, "I'll wash, you dry." Walking over to the sink, he tossed her a dish towel.

Alice was struck by the simplicity of it. No defining-moment speech, no spotlight on center stage, just this: two people washing up after supper. A family — of sorts. Maybe they'd work it out; maybe they wouldn't. But the least they could do was try.

When the dishwasher was stacked and the pots and pans washed and dried, Wes and Ian sat down at the kitchen table while she made coffee. She'd picked up a cake at Ingersoll's, but no one seemed much interested in dessert. She would freeze it for next time.

Next time. A picture formed in her mind: the four of them gathered about this table — Ian and Sam, she and Wes — sipping coffee in their stocking feet and nibbling on cake. Just as quickly the picture faded. Her mother and Ian would be together only on state occasions. *Didn't I make sure of that?*

She poured the coffee. "By the way, Ian, I also make a mean breakfast." She spoke casually. "Eggs, bacon, the works."

Ian stood up, his coffee untouched. He wasn't smiling, but he didn't look angry, either. "If the offer's still open I'll crash here and cut out early in the morning. You're right about it being a long drive."

Wes was noticeably relieved. "You can borrow a pair of my pajamas if you like," he called as Ian was heading for the doorway.

Ian turned, looking faintly amused. "Dad, I haven't worn pajamas since I was twelve."

"Just wait till you're my age." Wes flashed him a wry look. "Your son will be telling you the same thing."

They heard the door to the guest room click shut down the hall. Wes lowered his cup into its saucer, looking long and tenderly at Alice. He took her hand and brought it to his mouth, kissing her knuckles before unfurling her fingers, one by one, to plant a soft kiss on her palm.

"Have I told you lately that I love you?"

She smiled. "I never get tired of hearing it."

"Then you'll be hearing it a lot."

"That would suit me just fine."

After a moment he let go of her hand and pushed himself to his feet — a bit unsteadily. "Help an old man to bed?" He'd had a little too much to drink, she saw.

She saw, too, how it would be in the years to come. There would be nights when it wasn't about too much wine, when Wes would move a bit slower and lean on her more often. But for some reason the thought didn't bother her. *In sickness and in health . . .*

She rose, tucking his arm into hers. "My pleasure."

Alice was woken before dawn by the trilling of the phone. She bolted upright in the darkness, her heart pounding, the room pitching and yawing. *Something's wrong.* Why else would someone be calling at this hour?

She snatched up the receiver. " 'Lo?"

"It's me. Sorry I woke you."

Her sister. Who wouldn't be apologizing in a *real* emergency. Alice relaxed a bit, peering at the digital clock on the nightstand. "It's three a.m. What the hell is going on?"

"I'm down at the police station." Alice heard voices in the background, the muted jangling of phones. "It's Finch. I'll tell you all about it later on. That's not why I'm calling." Her sister took a deep breath. "It's Mom. I'm worried about her."

"Why? What happened?"

"Finch saw something tonight. Or I should say *someone*. Out at the convent. It's a long story — I can't go into it now. Let's just say it might be who the police are looking for."

Now Wes was awake, too, sitting up beside her, switching on the bedside lamp. "Who is it?" he asked groggily.

Alice cupped a hand over the receiver. "My sister."

"What's wrong?"

"That's what I'm trying to find out." Alice dropped her hand. "Laura, what does all this have to do with Mom?"

"Maybe nothing. I'm probably just being paranoid. But I've been calling and calling, and all I get is a busy signal."

"Her phone must be out of order."

"I figured as much." There was a pause in which Alice heard a door slam. "But I'd feel a whole lot better if someone checked up on her."

"What about the police?"

"That seems kind of extreme, doesn't it?"

Alice kicked off the covers. "I'm on my way." There was no real reason for alarm, but she felt anxious nonetheless. She was reaching into her closet for something to throw on when she abruptly slammed it shut. If her mother *was* in trouble there was no time to waste.

Wes was already out of bed, peeling off his pajama top and tugging on his crewneck sweater from the night before. "I'll drive."

They were halfway down the hall when a sleepy voice behind them called, "What's going on?"

Alice turned to find Ian in the doorway to the guest room, wearing only a pair of rumpled boxers. "Nothing," she told him. "Just . . . my mom's phone is out of order and Laura thought it'd be a good idea if we checked up on her. We're probably over-reacting but —"

Ian didn't let her finish. "I'll meet you out front."

The air outside was cool. Wes was backing the Mercedes out of the garage when Ian appeared in jeans and a sweat-shirt she couldn't help noticing was inside out. Then they were in the car, tearing down the steep canyon road at a speed that normally would have had Alice bracing herself against an impact.

Instead, she urged, "Can't you go any faster?"

"Not unless you want us all killed," Wes answered calmly.

Ian leaned over the seat. "How much farther?"

Alice twisted around to meet his anxious gaze. "Couple more miles." If he hadn't been out to her mother's new house he didn't know how isolated it was. "Can you imagine what she'll think when we all come bursting in on her?"

"Alice, is there something you're not telling me?" Ian's eyes searched her face.

She chose her words carefully, not wanting him to panic. "Look, this probably has nothing to do with it, but Laura was at the police station when she called. It seems Finch is being questioned about someone she saw who they think might be the Carson Springs killer."

"What does it have to do with Sam?"

"Nothing, I'm sure." It came out sounding less than certain.

She didn't need to add that a woman all alone out in the middle of nowhere would be at this killer's mercy. Ian had gotten the message — she saw it in the grim set of his jaw.

"Christ," he swore.

The road flattened and then they were swinging onto Falcon, where Wes bore down with a vengeance. The center line rushed up to wrap itself about Alice's throat. If anything should happen to her mother . . .

I'd never forgive myself.

Sam remained perfectly still, the thudding of her heart seeming to come from somewhere outside her, from an ocean fathoms below the floor on which she crouched. She could hear the dog's frantic barking — it sounded as if it were coming from the kitchen — an endless *roof-roof-roof.*

That's it, she thought. *First thing tomorrow it's back to your owner.*

All at once it occurred to her there might not *be* a tomorrow, and that the dog was the very last thing she ought to be thinking about right now. She started as if from a trance, icy fingers closing about her heart. *Please don't let it be who I think it is.* A thief she could handle. Anything, so long as the baby wasn't harmed.

The barking abruptly ceased. That's when she heard it: the faint crunch of broken glass. The invisible fingers squeezed tighter. She peeked up over the bed at the window, no more than a dozen feet away. If she could get to it and climb out . . .

She hadn't completed the thought when she was scrambling over the bed and across the room. She tugged on the sash, but it wouldn't budge. She yanked harder. Nothing.

Please God . . . oh please . . .

Hot panic clawed its way up her throat. Then she remembered the latch — *locked!* — and reached under the blinds, scrabbling wildly, metal slats clattering like cymbals.

The barking started up again. Now she couldn't hear a thing other than the dog's frantic *roof-roof-roof.* She glanced over her shoulder. The knife was sticking out from under the bed. She must have dropped it at some point, though she had no memory of doing so. Sam stared at it without really seeing it, a dreamy paralysis settling over her. Several seconds passed, seconds that to her were no more than a heartbeat.

The soft tread of footsteps just outside the door jolted her back into action. She shoved hard against the upper sash, and the window flew open, letting in a cool rush of air smelling faintly of cut grass. A faint pink blush lay along the horizon, like blood that hadn't quite washed out.

Sam had one leg over the sill when a cold hand closed over her arm.

Ian was the first to see the broken glass. When he'd heard the dog barking some instinct had made him race around back while his dad and Alice tried the front door. Now he stared in horror at what was left of the sliding glass door. More glass, like a dusting of sugar, was embedded in the discarded brick nearby.

A powerful dread swept through him.

Ian ducked inside, yelling at the top of his lungs, "Sam!" He skidded a little on the broken glass, his shoulder knocking loose a jagged shard still embedded in the frame. It guillotined down, splintering at his feet and nearly severing one of his toes. He barely noticed. *"Sam!"* he yelled again, dashing through the kitchen into the next room. Outside, he could hear bushes rustling and the slap of soles against concrete as his father and Alice raced around the side of the house, no doubt summoned by his shouts.

Something large and hairy came hurtling out of nowhere. Ian froze in the doorway as a large yellow dog, half crazed with excitement, threw itself at him, barking frantically. "Easy boy . . ." He pushed the dog away, which seemed more frightened than threatening. Where the hell was Sam?

As if in answer, he heard a muffled cry from down the hall.

The hand about her arm was cold. Icy as dead flesh. An image of Martin in his coffin flashed through her mind. But these fingers were alive. They yanked her off balance, and she tumbled to the floor with a breathless little cry. Reflexively, her knees jerked up to shield her belly.

Curled on her side, all she could see was a pair of blue pumps and skinny legs that traveled up, up before disappearing into the dark bell of a skirt. Then a face loomed into view. Horrid and bony, with hair blond and shiny as a doll's and pale blue eyes that seemed to stare sightlessly. Sam had seen that face but couldn't think where.

The woman began to recite tonelessly, "For a whore is a deep ditch, and a strange woman is a narrow pit . . . She also lieth in wait as for prey, and increaseth the transgressors among men . . ."

A knife glittered in her hand. Smaller than the one Sam had dropped — more like a switchblade. *Dear God.* She was inching away from it when a foot stamped down hard on her robe. Suddenly, she knew where she'd seen that face: at the convent, with Mother Ignatius.

"You've sinned." The queer, pale eyes dropped to Sam's belly. But not as if seeing her; as if looking through her. "And now His judgment is upon you."

"You . . . you don't even know me," Sam gasped.

"You've lain with a man not your husband, and now you're with child."

Fury rose, momentarily eclipsing her fear. "Who are you to judge me?"

Incredibly, the woman shook her head as if in regret. "It's the Lord's vengeance, not mine. I am merely His instrument." She spoke as quietly as if in church, making the sign of the cross. "Don't be afraid. I will be quick and merciful as with the others."

Others? Oh God.

The knife slashed down in a gleaming arc. Sam rolled away with a cry, feeling it tear through her robe, inches from her ribcage, before sinking onto the floor with a muffled *thud.* The room faded, then swam back into focus.

She grabbed for the knife, but the woman was quicker. She lunged to free it with a grunt of expelled breath that smelled faintly, and absurdly, of peanut butter. In her new, queerly heightened state of awareness Sam was acutely aware of everything — the scent of floor wax, a loose thread straggling from the quilt, the dust kitties under the bed.

I'm going to die, she thought. And, strangely, that was okay.

Then she remembered the baby. She mustn't let anything happen to the baby. She was rolling into a crouch when she heard a deep voice outside the room cry, *"Sam!"*

Her attacker froze, knife suspended in midair. At that precise moment Sam's gaze fell on the lamp cord snaking across the rug. She grabbed hold and gave a sharp tug. The lamp toppled to the floor, one of its bulbs exploding like a miniature bomb going off. The woman jumped back with a yelp, a tiny missile of broken glass embedded in her arm. She swatted at it as she might have a bee, blood trickling down her arm, smearing into something that resembled — Sam's overtaxed mind made another nimble leap into the absurd — the Nike swoosh.

Then her mind clicked back into gear, and she was on her feet making a dash for the door. She'd have made it, too, if her feet hadn't become tangled in the robe's trailing sash. She stumbled and pitched forward, grabbing hold of the bed frame to keep from falling. The woman took advantage and lunged, tackling her about the waist. Sam struggled against arms stronger than hers, fighting to keep from being dragged to the floor. This time, if she went down, she'd die. Only the thought of the baby gave her a strength she wouldn't have believed she possessed.

"Sam!" Louder this time.

She shrieked, but only a high whistle emerged.

Down the hallway the *roof-roof-roof* of Max barking was a staccato beat to the thud of racing footsteps.

The scene was out of a horror movie. Ian, momentarily blinded by the toppled lamp's glare, saw only the silhouettes on the wall, contracting and expanding like in some bizarre shadow play. Two figures caught, swaying, in what appeared a lover's embrace. Then he saw that one of the figures was Sam. He barely recognized her.

She managed to struggle free. Her robe

trailing from one arm, she bent to snatch something from the floor — a knife, he saw. She held it in front of her, arms extended, crying shrilly, "Not the baby. I won't let you hurt the baby!"

Her attacker advanced — a woman in a blond wig skewed at an angle, lipstick smeared in a way that made her appear to be mordantly grinning. As she stepped in front of the lamp, her long shadow angled up the wall onto the ceiling: an enormous insect about to gobble its prey.

Then Ian was flying across the room, hurling himself at her. They grappled, and he felt a flicker of surprise at her strength: It was almost inhuman. His fist scythed in the roundhouse blow taught to him aeons ago by his father. There was a cracking sound, like a pencil snapping in two, and the blond head jerked back, eyes rolling to white. He caught a glimpse of pale red hair under the wig as she buckled to the floor.

Then Sam was in his arms, shivering, her teeth chattering as if with fever. "Sh-she . . . she . . . was g-going to hurt the b-baby."

"The baby's fine. You're fine," he soothed, stroking the back of her head. "Everything's going to be okay. I'm here now." He tightened his arms about her, nearly overcome by a wave of lightheadedness at the thought of how close he'd come to losing her.

In the storm that followed — his father and Alice bursting into the room, followed a short while later by the police — a single thought stood clear in Ian's mind, like a beacon atop a lighthouse: *never again*. Never again would he be someplace else when he ought to be with Sam. This was where he belonged, this house . . . or some other. Man and wife, or live-in lovers. It didn't matter. As long as they were together.

From the Los Angeles Times

NUN CHARGED IN TWO DEATHS

In a bizarre twist, the arrest of a local nun in Carson Springs, CA, during what police are calling an assault with intent to kill, could lead to murder charges in connection with the stabbing deaths last summer of a homeless man and a popular high school teacher in town. Sister Beatrice Kernshaw, 35, was taken into custody charged with breaking and entering the home of Samantha Kiley, 48, a local business owner, and violently attacking her. "I'll have nightmares for the rest of my life," Kiley said, "but thank God no one was hurt." The victim, four months pregnant, was admitted to the hospital for observation but released the following day.

Local authorities have uncovered evidence linking Kernshaw to the unsolved deaths of Kyle Heaton, 52, and Phoebe Linton, 31, and law enforcement sources say they expect the nun to be charged with their murders and with the attempted murder of Ms. Kiley. The suspect has been placed in the care of doctors at the Edith Brockwood Psychiatric Hospital in Ventura while she awaits trial. Experts have labeled her a paranoid schizophrenic with a history of mental illness. According to one family member, Kernshaw's father reportedly shot himself to death in 1969 following his divorce from her mother. As a teen she spent several years at a Catholic home for troubled youths.

Born Bernadette Kernshaw in Portland, Oregon, she took her vows as a Catholic nun in 1974. Prior to her arrest she resided at Our Lady of the Wayside, a convent known for its honey, sold under the label Blessed Bee. The mother superior issued no comment, except to say, "We must all pray for Sister Beatrice."

Chapter 19

As September gave way to October, life in Carson Springs slowly settled back to normal. Television and newspaper coverage of the sensational arrest slowed to a trickle, and a weary relief began to set in. Doors remained bolted at night (by now the habit was too ingrained), but joggers began to appear once more in the park and on remote roads after sunset. The occasional nighttime hitchhiker could be seen as well, thumb cocked, blinking at oncoming headlights. Talk that had centered around the bizarre arrest of Sister Beatrice moved on to other things: the weather, which had turned uncommonly brisk, and the music festival just two weeks away.

When Ian Carpenter moved in with Sam Kiley, it caused only a minor stir. People had grown used to seeing them strolling about town hand in hand, or quietly conversing at the Tree House: Sam, with her newly rounded belly, and Wes Carpenter's handsome young son, with his pierced ear and ponytail, looking at her the way every woman, young or old, dreams of being looked at. Even Marguerite Moore had to admit, albeit grudgingly, that the more you saw of them, the less you noticed the difference in their ages.

Alice could have told them as much. In nearly four months of marriage she'd never been happier. The only disagreement between her and Wes had been over whether or not to install a hot tub in place of the live oak their bedroom currently looked out on. Wes was in favor of it, she wasn't. For now the hot tub was on hold.

Things were going equally well with her career. As the new executive producer of CBS's *Shannon O'Brien Show* she was already making a name, with a six-figure salary to show for it.

Laura hadn't been sitting still, either. The week following Sister Beatrice's arrest she'd flown to New York with Finch, shepherding her through a round of questioning by police in another, unrelated case. A long discussion with social services had followed. When all the pieces had fallen into place Laura had been horrified to learn that since the age of two, when she was abandoned by her mother, Bethany Wells had been in no fewer than fourteen foster homes, the most recent that of a woman named Shirlee Stoeckle. It was Shirlee's live-in boyfriend, Lyle Kruger, a drug dealer with a history of priors, who'd unwittingly set the girl free.

The matter of his untimely death, the result of a drug deal gone sour, was resolved with surprising swiftness. The police had already made their arrest — a pair of low-level runners brought in months ago on another charge. At the time no one had connected Bethany to Lyle's death. If not for the duly filed missing person report, she might well have disappeared without a trace.

And now here they were, three weeks later, back in New York, this time on a wholly separate legal matter. They'd arrived the night before and by nine-thirty the following morning were in a cab on their way to the courthouse on Centre Street. All the preliminaries had been seen to. Laura's lawyer in Carson Springs, a woman with the unlikely name of Rhonda Talltree — part Irish, part Navajo, part junkyard dog, as she liked to joke — had been working in tandem with an attorney here. Gary Bloom, a courtly older man who'd fiddled with his hearing aid throughout most of their initial meeting, had turned out to be a wonderful resource. He'd guided them through the shoals of social services and in remarkably short order had even managed to arrange for a hearing — to which they were on their way now.

Laura reached for Finch's hand. "Nervous?"

She managed a faint smile. "A little."

"Don't be. Rhonda says it's going to be okay."

"What does she know?" Finch, slumped in her seat staring out the window at the gray buildings inching past, reminded Laura of a weary warrior buckling on a suit of armor for one more battle.

"She's been on the phone with Gary almost every day, for one thing."

"Yeah, well . . . we'll see."

"Look, the worst that could happen is that it'll take a little longer than we expected."

The girl shot her a weary look that seemed to sum up everything in a glance: waiting was all she knew. She'd spent her whole life waiting for a home that wasn't just temporary. Why should this be any different?

At the same time, Laura wondered if Finch was aware of the profound change that had taken place in her over these past few months. She studied her out of the corner of her eye. Finch was wearing a simple navy skirt and cotton sweater in a lighter shade of blue. In her ears were the small silver hoops her new friend, Andie, had given her for luck. She looked more than just pretty; she looked like a young woman on the cusp of bigger and better things.

"I wish . . ." Finch caught her lower lip in her teeth. "Nothing."

"What?"

"I wish we didn't have to go through all this."

Laura felt her throat catch, and thought, *You don't know how often I've wished it, too — that I could've been there from the beginning.* She smiled, squeezing the girl's hand. "After today it'll be a cinch. Rhonda says . . ."

"I know, I know . . . Rome wasn't built in a day." Rhonda's favorite expression.

Then the cab was pulling to a stop in front of the courthouse, a grandly imposing structure with its row of Ionic columns that seemed to echo the theme of ancient times. She'd seen photos, of course, but they hadn't done it justice or conveyed just how intimidating it was. She felt like a tiny fish about to be swallowed by a whale.

Inside the vast marble foyer, they waited in line interminably before passing through a metal detector. Beyond was a domed rotunda with acres of polished marble against which their footsteps echoed as they made their way to the elevator. This time it was Finch who reached for her hand, holding on as if for dear life.

"It'll only be the judge and the lawyer from social services," Laura reminded her. "And Mr. Bloom, of course. He said it should go pretty quickly. In and out."

Finch shot her a gently reproving glance. "You said that already."

"Sorry." Laura smiled. "Guess I'm a little nervous, too."

"It gets easier." The girl looked at her the way a big sister might, one with far more experience in these matters.

They stepped out of the elevator. The courtroom was halfway down a long circular corridor, and as Laura pushed her way in through the swinging double doors, she stopped short. Chatting with her lawyer were a familiar pair she never in a million years expected to see so far from home: Hector and Maude.

They spotted her and grinned, strolling

toward her and Finch as if they'd come from around the block, not three thousand miles away: Hector looking uncomfortable in a suit and tie, and Maude in something demure for a change — a slightly used designer suit from Ragtime. Laura began to laugh softly, shaking her head in disbelief.

Finch, looking as stunned as Laura, whispered, "What are you guys *doing* here?"

"We came to show our support." Maude stepped up to hug Finch.

Finch clung to her, then drew back. "How . . . ?"

"I had a little bit of money saved up." Hector slipped an arm about Laura's waist. "I thought it was about time I saw for myself what's so special about New York."

"You could've said something," Laura scolded.

"I wanted it to be a surprise."

As if each morning she woke to find his head on the pillow next to hers wasn't enough.

Then they were making their way to the front of the courtroom, Maude leading the way with her arm around Finch. The judge appeared a few minutes later, a stern-faced older woman who seemed to regard them incuriously, as if she'd seen and heard it all. Laura glanced at Ms. Hargrave from social services — dumpy and middle-aged, with frizzy brown hair — and felt some of the tension go out of her. If the attorney's bored expression was any indication, this would be a cinch.

When the formalities were dispensed with, Gary Bloom rose to address the bench. "Your Honor, my client, Ms. Kiley, has instituted formal adoption proceedings. Miss Wells has been in her care for the past four months — on an informal basis. We request that she be allowed to remain with Ms. Kiley in California until the process has been completed."

The lawyer from social services dragged herself to her feet, and Laura was stunned when she opened her mouth to say, "Your Honor, we appreciate Ms. Kiley's willingness in this matter, but we can't just hand out children like puppies to anyone who comes along. Miss Wells is a ward of state, and whether or not she or Ms. Kiley recognizes it, she's entitled to certain protections under the law. I'm recommending that she remain in New York in the interim." She paused to consult her notes. "We've arranged for a suitable, ah, foster home for the time being."

Laura bristled. The woman was making

it sound like a matter of days, when it could take *months,* and from a distance even longer. She could feel Finch trembling beside her and longed to put her fears to rest. But how? She felt utterly helpless.

Gary stopped fiddling with his hearing aid long enough to say it for them, "Your Honor, that would make *fifteen* foster homes in as many years. Hasn't this poor girl been through enough? We're not asking to cut corners — just that she be allowed to remain in Ms. Kiley's custody. Someone who has proven herself to be a more than fit guardian."

Ms. Hargrave injected sourly, "Your Honor, we won't *know* that to be the case until an evaluation has been —"

The judge cut her off. "Thank you, Ms. Hargrave, your objection has been noted." Her tone was firm, but when she looked at Finch, her hard expression softened. "I'm sure you have an opinion on all this, Miss Wells. Would you care to share it with us?"

The girl rose awkwardly to her feet, glancing about nervously, her dark-eyed gaze traveling from Laura to Maude then to Hector before settling on the judge. Shyly, she said, "I, uh, if it's okay with you I'd like to stay with Lau . . . I mean, Ms. Kiley."

The judge smiled. "Yes, I rather imagined so. But perhaps you can tell us why, in your own words."

Flags of color appeared on Finch's cheeks, and Laura was swept by a sudden fear that she'd freeze or retreat into her shell. But when the girl spoke her words rang clear. "She's nice. I don't mean, like, just nice. They're *all* nice in the beginning. Laura's really that way. Maude . . . and Hector, too." She smiled at them. "They made me feel like I belonged. Like I *mattered*. That has to count for something, doesn't it?"

Laura's heart swelled. She could feel Hector's hand on hers, squeezing hard, but his face was a blur. Then she blinked, and the world swam into focus. She realized a battle wasn't forthcoming when she glanced over and saw Ms. Hargrave slumping back in her seat, as if impatient for this to be over. Laura felt both relieved and strangely saddened. Finch — or Bethany Wells, as she was known — was just another case in an already heavy load, not even worth fighting for.

"I'm going to allow your motion, Mr. Bloom," the judge said. "I'm sure the California court will take your concerns into consideration, Ms. Hargrave, and see this through all the proper channels. In the interim, I believe it's in the best interests of this girl that she remain with Ms. Kiley. I see too many kids who get lost in the system. A system," she frowned at the frizzy-haired attorney, "that has failed most of them abysmally. Occasionally, when I come across someone like Ms. Kiley, I'm reminded of why we're all here on this earth. Tonight, I assure you, I'll sleep well knowing that." She banged her gavel and declared, "Case dismissed."

Laura looked over at Hector, who grinned as if he'd known all along how it would turn out. Maude was dabbing at her eyes with a crumpled tissue. Finch merely looked stunned. Months of worry and heartache had ended, not with a bang, but with a whimper.

Minutes later, they were making their way down the courthouse steps when Finch said in a voice soft with wonder, "I guess this means I'm staying."

"If you don't mind bunking with a dotty old lady," Maude croaked, reaching into her purse for a fresh Kleenex. Had anyone been trailing them, Laura thought, all they'd have had to do was follow the shredded tissue in Maude's wake.

Finch's mouth hooked up in a little

smile. "Beats a bus station bench. Even if you *do* snore."

Laura squinted up at the tall buildings that surrounded them, at the people rushing along the sidewalks below. It was a beautiful day, clear and cool, a day that suddenly felt rich with possibility.

"Anyone in the mood for sightseeing?" she said. "I have a sudden urge to see the Statue of Liberty."

Maude brightened. "I've always wanted to go to the top of the Empire State."

"I'd be up for just about anything as long as food's involved. I feel like I haven't eaten in a week." Hector draped an arm around Laura, and she brought her head to rest against his shoulder — a shoulder built to lean on. "What about you, Finch? What's your pleasure?"

The girl looked uncertainly from one to the other. "If it's okay with you, I mean if you don't mind too much . . . well, I'd like to go home." A tear made its way down one cheek. It was the first time Laura had seen her cry.

They'd have to change their tickets; they weren't due to leave until tomorrow. But Laura didn't hesitate. "Sure, why not? We can see Lady Liberty another time. After all, it's not as if she's going anywhere."

"The Empire State can wait, too," Maude warbled. "In fact, the view from here is just fine."

When Laura looked to Hector he was already hailing a cab.

Chapter 20

Everyone agreed it was the finest festival in years. Situated on the grounds of the theosophy institute high atop Pilgrim's Peak, it enjoyed three perfect days of sunny skies and temperatures in the low seventies. In the outdoor amphitheater overlooking the valley and distant Toyon Ridge, where in the early days of the institute Greek plays were staged, world-class musicians entertained the hundreds of people, sprawled on picnic blankets and propped in beach chairs, who'd come to hear them play.

Aubrey Roellinger, prematurely gray with a Toscanini-like mane, conducted the orchestra comprised of musicians from around the world. Yo-Yo Ma, the featured soloist, played Bach and Prokofiev. The Gay Men's Chorus performed Fauré's Requiem to a standing ovation. And a handful of talented newcomers were showcased as well in a program ranging from early baroque to a symphony composed by Roellinger himself. One musician in particular, seventeen-year-old Korean violinist, Yi-Jai Kim — a last-minute replacement — brought the crowd to its feet with her virtuoso performance of Mendelssohn's Violin Concerto in E Minor.

Tents had been set up along the shady drive, where local craftsmen hawked wares, many with a musical theme: handmade thumb pianos, a seemingly endless variety of wind chimes, music boxes that tinkled every popular melody. There were custom printed T-shirts and mugs, and CDs of featured performers. Even jugglers and mimes, and a young woman painting henna tattoos. The grand prize in the raffle that had raised thousands of dollars for next year's festival was a state-of-the-art stereo system.

The doctor on call was summoned only twice. Once for a little boy who'd broken his toe — the result of having tripped over a sprinkler head in one of the roped-off areas. And again for an elderly man thought to be having a heart attack who turned out to be suffering nothing more serious than a case of heartburn. No one fainted from heatstroke, like in previous years, and only one pregnant woman went into labor — though she refused to leave until the last note of Mozart's Symphony in C Minor had been played.

The worst mishaps suffered by musicians were a few broken strings, a bent ego here and there, and the brief stir caused by a Stradivarius that went briefly missing. It was found under a table, a casualty of absentmindedness rather than larceny.

Marguerite Moore, bustling about like a cruise director aboard the *QE II*, was in charge of ticket taking. Each day she wore a seemingly identical pantsuit in a different sherbet shade that after hours of scurrying about in search of lost tickets, bundles of misplaced programs, and names mysteriously missing from her list, was reduced to something resembling a soggy cone. Sam, on the other hand, managed to look as cool as the ice tea and lemonade served in the booth she was overseeing — despite being five months pregnant. Every so often she would glance up to find Marguerite glowering in her direction. For some reason, it didn't bother her in the least.

Times had changed. Her worst fears hadn't been realized, and she'd had her share of pleasant surprises, like former classmate Becky Spurlock, whom she'd bumped into the other day at the dry cleaners. Becky had confessed that Sam had given her the courage to divorce her husband, something she'd wanted to do for years.

"I know it's not the same as having a baby," she'd said, a blush creeping to the roots of her hennaed hair. "With Mac — well, let's just say I just don't want to wake up one day an old lady and realize I missed my chance."

Then there was Delilah Sims. Last week, she'd approached Sam and Ian at the Tree House, saying she'd heard about Ian's work and was interested in seeing some of his paintings.

"I'm having a show," he'd told her. "The opening's a week from Thursday. Why don't you come?"

"I'd love to," she'd said, looking as if she meant it.

Ian handed her a flyer. "The Blue Iguana Gallery."

Delilah's face fell. "Oh, it's in Santa Barbara."

Sam didn't know what the big deal was — Santa Barbara was only twenty minutes away. For a woman as sophisticated as Delilah — educated in the best private schools, with a trust fund rumored to be in the millions — it seemed more than a little odd.

"Why don't you drive over with us?" she

offered. There was something about raven-haired Delilah, who always looked a bit wan, that reminded her of Sleeping Beauty. Maybe all she needed was a little encouragement to awaken her to life's possibilities.

"I'll have to see. Can I let you know?"

Delilah's gaze strayed in the direction of David Ryback. Sam had often come across them immersed in quiet conversation about a book that one or the other had just read, and wondered if maybe David was a little in love with Delilah, too.

"If you decide to come, just give us a call," Ian said, scribbling their number on the back of the flyer. "We'll swing by and pick you up."

Then Sam, caught up in the wonder of something as simple — yet profound — as a shared phone number, had put it out of her head. She was surprised when Delilah phoned the day of the opening, apologizing for not letting them know sooner and asking if the offer was still open. She'd ended up buying two of Ian's paintings.

That was a week ago, and now the festival was behind her, too. Sam had been looking forward to a quiet weekend alone with Ian when Laura called to invite them for supper on Sunday. She'd sounded happier than she had in years, but Sam had caught a tiny note of apprehension as well. It would be their first time together as a family, including Ian, since the wedding.

It seemed ages since then, yet in other ways it was as if no time had passed. Her daughters had fallen back into the habit of calling and dropping by. Laura, as funny and affectionate as ever, while Alice's warmth seemed a tad bit forced. Sam's youngest, for whom there was a place for everything and everything was in its place, didn't quite know what to do with this new, unpredictable mother of hers who, these days, wasn't so quick to put others first. Yes, she thought, mothers are supposed to protect their children, throw themselves in front of a speeding car if need be . . . *when they're little*. But her daughters were grown now. With or without her, they'd survive.

They were pulling into Laura's drive when she turned to Ian. "Isn't this the part where the credits start to roll?" she asked, feeling a fluttering in her belly that definitely wasn't the baby.

"Movies end, families don't." He reached over and squeezed her hand. "Nervous?"

"It's silly, I know. It's just that this is the

first time we've all been together since the wedding. One, big happy family," she said with the appropriate dash of irony. "Think we can pull it off?"

"Depends."

"On what?"

"Your expectations." He turned his lazy smile on her, the smile that went through her like cool water through parched ground every time. "Rose-colored glasses can be dangerous."

"Meaning I shouldn't try too hard to make it fit the picture in my mind?"

"Something like that." He braked to a stop behind Alice's sporty red Carrera.

"What if reality isn't so hot?"

"Don't shoot the bear until you see it."

"I've changed," she said. "The *rules* have changed."

He shrugged. "So make new ones."

Ian was helping her see, on a daily basis, how that was possible. Not that they had it all figured out. They knew where some of the pieces fit; others were works in progress. For one thing, Sam had come to the realization that she didn't necessarily want or need a nine-to-five husband, since she was no longer in that mode herself. When their child was a little older they'd be free to travel. Meanwhile, Ian spent his days at the studio he'd rented nearby, while Sam was perfectly content to stay at home puttering about the garden. If occasionally he worked straight through supper and well into the night she found she didn't mind. She liked being alone, and besides, she always knew he'd make his way home eventually.

She unbuckled her seat belt and climbed out. Together they headed up the front path. The dogs charged out to greet them, tails wagging, Rocky stopping to pee with great flourish on a hydrangea. Laura stepped out onto the porch, followed by Hector. She wore a crisp yellow shirt and jeans that showed off her new slenderness, while Hector looked the same as always: solid as a fence post, as much a fixture as the ranch itself.

He clasped Sam's hand. "Sam, nice to see you. You're looking well." His eyes didn't automatically drop to her belly as most people's did, and she was nearly as grateful for that as for the warmth with which he greeted Ian. "Hey, how's it going? Nice piece in the paper. Nice picture, too." He winked at Sam, who blushed a little at the reminder. When the photographer who'd covered the opening had asked for a shot of them together, she'd thought it was just a throwaway.

"Hi, Mom. Hi, Ian." Laura kissed them both on their cheeks. "You're just in time. Alice and I can't agree on the corn bread. She says it's one teaspoon of baking powder, I say it's two."

"Make that three," Sam said.

Lupe's jalapeño corn bread had been a carefully guarded secret for years, until she'd finally confessed she'd never taken the trouble to write it down. Only after careful observation and some experimenting on her own was Sam able to master it.

She followed Laura and Hector inside, where the smell of roast beef wafted toward her. A bouquet of daisies sat in a chipped brown jug on the coffee table made from an old wooden storm shutter. A man's pair of cowboy boots was parked on the hearth beside Laura's. Two pairs of yellow eyes and the end of a twitching tail peeked from under the sofa.

In the kitchen Alice was measuring out flour, and Wes was rummaging in the freezer for an ice cube tray. Maude was involved in the delicate business of unmolding a Jell-O salad, with Finch hovering at her elbow. The table was set: Blue Willow plates, many with chipped rims;

flatware representing several different phases of Laura's life; glasses, no two alike. The embroidered tablecloth, Sam was pleased to note, was the one she'd come across while packing up her things — a long-forgotten wedding present from Aunt Florine and Uncle Pernell. She'd given it to Laura, who didn't fuss about spills and looked at stains the way she did at snapshots in photo albums, as fond memories of various occasions.

Sam walked over to kiss Alice, catching a whiff of some expensive scent. "Is that a new dress? It's a good color on you."

"I got it in Cabo." She looked pleased that Sam had noticed.

"Did you have a nice trip?" Sam asked.

"Wonderful." Alice shared a meaningful glance with Wes. "We even looked at a few condos."

"You two retiring already?" Laura teased.

"Yeah, sure — in about a hundred years." Another glance at Wes. "In the meantime, it'd be nice to get away now and then. I've always wanted a place on the beach. And when we're not there, you and Hector could use it." There was a slight beat before she added, "Mom and Ian, too."

Sam wanted to shake it loose, this last bit of awkwardness, the way she'd once shaken pebbles from her daughter's shoes. She found herself longing suddenly for the way it had been before, for the ease with which they used to banter. It hadn't been perfect then, either, but they could laugh and joke with no hidden wires to trip over. They could sit at a table where everyone automatically knew their places, and the only thing to throw you off balance was the occasional wobbly chair leg.

"What can I get you two to drink?" Hector seemed at ease playing host. "Ian, there's a beer in the fridge with your name on it."

Ian grinned. "You read my mind, buddy."

"Just water for me. I'll get it." Sam knew her way around Laura's kitchen as well as her own. As she filled her glass, she watched Maude give the copper mold a final shake, and the ring of green Jell-O flecked with fruit plop quivering onto the plate.

Sam had no sooner settled in at the table when one of the cats leaped into her lap, purring. She smiled, remembering Mami telling her that cats always seemed to find you when you were pregnant. She wondered if it was true.

Maude stepped back to admire her mold. "Well now, isn't that a sight? Almost too pretty to eat."

"We'll manage, I'm sure." Laura peeked into the oven before sliding out a sizzling pan. "All yours," she said to Alice, whose corn bread batter was all ready to go in. "Just watch for the hot spots."

"You've been saying that for years. When are you going to get a new oven?" Alice grumbled good-naturedly.

Laura shrugged. "When I get around to it."

Soon they were all gathered around the table. Laura had added the extra leaf, which meant plenty of elbow room as well as space underneath for the dogs and cats to roam. Wine was poured, platters and bowls passed around. Before long every plate was heaped full.

The roast was delicious. The jalapeño corn bread every bit as good as Lupe's. Even Maude's Jell-O mold got its share of praises, though privately Sam had always thought such things were mostly for show. By the time the second bottle of wine was uncorked, the mood was even more relaxed, and talk turned to the recent changes at Delarosa's.

"You know that line from the movie, 'Build it and they'll come?' Well, the same thing must apply to Web sites. The orders have been *pouring* in." Laura shook her head in amazement.

"We can hardly keep up," Finch said.

"And I owe it all to Alice." Laura raised her glass to her sister. "If it hadn't been for you, I don't know when I would've gotten around to it."

"You would have . . . in another hundred years," Alice teased.

"I guess I'm the one with egg on my face." Sam felt slightly abashed. "I shouldn't have dragged my heels all these years."

"It's not your fault, Mom," Laura was quick to defend her. "You're the wrong generation, that's all."

There was an awkward pause in which the clinking of forks seemed louder than usual. It was Sam who broke the silence. "In that case," she said lightly, "I should sign up for a computer class. It would beat bingo down at the senior citizen's center."

Everyone laughed, dissolving any last bit of tension.

Then Laura met Hector's eyes across the table and she cleared her throat. "By the way, everybody, I have something to announce. Hector and I are getting married."

A loud chorus of whoops went up. When the cries had subsided, Sam wiped her eyes with her napkin and said, "Goodness. That's the best news I've heard in ages."

"When's the wedding?" Alice wanted to know.

"We were thinking of December. January at the latest."

"A Christmas wedding. Oh, how wonderful!" Maude brought her hands together in a soundless little clap. "Can I be in charge of decorations?"

Even knowing how Maude went overboard at times, Sam wasn't at all surprised to hear her good-hearted daughter reply, "Sure. We'll all pitch in. It'll be fun."

"Laura asked me to be maid of honor." Finch darted an uncertain glance at Alice. "You don't mind, do you?"

"Not at all." Alice smiled at Laura.

Wes's chair scraped back and he rose to his feet. "I propose a toast." He lifted his wineglass. "To Laura and Hector. May you be as happy as Alice and I have been."

Glasses clinked. More wine was poured. Suddenly everyone was talking at once. Sam felt a wonderful sense of peace settle over her. It was just like the old days, only better. Precisely *because* they weren't stuck in one place. A family isn't static, she thought. It's a constantly flowing current that, like life itself, can take you to some surprising places.

Maude, a bit tipsy from the wine, lifted her glass. "I propose a toast to the baby, too."

Sam glanced at Laura out of the corner of her eye, but she didn't seem the least bit bothered. She merely smiled, the smile of a woman happy with her life just as it is. "To the baby," she said.

"I just hope it takes after Sam," Ian said.

Wes laughed knowingly, the laugh of a father who'd survived his son's teenage years.

"What about you, Alice?" Laura asked hopefully. "Any chance you'll change your mind and have one of your own?"

"I doubt it." Alice didn't look uncomfortable like before, merely pensive.

"Give it time," Laura said.

"Oh, believe me I will. A long, long time."

"I doubt I'll be thinking of grandchildren for a while," Sam said lightly. Her earlier self-consciousness seemed to have vanished. "Besides, I already have one."

She looked over at Finch, who smiled back tentatively. She was dressed in what

Sam supposed was the latest teenage fashion: a pair of slim-fitting jeans and fuzzy pink sweater that showed off the ring in her navel. Laura had confided that Finch spent hours on the phone every day after school gabbing with her best friend Andie Fitzgerald. But with everything else that'd been going on Sam hadn't had much chance to get to know her. She found herself very much looking forward to it now.

Then the table was cleared and coffee cups set out. A plate of freshly baked Toll House cookies made its way to the table. In the softly lit kitchen, with dirty dishes piled in the sink and dogs scratching at their feet, Sam felt the glow of shared affection spread out to fill every well-worn corner. Enough to go around in the years to come, to mend hurt feelings and battered pride, even bridge the occasional gap.

A family. For better or worse.

NOTE FROM THE AUTHOR

If you enjoyed this, or any of my other books, I'd love to hear from you. I can be reached at the following:

www.eileengoudge.com
or
eileeng@nyc.rr.com

Or, for those of you who prefer the old-fashioned method:

Eileen Goudge
P.O. Box 1396, Murray Hill Station
New York, NY 10016